By Terry Pratchett

The Dark Side of the Sun • *Strata*
Good Omens (with Neil Gaiman)
The Long Earth (with Stephen Baxter)
The Long War (with Stephen Baxter)

For Young Adults
The Carpet People
The Bromeliad Trilogy: *Truckers* • *Diggers* • *Wings*
The Johnny Maxwell Trilogy: *Only You Can Save Mankind*
Johnny and the Dead • *Johnny and the Bomb*
The Unadulterated Cat (illustrated by Gray Jollife)
Nation

The Discworld® Books
The Color of Magic • *The Light Fantastic* • *Equal Rites*
Mort • *Sourcery* • *Wyrd Sisters* • *Pyramids*
Guards! Guards! • *Eric* (with Josh Kirby) • *Moving Pictures*
Reaper Man • *Witches Abroad* • *Small Gods*
Lords and Ladies • *Men at Arms* • *Soul Music* • *Feet of Clay*
Interesting Times • *Maskerade* • *Hogfather* • *Jingo*
The Last Continent • *Carpe Jugulum* • *The Fifth Elephant*
The Truth • *Thief of Time* • *Night Watch*
Monstrous Regiment • *Going Postal* • *Thud!*
Where's My Cow? (illustrated by Melvyn Grant)
Making Money • *Unseen Academicals* • *Snuff*

The Last Hero (illustrated by Paul Kidby)
The Art of Discworld (illustrated by Paul Kidby)
The Streets of Ankh-Morpork (with Stephen Briggs)
The Discworld Companion (with Stephen Briggs)
The Discworld Mapp (with Stephen Briggs)
The Wit and Wisdom of Discworld (with Stephen Briggs)
The Discworld Graphic Novels: *The Color of Magic*
The Light of Fantastic

For Young Adults
The Amazing Maurice and His Educated Rodents
The Wee Free Men • *A Hat Full of Sky*
Wintersmith • *I Shall Wear Midnight*
The Illustrated Wee Free Men (illustrated by Stephen Player)

Terry Pratchett

Lords and Ladies

A Novel of Discworld®

HARPER

An Imprint of HarperCollins*Publishers*

This is a work of fiction. Names, characters, places, and incidents are products of the author's imagination or are used fictitiously and are not to be construed as real. Any resemblance to actual events, locales, organizations, or persons, living or dead, is entirely coincidental.

HARPER

An Imprint of HarperCollins*Publishers*
195 Broadway,
New York, NY 10007.

Copyright © 1992 by Terry and Lyn Pratchett
Terry Pratchett® and Discworld® are registered trademarks.
ISBN 978-0-06-223739-2

First Harper premium printing: November 2013
First HarperTorch mass market printing: November 2002
First HarperCollins mass market printing: October 1996
First HarperCollins paperback printing: October 1995

HarperCollins ® and Harper ® are registered trademarks of Harper-Collins Publishers.

Printed in the United States of America

Visit Harper paperbacks on the World Wide Web at
www.harpercollins.com

10 9

Author's Note

By and large, most Discworld books have stood by themselves, as complete books. It *helps* to have read them in some kind of order, but it's not essential.

This one is different. I can't ignore the history of what has gone before. Granny Weatherwax first turned up in *Equal Rites*. In *Wyrd Sisters* she became the unofficial head of a tiny coven consisting of the easy-going, much-married Nanny Ogg and young Magrat, she of the red nose and unkempt hair and tendency to be soppy about raindrops and roses and whiskers on kittens.

And what took place was a plot not unadjacent to that of a famous play about a Scottish king, which ended with Verence II becoming king of the little hilly, forested country of Lancre.

Technically this shouldn't have happened, since strictly speaking he was not the heir, but to the witches he looked like being the best man for the job and, as they say, all's well that ends well. It also ended with Magrat reaching a very tentative Understanding with Verence . . . very tentative indeed, since both of them were so shy they immediately forgot whatever it was they were going to say to one another whenever they met, and whenever either of them did manage to say anything the other one misunderstood it and took offense, and both of them spent a lot of time wondering what the other one was thinking. This might be love, or the next best thing.

In *Witches Abroad* the three witches had to travel halfway across the continent to face down the Godmother (who had made Destiny an offer it couldn't refuse).

This is the story of what happened when they came home.

NOW READ ON . . .

LOrdS aNd LAdies

Now read on . . .

When does it start?

There are very few starts. Oh, some things *seem* to be beginnings. The curtain goes up, the first pawn moves, the first shot is fired*—but *that's* not the start. The play, the game, the war is just a little window on a ribbon of events that may extend back thousands of years. The point is, there's always something *before*. It's *always* a case of Now Read On.

Much human ingenuity has gone into finding the ultimate Before.

The current state of knowledge can be summarized thus:

In the beginning, there was nothing, which exploded.

Other theories about the ultimate start involve gods creating the universe out of the ribs, entrails, and testicles of their father.** There are quite a lot of these. They are interesting, not for what they tell you about cosmology, but for what they say about

---

*Probably at the first pawn.

**Gods like a joke as much as anyone else.

people. Hey, kids, which part do you think they made *your* town out of?

But *this* story starts on the Discworld, which travels through space on the back of four giant elephants which stand on the shell of an enormous turtle and is not made of any bits of anyone's bodies.

But when to begin?

Thousands of years ago? When a great hot cascade of stones came screaming out of the sky, gouged a hole out of Copperhead Mountain, and flattened the forest for ten miles around?

The dwarfs dug them up, because they were made of a kind of iron, and dwarfs, contrary to general opinion, love iron more than gold. It's just that although there's more iron than gold it's harder to sing songs about. Dwarfs love iron.

And that's what the stones contained. The love of iron. A love so strong that it drew all iron things to itself. The three dwarfs who found the first of the rocks only got free by struggling out of their chain-mail trousers.

Many worlds are iron, at the core. But the Discworld is as coreless as a pancake.

On the Disc, if you enchant a needle it will point to the Hub, where the magical field is strongest. It's simple.

Elsewhere, on worlds designed with less imagination, the needle turns because of the love of iron.

At the time, the dwarfs and the humans had a very pressing need for the love of iron.

And now, spool time forward for thousands of years to a point fifty years or more before the ever-moving *now*, to a hillside and a young woman, running. Not running away from something, exactly, or precisely running toward anything, but running just fast enough to keep ahead of a young man although, of course, not so far ahead that he'll give up. Out from the trees and into the rushy valley where, on a slight rise in the ground, are the stones.

They're about man-height, and barely thicker than a fat man.

And somehow they don't seem *worth* it. If there's a stone circle you mustn't go near, the imagination suggests, then there should be big brooding trilithons and ancient altar stones screaming with the dark memory of blood-soaked sacrifice. Not these dull stubby lumps.

It will turn out that she was running a bit too fast this time, and in fact the young man in laughing pursuit will get lost and fed up and will eventually wander off back to the town alone. She does not, at this point, know this, but stands absentmindedly adjusting the flowers twined in her hair. It's been that kind of afternoon.

She knows about the stones. No one ever gets *told* about the stones. And no one is ever told not to go there, because those who refrain from talking about the stones also know how powerful is the attraction of prohibition. It's just that going to the stones is not . . . what we do. Especially if we're nice girls.

But what we have here is not a nice girl, as generally understood. For one thing, she's not beautiful. There's a certain set to the jaw and arch to the nose that might, with a following wind and in the right light, be called handsome by a good-natured liar.

Also, there's a certain glint in her eye generally possessed by those people who have found that they are more intelligent than most people around them but who haven't yet learned that one of the most intelligent things they can do is prevent said people ever finding this out. Along with the nose, this gives her a piercing expression which is extremely disconcerting. It's not a face you can talk to. Open your mouth and you're suddenly the focus of a penetrating stare which declares: what you're about to say had better be interesting.

Now the eight little stones on their little hill are being subjected to the same penetrating gaze.

Hmm.

And then she approaches, cautiously. It's not the caution of a rabbit about to run. It's closer to the way a hunter moves.

She puts her hands on her hips, such as they are.

There's a skylark in the hot summer sky. Apart from that, there's no sound. Down in the little valley, and higher in the hills, grasshoppers are sizzling and bees are buzzing and the grass is alive with micro-noise. But it's always quiet around the stones.

"I'm here," she says. "Show me."

A figure of a dark-haired woman in a red dress appears inside the circle. The circle is wide enough to throw a stone across, but somehow the figure manages to approach from a great distance.

Other people would have run away. But the girl doesn't, and the woman in the circle is immediately interested.

"So you're real, then."

"Of course. What is your name, girl?"

"Esmerelda."

"And what do you want?"

"I don't want anything."

"Everyone wants something. Otherwise, why are *you* here?"

"I just wanted to find out if you was real."

"To you, certainly . . . you have *good* sight."

The girl nods. You could bounce rocks off her pride.

"And now you have learned this," said the woman in the circle, "what is it that you really want?"

"Nothing."

"Really? Last week you went all the way up to the mountains above Copperhead to talk to the trolls. What did you want from them?"

The girl put her head on one side.

"How do you know I did that?"

"It's at the top of your mind, girl. Anyone could see it. Anyone with . . . *good* sight."

"I shall be able to do that one day," said the girl smugly.

"Who knows? Possibly. What did you want from the trolls?"

"I . . . wanted to talk to them. D'you know they think time goes backward? Because you can see the past, they say, and—"

The woman in the circle laughed.

"But they are like the stupid dwarfs! All they are interested in is pebbles. There is nothing of interest in pebbles."

The girl gives a kind of one-shoulder uni-shrug, as if indicating that pebbles may be full of quiet interest.

"Why can't you come out from between the stones?"

There was a distinct impression that this was the wrong question to have asked. The woman carefully ignored it.

"I can help you find far more than pebbles," she said.

"You can't come out of the circle, can you?"

"Let me give you what you want."

"I can go anywhere, but you're stuck in the circle," said the girl.

"*Can* you go anywhere?"

"When I am a witch I shall be able to go *anywhere*."

"But you'll never be a witch."

"What?"

"They say you won't listen. They say you can't keep your temper. They say you have no discipline."

The girl tossed her hair. "Oh, you know that too, do you? Well, they would say that, wouldn't they? But I mean to be a witch whatever they say. You can find things out for yourself. You don't have to listen to a lot of daft old ladies who've never had a life. And, circle lady, I shall be the best witch there has ever been."

"With my help, I believe you may," said the woman in the circle. "Your young man is looking for you, I think," she added mildly.

Another of those one-shoulder shrugs, indicating that the young man can go on looking all day.

"I will, will I?"

"You could be a great witch. You could be anything. Anything you want. Come into the circle. Let me show you."

The girl takes a few steps forward, and then hesitates. There is something about the woman's tone. The smile is pleasant and friendly, but there is something in the voice—too desperate, too urgent, too *hungry*.

"But I'm learning a lot—"

"Step through the stones *now*!"

The girl hesitates again.

"How do I know—"

"Circle time is nearly over! Think of what you can learn! *Now!*"

"But—"

"*Step through!*"

But that was a long time ago, in the past.* And besides, the bitch is . . .

. . . older.

A land of ice . . .

Not winter, because that presumes an autumn and perhaps one day a spring. This is a land of ice, not just a time of ice.

And three figures on horseback, looking down the snow-covered slope to a ring of eight stones. From this side they look much bigger.

You might watch the figures for some time before you realized what it was about them that was strange—stranger, that is, than their clothing. The

---

*Which is another country.

hot breath of their horses hung in the freezing air. But the breath of the riders did not.

"And this time," said the figure in the center, a woman in red, "there will be no defeat. The land will welcome us. It must hate humans now."

"But there were witches," said one of the other riders. "I remember the witches."

"Once, yes," said the woman. "But now . . . poor things, *poor* things. Scarce any power in them at all. And suggestible. Pliant minds. I have crept about, my deary. I have crept about o' nights. I know the witches they have now. Leave the witches to me."

"I remember the witches," said the third rider insistently. "Minds like . . . like metal."

"Not anymore. I tell you, leave them to me."

The Queen smiled benevolently at the stone circle.

"And then you can have them," she said. "For me, I rather fancy a mortal husband. A *special* mortal. A union of the worlds. To show them that this time we mean to stay."

"The King will not like that."

"And when has *that* ever mattered?"

"Never, lady."

"The time is right, Lankin. The circles are opening. Soon we can return."

The second rider leaned on the saddlehorn.

"And I can hunt again," it said. "When? *When?*"

"Soon," said the Queen. "Soon."

It was a dark night, the kind of darkness which is not simply explainable by absence of moon or stars, but the darkness that appears to flow in from somewhere else—so thick and tangible that maybe you could snatch a handful of air and squeeze the night out of it.

It was the kind of darkness which causes sheep to leap fences and dogs to skulk in kennels.

Yet the wind was warm, and not so much strong as loud—it howled around the forests and wailed in chimneys.

On nights like this, normal people would pull the covers over their head, sensing that there were times when the world belonged to something else. In the morning it would be human again; there would be fallen branches, a few tiles off the roof, but *human*. For now . . . better to snuggle down . . .

But there was one man awake.

Jason Ogg, master blacksmith and farrier, pumped the bellows of his forge once or twice for the look of the thing, and sat down on his anvil again. It was always warm in the forge, even with the wind whistling around the eaves.

He could shoe anything, could Jason Ogg. They'd brought him an ant once, for a joke, and he'd sat up all night with a magnifying glass and an anvil made out of the head of a pin. The ant was still around, somewhere—sometimes he could hear it clatter across the floor.

But tonight . . . well, tonight, in some way, he was going to pay the rent. Of course, he owned the forge. It had been passed down for generations. But there was more to a forge than bricks and mortar and iron. He couldn't put a name to it, but it was there. It was the difference between being a master farrier and just someone who bent iron in complicated ways for a living. And it had something to do

with iron. And something to do with being allowed
to be very good at his job. Some kind of rent.

One day his dad had taken him aside and explained what he had to do, on nights like this.

There'd be times, he said, there'd be times—and
he'd know when they were without being told—
there'd be times when someone would come with a
horse to shoe. Make them welcome. Shoe the horse.
Don't let your mind wander. And try not to think
about anything except horseshoes.

He'd got quite used to it now.

The wind rose, and somewhere there was the
creak of a tree going over.

The latch rattled.

Then there was a knock at the door. Once. Twice.

Jason Ogg picked up his blindfold and put it on.
That was important, his dad had said. It saved you
getting distracted.

He undid the door.

"Evening, m'lord," he said.

A WILD NIGHT.

He smelled wet horse as it was led into the forge,
hooves clattering on the stones.

"There's tea brewing on the forge and our Dreen
done us some biscuits in the tin with A Present from
Ankh-Morpork on it."

THANK YOU. I TRUST YOU ARE WELL.

"Yes, m'lord. I done the shoes already. Won't hold
you up long. I know you're . . . very busy, like."

He heard the click-click of footsteps cross the
floor to the old kitchen chair reserved for customers, or at least for the owners of customers.

Jason had laid the tools and the horseshoes and

the nails ready to hand on the bench beside the anvil. He wiped his hands on his apron, picked up a file, and set to work. He didn't like cold shoeing, but he'd shod horses ever since he was ten. He could do it by feel. He picked up a rasp and set to work.

And he had to admit it. It was the most obedient horse he'd ever encountered. Pity he'd never actually seen it. It'd be a pretty good horse, a horse like that . . .

His dad had said: don't try to sneak a look at it.

He heard the glug of the teapot and then the gling-glong sound of a spoon being stirred and then the clink as the spoon was laid down.

Never any sound, his dad had said. Except when he walks and talks, you'll never hear him make a sound. No smacking of lips, stuff like that.

No breathing.

Oh, and another thing. When you takes the old shoes off, don't chuck 'em in the corner for to go for melt with the other scrap. Keep 'em separate. Melt 'em separate. Keep a pot special for it, and make the new shoes out of that metal. Whatever else you do, never put that iron on another living thing.

In fact, Jason had saved one set of the old shoes for pitching contests at the various village fairs, and never lost when he used them. He won so often that it made him nervous, and now they spent most of their time hanging on a nail behind the door.

Sometimes the wind rattled the window frame, or made the coals crackle. A series of thumps and a squawk a little way off suggested that the chicken house at the end of the garden had parted company with the ground.

The customer's owner poured himself another cup of tea.

Jason finished one hoof and let it go. Then he held out his hand. The horse shifted its weight and raised the last hoof.

This was a horse in a million. Perhaps more.

Eventually, he had finished. Funny, that. It never seemed to take very long. Jason had no use for a clock, but he had a suspicion that a job which took the best part of an hour was *at the same time* over in a matter of minutes.

"There," he said. " 'Tis done."

THANK YOU. I MUST SAY THESE ARE VERY GOOD BISCUITS. HOW DO THEY GET THE BITS OF CHOCOLATE IN?

"Dunno, m'lord," said Jason, staring fixedly at the inside of his blindfold.

I MEAN, THE CHOCOLATE OUGHT TO MELT OUT WHEN THEY'RE BAKED. HOW DO THEY DO IT, DO YOU THINK?

" 'Tis probably a craft secret," said Jason. "I never asks that kind o' question."

GOOD MAN. VERY WISE. I MUST—

He had to ask, if only so's he'd always know that he had asked.

"M'lord?"

YES, MR. OGG?

"I *'as* got one question . . ."

YES, MR. OGG?

Jason ran his tongue over his lips.

"If I were to . . . take the blindfold off, what'd I see?"

There. It was done now.

There was a clicking sound on the flagstones, and a change in the air movement which suggested to Jason that the speaker was now standing in front of him.

ARE YOU A MAN OF FAITH, MR. OGG?

Jason gave this some swift consideration. Lancre was not knee-deep in religions. There were the Nine Day Wonderers, and the Strict Offlians, and there were various altars to small gods of one sort or another, tucked away in distant clearings. He'd never really felt the need, just like the dwarfs. Iron was iron and fire was fire—start getting metaphysical and you were scraping your thumb on the bottom of your hammer.

WHAT DO YOU REALLY HAVE *FAITH* IN, RIGHT AT THIS MOMENT?

He's inches away, Jason thought. I could reach out and touch . . .

There was a smell. It wasn't unpleasant. It was hardly anything at all. It was the smell of air in old forgotten rooms. If centuries could smell, then old ones would smell like that.

MR. OGG?

Jason swallowed.

"Well, m'lord," he said, "right now . . . I really *believe* in this blindfold."

GOOD MAN. GOOD MAN. AND NOW . . . I MUST BE GOING.

Jason heard the latch lift. There was a thud as the doors scraped back, driven by the wind, and then there was the sound of hooves on the cobbles again.

YOUR WORK, AS ALWAYS, IS SUPERB.

"Thank you, m'lord."

I SPEAK AS ONE CRAFTSMAN TO AN-OTHER.

"Thank you, m'lord."

WE WILL MEET AGAIN.

"Yes, m'lord."

WHEN NEXT MY HORSE NEEDS SHOEING.

"Yes, m'lord."

Jason closed the door and bolted it, although there was probably no point, when you thought about it.

But that was the bargain—you shod anything they brought to you, *anything*, and the payment was that you *could* shoe anything. There had always been a smith in Lancre, and everyone knew the smith in Lancre was a very powerful smith indeed.

It was an ancient bargain, and it had something to do with iron.

The wind slackened. Now it was a whisper around the horizons, as the sun rose.

This was the octarine grass country. Good growing country, especially for corn.

And here was a field of it, waving gently between the hedges. Not a big field. Not a remarkable one, really. It was just a field with corn in it, except of course during the winter, when there were just pigeons and crows in it.

The wind dropped.

The corn still waved. They weren't the normal swells of the wind. They spread out from the center of the field like ripples from a dropped stone.

The air sizzled and was filled with an angry buzzing.

Then, in the center of the field, rustling as it bent, the young corn lay down.

In a circle.

And in the sky the bees swarmed and teemed, buzzing angrily.

It was a few weeks to midsummer. The kingdom of Lancre dozed in the heat, which shimmered on the forests and the fields.

Three dots appeared in the sky.

After a while, they became identifiable as three female figures on broomsticks, flying in a manner reminiscent of the famous three plaster flying ducks.

Observe them closely.

The first one—let us call her the leader—flies sitting bolt upright, in defiance of air resistance, and seems to be winning. She has features that would generally be described as striking, or even handsome, but she couldn't be called beautiful, at least by anyone who didn't want their nose to grow by three feet.

The second is dumpy and bandy-legged with a face like an apple that's been left for too long and an expression of near-terminal good nature. She is playing a banjo and, until a better word comes to mind, singing. It is a song about a hedgehog.

Unlike the broomstick belonging to the first figure, which is more or less unburdened except for a sack or two, this one is overladen with things like fluffy purple toy donkeys, corkscrews in the shape of small boys urinating, bottles of wine in straw baskets, and other international cultural items. Nestling among them is the smelliest and most evil-minded cat in the world, currently asleep.

The third, and definitely the last, broomstick rider is also the youngest. Unlike the other two, who dress like ravens, she wears bright, cheerful clothes which don't suit her now and probably didn't even suit her ten years ago. She travels with an air of vague good-natured hopefulness. There are flowers in her hair but they're wilting slightly, just like her.

The three witches pass over the borders of Lancre, the kingdom, and very shortly afterward over the town of Lancre itself. They begin their descent over the moorlands beyond, eventually touching down near a standing stone which happens to mark the boundaries of their territories.

They're back.

And everything's all right again.

For about five minutes.

There was a badger in the privy.

Granny Weatherwax poked it with her broom until it got the message and lumbered off. Then she took down the key which hung on the nail beside the copy of last year's *Almanack And Booke Of Dayes*, and walked back up the path to her cottage.

A whole winter away! There'd be a lot to do. Go and pick the goats up from Mr. Skindle, get the spiders out of the chimney, fish the frogs out of the well, and generally get back into the business of minding everyone's business for them because there'd be no telling what business people'd get up to without a witch around . . .

But she could afford an hour with her feet up first.

There was a robin's nest in the kettle, too. The birds had got in through a broken window pane. She carefully took the kettle outside and wedged it over the door so's to be safe from weasels, and boiled up some water in a saucepan.

Then she wound up the clock. Witches didn't have much use for clocks, but she kept it for the tick . . . well, mainly for the tick. It made a place seem lived in. It had belonged to her mother, who'd wound it up every day.

It hadn't come as a surprise to her when her mother died, firstly because Esme Weatherwax was a witch and witches have an insight into the future and secondly because she was already pretty experienced in medicine and knew the signs. So she'd had a chance to prepare herself, and hadn't cried at all until the day afterward, when the clock stopped right in the middle of the funeral lunch. She'd dropped a tray of ham rolls and then had to go and sit by herself in the privy for a while, so that no one would see.

Time to think about that sort of thing, now. Time to think about the past . . .

The clock ticked. The water boiled. Granny Weatherwax fished a bag of tea from the meager luggage on her broomstick, and swilled out the teapot.

The fire settled down. The clamminess of a room unlived-in for months was gradually dispelled. The shadows lengthened.

Time to think about the past. Witches have an insight into the future. The business she'd have to mind soon enough would be her own . . .

And then she looked out of the window.

Nanny Ogg balanced carefully on a stool and ran a finger along the top of the dresser. Then she inspected the finger. It was spotless.

"Hummph," she said. "Seems to be moderately clean."

The daughters-in-law shivered with relief.

"So far," Nanny added.

The three young women drew together in their mute terror.

Her relationship with her daughters-in-law was the only stain on Nanny Ogg's otherwise amiable character. Sons-in-law were different—she could remember their names, even their birthdays, and they joined the family like overgrown chicks creeping under the wings of a broody bantam. And grandchildren were treasures, every one. But any woman incautious enough to marry an Ogg son might as well resign herself to a life of mental torture and nameless domestic servitude.

Nanny Ogg never did any housework herself, but she was the cause of housework in other people.

She got down from the stool and beamed at them.

"You kept the place quite nice," she said. "Well done."

Her smile faded.

"Under the bed in the spare room," she said. "Haven't looked under there yet, have I?"

Inquisitors would have thrown Nanny Ogg out of their ranks for being too nasty.

She turned as more members of the family filed into the room, and her face contorted into the misty grin with which she always greeted grandchildren.

Jason Ogg pushed his youngest son forward. This was Pewsey Ogg, aged four, who was holding something in his hands.

"What you got there, then?" said Nanny. "You can show your Nan."

Pewsey held it up.

"My word, you *have* been a—"

It happened right there, right then, right in front of her.

And then there was Magrat.

She'd been away eight months.

Now panic was setting in. Technically she was engaged to the king, Verence II. Well . . . not exactly *engaged*, as such. There was, she was almost sure, a general unspoken understanding that engagement was a definite option. Admittedly she'd kept on telling him that she was a free spirit and definitely didn't want to be tied down in any way, and of course this was the case, more or less, but . . . but . . .

But . . . well . . . eight months. Anything could have happened in eight months. She should have come straight back from Genua, but the other two had been enjoying themselves.

She wiped the dust off her mirror and examined

herself critically. Not a lot to work with, really. No matter what she did with her hair it took about three minutes for it to tangle itself up again, like a garden hosepipe left in a shed.* She'd bought herself a new green dress, but what had looked exciting and attractive on the plaster model looked like a furled umbrella on Magrat.

Whereas Verence had been here reigning for eight months. Of course, Lancre was so small that you couldn't lie down without a passport, but he was a genuine king and genuine kings tended to attract young women looking for career opportunities in the queening department.

She did her best with the dress and dragged a vengeful brush through her hair.

Then she went up to the castle.

Guard duty at Lancre castle was the province of anyone who didn't have much of anything else to do at the moment. On duty today was Nanny Ogg's youngest son Shawn, in ill-fitting chain-mail. He brought himself to what he probably thought was attention as Magrat pattered past, and then dropped his pike and hurried after her.

"Can you slow down a bit, please, miss?"

He overtook her, ran up the steps to the door, picked up a trumpet that was hanging from a nail by a bit of string, and blew an amateurish fanfare. Then he looked panicky again.

"Wait right there, miss, right there . . . count to five, and then knock," he said, and darted through the door, slamming it behind him.

---

*Which, no matter how carefully coiled, will always uncoil overnight and tie the lawnmower to the bicycles.

Magrat waited, and then tried the knocker.

After a few seconds Shawn opened the door. He was red in the face and had a powdered wig on back to front.

"Yeeeuss?" he drawled, and tried to look like a butler.

"You've still got your helmet on under the wig," said Magrat helpfully.

Shawn deflated. His eyes swiveled upward.

"Everyone at the haymaking?" said Magrat.

Shawn raised his wig, removed the helmet, and put the wig back. Then he distractedly put the helmet back on top of the wig.

"Yes, and Mr. Spriggins the butler is in bed with his trouble again," said Shawn. "There's only me, miss. *And* I've got to get the dinner started before I'm off 'ome because Mrs. Scorbic is poorly."

"You don't have to show me in," said Magrat. "I do know the way."

"No, it's got to be done proper," said Shawn. "You just keep movin' slow and leave it to me."

He ran on ahead and flung open some double doors—

"Meeeyisss Magraaaaat Garrrrrli-ick!"

—and scurried toward the next set of doors.

By the third pair he was out of breath, but he did his best.

"Meeeyisss . . . Magraaaaa . . . Garrrrrli-ick . . . His Majesteeeyyaa the Ki—Oh, bugger, *now* where's he gone?"

The throne room was empty.

They eventually found Verence II, King of Lancre, in the stable yard.

Some people are born to kingship. Some achieve kingship, or at least Arch-Generalissimo-Father-of-His-Countryship. But Verence had kingship thrust upon him. He hadn't been raised to it, and had only arrived at the throne by way of one of those complicated mix-ups of fraternity and parentage that are all too common in royal families.

He had in fact been raised to be a Fool, a man whose job it was to caper and tell jokes and have custard poured down his trousers. This had naturally given him a grave and solemn approach to life and a grim determination never to laugh at anything ever again, especially in the presence of custard.

In the role of ruler, then, he had started with the advantage of ignorance. No one had ever told him how to be a king, so he had to find out for himself. He'd sent off for books on the subject. Verence was a great believer in the usefulness of knowledge derived from books.

He had formed the unusual opinion that the job of a king is to make the kingdom a better place for everyone to live in.

Now he was inspecting a complicated piece of equipment. It had a pair of shafts for a horse, and the rest of it looked like a cartful of windmills.

He glanced up, and smiled in an absentminded way.

"Oh, hello," he said. "All back safe then?"

"Um—" Magrat began.

"It's a patent crop rotator," said Verence. He tapped the machine. "Just arrived from Ankh-Morpork. The wave of the future, you know. I've really been getting interested in agricultural improvement and soil efficiency. We'll really have to get cracking on this new three-field system."

Magrat was caught off balance.

"But I think we've only *got* three fields," she said, "and there isn't much soil in—"

"It's very important to maintain the correct relationship between grains, legumes, and roots," said Verence, raising his voice. "Also, I'm seriously considering clover. I should be interested to know what you think!"

"Um—"

"And I think we should do something about the pigs!" Verence shouted. "The Lancre Stripe! Is very hardy! But we could really bring the poundage up! By careful cross-breeding! With, say, the Sto Saddleback! I'm having a boar sent up—Shawn, will you *stop* blowing that *damn* trumpet!"

Shawn lowered the trumpet.

"I'm doin' a fanfare, your majesty."

"Yes, yes, but you're not supposed to go *on*. A few brief notes are a sufficiency." Verence sniffed. "And something's burning."

"Oh, blow . . . it's the carrots . . ." Shawn hurried away.

"That's better," said Verence. "Where were we?"

"Pigs, I think," said Magrat, "but I really came to—"

"It all comes down to the soil," said Verence. "Get the soil right, and everything else follows. Incidentally, I'm arranging the marriage for Midsummer Day. I thought you'd like that."

Magrat's mouth formed an O.

"We could move it, of course, but not too much because of the harvest," said Verence.

"I've had some invitations sent out already, to the more obvious guests," said Verence.

"And I thought it might be a nice idea to have some sort of fair or festival beforehand," said Verence.

"I asked Boggi's in Ankh-Morpork to send up their best dressmaker with a selection of materials and one of the maids is about your size and I think you'll be very pleased with the result," said Verence.

"And Mr. Ironfoundersson, the dwarf, came down the mountain *specially* to make the crown," said Verence.

"And my brother and Mr. Vittoller's Men can't come because they're touring Klatch, apparently, but Hwel the playsmith has written a special play for the wedding entertainment. Something even rustics can't muck up, he says," said Verence.

"So that's all settled then?" said Verence.

Finally, Magrat's voice returned from some distant apogee, slightly hoarse.

"Aren't you supposed to *ask* me?" she demanded.

"What? Um. No, actually," said Verence. "No. Kings don't ask. I looked it up. I'm the king, you see, and you are, no offense meant, a subject. I don't have to ask."

Magrat's mouth opened for the scream of rage but, at last, her brain jolted into operation.

Yes, it said, of *course* you can yell at him and sweep away. And he'll probably come after you.

Very probably.

Um.

Maybe not *that* probably. Because he might be a

nice little man with gentle runny eyes but he's also a king and he's been looking things up. But very probably quite probably.

But . . .

Do you want to bet the rest of your life? Isn't this what you wanted anyway? Isn't it what you came here hoping for? Really?

Verence was looking at her with some concern.

"Is it the witching?" he said. "You don't have to give that up entirely, of course. I've got a great respect for witches. And you can be a witch queen, although I think that means you have to wear rather revealing clothes and keep cats and give people poisoned apples. I read that somewhere. The witching's a problem, is it?"

"No," Magrat mumbled, "it's not that . . . um . . . did you mention a crown?"

"You've got to have a crown," said Verence. "Queens do. I looked it up."

Her brain cut in again. Queen Magrat, it suggested. It held up the mirror of the imagination . . .

"You're not upset, are you?" said Verence.

"What? Oh. No. Me? No."

"Good. That's all sorted out, then. I think that just about covers everything, don't you?"

"Um—"

Verence rubbed his hands together.

"We're doing some marvelous things with legumes," he said, as if he hadn't just completely rearranged Magrat's life without consulting her. "Beans, peas . . . you know. Nitrogen fixers. And marl and lime, of course. Scientific husbandry. Come and look at this."

He bounced away enthusiastically.

"You know," he said, "we could really make this kingdom *work*."

Magrat trailed after him.

So that was all settled, then. Not a proposal, just a statement. She hadn't been quite sure how the moment would be, even in the darkest hours of the night, but she'd had an idea that roses and sunsets and bluebirds might just possibly be involved. Clover had not figured largely. Beans and other leguminous nitrogen fixers were not a central feature.

On the other hand Magrat was, at the core, far more practical than most people believed who saw no further than her vague smile and collection of more than three hundred pieces of occult jewelry, none of which worked.

So this was how you got married to a king. It all got arranged for you. There were no white horses. The past flipped straight into the future, carrying you with it.

Perhaps that was normal. Kings were busy people. Magrat's experience of marrying them was limited.

"Where are we going?" she said.

"The old rose garden."

Ah . . . well, this was more like it.

Except that there weren't any roses. The walled garden had been stripped of its walks and arbors and was now waist high in green stalks with white flowers. Bees were furiously at work in the blossoms.

"Beans?" said Magrat.

"*Yes!* A specimen crop. I keep bringing the farmers up here to show them," said Verence. He sighed.

"They nod and mumble and smile but I'm afraid they just go off and do the same old things."

"I know," said Magrat. "The same thing happened when I tried to give people lessons in natural childbirth."

Verence raised an eyebrow. Even to him the thought of Magrat giving lessons in childbirth to the fecund and teak-faced women of Lancre was slightly unreal.

"Really? How had they been having babies before?" he said.

"Oh, any old way," said Magrat.

They looked at the little buzzing bean field.

"Of course, when you're queen, you won't need to—" Verence began.

It happened softly, almost like a kiss, as light as the touch of sunlight.

There was no wind, only a sudden heavy calmness that made the ears pop.

The stems bent and broke, and lay down in a circle.

The bees roared, and fled.

The three witches arrived at the standing stone together.

They didn't even bother with explanations. There were some things you *know*.

"In the middle of my bloody herbs!" said Granny Weatherwax.

"On the palace garden!" said Magrat.

"Poor little mite! And he was holding it up to show me, too!" said Nanny Ogg.

Granny Weatherwax paused.

"What're you talking about, Gytha Ogg?" she said.

"Our Pewsey was growing mustard-and-cress on a flannel for his Nan," said Nanny Ogg, patiently. "He shows it to me, right enough, and just as I bends down and—splat! Crop circle!"

"This," said Granny Weatherwax, "is serious. It's been years since they've been as bad as this. We all know what it means, don't we. What we've got—"

"Um," said Magrat.

"—to do now is—"

"Excuse me," said Magrat. There were some things you had to be told.

"*Yes?*"

"*I* don't know what it means," said Magrat. "I mean, old Goodie Whemper—"

"—maysherestinpeace—" the older witches chorused.

"—told me once that the circles were dangerous, but she never said anything about *why.*"

The older witches shared a glance.

"Never told you about the Dancers?" said Granny Weatherwax.

"Never told you about the Long Man?" said Nanny Ogg.

"What Dancers? You mean those old stones up on the moor?"

"All you need to know *right now,*" said Granny Weatherwax, "is that we've got to put a stop to Them."

"*What Them?*"

Granny radiated innocence . . .

"The circles, of course," she said.

"Oh, no," said Magrat. "I can tell by the way you

said it. You said Them as though it was some sort of curse. It wasn't just a them, it was a them with a capital The."

The old witches looked awkward again.

"And who's the Long Man?" said Magrat.

"We do not," said Granny, "ever talk about the Long Man."

"No harm in telling her about the Dancers, at any rate," mumbled Nanny Ogg.

"Yes, but . . . you know . . . I mean . . . she's Magrat," said Granny.

"What's that meant to mean?" Magrat demanded.

"You probably won't feel the same way about Them, is what I am saying," said Granny.

"We're talking about the—" Nanny Ogg began.

"Don't name 'em!"

"Yeah, right. Sorry."

"Mind you, a circle might not find the Dancers," said Granny. "We can always hope. Could be just random."

"But if one opens up inside the—" said Nanny Ogg.

Magrat snapped.

"You just do this on purpose! You talk in code the whole time! You always do this! But you won't be able to when I'm *queen*!"

That stopped them.

Nanny Ogg put her head on one side.

"Oh?" she said. "Young Verence popped the question, then?"

"Yes!"

"When's the happy event?" said Granny Weath-erwax, icily.

"Two weeks' time," said Magrat. "Midsummer Day."

"Bad choice, *bad* choice," said Nanny Ogg. "Shortest night o' the year—"

"Gytha Ogg!"

"And *you'll* be my subjects," said Magrat, ignoring this. "And you'll have to curtsy and everything!"

She knew as soon as she said it that it was stupid, but anger drove her on.

Granny Weatherwax's eyes narrowed.

"Hmm," she said. "We will, will we?"

"Yes, and if you don't," said Magrat, "you can get thrown in *prison*."

"My word," said Granny. "Deary deary me. I wouldn't like that. I wouldn't like that at all."

All three of them knew that the castle dungeons, which in any case had never been its most notable feature, were now totally unused. Verence II was the most amiable monarch in the history of Lancre. His subjects regarded him with the sort of good-natured contempt that is the fate of all those who work quietly and conscientiously for the public good. Besides, Verence would rather cut his own leg off than put a witch in prison, since it'd save trouble in the long run and probably be less painful.

"Queen Magrat, eh?" said Nanny Ogg, trying to lighten the atmosphere a bit. "Cor. Well, the old castle could do with a bit of lightening up—"

"Oh, it'll lighten up all right," said Granny.

"Well, *anyway*, I don't have to bother with this sort of thing," said Magrat. "Whatever it is. It's *your* business. I just shan't have time, I'm sure."

"I'm *sure* you can please yourself, your going-to-be-majesty," said Granny Weatherwax.

"Hah!" said Magrat. "I can! You can jol—you can *damn* well find another witch for Lancre! All right? Another soppy girl to do all the dreary work and never be told anything and be talked over the head of the whole time. I've got better things to do!"

"Better things than being a witch?" said Granny.

Magrat walked into it.

"Yes!"

"Oh, dear," murmured Nanny.

"Oh. Well, then I expect you'll be wanting to be off," said Granny, her voice like knives. "Back to your palace, I'll be bound."

"Yes!"

Magrat picked up her broomstick.

Granny's arm shot out very fast and grabbed the handle.

"Oh, no," she said, "you don't. Queens ride around in golden coaches and whatnot. Each to their own. Brooms is for *witches*."

"Now come on, you two," began Nanny Ogg, one of nature's mediators. "Anyway, someone can be a queen and a w—"

"Who cares?" said Magrat, dropping the broomstick. "I don't have to bother with that sort of thing anymore."

She turned, clutched at her dress, and ran. She became a figure outlined against the sunset.

"You daft old besom, Esme," said Nanny Ogg. "Just because she's getting wed."

"You know what she'd say if we told her," said Granny Weatherwax. "She'd get it all wrong. The

Gentry. Circles. She'd say it was . . . *nice*. Best for her if she's out of it."

"They ain't been active for years and years," said Nanny. "We'll need some help. I mean . . . when did *you* last go up to the Dancers?"

"You know how it is," said Granny. "When it's so quiet . . . you don't think about 'em."

"We ought to have kept 'em cleared."

"True."

"We better get up there first thing tomorrow," said Nanny Ogg.

"Yes."

"Better bring a sickle, too."

There isn't much of the kingdom of Lancre where you could drop a football and not have it roll away from you. Most of it is moorland and steeply forested hillside, giving way to sharp and ragged mountains where even trolls wouldn't go and valleys so deep that they have to pipe the sunlight in.

There was an overgrown path up to the moorland where the Dancers stood, even though it was only a few miles from the town. Hunters tracked up there sometimes, but only by accident. It wasn't that the hunting was bad but, well—

—there were the stones.

Stone circles were common enough everywhere in the mountains. Druids built them as weather computers and since it was always cheaper to build a new 33-MegaLith circle than upgrade an old slow one there were generally plenty of ancient ones around.

No druids ever came near the Dancers.

The stones weren't shaped. They weren't even

positioned in any particularly significant way. There wasn't any of that stuff about the sun striking the right stone at dawn on the right day. Someone had just dragged eight red rocks into a rough circle.

But the weather was different. People said that, if it started to rain, it always began to fall inside the circle a few seconds *after* it had started outside, as if the rain was coming from further away. If clouds crossed the sun, it'd be a moment or two before the light faded inside the circle.

William Scrope is going to die in a couple of minutes. It has to be said that he shouldn't have been hunting deer out of season, and especially not the fine stag he was tracking, and certainly not a fine stag of the Ramtop Red species, which is officially endangered although not as endangered, right now, as William Scrope.

It was ahead of him, pushing through the bracken, making so much noise that a blind man could have tracked it.

Scrope waded through after it.

Mist was still hanging around the stones, not in a blanket but in long raggedy strings.

The stag reached the circle now, and stopped. It trotted back and forth once or twice, and then looked up at Scrope.

He raised the crossbow.

The stag turned, and leapt between the stones.

There were only confused impressions from then on. The first was of—

—*distance*. The circle was a few yards across, it shouldn't suddenly appear to contain so much *distance*.

And the next was of—

—*speed*. Something was coming out of the circle, a white dot growing bigger and bigger.

He knew he'd aimed the bow. But it was whirled out of his hands as the thing struck, and suddenly there was only the sensation of—

—*peace*.

And the brief remembrance of pain.

William Scrope died.

William Scrope looked through his hands at the crushed bracken. The reason that it was crushed was that his own body was sprawled upon it.

His newly deceased eyes surveyed the landscape.

There are no delusions for the dead. Dying is like waking up after a really good party, when you have one or two seconds of innocent freedom before you recollect all the things you did last night which seemed so logical and hilarious at the time, and then you remember the really *amazing* thing you did with a lampshade and two balloons, which had them in *stitches*, and now you realize you're going to have to look a lot of people in the eye today and you're sober now and so are they but *you can both remember*.

"Oh," he said.

The landscape flowed around the stones. It was all so obvious now, when you saw it from the outside . . .

Obvious. No walls, only doors. No edges, only corners—

WILLIAM SCROPE.

"Yes?"

IF YOU WOULD PLEASE STEP THIS WAY.

"Are you a hunter?"

I LIKE TO THINK I AM A PICKER-UP OF UNCONSIDERED TRIFLES.

Death grinned hopefully. Scrope's post-physical brow furrowed.

"What? Like . . . sherry, custard . . . that sort of thing?"

Death sighed. Metaphors were wasted on people. Sometimes he felt that no one took him seriously enough.

I TAKE AWAY PEOPLE'S LIVES IS WHAT I MEAN, he said testily.

"Where to?"

WE SHALL HAVE TO SEE, WON'T WE?

William Scrope was already fading into the mist.

"That thing that got me—"

YES?

"I thought they were extinct!"

NO. THEY JUST WENT AWAY.

"Where to?"

Death extended a bony digit.

OVER *THERE*.

Magrat hadn't originally intended to move into the palace before the wedding, because people would talk. Admittedly a dozen people lived in the palace, which had a huge number of rooms, but she'd still be *under the same roof*, and that was good enough. Or bad enough.

That was before. Now her blood was sizzling. Let people talk. She had a pretty good idea which people they'd be, too. Which person, anyway. *Witch* person. Hah. Let them talk all they liked.

She got up early and packed her possessions, such

as they were. It wasn't exactly her cottage, and most of the furniture went with it. Witches came and went, but witches' cottages went on forever, usually with the same thatch they started with.

But she *did* own the set of magical knives, the mystic colored cords, the assorted grails and crucibles, and a box full of rings, necklaces, and bracelets heavy with the hermetic symbols of a dozen religions. She tipped them all into a sack.

Then there were the books. Goodie Whemper had been something of a bookworm among witches. There were almost a dozen. She hesitated about the books, and finally she let them stay on the shelves.

There was the statutory pointy hat. She'd never liked it anyway, and had always avoided wearing it. Into the sack with it.

She looked around wild-eyed until she spotted the small cauldron in the inglenook. That'd do. Into the sack with *that*, and then tie the neck with string.

On the way up to the palace she crossed the bridge over Lancre Gorge and tossed the sack into the river.

It bobbed for a moment in the strong current, and then sank.

She'd secretly hoped for a string of multicolored bubbles, or even a hiss. But it just sank. Just as if it wasn't anything very important.

Another world, another castle . . .

The elf galloped over the frozen moat, steam billowing from its black horse and from the thing it carried over its neck.

It rode up the steps and into the hall itself, where the Queen sat amidst her dreams . . .

"My lord Lankin?"

"A stag!"

It was still alive. Elves were skilled at leaving things alive, often for weeks.

"From out of the circle?"

"*Yes*, lady!"

"It's weakening. Did I not tell you?"

"How *long*? How *long*?"

"Soon. Soon. What went through the other way?" The elf tried to avoid her face.

"Your . . . pet, lady."

"No doubt it won't go far." The Queen laughed. "No doubt it will have an amusing time . . ."

It rained briefly at dawn.

There's nothing nastier to walk through than shoulder-high wet bracken. Well, there is. There are an uncountable number of things nastier to walk through, especially if they're shoulder-high. But here and now, thought Nanny Ogg, it was hard to think of more than one or two.

They hadn't landed inside the Dancers, of course. Even *birds* detoured rather than cross that airspace. Migrating spiders on gossamer threads floating half a mile up curved around it. Clouds split in two and flowed around it.

Mist hung around the stones. Sticky, damp mist.

Nanny hacked vaguely at the clinging bracken with her sickle.

"You there, Esme?" she muttered.

Granny Weatherwax's head rose from a clump of bracken a few feet away.

"There's been things going on," she said, in a cold and deliberate tone.

"Like what?"

"All the bracken and weeds is trampled around the stones. I reckon someone's been *dancing*."

Nanny Ogg gave this the same consideration as would a nuclear physicist who'd just been told that someone was banging two bits of sub-critical uranium together to keep warm.

"They *never*," she said.

"They have. And another thing . . ."

It was hard to imagine what other thing there could be, but Nanny Ogg said "Yes?" anyway.

"Someone got killed up here."

"Oh, no," moaned Nanny Ogg. "Not inside the circle too."

"Nope. Don't be daft. It was outside. A tall man. He had one leg longer'n the other. And a beard. He was probably a hunter."

"How'd you know all that?"

"I just trod on 'im."

The sun rose through the mists.

The morning rays were already caressing the ancient stones of Unseen University, premier college of wizardry, five hundred miles away.

Not that many wizards were aware of this.

For most of the wizards of Unseen University their lunch was the first meal of the day. They were not, by and large, breakfast people. The Archchancellor and the Librarian were the only two who knew what the dawn looked like from the front, and they tended to have the entire campus to themselves for several hours.

The Librarian was always up early because he was an orang-utan, and they are naturally early risers, although in his case he didn't bellow a few times to keep other males off his territory. He just unlocked the Library and fed the books.

And Mustrum Ridcully, the current Archchancellor, liked to wander around the sleepy buildings, nodding to the servants and leaving little notes for his subordinates, usually designed for no other purpose than to make it absolutely clear that he was up and attending to the business of the day while they were still fast asleep.*

Today, however, he had something else on his mind. More or less literally.

It was round. There was healthy growth all around it. He could swear it hadn't been there yesterday.

He turned his head this way and that, squinting at the reflection in the mirror of the *other* mirror he was holding above his head.

The next member of staff to wake up after Ridcully and the Librarian was the Bursar; not because

---

*This happens all the time, everywhere in the multiverse, even on cold planets awash with liquid methane. No one knows why it is, but in any group of employed individuals the only naturally early riser is *always* the office manager, who will *always* leave reproachful little notes (or, as it might be, engraved helium crystals) on the desks of their subordinates. In fact the only place this does not happen very often is the world Zyrix, and this is only because Zyrix has eighteen suns and it is only possible to be an early riser there once every 1,789.6 years, but even then, once every 1,789.6 years, resonating to some strange universal signal, smallminded employers slither down to the office with a tentacle full of small reproachful etched *frimpt* shells at the ready.

he was a naturally early riser, but because by around ten o'clock the Archchancellor's very limited supply of patience came to an end and he would stand at the bottom of the stairs and shout:

"Bursaaar!"

—until the Bursar appeared.

In fact it happened so often that the Bursar, a natural neurovore,* frequently found that he'd got up and dressed himself in his sleep several minutes before the bellow. On this occasion he was upright and fully clothed and halfway to the door before his eyes snapped open.

Ridcully never wasted time on small talk. It was always large talk or nothing.

"Yes, Archchancellor?" said the Bursar, glumly.

The Archchancellor removed his hat.

"What about this, then?" he demanded.

"Um, um, um . . . *what*, Archchancellor?"

"This, man! This!"

Close to panic, the Bursar stared desperately at the top of Ridcully's head.

"The what? Oh. The bald spot?"

"I have *not* got a bald spot!"

"Um, then—"

"I mean it wasn't there yesterday!"

"Ah. Well. Um." At a certain point something always snapped inside the Bursar, and he couldn't stop himself. "Of course these things do happen and my grandfather always swore by a mixture of honey and horse manure, he rubbed it on every day—"

"I'm *not* going bald!"

---

*He lived on his nerves.

A tic started to dance across the Bursar's face. The words started to come out by themselves, without the apparent intervention of his brain.

"—and then he got this device with a glass rod and, and, and you rubbed it with a silk cloth and—"

"I mean it's ridiculous! My family have never gone bald, except for one of my aunts!"

"—and, and, and then he'd collect morning dew and wash his head, and, and, and—"

Ridcully subsided. He was not an unkind man.

"What're you taking for it at the moment?" he murmured.

"Dried, dried, dried, dried," stuttered the Bursar.

"The old dried frog pills, right?"

"R-r-r-r."

"Left-hand pocket?"

"R-r-r-r."

"OK . . . right . . . swallow . . ."

They stared at one another for a moment.

The Bursar sagged.

"M-m-much better now, Archchancellor, thank you."

"Something's definitely happening, Bursar. I can feel it in my water."

"Anything you say, Archchancellor."

"Bursar?"

"Yes, Archchancellor?"

"You ain't a member of some secret society or somethin', are you?"

"Me? *No*, Archchancellor."

"Then it'd be a damn good idea to take your underpants off your head."

* * *

"Know him?" said Granny Weatherwax.

Nanny Ogg knew everyone in Lancre, even the forlorn thing on the bracken.

"It's William Scrope, from over Slice way," she said. "One of three brothers. He married that Palliard girl, remember? The one with the air-cooled teeth?"

"I hope the poor woman's got some respectable black clothes," said Granny Weatherwax.

"Looks like he's been stabbed," said Nanny. She turned the body over, gently but firmly. Corpses as such didn't worry her. Witches generally act as layers-out of the dead as well as midwives; there were plenty of people in Lancre for whom Nanny Ogg's face had been the first and last thing they'd ever seen, which had probably made all the bit in the middle seem quite uneventful by comparison.

"Right through," she said. "Stabbed right through. Blimey. Who'd do a thing like that?"

Both the witches turned to look at the stones.

"I don't know *what*, but I knows where it come from," said Granny.

Now Nanny Ogg could see that the bracken all around the stones was indeed well trodden down, and quite brown.

"I'm going to get to the bottom of this," said Granny.

"You'd better not go into—"

"I knows exactly where I should go, thank you."

There were eight stones in the Dancers. Three of them had names. Granny walked around the ring until she reached the one known as the Piper.

She removed a hatpin from among the many that

riveted her pointy hat to her hair and held it about six inches from the stone. Then she let it go, and watched what happened.

She went back to Nanny.

"There's still power there," she said. "Not much, but the ring is holding."

"But who'd be daft enough to come up here and dance around the stones?" said Nanny Ogg, and then, as a treacherous thought drifted across her mind, she added, "Magrat's been away with us the whole time."

"We shall have to find out," said Granny, setting her face in a grim smile. "Now help me up with the poor man."

Nanny Ogg bent to the task.

"Coo, he's heavy. We could've done with young Magrat up here."

"No. Flighty," said Granny Weatherwax. "Head easily turned."

"Nice girl, though."

"But soppy. She thinks you can lead your life as if fairy stories work and folk songs are really true. Not that I don't wish her every happiness."

"Hope she does all right as queen," said Nanny.

"We taught her everything she knows," said Granny Weatherwax.

"Yeah," said Nanny Ogg, as they disappeared into the bracken. "D'you think . . . maybe . . . ?"

"What?"

"D'you think maybe we ought to have taught her everything *we* know?"

"It'd take too long."

"Yeah, right."

* * *

It took a while for letters to get as far as the Archchancellor. The post tended to be picked up from the University gates by anyone who happened to be passing, and then left lying on a shelf somewhere or used as a pipe lighter or a bookmark or, in the case of the Librarian, as bedding.

This one had only taken two days, and was quite intact apart from a couple of cup rings and a bananary fingerprint. It arrived on the table along with the other post while the faculty were at breakfast. The Dean opened it with a spoon.

"Anyone here know where Lancre is?" he said.

"Why?" said Ridcully, looking up sharply.

"Some king's getting married and wants us to come."

"Oh dear, oh dear," said the Lecturer in Recent Runes. "Some tinpot king gets wed and he wants *us* to come?"

"It's up in the mountains," said the Archchancellor, quietly. "Good trout fishin' in those parts, as I recall. My word. Lancre. Good grief. Hadn't thought about the place in years. You know, there's glacier lakes up there where the fish've never seen a rod. Lancre. Yes."

"And it's far too far," said the Lecturer in Recent Runes.

Ridcully wasn't listening. "And there's deer. Thousands of head of deer. And elk. Wolves all over the place. Mountain lions too, I shouldn't wonder. I heard that Ice Eagles have been seen up there again, too."

His eyes gleamed.

"There's only half a dozen of 'em left," he said.

Mustrum Ridcully did a lot for rare species. For one thing, he kept them rare.

"It's the back of beyond," said the Dean. "Right off the edge of the map."

"Used to stay with my uncle up there, in the holidays," said Ridcully, his eyes misty with distance. "Great days I had up there. Great days. The summers up there . . . and the sky's a deeper blue than anywhere else, it's very . . . and the grass . . . and . . ."

He returned abruptly from the landscapes of memory.

"Got to go, then," he said. "Duty calls. Head of state gettin' married. Important occasion. Got to have a few wizards there. Look of the thing. Nobblyess obligay."

"Well, *I'm* not going," said the Dean. "It's not natural, the countryside. Far too many trees. Never could stand it."

"The Bursar could do with an outing," said Ridcully. "Seems a bit jumpy just lately, can't imagine why." He leaned forward to look along the High Table. "Bursaaar!"

The Bursar dropped his spoon into his oatmeal.

"See what I mean?" said Ridcully. "Bundle o' nerves the whole time. I WAS SAYING YOU COULD DO WITH SOME FRESH AIR, BURSAR." He nudged the Dean heavily. "Hope he's not going off his rocker, poor fella," he said, in what he chose to believe was a whisper. "Spends too much time indoors, if you get my drift."

The Dean, who went outdoors about once a month, shrugged his shoulders.

"I EXPECT YOU'D LIKE A LITTLE TIME

AWAY FROM THE UNIVERSITY, EH?" said the Archchancellor, nodding and grimacing madly. "Peace and quiet? Healthy country livin'?"

"I, I, I, I should like that very much, Archchancellor," said the Bursar, hope rising in his face like an autumn mushroom.

"Good man. Good man. You shall come with me," said Ridcully, beaming.

The Bursar's expression froze.

"Got to be someone else, too," said Ridcully. "Volunteers, anyone?"

The wizards, townies to a man, bent industriously over their food. They always bent industriously over their food in any case, but this time they were doing it to avoid catching Ridcully's eye.

"What about the Librarian?" said the Lecturer in Recent Runes, throwing a random victim to the wolves.

There was a sudden babble of relieved agreement.

"Good choice," said the Dean. "Just the thing for him. Countryside. Trees. And . . . and . . . trees."

"Mountain air," said the Lecturer in Recent Runes.

"Yes, he's been looking peaky lately," said the Reader in Invisible Writings.

"It'd be a real treat for him," said the Lecturer in Recent Runes.

"Home away from home, I expect," said the Dean. "Trees all over the place."

They all looked expectantly at the Archchancellor.

"He doesn't wear clothes," said Ridcully. "And he goes 'ook' all the time."

"He does wear the old green robe thing," said the Dean.

"Only when he's had a bath."

Ridcully rubbed his beard. In fact he quite liked the Librarian, who never argued with him and always kept himself in shape, even if that shape was a pear shape. It was the right shape for an orang-utan.

The thing about the Librarian was that no one *noticed* he was an orang-utan anymore, unless a visitor to the University happened to point it out. In which case someone would say, "Oh, yes. Some kind of magical accident, wasn't it? Pretty sure it was something like that. One minute human, next minute an ape. Funny thing, really . . . can't remember what he looked like before. I mean, he *must* have been human, I suppose. Always thought of him as an ape, really. It's more *him*."

And indeed it had been an accident among the potent and magical books of the University library that had as it were bounced the Librarian's genotype down the evolutionary tree and back up a different branch, with the significant difference that now he could hang on to it upside down with his feet.

"Oh, all right," said the Archchancellor. "But he's got to wear something during the ceremony, if only for the sake of the poor bride."

There was a whimper from the Bursar.

All the wizards turned toward him.

His spoon landed on the floor with a small thud. It was wooden. The wizards had gently prevented him from having metal cutlery since what was now known as the Unfortunate Incident At Dinner.

"A-a-a-a," gurgled the Bursar, trying to push himself away from the table.

"Dried frog pills," said the Archchancellor. "Someone fish 'em out of his pocket."

The wizards didn't rush this. You could find anything in a wizard's pocket—peas, unreasonable things with legs, small experimental universes, anything . . .

The Reader in Invisible Writings craned to see what had unglued his colleague.

"Here, look at his porridge," he said.

There was a perfect round depression in the oatmeal.

"Oh dear, *another* crop circle," said the Dean.

The wizards relaxed.

"Damn things turning up everywhere this year," said the Archchancellor. He hadn't taken his hat off to eat the meal. This was because it was holding down a poultice of honey and horse manure and a small mouse-powered electrostatic generator he'd got those clever young fellas in the High Energy Magic research building to knock together for him, clever fellas they were, one day he might even understand half of what they were always gabblin' on about . . .

In the meantime, he'd keep his hat on.

"Particularly strong, too," said the Dean. "The gardener told me yesterday they're playing merry hell with the cabbages."

"I thought them things only turned up out in fields and things," said Ridcully. "Perfectly normal natural phenomenon."

"If there is a suitably high flux level, the intercontinuum pressure can probably overcome quite a high base reality quotient," said the Reader in Invisible Writings.

The conversation stopped. Everyone turned to look at this most wretched and least senior member of the staff.

The Archancellor glowered.

"I don't even want you to *begin* to start explainin' that," he said. "You're probably goin' to go on about the universe bein' a rubber sheet with weights on it again, right?"

"Not exactly a—"

"And the word 'quantum' is hurryin' toward your lips again," said Ridcully.

"Well, the—"

"*And* 'continuinuinuum' too, I expect," said Ridcully.

The Reader in Invisible Writings, a young wizard whose name was Ponder Stibbons, sighed deeply.

"No, Archchancellor, I was merely pointing out—"

"It's not wormholes again, is it?"

Stibbons gave up. Using a metaphor in front of a man as unimaginative as Ridcully was like a red rag to a bu—was like putting something very annoying in front of someone who was annoyed by it.

It was very hard, being a reader in Invisible Writings.*

"I reckon you'd better come too," said Ridcully.

---

*The study of invisible writings was a new discipline made available by the discovery of the bi-directional nature of Library-Space. The thaumic mathematics are complex, but boil down to the fact that all books, everywhere, affect all other books. This is obvious: books inspire other books written in the future, and cite books written in the past. But the General Theory** of L-Space suggests that, in that case, the contents of books *as yet unwritten* can be deduced from books now in existence.

**There's a Special Theory as well, but no one bothers with it much because it's self-evidently a load of marsh gas.

"Me, Archchancellor?"

"Can't have you skulking around the place inventing millions of other universes that're too small to see and all the rest of that continuinuinuum stuff," said Ridcully. "Anyway, I shall need someone to carry my rods and crossbo—my stuff," he corrected himself.

Stibbons stared at his plate. It was no good arguing. What he had really wanted out of life was to spend the next hundred years of it in the University, eating big meals and not moving much in between them. He was a plump young man with a complexion the color of something that lives under a rock. People were always telling him to make something of his life, and that's what he wanted to do. He wanted to make a bed of it.

"But, Archchancellor," said the Lecturer in Recent Runes, "it's *still* too damn far."

"Nonsense," said Ridcully. "They've got that new turnpike open all the way to Sto Helit now. Coaches every Wednesday, reg'lar. Bursaaar! Oh, give him a dried frog pill, someone . . . Mr. Stibbons, if you could happen to find yourself in this universe for five minutes, go and arrange some tickets. There. All sorted out, right?"

Magrat woke up.

And knew she wasn't a witch anymore. The feeling just crept over her, as part of the normal stock-taking that any body automatically does in the first seconds of emergence from the pit of dreams: arms: 2, legs: 2, existential dread: 58%, randomized guilt: 94%, witchcraft level: 00.00.

The point was, she couldn't remember ever being anything else. She'd always been a witch. Magrat Garlick, third witch, that was what she was. The soft one.

She knew she'd never been much good at it. Oh, she could do some spells and do them quite well, and she was good at herbs, but she wasn't a witch *in the bone* like the old ones. They made sure she knew it.

Well, she'd just have to learn queening. At least she was the only one in Lancre. No one'd be looking over her shoulder the whole time, saying things like, "You ain't holding that scepter *right*!"

Right . . .

Someone had stolen her clothes in the night.

She got up in her nightshirt and hopped over the cold flagstones to the door. She was halfway there when it opened of its own accord.

She recognized the small dark girl that came in, barely visible behind a stack of linen. Most people in Lancre knew everyone else.

"Millie Chillum?"

The linen bobbed a curtsy.

"Yes'm?"

Magrat lifted up part of the stack.

"It's me, Magrat," she said. "Hello."

"Yes'm." Another bob.

"What's up with you, Millie?"

"Yes'm." Bob, bob.

"I said it's *me*. You don't have to look at me like that."

"Yes'm."

The nervous bobbing continued. Magrat found her own knees beginning to jerk in sympathy but as it were behind the beat, so that as she was bobbing down she overtook the girl bobbing up.

"If you say 'yes'm' again, it will go very hard with you," she managed, as she went past.

"Y—right, your majesty, m'm."

Faint light began to dawn.

"I'm not queen yet, Millie. And you've known me for twenty years," panted Magrat, on the way up.

"Yes'm. But you're going to *be* queen. So me mam told me I was to be respectful," said Millie, still curtsying nervously.

"Oh. Well. All right, then. Where are my clothes?"

"Got 'em here, your pre-majesty."

"They're not mine. And please stop going up and down all the time. I feel a bit sick."

"The king ordered 'em from Sto Helit special, m'm."

"Did he, eh? How long ago?"

"Dunno, m'm."

He *knew* I was coming home, thought Magrat. How? What's going on here?

There was a good deal more lace than Magrat was used to, but that was, as it were, the icing on the cake. Magrat normally wore a simple dress with not much underneath it except Magrat. Ladies of quality couldn't get away with that kind of thing. Millie had been provided with a sort of technical diagram, but it wasn't much help.

They studied it for some time.

"This is a standard queen outfit, then?"

"Couldn't say, m'm. I think his majesty just sent 'em a lot of money and said to send you everything."

They spread out the bits on the floor.

"Is this the pantoffle?"

Outside, on the battlements, the guard changed. In fact he changed into his gardening apron and went off to hoe the beans. Inside, there was considerable sartorial discussion.

"I think you've got it up the wrong way, m'm. Which bit's the farthingale?"

"Says here Insert Tabbe A into Slotte B. Can't find Slotte B."

"These're like *saddlebags*. I'm not wearing *these*. And this thing?"

"A ruff, m'm. Um. They're all the rage in Sto Helit, my brother says."

"You mean they make people angry? And what's this?"

"Brocade, I think."

"It's like *cardboard*. Do I have to wear this sort of thing *everyday*?"

"Don't know, I'm sure, m'm."

"But Verence just trots around in leather gaiters and an old jacket!"

"Ah, but you're queen. Queens can't do that sort of thing. Everyone knows that, m'm. It's all right for kings to go wandering around with their arse half out their trous—"

She rammed her hand over her mouth.

"It's all right," said Magrat. "I'm sure even kings have . . . tops to their legs just like everyone else. Just go on with what you were saying."

Millie had gone bright red.

"I mean, I mean, I mean, queens has got to be ladylike," she managed. "The king got books about it. Ettiquetty and stuff."

Magrat surveyed herself critically in the mirror.

"It really suits you, your soon-going-to-be-majesty," said Millie.

Magrat turned this way and that.

"My hair's a mess," she said, after a while.

"Please m'm, the king said he's having a hair-dresser come all the way from Ankh-Morpork, m'm. For the wedding."

Magrat patted a tress into place. It was beginning to dawn on her that being a queen was a whole new life.

"My word," she said. "And what happens now?"

"Dunno, m'm."

"What's the king doing?"

"Oh, he had breakfast early and buggered off over to Slice to show old Muckloe how to breed his pigs out of a book."

"So what do *I* do? What's my *job*?"

Millie looked puzzled although this did not involve much of a change in her general expression.

"Dunno, m'm. Reigning, I suppose. Walking around in the garden. Holding court. Doin' tapestry. That's very popular among queens. And then . . . er . . . later on there's the royal succession . . ."

"At the moment," said Magrat firmly, "we'll have a go at the tapestry."

Ridcully was having difficulty with the Librarian.

"I happen to be your Archchancellor, sir!"

"Oook."

"You'll *like* it up there! Fresh air! Bags of trees! More woods than you can shake a stick at!"

"Oook!"

"Come down this minute!"

"Oook!"

"The books'll be quite safe here during the holidays. Good grief, it's hard enough to get students to come in here at the best of times—"

"Oook!"

Ridcully glared at the Librarian, who was hanging by his toes from the top shelf of Parazoology *Ba* to *Mn*.

"Oh, well," he said, his voice suddenly low and cunning, "it's a great shame, in the circumstances. They've got a pretty good library in Lancre castle, I heard. Well, they *call* it a library—it's just a lot of old books. Never had a catalogue near 'em, apparently."

"Oook?"

"Thousands of books. Someone told me there's incunibles, too. Shame, really, you not wanting to see them."

Ridcully's voice could have greased axles.

"Oook?"

"But I can see your mind is quite made up. So I shall be going. Farewell."

Ridcully paused outside the Library door, counting under his breath. He'd reached "three" when the Librarian knuckled through at high speed, caught by the incunibles.

"So that'll be four tickets, then?" said Ridcully.

Granny Weatherwax set about finding out what had been happening around the stones in her own distinctive way.

People underestimate bees.

Granny Weatherwax didn't. She had half a dozen hives of them and knew, for example, there is no such creature as an individual bee. But there is such a creature as a swarm, whose component cells are just a bit more mobile than those of, say, the common whelk. Swarms see everything and sense a lot more, and they can remember things for years, although their memory tends to be external and built out of wax. A honeycomb is a hive's memory—the placement of egg cells, pollen cells, queen cells, honey cells, different *types* of honey, are all part of the memory array.

And then there are the big fat drones. People think all they do is hang around the hive all year, waiting for those few brief minutes when the queen even notices their existence, but that doesn't explain why they've got more sense organs than the roof of the CIA building.

Granny didn't really *keep* bees. She took some old wax every year, for candles, and the occasional pound of honey that the hives felt they could spare, but mainly she had them for someone to talk to.

For the first time since she'd returned home, she went to the hives.

And stared.

Bees were boiling out of the entrances. The thrum of wings filled the normally calm little patch behind the raspberry bushes. Brown bodies zipped through the air like horizontal hail.

She wished she knew why.

Bees were her one failure. There wasn't a mind in Lancre she couldn't Borrow. She could even see the world through the eyes of earthworms.* But a swarm, a mind made up of thousands of mobile parts, was beyond her. It was the toughest test of all. She'd tried over and over again to ride on one, to see the world through ten thousand pairs of multi-faceted eyes all at once, and all she'd ever got was a migraine and an inclination to make love to flowers.

But you could tell a lot from just watching bees. The activity, the direction, the way the guard bees acted . . .

They were acting *extremely worried*.

So she went for a lie down, as only Granny Weatherwax knew how.

Nanny Ogg tried a different way, which didn't have much to do with witchcraft but *did* have a lot to do with her general Oggishness.

She sat for a while in her spotless kitchen, drinking rum and smoking her foul pipe and staring at the paintings on the wall. They had been done by her youngest grandchildren in a dozen shades of mud, most of them of blobby stick figures with the word GRAN blobbily blobbed in underneath in muddy blobby letters.

In front of her the cat Greebo, glad to be home again, lay on his back with all four paws in the air, doing his celebrated something-found-in-the-gutter impersonation.

Finally Nanny got up and ambled thoughtfully down to Jason Ogg's smithy.

---

*It was largely dark.

A smithy always occupied an important position in the villages, doing the duty of town hall, meeting room, and general clearing house for gossip. Several men were lounging around in it now, filling in time between the normal Lancre occupations of poaching and watching the women do the work.

"Jason Ogg, I wants a *word* with you."

The smithy emptied like magic. It was probably something in Nanny Ogg's tone of voice. But Nanny reached out and grabbed one man by the arm as he tried to go past at a sort of stumbling crouch.

"I'm *glad* I've run into you, Mr. Quarney," she said. "Don't rush off. Store doing all right, is it?"

Lancre's only storekeeper gave her the look a threelegged mouse gives an athletic cat. Nevertheless, he tried.

"Oh, terrible bad, terrible bad business is right now, Mrs. Ogg."

"Same as normal, eh?"

Mr. Quarney's expression was pleading. He knew he wasn't going to get out without *something*, he just wanted to know what it was.

"Well, now," said Nanny, "you know the widow Scrope, lives over in Slice?"

Quarney's mouth opened.

"She's not a widow," he said. "She—"

"Bet you half a dollar?" said Nanny.

Quarney's mouth stayed open, and around it the rest of his face recomposed itself in an expression of fascinated horror.

"So she's to be allowed credit, right, until she gets the farm on its feet," said Nanny, in the silence. Quarney nodded mutely.

"That goes for the rest of you men listening outside the door," said Nanny, raising her voice. "Dropping a cut of meat on her doorstep once a week wouldn't come amiss, eh? And she'll probably want extra help come harvest. I knows I can depend on you all. Now, off you go . . ."

They ran for it, leaving Nanny Ogg standing triumphantly in the doorway.

Jason Ogg looked at her hopelessly, a fifteen-stone man reduced to a four-year-old boy.

"Jason?"

"I got to do this bit of brazing for old—"

"So," said Nanny, ignoring him, "what's been happening in these parts while we've been away, my lad?"

Jason poked at the fire distractedly with an iron bar.

"Oh, well, us had a big whirlwind on Hogswatch-night and one of Mother Peason's hens laid the same egg three times, and old Poorchick's cow gave birth to a seven-headed snake, and there was a rain of frogs over in Slice—"

"Been pretty normal, then," said Nanny Ogg. She refilled her pipe in a casual but meaningful way.

"All very quiet, really," said Jason. He pulled the bar out of the fire, laid it on the anvil, and raised his hammer.

"I'll find out sooner or later, you know," said Nanny Ogg.

Jason didn't turn his head, but his hammer stopped in mid-air.

"I always does, you know," said Nanny Ogg.

The iron cooled from the color of fresh straw to bright red.

"You knows you always feels better for telling your old mum," said Nanny Ogg.

The iron cooled from red to spitting black. But Jason, used all day to the searing heat of a forge, seemed to be uncomfortably warm.

"I should beat it up before it gets cold," said Nanny Ogg.

"Weren't my fault, Mum! How could I stop 'em?"

Nanny sat back in the chair, smiling happily.

"What them would these be, my son?"

"That young Diamanda and that Perdita and that girl with the red hair from over in Bad Ass and them others. I *says* to old Peason, I says you'd have something to say, I *tole* 'em Mistress Weatherwax'd get her knic—would definitely be sarcastic when she found out," said Jason. "But they just laughs. They said they could teach 'emselves witching."

Nanny nodded. Actually, they were quite right. You *could* teach yourself witchcraft. But both the teacher and the pupil had to be the right kind of person.

"Diamanda?" she said. "Don't recall the name."

"Really she's Lucy Tockley," said Jason. "She says Diamanda is more . . . more witchy."

"Ah. The one that wears the big floppy felt hat?"

"Yes, Mum."

"She's the one that paints her nails black, too?"

"Yes, Mum."

"Old Tockley sent her off to school, didn't he?"

"Yes, Mum. She came back while you was gone."

"Ah."

Nanny Ogg lit her pipe from the forge. Floppy hat and black nails and education. Oh, dear.

"How many of these gels are there, then?" she said.

"Bout half a dozen. But they'm *good* at it, Mum."

"Yeah?"

"And it ain't as if they've been doing anything bad."

Nanny Ogg stared reflectively at the glow in the forge.

There was a bottomless quality to Nanny Ogg's silences. And also a certain directional component. Jason was quite clear that the silence was being aimed at him.

He always fell for it. He tried to fill it up.

"And that Diamanda's been properly educated," he said. "She knows some lovely words."

Silence.

"And I knows you've always said there weren't enough young girls interested in learnin' witching these days," said Jason. He removed the iron bar and hit it a few times, for the look of the thing.

More silence flowed in Jason's direction.

"They goes and dances up in the mountains every full moon."

Nanny Ogg removed her pipe and inspected the bowl carefully.

"People do say," said Jason, lowering his voice, "that they dances in the altogether."

"Altogether what?" said Nanny Ogg.

"You know, Mum. In the nudd."

"Cor. There's a thing. Anyone see where they go?"

"Nah. Weaver the thatcher says they always gives him the slip."

"Jason?"

"Yes, Mum?"

"They bin dancin' around the stones."

Jason hit his thumb.

There were a number of gods in the mountains and forests of Lancre. One of them was known as Herne the Hunted. He was a god of the chase and the hunt. More or less.

Most gods are created and sustained by belief and hope. Hunters danced in animal skins and created gods of the chase, who tended to be hearty and boisterous with the tact of a tidal wave. But they are not the only gods of hunting. The prey has an occult voice too, as the blood pounds and the hounds bay. Herne was the god of the chased and the hunted and all small animals whose ultimate destiny is to be an abrupt damp squeak.

He was about three feet high with rabbit ears and very small horns. But he did have an extremely good turn of speed, and was using it to the full as he tore madly through the woods.

"They're coming! They're coming! *They're all coming back!*"

"Who are?" said Jason Ogg. He was holding his thumb in the water trough.

Nanny Ogg sighed.

"*Them,*" she said. "You know. *Them.* We ain't certain, but . . ."

"Who's Them?"

Nanny hesitated. There were some things you didn't tell ordinary people. On the other hand, Jason was a blacksmith, which meant he wasn't ordinary. Blacksmiths had to keep secrets. And he was family; Nanny Ogg had had an adventurous youth and wasn't very good at counting, but she was pretty certain he was her son.

"You see," she said, waving her hands vaguely, "them stones . . . the Dancers . . . see, in the old days . . . see, once upon a time . . ."

She stopped, and tried again to explain the essentially fractal nature of reality.

"Like . . . there's some places that're *thinner* than others, where the old doorways used to be, well, not doorways, never exactly understood it myself, not doorways as such, more places where the world is *thinner* . . . Anyway, the thing *is*, the Dancers . . . are a kind of fence . . . we, well, when I say *we* I mean thousands of years ago . . . I mean, but they're not just stones, they're some kind of thunderbolt iron but . . . there's things like tides, only not with water, it's when worlds get closer together'n you can nearly step between 'em . . . anyway, if people've been hangin' around the stones, playin' around . . . then *They'll* be back, if we're not careful."

"What They?"

"That's the whole trouble," said Nanny, miserably. "If I tells you, you'll get it all wrong. They lives on the other side of the Dancers."

Her son stared at her. Then a faint grin of realization wandered across his face.

"Ah," he said. "I knows. I heard them wizards down in Ankh is always accidentally rippin' holes in this fabric o' reality they got down there, and you get them horrible things coming out o' the Dungeon Dimensions. Huge buggers with dozens o' eyeballs and more legs'n a Morris team." He gripped his No. 5 hammer. "Don't you worry, Mum. If they starts poppin' out here, we'll soon—"

"No, it *ain't* like that," said Nanny. "Those live *outside*. But Them lives . . . over there."

Jason looked completely lost.

Nanny shrugged. She'd have to tell someone, sooner or later.

"The Lords and Ladies," she said.

"Who're they?"

Nanny looked around. But, after all, this was a forge. There had been a forge here long before there was a castle, long before there was even a kingdom. There were horseshoes everywhere. Iron had entered the very walls. It wasn't just a place of iron, it was a place where iron died and was reborn. If you couldn't speak the words here, you couldn't speak 'em anywhere.

Even so, she'd rather not.

"*You* know," she said. "The Fair Folk. The Gentry. The Shining Ones. The Star People. *You* know."

"What?"

Nanny put her hand on the anvil, just in case, and said the word.

Jason's frown very gently cleared, at about the same speed as a sunrise.

"Them?" he said. "But aren't they nice and—?"

"See?" said Nanny. "I *told* you you'd get it wrong!"

"*How* much?" said Ridcully.

The coachman shrugged.

"Take it or leave it," he said.

"I'm sorry, sir," said Ponder Stibbons. "It's the only coach."

"Fifty dollars each is daylight robbery!"

"No," said the coachman patiently. "Daylight robbery," he said, in the authoritative tones of the experienced, "is when someone steps out into the road with an arrow pointing at us and then all his friends swings down from the rocks and trees and take away all our money and things. And then there's nighttime robbery, which is like daytime robbery except they set fire to the coach so's they can see what they're about. Twilight robbery, now, your basic twilight robbery is—"

"Are you saying," said Ridcully, "that getting robbed is included in the *price*?"

"Bandits' Guild," said the coachman. "Forty dollars per head, see. It's a kind of flat rate."

"What happens if we don't pay it?" said Ridcully.

"You end up flat."

The wizards went into a huddle.

"We've got a hundred and fifty dollars," said Ridcully. "We can't get any more out of the safe because the Bursar ate the key yesterday."

"Can I try an idea, sir?" said Ponder.

"All right."

Ponder gave the coachman a bright smile.

"Pets travel free?" he suggested.

"Oook?"

Nanny Ogg's broomstick skimmed a few feet above the forest paths, cornering so fast that her boots scraped through the leaves. She leapt off at Granny Weatherwax's cottage so quickly that she didn't switch it off, and it kept going until it stuck in the privy.

The door was open.

"Cooee?"

Nanny glanced into the scullery, and then thumped up the small narrow staircase.

Granny Weatherwax was stretched rigid on her bed. Her face was gray, her skin was cold.

People had discovered her like this before, and it always caused embarrassment. So now she reassured visitors but tempted fate by always holding, in her rigid hands, a small handwritten sign which read:

I ATE'NT DEAD.

The window was propped open with a piece of wood.

"Ah," said Nanny, far more for her own benefit than for anyone else's, "I sees you're out. I'll, I'll, I'll just put the kettle on, shall I, and wait 'til you comes back?"

Esme's skill at Borrowing unnerved her. It was all very well entering the minds of animals and such, but too many witches had never come back. For several years Nanny had put out lumps of fat and bacon rind for a bluetit that she was sure was old Granny Postalute, who'd gone out Borrowing one day and never came back. Insofar as a witch could consider things uncanny, Nanny Ogg considered it uncanny.

She went back down to the scullery and lowered a bucket down the well, remembering to fish the newts out this time before she boiled the kettle.

Then she watched the garden.

After a while a small shape flittered across it, heading for the upstairs window.

Nanny poured out the tea. She carefully took one spoonful of sugar out of the sugar basin, tipped the *rest* of the sugar into her cup, put the spoonful back in the basin, put both cups on a tray, and climbed the stairs.

Granny Weatherwax was sitting up in her bed.

Nanny looked around.

There was a large bat hanging upside down from a beam.

Granny Weatherwax rubbed her ears.

"Shove the po under it, will you, Gytha?" she mumbled. "They're a devil for excusing themselves on the carpet."

Nanny unearthed the shyest article of Granny Weatherwax's bedroom crockery and moved it across the rug with her foot.

"I brought you a cup of tea," she said.

"Good job, too. Mouth tastes of moths," said Granny.

"Thought you did owls at night?" said Nanny.

"Yeah, but you ends up for days trying to twist your head right round," said Granny. "At least bats always faces the same way. Tried rabbits first off, but you know what they are for remembering things. Anyway, you know what *they* thinks about the whole time. They're famous for it."

"Grass."

"Right."

"Find out anything?" said Nanny.

"Half a dozen people have been going up there. Every full moon!" said Granny. "Gels, by the shape of them. You only see silhouettes, with bats."

"You done well there," said Nanny, carefully. "Girls from round here, you reckon?"

"Got to be. They ain't using broomsticks."

Nanny Ogg sighed.

"There's Agnes Nitt, old Threepenny's daughter," she said. "And the Tockley girl. And some others."

Granny Weatherwax looked at her with her mouth open.

"I asked our Jason," she said. "Sorry."

The bat burped. Granny genteelly covered her hand with her mouth.

"I'm a silly old fool, ain't I?" she said, after a while.

"No, no," said Nanny. "Borrowing's a real skill. You're really good at it."

"Prideful, that's what I am. Once upon a time I'd of thought of asking people, too, instead of fooling around being a bat."

"Our Jason wouldn't have told you. He only told me 'cos I would've made 'is life a living hell if he didn't," said Nanny Ogg. "That's what a mother's for."

"I'm losing my touch, that's what it is. Getting old, Gytha."

"You're as old as you feel, that's what I always say."

"That's what I mean."

Nanny Ogg looked worried.

"Supposing Magrat'd been here," said Granny. "She'd see me being daft."

"Well, she's safe in the castle," said Nanny. "Learning how to be queen."

"At least the thing about queening," said Granny, "is that no one notices if you're doing it wrong. It *has* to be right 'cos it's *you* doing it."

"S'funny, royalty," said Nanny. "It's like magic. You take some girl with a bum like two pigs in a blanket and a head full of air and then she marries a king or a prince or someone and suddenly she's this radiant right royal princess. It's a funny old world."

"I ain't going to kowtow to her, mind," said Granny.

"You never kowtow to anyone anyway," said Nanny Ogg patiently. "You never bowed to the old king. You barely gives young Verence a nod. You never kowtows to anyone ever, anyway."

"That's right!" said Granny. "That's part of being a witch, that is."

Nanny relaxed a bit. Granny being an old woman made her uneasy. Granny in her normal state of barely controlled anger was far more her old self.

Granny stood up.

"Old Tockley's girl, eh?"

"That's right."

"Her mother was a Keeble, wasn't she? Fine woman, as I recall."

"Yeah, but when she died the old man sent her off to Sto Lat to school."

"Don't hold with schools," said Granny Weatherwax. "They gets in the way of education. All them books. Books? What good are they? There's too much reading these days. We never had time to read when we was young, I know that."

"We were too busy makin' our own entertainment."

"Right. Come on—we ain't got much time."

"What d'you mean?"

"It's not just the girls. There's something out there, too. Some kind of mind, movin' around."

Granny shivered. She'd been aware of it in the same way that a skilled hunter, moving through the hills, is aware of another hunter—by the silences where there should have been noise, by the trampling of a stem, by the anger of the bees.

Nanny Ogg had never liked the idea of Borrowing, and Magrat had always refused even to give it a try. The old witches on the other side of the mountain had too much trouble with inconvenient in-body experiences to cope with the out-of-body kind. So Granny was used to having the mental dimension to herself.

There was a mind moving around in the kingdom, and Granny Weatherwax didn't understand it.

She Borrowed. You had to be careful. It was like a drug. You could ride the minds of animals and birds, but never bees, steering them gently, seeing through their eyes. Granny Weatherwax had many times flicked through the channels of consciousness around her. It was, to her, part of the heart of witchcraft. To see through other eyes . . .

. . . through the eyes of gnats, seeing the slow patterns of time in the fast pattern of one day, their minds traveling rapidly as lightning . . .

. . . to listen with the body of a beetle, so that the world is a three-dimensional pattern of vibrations . . .

. . . to see with the nose of a dog, all smells now colors . . .

But there was a price. No one asked you to pay it, but the very *absence* of demand was a moral obligation. You tended not to swat. You dug lightly. You fed the dog. You paid. You *cared*; not because it was kind or good, but because it was right. You left nothing but memories, you took nothing but experience.

But this other roving intelligence . . . it'd go in

and out of another mind like a chainsaw, taking, taking, taking. She could sense the shape of it, the predatory shape, all cruelty and cool unkindness; a mind full of intelligence, that'd use other living things and hurt them because it was fun.

She could put a name to a mind like that.

Elf.

Branches thrashed high in the trees.

Granny and Nanny strode through the forest. At least, Granny Weatherwax strode. Nanny Ogg scurried.

"The Lords and Ladies are trying to find a way," said Granny. "And there's something else. Something's already come through. Some kind of animal from the other side. Scrope chased a deer into the circle and the thing must have been there, and they always used to say something can come through if something goes the other way—"

"What thing?"

"You know what a bat's eyesight is like. Just a big shape is all it saw. Something killed old Scrope. It's still around. Not an . . . not one o' the Lords and Ladies," said Granny, "but something from El . . . that place."

Nanny looked at the shadows. There are a lot of shadows in a forest at night.

"Ain't you scared?" she said.

Granny cracked her knuckles.

"No. But I hope it is."

"Ooo, it's true what they say. You're a prideful one, Esmerelda Weatherwax."

"Who says that?"

"Well, you did. Just now."

"I wasn't feeling well."

Other people would probably say: I wasn't myself. But Granny Weatherwax didn't have anyone else to be.

The two witches hurried on through the gale.

From the shelter of a thorn thicket, the unicorn watched them go.

Diamanda Tockley did indeed wear a floppy black velvet hat. It had a veil, too.

Perdita Nitt, who had once been merely Agnes Nitt before she got witchcraft, wore a black hat with a veil too, because Diamanda did. Both of them were seventeen. And she wished she was naturally skinny, like Diamanda, but if you can't be skinny you can at least look unhealthy. So she wore so much thick white makeup in order to conceal her naturally rosy complexion that if she turned around suddenly her face would probably end up on the back of her head.

They'd done the Raising of the Cone of Power, and some candle magic, and some scrying. Now Diamanda was showing them how to do the cards.

She said they contained the distilled wisdom of the Ancients. Perdita had found herself treacherously wondering who these Ancients were—they clearly weren't the same as *old people*, who were stupid, Diamanda said, but she wasn't quite clear why they were wiser than, say, modern people.

Also, she didn't understand what the Feminine Principle was. And she wasn't too clear about this Inner Self business. She was coming to suspect that she didn't have one.

And she wished she could do her eyes like Diamanda did.

And she wished she could wear heels like Diamanda did.

Amanita DeVice had told her that Diamanda slept in a real coffin.

She wished she had the nerve to have a dagger-and-skull tattoo on her arm like Amanita did, even if it *was* only in ordinary ink and she had to wash it off every night in case her mother saw it.

A tiny, nasty voice from Perdita's inner self suggested that Amanita wasn't a good choice of name.

Or Perdita, for that matter.

And it said that maybe Perdita shouldn't meddle with things she didn't understand.

The trouble was, she knew, that this meant nearly everything.

She wished she could wear black lace like Diamanda did.

Diamanda got results.

Perdita wouldn't have believed it. She'd always known about witches, of course. They were old women who dressed like crows, except for Magrat Garlick, who was frankly *mental* and always looked as if she was going to burst into tears. Perdita remembered Magrat bringing a guitar to a Hogswatchnight party once and singing wobbly folk songs with her eyes shut in a way that suggested that she really believed in them. She hadn't been able to play, but this was all right because she couldn't sing, either. People had applauded because, well, what else could you do?

But Diamanda had read books. She knew about

stuff. Raising power at the stones, for one thing. It really worked.

Currently she was showing them the cards.

The wind had got up again tonight. It rattled the shutters and made soot fall down the chimney. It seemed to Perdita that it had blown all the shadows into the corners of the room—

"Are you paying attention, sister?" said Diamanda coldly.

That was another thing. You had to call one another 'sister,' out of fraternity.

"Yes, Diamanda," she said, meekly.

"*This* is the Moon," Diamanda repeated, "for those who weren't paying attention." She held up the card. "And what do we see here—you, Muscara?"

"Um . . . it's got a picture of the moon on it?" said Muscara (*née* Susan) in a hopeful voice.

"Of course it's not the *moon*. It's a nonmimetic convention, not tied to a conventional referencing system, *actually*," said Diamanda.

"Ah."

A gust rocked the cottage. The door burst open and slammed back against the wall, giving a glimpse of cloud-wracked sky in which a nonmimetic convention was showing a crescent.

Diamanda waved a hand. There was a brief flash of octarine light. The door jerked shut. Diamanda smiled in what Perdita thought of as her cool, knowing way.

She placed the card on the black velvet cloth in front of her.

Perdita looked at it gloomily. It was all very pretty, the cards were colored like little pasteboard jewels, and they had interesting names. But that little traitor voice whispered: how the hell can they know what the future holds? Cardboard isn't very bright.

On the other hand, the coven *was* helping people . . . more or less. Raising power and all that sort of thing. Oh dear, supposing she asks *me*?

Perdita realized that she was feeling worried. Something was wrong. It had just gone wrong. She didn't know what it was, but it had gone wrong now. She looked up.

"Blessings be upon this house," said Granny Weatherwax.

In much the same tone of voice have people said, "Eat hot lead, Kincaid," and, "I expect you're wondering after all that excitement whether I've got any balloons and lampshades left."

Diamanda's mouth dropped open.

" 'Ere, you're doing that wrong. You don't want to muck about with a hand like that," said Nanny Ogg helpfully, looking over her shoulder. "You've got a Double Onion there."

"Who are *you*?"

Suddenly they were there. Perdita thought: one minute there's shadows, the next minute they were *there*, solid as anything.

"What's all the chalk on the floor, then?" said Nanny Ogg. "You've got all chalk on the floor. And heathen writing. Not that I've got anything against heathens," she added. She appeared to think about it. "I'm practic'ly one," she added further, "but I don't write on the floor. What'd you want to write all on the floor for?" She nudged Perdita. "You'll never get the chalk out," she said, "it gets right into the grain."

"Um, it's a magic circle," said Perdita. "Um, hello, Mrs. Ogg. Um. It's to keep bad influences away . . ."

Granny Weatherwax leaned forward slightly.

"Tell me, my dear," she said to Diamanda, "do you think it's working?"

She leaned forward further.

Diamanda leaned backward.

And then slowly leaned forward again.

They ended up nose to nose.

"Who's this?" said Diamanda, out of the corner of her mouth.

"Um, it's Granny Weatherwax," said Perdita. "Um. She's a witch, um . . ."

"What level?" said Diamanda.

Nanny Ogg looked around for something to hide behind. Granny Weatherwax's eyebrow twitched.

"Levels, eh?" she said. "Well, I suppose I'm level one."

"Just starting?" said Diamanda.

"Oh dear. Tell you what," said Nanny Ogg quietly to Perdita, "if we was to turn the table over, we could probably hide behind it, no problem."

But to herself she was thinking: Esme can never resist a challenge. None of us can. You ain't a witch if you ain't got self-confidence. But we're not getting any younger. It's like being a hired swordfighter, being a top witch. You think you're good, but you know there's got to be someone younger, practicing every day, polishing up their craft, and one day you're walkin' down the road and you hears this voice behind you sayin': go for your toad, or similar.

Even for Esme. Sooner or later, she'll come up against someone faster on the craftiness than she is.

"Oh, yes," said Granny, quietly. "Just starting. Every day, just starting."

Nanny Ogg thought: but it won't be today.

"You stupid old woman," said Diamanda, "you don't frighten me. Oh, yes. I know all about the way you old ones frighten superstitious peasants, *actually*. Muttering and squinting. It's all in the mind. Simple psychology. It's not *real* witchcraft."

"I'll, er, I'll just go into the scullery and, er, see if I can fill any buckets with water, shall I?" said Nanny Ogg, to no one in particular.

"I 'spect you'd know *all* about witchcraft," said Granny Weatherwax.

"I'm studying, yes," said Diamanda.

Nanny Ogg realized that she had removed her own hat and was biting nervously at the brim.

"I 'spect you're *really* good at it," said Granny Weatherwax.

"Quite good," said Diamanda.

"*Show me.*"

She *is* good, thought Nanny Ogg. She's been facing down Esme's stare for more'n a minute. Even *snakes* generally give up after a minute.

If a fly had darted through the few inches of space between their stares it would have flashed into flame in the air.

"I learned my craft from Nanny Gripes," said Granny Weatherwax, "who learned it from Goody Heggety, who got it from Nanna Plumb, who was taught it by Black Aliss, who—"

"So what you're saying *is*," said Diamanda, loading the words into the sentence like cartridges in a chamber, "that *no one* has *actually* learned anything *new*?"

The silence that followed was broken by Nanny Ogg saying: "Bugger, I've bitten right through the brim. Right through."

"I *see*," said Granny Weatherwax.

"Look," said Nanny Ogg hurriedly, nudging the trembling Perdita, "right through the lining and everything. Two dollars and curing his pig that hat cost me. That's two dollars and a pig cure I shan't see again in a hurry."

"So you can just go away, old woman," said Diamanda.

"But we ought to meet again," said Granny Weatherwax.

The old witch and the young witch weighed one another up.

"Midnight?" said Diamanda.

"Midnight? Nothing special about midnight. Practic'ly anyone can be a witch at midnight," said Granny Weatherwax. "How about noon?"

"Certainly. What are we fighting for?" said Diamanda.

"Fighting? We ain't *fighting*. We're just showing each other what we can do. Friendly like," said Granny Weatherwax.

She stood up.

"I'd better be goin'," she said. "Us old people need our sleep, you know how it is."

"And what does the winner get?" said Diamanda. There was just a trace of uncertainty in her voice now. It was very faint, on the Richter scale of doubt it was probably no more than a plastic teacup five miles away falling off a low shelf onto a carpet, but it was there.

"Oh, the winner gets to win," said Granny Weatherwax. "That's what it's all about. Don't bother to see us out. You didn't see us in."

The door slammed back.

"Simple psychokinesis," said Diamanda.

"Oh, well. That's all right then," said Granny Weatherwax, disappearing into the night. "Explains it all, that does."

There used to be such simple directions, back in the days before they invented parallel universes—Up and Down, Right and Left, Backward and Forward, Past and Future . . .

But normal directions don't work in the multiverse, which has far too many dimensions for anyone to find their way. So new ones have to be invented so that the way *can* be found.

Like: East of the Sun, West of the Moon.

Or: Behind the North Wind.

Or: At the Back of Beyond.

Or: There and Back Again.

Or: Beyond the Fields We Know.

And sometimes there's a short cut. A door or a gate. Some standing stones, a tree cleft by lightning, a filing cabinet.

Maybe just a spot on some moorland somewhere . . .

A place where *there* is very nearly *here*.

Nearly, but not quite. There's enough leakage to make pendulums swing and psychics get nasty headaches, to give a house a reputation for being haunted, to make the occasional pot hurl across a room. There's enough leakage to make the drones fly guard.

Oh, yes. The drones.

There are things called drone assemblies. Sometimes, on fine summer days, the drones from hives for miles around will congregate in some spot, and fly circles in the air, buzzing like tiny early warning systems, which is what they are.

Bees are sensible. It's a human word. But bees are creatures of order, and programmed into their very genes is a hatred of chaos.

If some people once knew where such a spot was, if they had experience of what happens when here and there become entangled, then they might—if they knew how—mark such a spot with certain stones.

In the hope that enough daft buggers would take it as a warning, and keep away.

"Well, what'd you think?" said Granny, as the witches hurried home.

"The little fat quiet one's got a bit of natural talent," said Nanny Ogg. "I could feel it. The rest of 'em are just along for the excitement, to my mind. Playing at witches. You know, ooh-jar boards and cards and wearing black lace gloves with no fingers to 'em and paddlin' with the occult."

"I don't hold with paddlin' with the occult," said Granny firmly. "Once you start paddlin' with the occult you start believing in spirits, and when you start believing in spirits you start believing in demons, and then before you know where you are you're believing in gods. And then you're in *trouble*."

"But all them things exist," said Nanny Ogg.

"That's no call to go around believing in them. It only encourages 'em."

Granny Weatherwax slowed to a walk.

"What about *her*?" she said.

"What exactly about her do you mean?"

"You felt the power there?"

"Oh, yeah. Made my hair stand on end."

"Someone gave it to her, and I know who. Just a slip of a gel with a head full of wet ideas out of books, and suddenly she's got the power and don't know how to deal with it. Cards! Candles! That's not witchcraft, that's just party games. Paddlin' with the occult. Did you see she'd got black finger-nails?"

"Well, mine ain't so clean—"

"I mean painted."

"I used to paint my toenails red when I was young," said Nanny, wistfully.

"Toenails is different. So's red. Anyway," said Granny, "you only did it to appear allurin'."

"It worked, too."

"Hah!"

They walked along in silence for a bit.

"I felt a *lot* of power there," Nanny Ogg said, eventually.

"Yes. I know."

"A lot."

"Yes."

"I'm not saying you couldn't beat her," said Nanny quickly. "I'm not saying that. But I don't reckon I could, and it seemed to me it'd raise a bit of a sweat even on you. You'll have to hurt her to beat her."

"I'm losin' my judgment, aren't I?"

"Oh, I—"

"She *riled* me, Gytha. Couldn't help myself. Now I've got to duel with a gel of seventeen, and if I wins I'm a wicked bullyin' old witch, and if I loses . . ."

She kicked up a drift of old leaves.

"Can't stop myself, that's my trouble."

Nanny Ogg said nothing.

"And I loses my temper over the least little—"

"Yes, but—"

"I hadn't finished talkin'."

"Sorry, Esme."

A bat fluttered by. Granny nodded to it.

"Heard how Magrat's getting along?" she said, in a tone of voice which forced casualness embraced like a corset.

"Settling in fine, our Shawn says."

"Right."

They reached a crossroads; the white dust glowed very faintly in the moonlight. One way led into Lancre, where Nanny Ogg lived. Another eventually got lost in the forest, became a footpath, then a track, and eventually reached Granny Weatherwax's cottage.

"When shall we . . . *two* . . . meet again?" said Nanny Ogg.

"Listen," said Granny Weatherwax. "She's well out of it, d'you hear? She'll be a lot happier as a queen!"

"I never said nothing," said Nanny Ogg mildly.

"I know you never! I could *hear* you not saying

anything! You've got the loudest silences I ever did hear from anyone who wasn't dead!"

"See you about eleven o'clock, then?"

"Right!"

The wind got up again as Granny walked along the track to her cottage.

She knew she was on edge. There was just too much to do. She'd got Magrat sorted out, and Nanny could look after herself, but the Lords and the Ladies . . . she hadn't counted on them.

The point was . . .

The point was that Granny Weatherwax had a feeling she was going to die. This was beginning to get on her nerves.

Knowing the time of your death is one of those strange bonuses that comes with being a true magic user. And, on the whole, it *is* a bonus.

Many a wizard has passed away happily drinking the last of his wine cellar and incidentally owing very large sums of money.

Granny Weatherwax had always wondered how it felt, what it was that you suddenly saw looming up. And what it turned out to be was a blankness.

People think that they live life as a moving dot traveling from the Past into the Future, with memory streaming out behind them like some kind of mental cometary tail. But memory spreads out in front as well as behind. It's just that most humans aren't good at dealing with it, and so it arrives as premonitions, forebodings, intuitions, and hunches. Witches *are* good at dealing with it, and to suddenly find a blank where these tendrils of the future should be has much the same effect on a witch as emerging from a cloud bank and seeing a team of sherpas looking down on him does on an airline pilot.

She'd got a few days, and then that was it. She'd always expected to have a bit of time to herself, get the garden in order, have a good clean up around the place so that whatever witch took over wouldn't think she'd been a sloven, pick out a decent burial plot, and then spend some time sitting out in the rocking chair, doing nothing at all except looking at the trees and thinking about the past. Now . . . no chance.

And other things were happening. Her memory seemed to be playing up. Perhaps this is what happened. Perhaps you just drained away toward the end, like old Nanny Gripes, who ended up putting the cat on the stove and the kettle out for the night.

Granny shut the door behind her and lit a candle.

There was a box in the dresser drawer. She opened it on the kitchen table and took out the carefully folded piece of paper. There was a pen and ink in there, too.

After some thought, she picked up where she had left off:

. . . and to my friend Gytha Ogg I leave my bedde and the rag rugge the smith in Bad Ass made for me, and the matchin jug and basin and wosfname sett she always had her eye on, and my broomstick what will be Right as Rain with a bit of work.

To Magrat Garlick I leave the Contentes elsewhere in this box, my silver tea service with the milk jug in the shape of a humerous cow what is an Heir Loom, also the Clocke what belonged to my mother, but I charge her always to keep it wound, for when the clocke stops—

There was a noise outside.

If anyone else had been in the room with her Granny Weatherwax would have thrown open the door boldly, but she was by herself. She picked up the poker very carefully, moved surprisingly soundlessly to the door given the nature of her boots, and listened intently.

There was something in the garden.

It wasn't much of a garden. There were the Herbs, and the soft fruit bushes, a bit of lawn and, of course, the beehives. And it was open to the woods. The local wildlife knew better than to invade a witch's garden.

Granny opened the door carefully.

The moon was setting. Pale silver light turned the world into monochrome.

There was a unicorn on the lawn. The stink of it hit her.

Granny advanced, holding the poker in front of her. The unicorn backed away, and pawed at the ground.

Granny saw the future plain. She already knew the *when*. Now she was beginning to apprehend the *how*.

"So," she said, under her breath, "I knows where *you* came from. And you can damn well get back there."

The thing made a feint at her, but the poker swung toward it.

"Can't stand the iron, eh? Well, just you trot back to your mistress and tell her that we know all about iron in Lancre. And I knows about her. She's to keep away, understand? This is my place!"

* * *

Then it was moonlight. Now it was day.

There was quite a crowd in what passed for Lancre's main square. Not much happened in Lancre anyway, and a duel between witches was a sight worth seeing.

Granny Weatherwax arrived at a quarter to noon. Nanny Ogg was waiting on a bench by the tavern. She had a towel around her neck, and was carrying a bucket of water in which floated a sponge.

"What's that for?" said Granny.

"Half time. And I done you a plate of oranges."

She held up the plate. Granny snorted.

"You look as if you could do with eating something, anyway," said Nanny. "You don't look as if you've had anything today . . ."

She glanced down at Granny's boots, and the grubby hem of her long black dress. There were scraps of bracken and bits of heather caught on it.

"You daft old besom!" she hissed. "What've you been *doing*!"

"I had to—"

"You've been up at the Stones, haven't you! Trying to hold back the Gentry."

"Of course," said Granny. Her voice wasn't faint. She wasn't swaying. But her voice wasn't faint and she wasn't swaying, Nanny Ogg could see, because Granny Weatherwax's body was in the grip of Granny Weatherwax's mind.

"Someone's got to," she added.

"You could have come and asked me!"

"You'd have talked me out of it."

Nanny Ogg leaned forward.

"You all right, Esme?"

"Fine! I'm fine! Nothing wrong with me, all right?"

"Have you had any sleep at all?" she said.

"Well—"

"You haven't, have you? And then you think you can just stroll down here and confound this girl, just like that?"

"I don't know," said Granny Weatherwax.

Nanny Ogg looked hard at her.

"You don't, do you?" she said, in a softer tone of voice. "Oh, well . . . you better sit down here, before you fall down. Suck an orange. They'll be here in a few minutes."

"No she won't," said Granny. "She'll be late."

"How d'you know?"

"No good making an entrance if everyone isn't there to see you, is it? That's headology."

In fact the young coven arrived at twenty past twelve, and took up station on the steps of the market pentangle on the other side of the square.

"Look at 'em," said Granny Weatherwax. "All in black, again."

"Well, we wear black too," said Nanny Ogg the reasonable.

"Only 'cos it's respectable and serviceable," said Granny morosely. "Not because it's romantic. Hah. The Lords and Ladies might as well be here already."

After some eye contact, Nanny Ogg ambled across the square and met Perdita in the middle. The young would-be witch looked worried under her makeup. She held a black lace handkerchief in her hands, and was twisting it nervously.

"Morning, Mrs. Ogg," she said.

"Afternoon, Agnes."

"Um. What happens now?"

Nanny Ogg took out her pipe and scratched her ear with it.

"Dunno. Up to you, I suppose."

"Diamanda says why does it have to be here and now?"

"So's everyone can see," said Nanny Ogg. "That's the point, ain't it? Nothing hole and corner about it. Everyone's got to know who's best at witchcraft. The whole town. Everyone sees the winner win and the loser lose. That way there's no argument, eh?"

Perdita glanced toward the tavern. Granny Weatherwax had dozed off.

"Quietly confident," said Nanny Ogg, crossing her fingers behind her back.

"Um, what happens to the loser?" said Perdita.

"Nothing, really," said Nanny Ogg. "Generally she leaves the place. You can't be a witch if people've seen you beat."

"Diamanda says she doesn't want to hurt the old lady too much," said Perdita. "Just teach her a lesson."

"That's nice. Esme's a quick learner."

"Um. I wish this wasn't happening, Mrs. Ogg."

"That's nice."

"Diamanda says Mistress Weatherwax has got a very impressive stare, Mrs. Ogg."

"That's nice."

"So the test is . . . just staring, Mrs. Ogg."

Nanny put her pipe in her mouth.

"You mean the old first-one-to-blink-or-look-away challenge?"

"Um, yes."

"Right." Nanny thought about it, and shrugged. "Right. But we'd better do a magic circle first. Don't want anyone else getting hurt, do we?"

"Do you mean using Skorhian Runes or the Triple Invocation octogram?" said Perdita.

Nanny Ogg put her head on one side.

"Never heard of them things, dear," she said. "I always does a magic circle like this . . ."

She sidled crabwise away from the fat girl, dragging one toe in the dust. She edged around in a rough circle about fifteen feet across, still dragging her boot, until she backed into Perdita.

"Sorry. There. Done it."

"*That's* a magic circle?"

"Right. People can come to harm else. All kinds of magic zipping around the place when witches fight."

"But you didn't chant or *anything*."

"No?"

"There has to be a chant, doesn't there?"

"Dunno. Never done one."

"Oh."

"I could sing you a comic song if you likes," said Nanny helpfully.

"Um, no. Um." Perdita had never heard Nanny sing, but news gets around.

"I like your black lace hanky," said Nanny, not a bit abashed. "Very good for not showing the bogies."

Perdita stared at the circle as though hypnotized. "Um. Shall we start, then?"

"Right."

Nanny Ogg scurried back to the bench and elbowed Granny in the ribs.

"Wake up!"

Granny opened an eye.

"I weren't asleep, I was just resting me eyes."

"All you've got to do is stare her down!"

"At least she knows about the importance of the stare, then. Hah! Who does she think she is? I've been staring at people all my life!"

"Yes, that's what's bothering me—*aaahh . . . who's Nana's little boy, then?*"

The rest of the Ogg clan had arrived.

Granny Weatherwax personally disliked young Pewsey. She disliked all small children, which is why she got on with them so well. In Pewsey's case, she felt that no one should be allowed to wander around in just a vest even if they were four years old. And the child had a permanently runny nose and ought to be provided with a handkerchief or, failing that, a cork.

Nanny Ogg, on the other hand, was instant putty in the hands of any grandchild, even one as sticky as Pewsey.

"Want sweetie," growled Pewsey, in that curiously deep voice some young children have.

"Just in a moment, my duck, I'm talking to the lady," Nanny Ogg fluted.

"Want sweetie *now*."

"Bugger off, my precious, Nana's busy right this minute."

Pewsey pulled hard on Nanny Ogg's skirts.

"*Now* sweetie *now!*"

Granny Weatherwax leaned down until her impressive nose was about level with Pewsey's gushing one.

"If you don't go away," she said gravely, "I will personally rip your head off and fill it with snakes."

"There!" said Nanny Ogg. "There's lots of poor children in Klatch that'd be *grateful* for a curse like that."

Pewsey's little face, after a second or two of uncertainty, split into a pumpkin grin.

"Funny lady," he said.

"Tell you what," said Nanny, patting Pewsey on the head and then absentmindedly wiping her hand on her dress, "you see them young ladies on the other side of the square? They've got *lots* of sweeties."

Pewsey waddled off.

"That's germ warfare, that is," said Granny Weatherwax.

"Come on," said Nanny. "Our Jason's put a couple of chairs in the circle. You sure you're all right?"

"I'll do."

Perdita Nitt traipsed across the road again.

"Er . . . Mrs. Ogg?"

"Yes, dear?"

"Er. Diamanda says you don't understand, she says they won't be trying to outstare one another . . ."

Magrat was bored. She'd never been bored when she was a witch. Permanently bewildered and overworked *yes*, but not bored.

She kept telling herself it'd probably be better when she really *was* queen, although she couldn't quite see how. In the meantime she wandered aimlessly through the castle's many rooms, the swishing of her dress almost unheard above the background roar of the turbines of tedium:

—humdrumhumdrumhumdrum—

She'd spent the whole morning trying to learn to do tapestry, because Millie assured her that's what queens did, and the sampler with its message "Gods bless this Hosue" was even now lying forlornly on her chair.

In the Long Gallery were huge tapestries of ancient battles, done by previous bored regal incumbents; it was amazing how all the fighters had been persuaded to stay still long enough. And she'd looked at the many, many paintings of the queens themselves, all of them pretty, all of them well-dressed according to the fashion of their times, and all of them bored out of their tiny well-shaped skulls.

Finally she went back to the solar. This was the big room on top of the main tower. In theory, it was there to catch the sun. It did. It also caught the wind and the rain. It was a sort of drift net for anything the sky happened to throw.

She yanked on the bellpull that in theory summoned a servant. Nothing happened. After a couple of further pulls, and secretly glad of the exercise, she went down to the kitchen. She would have liked to spend more time there. It was always warm and there was generally someone to talk to. But nobbly-ess obligay—queens had to live Above Stairs.

Below Stairs there was only Shawn Ogg, who was cleaning the oven of the huge iron stove and reflecting that this was no job for a military man.

"Where's everyone gone?"

Shawn leapt up, banging his head on the stove.

"Ow! Sorry, miss! Um! Everyone's . . . everyone's down in the square, miss. I'm only here because

Mrs. Scorbic said she'd have my hide if I didn't get all the yuk off."

"What's happening in the square, then?"

"They say there's a couple of witches having a real set-to, miss."

"What? Not your mother and Granny Weatherwax!"

"Oh no, miss. Some new witch."

"In Lancre? A *new* witch?"

"I think that's what Mum said."

"I'm going to have a look."

"Oh, I don't think that'd be a good idea, miss," said Shawn.

Magrat drew herself up regally.

"We happen to be Queen," she said. "Nearly. So you don't tell one one can't do things, or one'll have you cleaning the privies!"

"But I *does* clean the privies," said Shawn, in a reasonable voice. "Even the garderobe—"

"And *that's* going to go, for a start," said Magrat, shuddering. "One's *seen* it."

"Doesn't bother me, miss, it'll give me Wednesday afternoons free," said Shawn, "but what I meant was, you'll have to wait till I've gone down to the armory to fetch my horn for the fanfare."

"One won't need a fanfare, thank you very much."

"But you got to have a fanfare, miss."

"One can blow my own trumpet, thank you."

"Yes, miss."

"Miss what?"

"Miss Queen."

"And don't you forget it."

* * *

Magrat arrived at as near to a run as was possible in the queen outfit, which ought to have had castors.

She found a circle of several hundred people and, near the edge, a very pensive Nanny Ogg.

"What's happening, Nanny?"

Nanny turned.

"Oops, sorry. Didn't hear no fanfare," she said. "I'd curtsy, only it's my legs."

Magrat looked past her at the two seated figures in the circle.

"What're they doing?"

"Staring contest."

"But they're looking at the sky."

"Bugger that Diamanda girl! She's got Esme trying to outstare the sun," said Nanny Ogg. "No looking away, no blinking . . ."

"How long have they been doing it?"

"About an hour," said Nanny gloomily.

"That's terrible!"

"It's bloody stupid is what it is," said Nanny. "Can't think what's got into Esme. As if power's all there is to witching! *She* knows that. Witching's not power, it's how you harness it."

There was a pale gold haze over the circle, from magical fallout.

"They'll have to stop at sunset," said Magrat.

"Esme won't last until sunset," said Nanny. "Look at her. All slumped up."

"I suppose you couldn't use some magic to—" Magrat began.

"Talk sense," said Nanny. "If Esme found out, she'd kick me round the kingdom. Anyway, the others'd spot it."

"Perhaps we could create a small cloud or something?" said Magrat.

"No! That's cheating!"

"Well, *you* always cheat."

"I cheat for myself. You can't cheat for other people."

Granny Weatherwax slumped again.

"I could have it stopped," said Magrat.

"You'd make an enemy for life."

"I thought Granny *was* my enemy for life."

"If you think that, my girl, you've got no understanding," said Nanny. "One day you'll find out Esme Weatherwax is the best friend you ever had."

"But we've got to do something! Can't you think of *anything*?"

Nanny Ogg looked thoughtfully at the circle. Occasionally a little wisp of smoke curled up from her pipe.

The magical duel was subsequently recorded in Birdwhistle's book *Legendes and Antiquities of the Ramptops* and went as follows:

"*The duel beinge ninety minutes advanced, a small boy child upon a sudden ran across the square and stept within the magic circle, whereup he fell down with a terrible scream also a flash. The olde witche looked around, got out of her chair, picked him up, and carried him to his grandmother, then went back to her seat, whilom the young witch never averted her eyes from the Sunne. But the other young witches stopped the duel averring, Look, Diamanda has wonne, the reason being, Weatherwax looked away. Whereupon the child's grandmother said in a loude voice, Oh yes? Pulle the other onne, it have got*

*bells on. This is not a conteft about power, you stupid
girls, it is a contest about witchcraft, do you not even
begin to know what being a witch IS?*

*"Is a witch someone who would look round when she
heard a child scream?*

"And the townspeople said, Yess!"

"That was *wonderful*," said Mrs. Quarney, the storekeeper's wife. "The whole town cheered. A true
miffic quality."

They were in the tavern's back room. Granny
Weatherwax was lying on a bench with a damp
towel over her face.

"Yes, it was, wasn't it?" said Magrat.

"That girl was left without a leg to stand on, everyone says."

"Yes," said Magrat.

"Strutted off with her nose in a sling, as they say."

"Yes," said Magrat.

"Is the little boy all right?"

They all looked at Pewsey, who was sitting in a
suspicious puddle on the floor in the corner with a
bag of sweets and a sticky ring around his mouth.

"Right as rain," said Nanny Ogg. "Nothing
worse'n a bit of sunburn. He screams his head off at
the least little thing, bless him," she said proudly, as
if this was some kind of rare talent.

"Gytha?" said Granny, from under the towel.

"Yes?"

"You knows I don't normally touch strong licker,
but I've heard you mention the use of brandy for
medicinal purposes."

"Coming right up."

Granny raised her towel and focused one eye on Magrat.

"Good afternoon, your pre-majesty," she said. "Come to be gracious at me, have you?"

"Well done," said Magrat, coldly. "Can one have a word with you, Na—Mrs. Ogg? Outside?"

"Right you are, your queen," said Nanny.

In the alley outside Magrat spun around with her mouth open.

"You—"

Nanny held up her hand.

"I know what you're going to say," she said. "But there wasn't any danger to the little mite."

"But you—"

"Me?" said Nanny. "I hardly did *anything*. They didn't know he was going to run into the circle, did they? They both reacted just like they normally would, didn't they? Fair's fair."

"Well, in a way, but—"

"No one *cheated*," said Nanny.

Margrat sagged into silence. Nanny patted her on the shoulder.

"So you won't be telling anyone you saw me wave the bag of sweets at him, will you?" she said.

"No, Nanny."

"There's a good going-to-be-queen."

"Nanny?"

"Yes, dear?"

Magrat took a deep breath.

"How did Verence know when we were coming back?"

It seemed to Magrat that Nanny thought for just a few seconds too long.

"Couldn't say," she said at last. "Kings are a bit magical, mind. They can cure dandruff and that. Probably he woke up one morning and his royal prerogative gave him a tickle."

The trouble with Nanny Ogg was that she *always* looked as if she was lying. Nanny Ogg had a pragmatic attitude to the truth; she told it if it was convenient and she couldn't be bothered to make up something more interesting.

"Keeping busy up there, are you?" she said.

"One's doing very *well*, thank you," said Magrat, with what she hoped was queenly *hauteur*.

"Which one?" said Nanny.

"Which one what?"

"Which one's doing very well?"

"Me!"

"You should have said," said Nanny, her face poker straight. "So long as you're keeping busy, that's the important thing."

"He *knew* we were coming back," said Magrat firmly. "He'd even got the invitations sorted out. Oh, by the way . . . there's one for you—"

"I know, one got it this morning," said Nanny. "Got all that fancy nibbling on the edges and gold and everything. Who's Ruservup?"

Magrat had long ago got a handle on Nanny Ogg's world-view.

"RSVP," she said. "It means you ought to say if you're coming."

"Oh, one'll be along all right, catch one staying away," said Nanny. "Has one's Jason sent one *his* invite yet? Thought not. Not a skilled man with a pen, our Jason."

"Invitation to what?" said Magrat. She was getting fed up with ones.

"Didn't Verence tell one?" said Nanny. "It's a special play that's been written special for you."

"Oh, yes," said Magrat. "The Entertainment."

"Right," said Nanny. "It's going to be on Midsummer's Eve."

"It's got to be special, on Midsummer's Eve," said Jason Ogg.

The door to the smithy had been bolted shut. Within were the eight members of the Lancre Morris Men, six times winners of the Fifteen Mountains All-Comers Morris Championship,* now getting to grips with a new art form.

"I feel a right twit," said Bestiality Carter, Lancre's only baker. "A dress on! I just hope my wife doesn't see me!"

"Says here," said Jason Ogg, his enormous forefinger hesitantly tracing its way along the page, "that it's a beaut-i-ful story of the love of the Queen of the Fairies—that's you, Bestiality—"

"—thank you very much—"

"—for a mortal man. Plus a hum-our-rus int-ter-lude with Comic Artisans . . ."

"What's an artisan?" said Weaver the thatcher.

"Dunno. Type of well, I reckon." Jason scratched his head. "Yeah. They've got 'em down on the plains. I repaired a pump for one once. Artisan wells."

"What's comic about them?"

"Maybe people fall down 'em in a funny way?"

---

*Three times outright, once after eleven hours extra time, and twice when the other finalists ran away.

"Why can't we do a Morris like normal?" said Obidiah Carpenter the tailor.*

"Morris is for every day," said Jason. "We got to do something cultural. This come all the way from Ankh-Morpork."

"We could do the Stick and Bucket Dance," volunteered Baker the weaver.

"*No one* is to do the Stick and Bucket Dance ever again," said Jason. "Old Mr. Thrum still walks with a limp, and it were three months ago."

Weaver the thatcher squinted at his copy of the script.

"Who's this bugger *Exeunt Omnes*?" he said.

"I don't think much of my part," said Carpenter, "it's too small."

"It's his poor wife I feel sorry for," said Weaver, automatically.

"Why?" said Jason.†

"And why's there got to be a lion in it?" said Baker the weaver.

" 'Cos it's a play!" said Jason. "No one'd want to see it if it had a . . . a *donkey* in it! Oi can just see people comin' to see a play 'cos it had a *donkey* in it. This play was written by a real playsmith! Hah, I can just see a real playsmith putting *donkeys* in a play! He says he'll be very interested to hear how we get on! Now just you all shut up!"

---

*Who was also general poacher, cess-pit cleaner, and approximate carpenter.**

**"With a couple of nails it'll stay up all right."

†The thing about iron is that you generally don't have to think fast in dealing with it.

"I don't *feel* like the Queen of the Fairies," moaned Bestiality Carter.*

"You'll grow into it," said Weaver.

"I hope not."

"And you've got to rehearse," said Jason.

"There's no room," said Thatcher the carter.

"Well, I ain't doin' it where anyone else can see," said Bestiality. "Even if we go out in the woods somewhere, people'll be bound to see. Me in a dress!"

"They won't recognize you in your makeup," said Weaver.

"*Makeup?*"

"Yeah, and your wig," said Tailor the other weaver.

"He's right, though," said Weaver. "If we're going to make fools of ourselves, I don't want no one to see me until we're *good* at it."

"Somewhere off the beaten track, like," said Thatcher the carter.

"Out in the country," said Tinker the tinker.

"Where no one goes," said Carter.

Jason scratched his cheese-grater chin. He was bound to think of somewhere.

---

*Well, it's like this . . . The Carter parents were a quiet and respectable Lancre family who got into a bit of a mix-up when it came to naming their children. First, they had four daughters, who were christened Hope, Chastity, Prudence, and Charity, because naming girls after virtues is an ancient and unremarkable tradition. Then their first son was born and out of some misplaced idea about how this naming business was done he was called Anger Carter, followed later by Jealousy Carter, Bestiality Carter, and Covetousness Carter. Life being what it is, Hope turned out to be a depressive, Chastity was enjoying life as a lady of negotiable affection in Ankh-Morpork, Prudence had thirteen children, and Charity expected to get a dollar's change out of seventy-five pence—whereas the boys had grown into amiable, well-tempered men, and Bestiality Carter was, for example, very kind to animals.

"And *who*'s going to play Exeunt Omnes?" said Weaver. "He doesn't have much to say, does he?"

The coach rattled across the featureless plains. The land between Ankh-Morpork and the Ramtops was fertile, well-cultivated and dull, dull, dull. Travel broadens the mind. This landscape broadened the mind because the mind just flowed out from the ears like porridge. It was the kind of landscape where, if you saw a distant figure cutting cabbages, you'd watch him until he was out of sight because there was simply nothing else for the eye to do.

"I spy," said the Bursar, "with my little eye, something beginning with . . . H."

"Oook."

"No."

"Horizon," said Ponder.

"You guessed!"

"Of course I guessed. I'm supposed to guess. We've had S for Sky, C for Cabbage, O for . . . for Ook, and there's nothing *else*."

"I'm not going to play anymore if you're going to guess." The Bursar pulled his hat down over his ears and tried to curl up on the hard seat.

"There'll be lots to see in Lancre," said the Archchancellor. "The only piece of flat land they've got up there is in a museum."

Ponder said nothing.

"Used to spend whole summers up there," said Ridcully. He sighed. "You know . . . things could have been very different."

Ridcully looked around. If you're going to relate

an intimate piece of personal history, you want to be sure it's going to be heard.

The Librarian looked out at the jolting scenery. He was sulking. This had a lot to do with the new bright blue collar around his neck with the word "PONGO" on it. Someone was going to suffer for this.

The Bursar was trying to use his hat like a limpet uses its shell.

"There was this girl."

Ponder Stibbons, chosen by a cruel fate to be the only one listening, looked surprised. He was aware that, technically, even the Archchancellor had been young once. After all, it was just a matter of time. Common sense suggested that wizards didn't flash into existence aged seventy and weighing nineteen stone. But common sense needed reminding.

He felt he ought to say something.

"Pretty, was she, sir?" he said.

"No. No, I can't say she was. *Striking.* That's the word. Tall. Hair so blond it was nearly white. And eyes like gimlets, I tell you."

Ponder tried to work this out.

"You don't mean that dwarf who runs the delicatessen in—" he began.

"I *mean* you always got the impression she could see right through you," said Ridcully, slightly more sharply than he had intended. "And she could run . . ."

He lapsed into silence again, staring at the newsreels of memory.

"I would've married her, you know," he said.

Ponder said nothing. When you're a cork in

someone else's stream of consciousness, all you can do is spin and bob in the eddies.

"What a summer," murmured Ridcully. "Very like this one, really. Crop circles were bursting like raindrops. And . . . well, I was having doubts, you know. Magic didn't seem to be enough. I was a bit . . . lost. I'd have given it all up for her. Every blasted octogram and magic spell. Without a second thought. You know when they say things like 'she had a laugh like a mountain stream'?"

"I'm not *personally* familiar with it," said Ponder, "but I have read poetry that—"

"Load of cobblers, poetry," said Ridcully. "I've listened to mountain streams and they just go trickle, trickle, gurgle. And you get them things in them, you know, insect things with little . . . anyway. Doesn't sound like laughter at all, is my point. Poets always get it wrong. 'S'like 'she had lips like cherries.' Small, round, and got a stone in the middle? Hah!"

He shut his eyes. After a while Ponder said, "So what happened, sir?"

"What?"

"The girl you were telling me about."

"What girl?"

"This girl."

"Oh, that girl. Oh, she turned me down. Said there were things she wanted to do. Said there'd be time enough."

There was another pause.

"What happened then?" Ponder prompted.

"Happened? What d'you think happened? I went off and studied. Term started. Wrote her a lot of letters but she never answered 'em. Probably never got 'em, they probably eat the mail up there. Next year I was studying all summer and never had time to go back. Never *did* go back. Exams and so on. Expect she's dead now, or some fat old granny with a dozen kids. Would've wed her like a shot. Like a *shot*." Ridcully scratched his head. "Hah . . . just wish I could remember her name . . ."

He stretched out with his feet on the Bursar.

" 'S'funny, that," he said. "Can't even remember her name. Hah! She could outrun a horse—"

"Kneel and deliver!"

The coach rattled to a halt.

Ridcully opened an eye.

"What's that?" he said.

Ponder jerked awake from a reverie of lips like mountain streams and looked out of the window.

"I think," he said, "it's a very small highwayman."

The coachman peered down at the figure in the road. It was hard to see much from this angle, because of the short body and the wide hat. It was like looking at a well-dressed mushroom with a feather in it.

"I do apologize for this," said the very small highwayman. "I find myself a little short."

The coachman sighed and put down the reins. Properly arranged holdups by the Bandits' Guild were one thing, but he was blowed if he was going to be threatened by an outlaw that came up to his waist and didn't even have a crossbow.

"You little bastard," he said. "I'm going to knock your block off."

He peered closer.

"What's that on your back? A hump?"

"Ah, you've noticed the stepladder," said the low highwayman. "Let me demonstrate—"

"What's happening?" said Ridcully, back in the coach.

"Um, a dwarf has just climbed up a small stepladder and kicked the coachman in the middle of the road," said Ponder.

"That's something you don't see every day," said Ridcully. He looked happy. Up to now, the journey had been quite uneventful.

"Now he's coming toward us."

"Oh, good."

The highwayman stepped over the groaning body of the driver and marched toward the door of the coach, dragging his stepladder behind him.

He opened the door.

"Your money or, I'm sorry to say, your—"

A blast of octarine fire blew his hat off.

The dwarf's expression did not change.

"I wonder if I might be allowed to rephrase my demands?"

Ridcully looked the elegantly dressed stranger up and down or, rather, down and further down.

"You don't look like a dwarf," he said, "apart from the height, that is."

"Don't look like a dwarf apart from the height?"

"I mean, the helmet and iron boots department is among those you are lacking in," said Ridcully.

The dwarf bowed and produced a slip of pasteboard from one grubby but lace-clad sleeve.

"My card," he said.

It read:

Giamo Casanunda
WORLD'S SECOND GREATEST LOVER
"We Never Sleep"

| FINEST SWORDSMAN | SOLDIER OF FORTUNE |
| OUTRAGEOUS LIAR | STEPLADDERS REPAIRED |

Ponder peered over Ridcully's shoulder.

"Are you really an outrageous liar?"

"No."

"Why are you trying to rob coaches, then?"

"I am afraid I was waylaid by bandits."

"But it says here," said Ridcully, "that you are a finest swordsman."

"I was outnumbered."

"How many of them were there?"

"Three million."

"Hop in," said Ridcully.

Casanunda threw his stepladder into the coach and then peered into the gloom.

"Is that an ape asleep in there?"

"Yes."

The Librarian opened one eye.

"What about the smell?"

"He won't mind."

"Hadn't you better apologize to the coachman?" said Ponder.

"No, but I could kick him again harder if he likes."

"And that's the Bursar," said Ridcully, pointing to Exhibit B, who was sleeping the sleep of the near-terminally overdosed on dried frog pills. "Hey,

Bursar? Bursssaaar? No, he's out like a light. Just push him under the seat. Can you play Cripple Mr. Onion?"

"Not very well."

"Capital!"

Half an hour later Ridcully owed the dwarf $8,000.

"But I put it on my visiting card," Casanunda pointed out. "Outrageous liar. Right there."

"Yes, but I thought you were lying!"

Ridcully sighed and, to Ponder's amazement, produced a bag of coins from some inner recess. They were large coins and looked suspiciously realistic and golden.

Casanunda might have been a libidinous soldier of fortune by profession but he was a dwarf by genetics, and there are some things dwarfs *know*.

"Hmm," he said. "You don't have 'outrageous liar' on *your* visiting card, by any chance?"

"No!" said Ridcully excitedly.

"It's just that I can recognize chocolate money when I see it."

"You know," said Ponder, as the coach jolted along a canyon, "this reminds me of that famous logical puzzle."

"What logical puzzle?" said the Archchancellor.

"Well," said Ponder, gratified at the attention, "it appears that there was this man, right, who had to choose between going through two doors, apparently, and the guard on one door always told the truth and the guard on the other door always told a lie, and the thing *was*, behind one door was certain death, and behind the other door was freedom, and he didn't know which guard was which, and he could only ask them one question and so: what did he ask?"

The coach bounced over a pothole. The Librarian turned over in his sleep.

"Sounds like Psychotic Lord Hargon of Quirm to me," said Ridcully, after a while.

"That's right," said Casanunda. "He was a devil for jokes like that. How many students can you get in an Iron Maiden, that kind of thing."

"So this was at his place, then, was it?" said Ridcully.

"What? I don't know," said Ponder.

"Why not? You seem to know all about it."

"I don't think it was *anywhere*. It's a *puzzle*."

"Hang on," said Casanunda, "I think I've worked it out. One question, right?"

"Yes," said Ponder, relieved.

"And he can ask either guard?"

"*Yes.*"

"Oh, right. Well, in that case he goes up to the smallest guard and says, 'Tell me which is the door to freedom if you don't want to see the color of your kidneys and incidentally I'm walking through it *behind* you, so if you're trying for the Mr. Clever Award just remember who's going through it *first.*' "

"No, no, no!"

"Sounds logical to me," said Ridcully. "Very good thinking."

"But you haven't got a weapon!"

"Yes I have. I wrested it from the guard while he was considering the question," said Casanunda.

"Clever," said Ridcully. "Now *that*, Mr. Stibbons,

is logical thought. You could learn a lot from this man—"

"—dwarf—"

"—sorry, dwarf. *He* doesn't go on about parasite universes all the time."

"Parallel!" snapped Ponder, who had developed a very strong suspicion that Ridcully was getting it wrong on purpose.

"Which ones are the parasite ones, then?"

"There aren't any! I mean, there aren't any, Archchancellor.* *Parallel* universes, I said. Universes where things didn't happen like—" He hesitated. "Well, you know that girl?"

"What girl?"

"The girl you wanted to marry?"

"How'd you know that?"

"You were talking about her just after lunch."

"Was I? More fool me. Well, what about her?"

"Well . . . in a way, you *did* marry her," said Ponder.

Ridcully shook his head. "Nope. Pretty certain I didn't. You remember that sort of thing."

"Ah, but not in *this* universe—"

The Librarian opened one eye.

"You suggestin' I nipped into some other universe to get married?" said Ridcully.

"No! I mean, you got married in that universe and not in this universe," said Ponder.

"Did I? What? A proper ceremony and everything?"

"Yes!"

"Hmm." Ridcully stroked his beard. "You sure?"

---

*Ponder was one hundred percent wrong about this.

"Certain, Archchancellor."

"My word! I never knew that."

Ponder felt he was getting somewhere.

"So—"

"Yes?"

"Why don't I remember it?"

Ponder had been ready for this.

"Because the you in the other universe is different from the you here," he said. "It was a different you that got married. He's probably settled down somewhere. He's probably a great-grandad by now."

"He never writes, I know that," said Ridcully. "And the bastard never invited me to the wedding."

"Who?"

"Him."

"But he's you!"

"Is he? Huh! You'd think *I'd* think of *me*, wouldn't you? What a bastard!"

It wasn't that Ridcully was stupid. Truly stupid wizards have the life expectancy of a glass hammer. He had quite a powerful intellect, but it was powerful like a locomotive, and ran on rails and was therefore almost impossible to steer.

There are indeed such things as parallel universes, although parallel is hardly the right word— universes swoop and spiral around one another like some mad weaving machine or a squadron of Yossarians with middle-ear trouble.

And they branch. But, and this is important, not all the time. The universe doesn't much care if you tread on a butterfly. There are plenty more butterflies. Gods might note the fall of a sparrow but they don't make any effort to catch them.

Shoot the dictator and prevent the war? But the dictator is merely the tip of the whole festering boil of social pus from which dictators emerge; shoot one, and there'll be another one along in a minute. Shoot him too? Why not shoot everyone and invade Poland? In fifty years', thirty years', ten years' time the world will be very nearly back on its old course. History always has a great weight of inertia.

Almost always . . .

At circle time, when the walls between *this* and *that* are thinner, when there are all sorts of strange leakages . . . Ah, *then* choices are made, *then* the universe can be sent careening down a different leg of the well-known Trousers of Time.

But there are also stagnant pools, universes cut off from past and future. They have to steal pasts and futures from other universes; their only hope is to batten on to the dynamic universes as they pass through the fragile period, as remora fish hang on to a passing shark. These are the parasite universes and, when the crop circles burst like raindrops, they have their chance . . .

Lancre castle was far bigger than it needed to be. It wasn't as if Lancre could have been bigger at one time; inhospitable mountains crowded it on three sides, and a more or less sheer drop occupied where the fourth side would have been if a sheer drop hadn't been there. As far as anyone knew, the mountains didn't belong to anyone. They were just mountains.

The castle rambled everywhere. No one even knew how far the cellars went.

These days everyone lived in the turrets and halls near the gate.

"I mean, look at the crenellations," said Magrat.

"What, m'm?"

"The cut-out bits on top of the walls. You could hold off an army here."

"That's what a castle's for, isn't it, m'm?"

Magrat sighed. "Can we stop the 'm'm', please? It makes you sound uncertain."

"Mm, m'm?"

"I mean, who is there to fight up here? Not even trolls could come over the mountains, and anyone coming up the road is asking for a rock on the head. Besides, you only have to cut down Lancre bridge."

"Dunno, m'm. Kings've got to have castles, I s'pose."

"Don't you ever *wonder* about anything, you stupid girl?"

"What good does that do, m'm?"

I called her a stupid girl, thought Magrat. Royalty is rubbing off on me.

"Oh, well," she said, "where've we got to?"

"We're going to need two thousand yards of the blue chintz material with the little white flowers," said Millie.

"And we haven't even measured *half* the windows yet," said Magrat, rolling up the tape measure.

She looked down the length of the Long Gallery. The thing about it, the thing that made it so noticeable, the *first* thing anyone noticed about it, was that it was very long. It shared certain distinctive traits with the Great Hall and the Deep Dungeons. Its name was a perfectly accurate description. And it would be, as Nanny Ogg would say, a bugger to carpet.

"Why? Why a castle in Lancre?" she said, mainly to herself, because talking to Millie *was* like talking to yourself. "We've never fought anyone. Apart from outside the tavern on a Saturday night."

"Couldn't say, I'm sure, m'm," said Millie.

Magrat sighed.

"Where's the king today?"

"He's opening Parliament, m'm."

"Hah! Parliament!"

Which had been another of Verence's ideas. He'd tried to introduce Ephebian democracy to Lancre, giving the vote to everyone, or at least everyone *"who be of good report and who be male and hath forty years and owneth a hosue* worth more than three and a half goats a year,"* because there's no sense in being stupid about things and giving the vote to people who were poor or criminal or insane or female, who'd only use it irresponsibly. It worked, more or less, although the Members of Parliament only turned up when they felt like it and in any case no one ever wrote anything down and, besides, no one ever disagreed with whatever Verence said because he was King. What's the point of having a king, they thought, if you have to rule yourself? He should do his job, even if he couldn't spell properly. No one was asking *him* to thatch roofs or milk cows, were they?

"I'm bored, Millie. Bored, bored, bored. I'm going for a walk in the gardens."

"Shall I fetch Shawn with the trumpet?"

---

*Verence and Magrat had a lot in common, really.

"Not if you want to live."

Not all the gardens had been dug up for agricultural experiments. There was, for example, the herb garden. To Magrat's expert eye it was a pretty poor herb garden, since it just contained plants that flavored food. And at that Mrs. Scorbic's repertoire stopped short at mint and sage. There wasn't a sprig of vervain or yarrow or Old Man's Trousers anywhere in it.

And there was the famous maze or, at least, it would be a famous maze. Verence had planted it because he'd heard that stately castles should have a maze and everyone agreed that, once the bushes were a bit higher than their current height of about one foot, it would indeed be a very famous maze and people would be able to get lost in it without having to shut their eyes and bend down.

Magrat drifted disconsolately along the gravel path, her huge wide dress leaving a smooth trail.

There was a scream from the other side of the hedge, but Magrat recognized the voice. There were certain traditions in Lancre castle which she had learned.

"Good morning, Hodgesaargh," she said.

The castle falconer appeared around the corner, dabbing at his face with a handkerchief. On his other arm, claws gripping like a torture instrument, was a bird. Evil red eyes glared at Magrat over a razor-sharp beak.

"I've got a new hawk," said Hodgesaargh proudly. "It's a Lancre crowhawk. They've never been tamed before. I'm taming it. I've already stopped it pecking myooooow—"

He flailed the hawk madly against the wall until it let go of his nose.

Strictly speaking, Hodgesaargh wasn't his real name. On the other hand, on the basis that someone's real name is the name they introduce themselves to you by, he was definitely Hodgesaargh.

This was because the hawks and falcons in the castle mews were all Lancre birds and therefore naturally possessed of a certain "sod you" independence of mind. After much patient breeding and training Hodgesaargh had managed to get them to let go of someone's wrist, and now he was working on stopping them viciously attacking the person who had just been holding them, i.e., invariably Hodgesaargh. He was nevertheless a remarkably optimistic and good-natured man who lived for the day when his hawks would be the finest in the world. The hawks lived for the day when they could eat his *other* ear.

"I can see you're doing very well," said Magrat. "You don't think, do you, that they might respond better to cruelty?"

"Oh, no, miss," said Hodgesaargh, "you have to be kind. You have to build up a bond, you see. If they don't trust you theyaaaagh—"

"I'll just leave you to get on with it then, shall I?" said Magrat, as feathers filled the air.

Magrat had been gloomily unsurprised to learn that there was a precise class and gender distinction in falconry—Verence, being king, was allowed a gyrfalcon, whatever the hell that was, any earls in the vicinity could fly a peregrine, and priests were allowed sparrowhawks. Commoners were just about allowed a stick to throw.* Magrat found herself wondering what Nanny Ogg would be allowed—a small chicken on a spring, probably.

There was no specific falcon for a witch but, as a queen, the Lancre rules of falconry allowed her to fly the wowhawk or Lappet-faced Worrier. It was small and shortsighted and preferred to walk everywhere. It fainted at the sight of blood. And about twenty wowhawks could kill a pigeon, if it was a sick pigeon. She'd spent an hour with one on her wrist. It had wheezed at her, and eventually it had dozed off upside down.

But at least Hodgesaargh had a job to do. The castle was full of people doing jobs. Everyone had something useful to do except Magrat. She just had to exist. Of course, everyone would talk to her, provided she talked to them first. But she was always interrupting something important. Apart from ensuring the royal succession, which Verence had sent off for a book about, she—

"You just keep back there, girl. You don't want to come no further," said a voice.

Magrat bridled.

"Girl? One happens to be very nearly of the royal blood by marriage!"

"Maybe, but the bees don't know that," said the voice.

Magrat stopped.

She'd stepped out beyond what were the gardens from the point of view of the royal family and into what were the gardens from the point of view of ev-

---

*If it wasn't a *big* stick.

eryone else—beyond the world of hedges and topi-
ary and herb gardens and into the world of old sheds,
piles of flowerpots, compost and, just here, beehives.

One of the hives had the lid off. Beside it, in the
middle of a brown cloud, smoking his special bee
pipe, was Mr. Brooks.

"Oh," she said, "it's you, Mr. Brooks."

Technically, Mr. Brooks was the Royal Beekeeper. But the relationship was a careful one. For
one thing, although most of the staff were called by
their last names Mr. Brooks shared with the cook
and the butler the privilege of an honorific. Because
Mr. Brooks had secret powers. He knew all about
honey flows and the mating of queens. He knew
about swarms, and how to destroy wasps' nests. He
got the general respect shown to those, like witches
and blacksmiths, whose responsibilities are not entirely to the world of the humdrum and everyday—
people who, in fact, know things that others don't
about things that others can't fathom. And he was
generally found doing something fiddly with the
hives, ambling across the kingdom in pursuit of a
swarm, or smoking his pipe in his secret shed which
smelled of old honey and wasp poison. You didn't
offend Mr. Brooks, not unless you wanted swarms
in your privy while he sat cackling in his shed.

He carefully replaced the lid on the hive and
walked away. A few bees escaped from the gaping
holes in his beekeeping veil.

"Afternoon, your ladyship," he conceded.

"Hello, Mr. Brooks. What've you been doing?"

Mr. Brooks opened the door of his secret shed,
and rummaged about inside.

"They're late swarming," said the beekeeper. "I was just checking up on 'em. Fancy a cup of tea, girl?"

You couldn't stand on ceremony with Mr. Brooks. He treated everyone as an equal, or more often as a slight inferior; it probably came of ruling thousands, every day. And at least she could talk to him. Mr. Brooks had always seemed to her as close to a witch as it was possible to be while still being male.

The shed was stuffed full of bits of hive, mysterious torture instruments for extracting honey, old jars, and a small stove on which a grubby teapot steamed next to a huge saucepan.

He took her silence for acceptance, and poured out two mugs.

"Is it herbal?" she quavered.

"Buggered if I know. It's just brown leaves out of a tin."

Magrat looked uncertainly into a mug which pure tannin was staining brown. But she rallied. One thing you had to do when you were queen, she knew, was Put Commoners at their Ease. She cast around for some easeful question.

"It must be very interesting, being a beekeeper," she said.

"Yes. It is."

"One's often wondered—"

"What?"

"How do you actually milk them?"

The unicorn prowled through the forest. It felt blind, and out of place. This wasn't a proper land. The sky was blue, not flaming with all the colors of the aurora. And time was passing. To a creature not born subject to time, it was a sensation not unakin to falling.

It could feel its mistress inside its head, too. That was worse even than the passing of time.

In short, it was mad.

Magrat sat with her mouth open.

"I thought queens were *born*," she said.

"Oh, no," said Mr. Brooks. "There ain't no such thing as a queen egg. The bees just decides to feed one of 'em up as a queen. Feeds 'em royal jelly."

"What happens if they don't?"

"Then it just becomes an ordinary worker, your ladyship," said Mr. Brooks, with a suspiciously republican grin.

Lucky for it, Magrat thought.

"So they have a new queen, and then what happens to the old one?"

"Usually the old girl swarms," said Mr. Brooks. "Pushes off and takes some of the colony with her. I must've seen a thousand swarms, me. Never seen a Royal swarm, though."

"What's a Royal swarm?"

"Can't say for sure. It's in some of the old bee books. A swarm of swarms. It's something to see, they say." The old beekeeper looked wistful for a moment.

"'Course," he went on, righting himself, "the *real* fun starts if the weather's bad and the ole queen can't swarm, right?" He moved his hand in a sly circular motion. "What happens then *is*, the two queens— that's the old queen, right? and the new queen—the two queens start astalkin' one another among the combs, with the rain adrummin' on the roof of the hive, and the business of the hive agoin' on all around them," Mr. Brooks moved his hands graphically, and Magrat leaned forward, "all among the combs, the drones all hummin', and all the time they can sense one another, 'cos they can tell, see, and then they spots one another and—"

"Yes? Yes?" said Magrat, leaning forward.

"Slash! Stab!"

Magrat hit her head on the wall of the hut.

"Can't have more'n one queen in a hive," said Mr. Brooks calmly.

Magrat looked out at the hives. She'd always liked the look of beehives, up until now.

"Many's the time I've found a dead queen in front of the hive after a spell of wet weather," said Mr. Brooks, happily. "Can't abide another queen around the place, you know. And it's a right old battle, too. The old queen's more cunnin'. But the new queen, she's *really* got everything to fight for."

"Sorry?"

"If she wants to be mated."

"Oh."

"But it gets really interestin' in the autumn," said Mr. Brooks. "Hive don't need any dead weight in the winter, see, and there's all these drones hangin' around not doing anything, so the workers drag all the drones down to the hive entrance, see, and they bite their—"

"Stop! This is horrible!" said Magrat. "I thought beekeeping was, well, *nice*."

"Of course, that's around the time of year when

the bees wear out," said Mr. Brooks. "What happens is, see, your basic bee, why, it works 'til it can't work no more, and you'll see a lot of old workers acrawlin' around in front of the hive 'cos—"

"Stop it! Honestly, this is too much. I'm queen, you know. Almost."

"Sorry, miss," said Mr. Brooks. "I thought you wanted to know a bit about beekeeping."

"Yes, but not *this*!"

Magrat swept out.

"Oh, I dunno," said Mr. Brooks. "Does you good to get close to Nature."

He shook his head cheerfully as she disappeared among the hedges.

"Can't have more than one queen in a hive," he said. "Slash! Stab! Hehheh!"

From somewhere in the distance came the scream of Hodgesaargh as nature got close to him.

Crop circles opened everywhere.

Now the universes swung into line. They ceased their boiling spaghetti dance and, to pass through this chicane of history, charged forward neck and neck in their race across the rubber sheet of incontinent Time.

At such time, as Ponder Stibbons dimly perceived, they had an effect on one another—shafts of reality crackled back and forward as the universes jostled for position.

If you were someone who had trained their mind to be the finest of receivers, and were running it at the moment with the gain turned up until the knob broke, you might pick up some very strange signals indeed . . .

The clock ticked.

Granny Weatherwax sat in front of the open box, reading. Occasionally she stopped and closed her eyes and pinched her nose.

Not knowing the future was bad enough, but at least she understood why. Now she was getting flashes of *déjà vu*. It had been going on all week. But they weren't her *déjà vus*. She was getting them for the first time, as it were—flashes of memory that couldn't have existed. *Couldn't* have existed. She was Esme Weatherwax, sane as a brick, always had been, she'd *never* been—

There was a knock at the door.

She blinked, glad to be free of those thoughts. It took her a second or two to focus on the present. Then she folded up the paper, slipped it into its envelope, pushed the envelope back into its bundle, put the bundle into the box, locked the box with a small key which she hung over the fireplace, and walked to the door. She did a last-minute check to make sure she hadn't absentmindedly taken all her clothes off, or something, and opened it.

"Evenin'," said Nanny Ogg, holding out a bowl with a cloth over it, "I've brung you some—"

Granny Weatherwax was looking past her.

"Who're these people?" she said.

The three girls looked embarrassed.

"See, they came round my house and said—" Nanny Ogg began.

"Don't tell me. Let me guess," said Granny. She strode out, and inspected the trio.

"Well, well, well," she said. "My word. My word. Three girls who want to be witches, am I right?" Her voice went falsetto. "'Oh, please, Mrs. Ogg, we has seen the error of our ways, we want to learn *proper* witchcraft.' Yes?"

"Yes. Something like that," said Nanny. "But—"

"This is witchcraft," said Granny Weatherwax. "It's not . . . it's not a game of *conkers*. Oh, deary, deary me."

She walked along the very short row of trembling girls.

"What's your name, girl?"

"Magenta Frottidge, ma'am."

"I bet that's not what your mum calls you?"

Magenta looked at her feet.

"She calls me Violet, ma'am."

"Well, it's a better color than magenta," said Granny. "Want to be a bit mysterious, eh? Want to make folks feel you got a grip on the occult? Can you do magic? Your friend taught you anything, did she? Knock my hat off."

"What, ma'am?"

Granny Weatherwax stood back, and turned around.

"Knock it off. I ain't trying to stop you. Go on."

Magenta-shading-to-Violet shaded to pink.

"Er . . . I never got the hang of the psycho-thingy . . ."

"Oh, dear. Well, just let's see what the rest can do . . . Who're you, girl?"

"Amanita, ma'am."

"Such a *pretty* name. Let's see what you can do."

Amanita looked around nervously.

"I, er, don't think I can while you're watching me—" she began.

"That's a shame. What about you, on the end?"

"Agnes Nitt," said Agnes, who was much faster on the uptake than the other two and saw that there was no point in pushing Perdita.

"Go on, then. Try."

Agnes concentrated.

"Oh, deary, deary me," said Granny. "And my hat's still on. Show them, Gytha."

Nanny Ogg sighed, picked up a piece of fallen branch, and hurled it at Granny's hat. Granny caught the stick in mid-air.

"But, but—you said we had to use magic—" Amanita began.

"No, I didn't," said Granny.

"But *anyone* could have done *that*," said Magenta.

"Yes, but that's not the point," said Granny. "The point is that you didn't." She smiled, which was unusual for her. "Look, I don't want to be nasty to you. You're young. The world's full of things you could be doing. You don't want to be witches. Not if you knew what it means. Now just go away. Go home. Don't try the paranormal until you know what's normal. Go on. Run along."

"But that's just trickery! That's what Diamanda said! You just use words and trickery—" Magenta protested.

Granny raised a hand.

In the trees, the birds stopped singing.

"Gytha?"

Nanny Ogg gripped her own hat brim defensively. "Esme, listen, this hat cost me two whole dollars—"

The boom echoed through the woods.

Bits of hat lining zigzagged gently out of the sky.

Granny pointed her finger at the girls, who tried to lean out of the way.

"Now," she said, "why don't you go and see to your friend? She was beat. She probably ain't very happy. That's no time to go leaving people."

They still stared at her. Her finger seemed to fascinate them.

"I just *asked* you to go home. Perfectly reasonable voice. Do you want me to *shout*?"

They turned and ran.

Nanny Ogg glumly pushed her hand through the stricken hat brim.

"It took me ages to get that pig cure together," she mumbled. "You need eight types of leaves. Willow leaves, tansy leaves, Old Man's Trousers leaves . . . I was collecting 'em all day. It's not as though leaves grow on trees—"

Granny Weatherwax watched the disappearing girls.

Nanny Ogg paused. Then she said: "Takes you back, eh? I remember when I was fifteen, standing in front of old Biddy Spective, and she said in that voice of hers, 'You want to be a *what*?' and I was that frightened I near widd—"

"I never stood in front of no one," said Granny Weatherwax distantly. "I camped on old Nanny Gripes' garden until she promised to tell me everything she knew. Hah. That took her a week *and* I had the afternoons free."

"You mean you weren't Chosen?"

"Me? No. I chose," said Granny. The face she turned to Nanny Ogg was one she wouldn't forget in a hurry, although she might try. "I chose, Gytha Ogg. And I want that you should know this right now. Whatever happens. I ain't never regretted anything. Never regretted one single thing. Right?"

"If you say so, Esme."

What is magic?

There is the wizards' explanation, which comes in two forms, depending on the age of the wizard. Older wizards talk about candles, circles, planets, stars, bananas, chants, runes, and the importance of having at least four good meals every day. Younger wizards, particularly the pale ones who spend most of their time in the High Energy Magic building,[*] chatter at length about fluxes in the morphic nature of the universe, the essentially impermanent quality of even the most apparently rigid time-space framework, the implausibility of reality, and so on: what this means is that they have got hold of something hot and are gabbling the physics as they go along . . .

It was almost midnight. Diamanda ran up the hill toward the Dancers, the briars and heather tearing at her dress.

The humiliation banged back and forth in her

[*]It was here that the thaum, hitherto believed to be the smallest possible particle of magic, was successfully demonstrated to be made up of *resons*[**] or reality fragments. Currently research indicates that each reson is itself made up of a combination of at least five "flavors," known as "up," "down," "sideways," "sex appeal," and "peppermint."

[**]Lit: "Thing-ies."

skull. Stupid *malicious* old women! And stupid *people*, too! She'd won. According to the rules, she'd won! But everyone had laughed at her.

That stung. The recollection of those stupid faces, all grinning. And everyone supporting those horrible old women, who had no idea about the meaning of witchcraft and what it could *become*.

She'd show them.

Ahead of her, the Dancers were dark against the moonlit clouds.

Nanny Ogg looked under her bed in case there was a man there. Well, you never knew your luck.

She was going to have an early night. It had been a busy day.

There was a jar of boiled sweets by her bed, and a thick glass bottle of the clear fluid from her complicated still out behind the woodshed. It wasn't exactly whiskey, and it wasn't exactly gin, but it *was* exactly 90° proof, and a great comfort during those worrying moments that sometimes occurred around 3 A.M. when you woke up and forgot who you were. After a glass of the clear liquid you still didn't remember who you were, but that was all right now because you were someone else anyway.

She plumped up the four pillows, kicked her fluffy slippers into the corner, and pulled the blankets over her head, creating a small, warm, and slightly rank cave. She sucked a boiled sweet; Nanny had only one tooth left, and that had taken all she could throw at it for many years, so a sweet at bedtime wasn't going to worry it much.

After a few seconds a sense of pressure on her

feet indicated that the cat Greebo had taken up his accustomed place on the end of the bed. Greebo always slept on Nanny's bed; the way he'd affectionately try to claw your eyeballs out in the morning was as good as an alarm clock. But she always left a window open all night in case he wanted to go out and disembowel something, bless him.

Well, well. Elves. (They couldn't hear you say the word *inside your head*, anyway. At least, not unless they were real close.) She really thought they'd seen the last of them. How long was it, now? Must be hundreds and hundreds of years, maybe thousands. Witches didn't like to talk about it, because they'd made a big mistake about the elves. They'd seen through the buggers in the end, of course, but it had been a close thing. And there'd been a lot of witches in those days. They'd been able to stop them at every turn, make life in this world too hot for them. Fought them with iron. Nothing elvish could stand iron. It blinded them, or something. Blinded them all over.

There weren't many witches now. Not *proper* witches. More of a problem, though, was that people didn't seem to be able to remember what it was *like* with the elves around. Life was certainly more interesting then, but usually because it was shorter. And it was more colorful, if you liked the color of blood. It got so people didn't even dare talk openly about the bastards.

You said: The Shining Ones. You said: The Fair Folk. And you spat, and touched iron. But generations later, you forgot about the spitting and the iron, and you forgot why you used those names for them, and you remembered only that they were beautiful.

Yes, there'd been a lot of witches in them days. Too many women found an empty cradle, or a husband that never came home from the hunt. Had *been* the hunt.

Elves! The bastards . . . and yet . . . and yet . . . somehow, yes, they did things to memory.

Nanny Ogg turned over in bed. Greebo growled in protest.

Take dwarfs and trolls, for e.g. People said: Oh, you can't trust 'em, trolls are OK if you've got 'em in front of you, and some of 'em are decent enough in their way, but they're cowardly and stupid, and as for dwarfs, well, they're greedy and devious devils, all right, fair enough, sometimes you meet one of the clever little sods that's not too bad, but overall they're no better'n trolls, in fact—

—they're just like *us*.

But they ain't any prettier to look at and they've got no *style*. And we're stupid, and the memory plays tricks, and we remember the elves for their beauty and the way they move, and forget what they *were*. We're like mice saying, "Say what you like, cats have got real *style*."

People never quaked in their beds for fear of dwarfs. They never hid under the stairs from trolls. They might have chased 'em out of the henhouse, but trolls and dwarfs were never any more than a bloody nuisance. They were never a terror in the night.

We only remembers that the elves sang. We forgets what it was they were singing about.

Nanny Ogg turned over again. There was a slithering noise from the end of the bed, and a muffled yowl as Greebo hit the floor.

And Nanny sat up.

"Get your walking paws on, young fella-me-lad. We're going out."

As she passed through the midnight kitchen she paused, took one of the big black flatirons from the hob by the fire, and attached it to a length of clothesline.

For all her life she'd walked at night through Lancre with no thought of carrying a weapon of any sort. Of course, for most of that time she'd recognizably been a witch, and any importunate prowler would've ended up taking his essentials away in a paper bag, but even so it was generally true of any woman in Lancre. Man too, come to that.

Now she could sense her own fear.

The elves were coming back all right, casting their shadows before them.

Diamanda reached the crest of the hill.

She paused. She wouldn't put it past that old Weatherwax woman to have followed her. She felt sure there had been something tracking her in the woods.

There was no one else around.

She turned.

"Evenin', miss."

"You? You *did* follow me!"

Granny got to her feet from the shadow of the Piper, where she had been sitting quite invisibly in the blackness.

"Learned that from my dad," she said. "When he went hunting. He always used to say a bad hunter chases, a good hunter waits."

"Oh? So you're *hunting* me now?"

"No. I was just waiting. I knew you'd come up here. You haven't got anywhere else to go. You've come to call her, haven't you? Let me see your hands."

It wasn't a request, it was a command. Diamanda found her hands moving of their own accord. Before she could pull them back the old woman had grabbed them and held them firmly; her skin felt like sacking.

"Never done a hard day's work in your life, have you?" said Granny, pleasantly. "Never picked cabbages with the ice on 'em, or dug a grave, or milked a cow, or laid out a corpse."

"You don't have to do all that to be a witch!" Diamanda snapped.

"Did I say so? And let me tell you something. About beautiful women in red with stars in their hair. And probably moons, too. And voices in your head when you slept. And power when you came up here. She offered you lots of power, I expect. All you wanted. For free."

Diamanda was silent.

"Because it happened before. There's always someone who'll listen." Granny Weatherwax's eyes seemed to lose their focus.

"When you're lonely, and people around you seem too stupid for words, and the world is full of secrets that no one'll tell you . . ."

"Are you reading my mind?"

"Yours?" Granny's attention snapped back, and her voice lost its distant quality. "Hah! Flowers and suchlike. Dancing about without yer drawers on. Mucking about with cards and bits of string. And it worked, I expect. She gave you power, for a while. Oh, she must have laughed. And then there is less power and more price. And then no power, and you're payin' every day. They always take more than they give. And what they give has less than no value. And they end up taking everything. What they like to get from us is our fear. What they want from us most of all is our belief. If you call them, they will come. You'll give them a channel if you call them here, at circle time, where the world's thin enough to hear. The power in the Dancers is weak enough now as it is. And I'm not having the . . . the Lords and Ladies back."

Diamanda opened her mouth.

"I ain't finished yet. You're a bright girl. Lots of things you could be doing. But you don't want to be a witch. It's not an easy life."

"You mad old woman, you've got it all wrong! Elves aren't like that—"

"Don't say the word. Don't say the word. They come when called."

"Good! Elf, elf, elf! Elf—"

Granny slapped her face, hard.

"Even you knows that's stupid and childish," she said. "Now you listen to me. If you stay here, there's to be none of this stuff anymore. Or you can go somewhere else and find a future, be a great lady, you've got the mind for it. And maybe you'll come back in ten years loaded down with jewels and stuff, and lord it over all us stay-at-homes, and that will be fine. But if you stay here and keep trying to call the . . . Lords and Ladies, then you'll be up against me again. Not playing stupid games in the daylight, but *real* witchcraft. Not messing around with moons and circles, but the true stuff, out of the blood and the bone and out of the head. And you don't know *nothin'* about that. Right? And it don't allow for mercy."

Diamanda looked up. Her face was red where the slap had landed.

"Go?" she said.

Granny reacted a second too late.

Diamanda darted between the stones.

"You stupid child! Not *that* way!"

The figure was already getting smaller, even though it appeared to be only a few feet away.

"Oh, drat!"

Granny dived after her, and heard her skirt rip as the pocket tore. The poker she'd brought along whirred away and clanked against one of the Dancers.

There was a series of jerks and *tings* as the hobnails tore out of her boots and sped toward the stones.

No iron could go through the stones, no iron at all.

Granny was already racing over the turf when she realized what that meant. But it didn't matter. She'd made a choice.

There was a feeling of dislocation, as directions danced and twirled around. And then snow underfoot. It was white. It had to be white, because it was snow. But patterns of color moved across it, reflecting the wild dance of the permanent aurora in the sky.

Diamanda was struggling. Her footwear was barely suitable for a city summer, and certainly not for a foot of snow. Whereas Granny Weatherwax's boots, even without their hobnails, could have survived a trot across lava.

Even so, the muscles that were propelling them had been doing it for too long. Diamanda was outrunning her.

More snow was falling, out of a night sky. There was a ring of riders waiting a little way from the stones, with the Queen slightly ahead. Every witch knew her, or the shape of her.

Diamanda tripped and fell, and then managed to bring herself up to a kneeling position.

Granny stopped.

The Queen's horse whinnied.

"Kneel before your Queen, you," said the elf. She was wearing red, with a copper crown in her hair.

"Shan't. Won't," said Granny Weatherwax.

"You are in my kingdom, woman," said the Queen. "You do not come or go without the leave of me. You will kneel!"

"I come and go without the leave of *anyone*," said Granny Weatherwax. "Never done it before, ain't starting now."

She put a hand on Diamanda's shoulder.

"These are your elves," she said. "Beautiful, ain't they?"

The warriors must have been more than two meters tall. They did not wear clothes so much as items strung together—scraps of fur, bronze plates, strings of brightly colored feathers. Blue and green tattoos covered most of their exposed skin. Several of them held drawn bows, the tips of their arrows following Granny's every move.

Their hair massed around their heads like a halo, thick with grease. And although their faces were indeed the most beautiful Diamanda had ever seen, it was beginning to creep over her that there was something subtly wrong, some quirk of expression that did not quite fit.

"The only reason we're still alive now is that we're more fun alive than dead," said Granny's voice behind her.

"You know you shouldn't listen to the crabbed old woman," said the Queen. "What can she offer?"

"More than snow in summertime," said Granny. "Look at their eyes. Look at their eyes."

The Queen dismounted.

"Take my hand, child," she said.

Diamanda stuck out a hand gingerly.

There *was* something about the eyes. It wasn't the shape or the color. There was no evil glint. But there was . . .

. . . a look. It was such a look that a microbe might encounter if it could see up from the bottom end of the microscope. It said: You are nothing. It said: You are flawed, you have no value. It said: You are animal. It said: Perhaps you may be a pet, or perhaps you may be a quarry. It said: And the choice is not yours.

She tried to pull her hand away.

"Get out of her mind, old crone."

Granny's face was running with sweat.

"I ain't in her mind, elf. I'm keeping *you* out."

The Queen smiled. It was the most beautiful smile Diamanda had ever seen.

"And you have some power, too. Amazing. I never thought you'd amount to anything, Esmerelda Weatherwax. But it's no good here. Kill them both. But not at the same time. Let the other one watch."

She climbed on to her horse again, turned it around, and galloped off.

Two of the elves dismounted, drawing thin bronze daggers from their belts.

"Well, that's about it, then," said Granny Weatherwax, as the warriors approached. She dropped her voice.

"When the time comes," she said, "run."

"What time?"

"You'll know."

Granny fell to her knees as the elves approached.

"Oh, deary me, oh spare my life, I am but a poor old woman and skinny also," she said. "Oh spare my life, young sir. Oh lawks."

She curled up, sobbing. Diamanda looked at her in astonishment, not least at how anyone could expect to get away with something like that.

Elves had been away from humans for a long time. The first elf reached her, hauled her up by her shoulder, and got a doubled-handed, bony-knuckled punch in an area that Nanny Ogg would be surprised that Esme Weatherwax even knew about.

Diamanda was already running. Granny's elbow caught the other elf in the chest as she set off after her.

Behind her, she heard the merry laughter of the elves.

Diamanda had been surprised at Granny's old lady act. She was far more surprised when Granny drew level. But Granny had more to run away from.

"They've got horses!"

Granny nodded. And it's true that horses go faster than people, but it's not instantly obvious to everyone that this is only true over moderate distances. Over short distances a determined human can outrun a horse, because they've only got half as many legs to sort out.

Granny reached over and gripped Diamanda's arm.

"Head for the gap between the Piper and the Drummer!"

"Which ones are they?"

"You don't even know *that?*"

Humans can outrun a horse, indeed. It was preying on Granny Weatherwax's mind that no one can outrun an arrow.

Something whined past her ear.

The circle of stones seemed as far away as ever.

Nothing for it. It oughtn't to be possible. She'd only ever tried it seriously when she was lying down, or at least when she had something to lean against.

She tried it now . . .

There were four elves chasing them. She didn't even think about looking into their minds. But the horses . . . ah, the horses . . .

They were carnivores, minds like an arrowhead.

The rules of Borrowing were: you didn't hurt, you just rode inside their heads, you didn't *involve* the subject in any way . . .

Well, not so much a *rule*, as such, more of a general guideline.

A stone-tipped arrow went through her hat.

Hardly really a guideline, even.

In fact, not even—

Oh, *drat*.

She plunged into the lead horse's mind, down through the layers of barely controlled madness which is what is inside even a normal horse's brain. For a moment she looked out through its bloodshot eyes at her own figure, staggering through the snow. For a moment she was trying to control six legs at once, two of them in a separate body.

In terms of difficulty, playing one tune on a musical instrument and singing a totally different one* was a stroll in the country by comparison.

She knew she couldn't do it for more than a few seconds before total confusion overwhelmed mind and body. But a second was all she needed. She let the confusion arise, dumped it in its entirety in the horse's mind, and withdrew sharply, picking up control of her own body as it began to fall.

There was one horrible moment in the horse's head.

It wasn't sure what it was, or how it had got there. More importantly, it didn't know how many legs it had. There was a choice of two or four, or possibly even six. It compromised on three.

Granny heard it scream and collapse noisily, by the sound of things taking a couple of others with it.

"Hah!"

She risked a look sideways at Diamanda.

Who wasn't there.

---

*Except for Nanny Ogg, who did it all the time, although not on purpose.

She was in the snow some way back, trying with difficulty to get to her feet. The face she turned to Granny was as pale as the snow.

There was an arrow sticking out of her shoulder.

Granny darted back, grabbed the girl and hauled her upright.

"Come on! Nearly there!"

"Can't r'n . . . c'ld . . ."

Diamanda slumped forward. Granny caught her before she hit the snow and, with a grunt of effort, slung her over her shoulder.

A few more steps, and all she had to do was fall forwar . . .

A clawed hand snatched at her dress . . .

And three figures fell, rolling over and over in the summer bracken.

The elf was first to its feet, looking around in dazed triumph. It already had a long copper knife in its hand.

It focused on Granny, who had landed on her back. She could smell the rankness of it as it raised the knife, and she sought desperately for a way into its head . . .

Something flashed past her vision.

A length of rope had caught the elf's neck, and went tight as something swished through the air. The creature stared in horror as a flatiron whirred a few feet away from its face and swung past its ear, winding around and around with increasing speed but a decreasing orbital radius until it connected heavily with the back of the elf's head, lifting it off its feet and dropping it heavily on the turf.

Nanny Ogg appeared in Granny's vision.

"Cor, it doesn't half whiff, don't it?" she said. "You can smell elves a mile off."

Granny scrambled upright.

There was nothing but grass inside the circle. No snow, no elves.

She turned to Diamanda. So did Nanny. The girl was lying unconscious.

"Elf-shot," said Granny.

"Oh, bugger."

"The point's still in there."

Nanny scratched her head.

"I could probably get the point out, no problem," she said, "but I don't know about the poison . . . we could tie a tourniquet around the affected part."

"Hah! Her neck'd be favorite, then."

Granny sat down with her chin on her knees. Her shoulders ached.

"Got to get me breath back," she said.

Images swam in the forefront of her mind. Here it came again. She knew there were such things as alternative futures, after all, that's what the future *meant*. But she'd never heard of alternative pasts. She could remember having just gone through the stones, if she concentrated. But she could remember other things. She could remember being in bed in her own house, but that was it, it was a house, not a cottage, but she was *her*, they were her *own* memories . . . she had a nagging feeling that she was asleep, right now . . .

Dully, she tried to focus on Nanny Ogg. There was something comfortingly solid about Gytha Ogg.

Nanny had produced a penknife.

"What the hell are you doing?"

"Going to put it out of its misery, Esme."

"Doesn't look miserable to me."

Nanny Ogg's eyes gleamed speculatively.

"Could soon arrange that, Esme."

"Don't go torturing it just because it's lying down, Gytha."

"Damn well ain't waiting for it to stand up again, Esme."

"*Gytha.*"

"Well, they used to carry off babies. I ain't having that again. The thought of someone carrying off our Pewsey—"

"Even elves ain't that daft. Never seen such a sticky child in all my life."

Granny pulled gently at Diamanda's eyelid.

"Out cold," she said. "Off playing with the fairies."

She picked the girl up. "Come on. I'll carry her, you bring Mr. Tinkerbell."

"That was brave of you, carrying her over your shoulder," said Nanny. "With them elves firing arrows, too."

"And it meant less chance of one hitting me, too," said Granny.

Nanny Ogg was shocked.

"What? You never thought that, did you?"

"Well, she'd been hit already. If *I'd* been hit too, neither of us'd get out," said Granny, simply.

"But that's—that's a bit *heartless*, Esme."

"Heartless it may be, but headless it ain't. I've never claimed to be nice, just to be sensible. No need to look like that. Now, are you coming or are you going to stand there with your mouth open all day?"

Nanny closed her mouth, and then opened it again to say:

"What're you going to do?"

"Well, do *you* know how to cure her?"

"Me? No!"

"Right! Me neither. But I know someone who might know," she said. "And we can shove *him* in the dungeons for now. Lots of iron bars down there. That should keep him quiet."

"How'd he get through?"

"He was holding on to me. I don't know how it works. Maybe the stone . . . force opens to let humans through, or something. Just so long as his friends stay inside, that's all I'm bothered about."

Nanny heaved the unconscious elf on to her shoulders without much effort.*

"Smells worse than the bottom of a goat's bed," she said. "It's a bath for me when I get home."

"Oh, dear," said Granny. "It gets worse, don't it?"

What is magic?

Then there is the witches' explanation, which comes in two forms, depending on the age of the witch. Older witches hardly put words to it at all, but may suspect in their hearts that the universe really doesn't know what the hell is going on and consists of a zillion trillion billion possibilities, and could become any one of them if a trained mind rigid with quantum certainty was inserted in the crack and *twisted*; that, if you really had to make

---

*As has been pointed out earlier in the Discworld chronicles, entire agricultural economies have been based on the lifting power of little old ladies in black dresses.

someone's hat explode, all you needed to do was *twist* into that universe where a large number of hat molecules all decide at the same time to bounce off in different directions.

Younger witches, on the other hand, talk about it all the time and believe it involves crystals, mystic forces, and dancing about without yer drawers on.

Everyone may be right, all at the same time. That's the thing about quantum.

It was early morning. Shawn Ogg was on guard on the battlements of Lancre castle, all that stood between the inmates and any mighty barbarian hordes that might be in the area.

He enjoyed the military life. Sometimes he wished a small horde would attack, just so's he could Save the Day. He daydreamed of leading an army into battle, and wished the king would get one.

A brief scream indicated that Hodgesaargh was giving his charges their morning finger.

Shawn ignored the noise. It was part of the background hum of the castle. He was passing the time by seeing how long he could hold his breath.

He had any amount of ways of passing the time, since guard duty in Lancre involved such an awful lot of it. There was Getting The Nostrils Really *Clean*, that was a good one. Or Farting Tunes. Or Standing On One Leg. Holding His Breath and Counting was something he fell back on when he couldn't think of anything else and his meals hadn't been too rich in carbohydrates.

There were a couple of loud creaks from the door knocker, far below. There was so much rust on it now that the only way it could be coaxed into making any sound was to lift it up, which made it squeak, and then force it mightily downward, which caused another squeak and, if the visitor was lucky, a faint thud.

Shawn took a deep breath and leaned over the battlements.

"Halt! Who Goes There?" he said.

A ringing voice came up from below.

"It's me, Shawn. Your mum."

"Oh, hello, Mum. Hello, Mistress Weatherwax."

"Let us in, there's a good boy."

"Friend or Foe?"

"What?"

"It's what I've got to say, Mum. It's official. And then you've got to say Friend."

"I'm your *mum*."

"You've got to do it properly, Mum," said Shawn, in the wretched tones of one who knows he's going to lose no matter what happens next, "otherwise what's the point?"

"It's going to be Foe in a minute, my lad."

"Oooaaaww, *Mum!*"

"Oh, all right. Friend, then."

"Yes, but you could just be saying that—"

"Let us in right now, Shawn Ogg."

Shawn saluted, slightly stunning himself with the butt of his spear.

"Right you are, Mistress Weatherwax."

His round, honest face disappeared from view. After a minute or two they heard the creaking of the portcullis.

"How did you do that?" said Nanny Ogg.

"Simple," said Granny. "He knows *you* wouldn't make his daft head explode."

"Well, *I* know *you* wouldn't, too."

"No you don't. You just know I ain't done it up to now."

Magrat had thought this sort of thing was just a joke, but it was true. The castle's Great Hall had one long, one *very* long dining table, and she and Verence sat at either end of it.

It was all to do with etiquette.

The king had to sit at the head of the table. That was obvious. But if she sat on one side of him it made them both uneasy, because they had to keep turning to talk to each other. Opposite ends and shouting was the only way.

Then there was the logistics of the sideboard. Again, the easy option—them just going over and helping themselves—was out of the question. If kings went round putting their own food on their own plate, the whole system of monarchy would come crashing down.

Unfortunately, this meant that service had to be by means of Mr. Spriggins the butler, who had a bad memory, a nervous twitch and a rubber knee, and a sort of medieval elevator system that connected with the kitchen and sounded like the rattle of a tumbril. The elevator shaft was a kind of heat sink. Hot food was cold by the time it arrived. Cold food got colder. No one knew what would happen to ice cream, but it would probably involve some rewriting of the laws of thermodynamics.

Also, the cook couldn't get the hang of vegetarianism. The traditional palace cuisine was heavy in artery-clogging dishes so full of saturated fats that they oozed out in great wobbly globules. Vegetables existed as things to soak up spare gravy, and were generally boiled to a uniform shade of yellow in any case. Magrat had tried explaining things to Mrs. Scorbic the cook, but the woman's three chins wobbled so menacingly at words like "vitamins" that she'd made an excuse to back out of the kitchen.

At the moment she was making do with an apple. The cook knew about apples. They were big roasted floury things scooped out and filled with raisins and cream. So Magrat had resorted to stealing a raw one from the apple loft. She was also plotting to find out where the carrots were kept.

Verence was distantly visible behind the silver candlesticks and a pile of account books.

Occasionally they looked up and smiled at each other. At least, it looked like a smile but it was a little hard to be sure at this distance.

Apparently he'd just said something.

Magrat cupped her hands around her mouth.

"Pardon?"

"We need a—"

"Sorry?"

"What?"

"What?"

Finally Magrat got up and waited while Spriggins, purple in the face with the effort, moved her chair down toward Verence. She could have done it herself, but it wasn't what queens did.

"We ought to have a Poet Laureate," said Verence, marking his place in a book. "Kingdoms have to have one. They write poems for special celebrations."

"Yes?"

"I thought perhaps Mrs. Ogg? I hear she's quite an amusing songstress."

Magrat kept a straight face.

"I . . . er . . . I think she knows lots of rhymes for *certain* words," she said.

"Apparently the going rate is fourpence a year and a butt of sack," said Verence, peering at the page. "Or it may be a sack of butt."

"What exactly will she have to do?" said Magrat.

"It says here the role of the Poet Laureate is to recite poems on State occasions," said Verence.

Magrat had witnessed some of Nanny Ogg's humorous recitations, especially the ones with the gestures. She nodded gravely.

"Provided," she said, "and I want to be absolutely sure you understand me on this, *provided* she takes up her post *after* the wedding."

"Oh, dear? Really?"

"*After* the wedding."

"Oh."

"Trust me."

"Well, of course, if it makes you happy—"

There was a commotion outside the double doors, which were flung back. Nanny Ogg and Granny Weatherwax stamped in, with Shawn trying to overtake them.

"Oooaaww, *Mum*! I'm supposed to go in first to say who it is!"

"We'll tell them who we are. Wotcha, your majesties," said Nanny.

"Blessing be upon this castle," said Granny. "Magrat, there's some doctorin' needs doing. Here."

Granny swept a candlestick and some crockery on to the floor with a dramatic motion and laid Diamanda on the table. In fact there were several acres of table totally devoid of any obstruction, but there's no sense in making an entrance unless you're prepared to make a mess.

"But I thought she was fighting you yesterday!" said Magrat.

"Makes no difference," said Granny. "Morning, your majesty."

King Verence nodded. Some kings would have shouted for the guards at this point but Verence did not because he was sensible, this was Granny Weatherwax and in any case the only available guard was Shawn Ogg, who was trying to straighten out his trumpet.

Nanny Ogg had drifted over to the sideboard. It wasn't that she was callous, but it had been a busy few hours and there was a lot of breakfast that no one seemed to be interested in.

"What happened to her?" said Magrat, inspecting the girl carefully.

Granny looked around the room. Suits of armor, shields hanging on the walls, rusty old swords and pikes . . . probably enough iron here . . .

"She was shot by an elf—"

"But—" said Magrat and Verence at the same time.

"Don't ask questions now, got no time. Shot by an elf. Them horrible arrows of theirs. They make the mind go wandering off all by itself. Now—can you do anything?"

Despite her better nature, Magrat felt a spark of righteous ire.

"Oh, so suddenly I'm a witch again when you—"

Granny Weatherwax sighed.

"No time for *that*, either," she said. "I'm just askin'. All you have to do is say no. Then I'll take her away and won't bother you again."

The quietness of her voice was so unexpected that Magrat tripped over her own anger, and tried to right herself.

"I wasn't saying I *wouldn't*, I was just—"

"Good."

There was a series of clangs as Nanny Ogg lifted the silver tureen lids.

"Hey, they've got three kinds of eggs!"

"Well, there's no fever," said Magrat. "Slow pulse. Eyes unfocused. Shawn?"

"Yes, Miss Queen?"

"Boiled, scrambled, *and* fried. That's what I call posh."

"Run down to my cottage and bring back all the books you can find. I'm sure I read something about this once, Granny. Shawn?"

Shawn paused halfway to the door.

"Yes, Miss Queen?"

"On your way out, stop off in the kitchens and ask them to boil up a lot of water. We can start by getting the wound clean, at any rate. But look, elves—"

"I'll let you get on with it, then," said Granny, turning away. "Can I have a word with you, your majesty? There's something downstairs you ought to see."

"I shall need some help," said Magrat.

"Nanny'll do it."

"That's me," said Nanny indistinctly, spraying crumbs.

"*What* are you eating?"

"Fried egg and ketchup sandwich," said Nanny happily.

"You better get the cook to boil you, too," said Magrat, rolling up her sleeves. "Go and see her." She looked at the wound. "And see if she's got any mouldy bread. . . ."

The basic unit of wizardry is the Order or the College or, of course, the University.

The basic unit of witchcraft is the witch, but the basic *continuous* unit, as has already been indicated, is the cottage.

A witch's cottage is a very specific architectural item. It is not exactly built, but put together over the years as the areas of repair join up, like a sock made entirely of darns. The chimney twists like a corkscrew. The roof is thatch so old that small but flourishing trees are growing in it, the floors are switchbacks, it creaks at night like a tea clipper in a gale. If at least two walls aren't shored up with balks of timber then it's not a true witch's cottage at all, but merely the home of some daft old bat who reads tea leaves and talks to her cat.

Cottages tend to attract similar kinds of witches. It's natural. Every witch trains up one or two young witches in their life, and when in the course of mortal time the cottage becomes vacant it's only sense for one of them to move in.

Magrat's cottage traditionally housed thoughtful witches who noticed things and wrote things down. Which herbs were better than others for headaches, fragments of old stories, odds and ends like that.

There were a dozen books of tiny handwriting and drawings, the occasional interesting flower or unusual frog pressed carefully between the pages.

It was a cottage of *questioning* witches, research witches. Eye of *what* newt? What *species* of ravined salt-sea shark? It's all very well a potion calling for Love-in-idleness, but which of the thirty-seven common plants called by that name in various parts of the continent was actually *meant*?

The reason that Granny Weatherwax was a better witch than Magrat was that she knew that in witchcraft it didn't matter a damn which one it was, or even if it was a piece of grass.

The reason that Magrat was a better doctor than Granny was that she thought it did.

The coach slowed to a halt in front of the barricade across the road.

The bandit chieftain adjusted his eyepatch. He had two good eyes, but people respect uniforms. Then he strolled toward the coach.

"Morning, Jim. What've we got today, then?"

"Uh. This could be difficult," said the coachman. "Uh, there's a handful of wizards. And a dwarf. And an ape." He rubbed his head, and winced. "Yes. Definitely an ape. Not, and I think I should make this clear, any other kind of man-shaped thing with hair on."

"You all right, Jim?"

"I've had this lot ever since Ankh-Morpork. Don't talk to *me* about dried frog pills."

The bandit chief raised his eyebrows.

"All right. I won't."

He knocked on the coach door. The window slid down.

"I wouldn't like you to think of this as a robbery," he said. "I'd like you to think of it more as a colorful anecdote you might enjoy telling your grandchildren about."

A voice from within said, "That's him! He stole my horse!"

A wizard's staff poked out. The chieftain saw the knob on the end.

"Now, then," he said, pleasantly. "I know the rules. Wizards aren't allowed to use magic against civilians except in genuine life-threatening situa—"

There was a burst of octarine light.

"Actually, it's not a rule," said Ridcully. "It's more a guideline." He turned to Ponder Stibbons. "Interestin' use of Stacklady's Morphic Resonator here, I hope you noticed."

Ponder looked down.

The chieftain had been turned into a pumpkin although, in accordance with the rules of universal humor, he still had his hat on.

"And now," said Ridcully, "I'd be obliged if all you fellows hidin' behind the rocks and things would just step out where I can see you. Very good. Mr. Stibbons, you and the Librarian just pass around with the hat, please."

"But this is robbery!" said the coachman. "And you've turned him into a fruit!"

"A vegetable," said Ridcully. "Anyway, it'll wear off in a couple of hours."

"And I'm owed a horse," said Casanunda.

The bandits paid up, reluctantly handing over money to Ponder and reluctantly but *very quickly* handing over money to the Librarian.

"There's almost three hundred dollars, sir," said Ponder.

"And a horse, remember. In fact, there were two horses. I'd forgotten about the other horse until now."

"Capital! We're in pocket on the trip. So if these gentlemen would just remove the roadblock, we'll be on our way."

"In fact, there was a third horse I've just remembered about."

"This isn't what you're supposed to do! You're supposed to be robbed!" shouted the coachman.

Ridcully pushed him off the board.

"We're on holiday," he said.

The coach rattled away. There was a distant cry of "And four horses, don't forget" before it rounded a bend.

The pumpkin developed a mouth.

"Have they gone?"

"Yes, boss."

"Roll me into the shade, will you? And no one say anything about this ever again. Has anyone got any dried frog pills?"

Verence II respected witches. They'd put him on the throne. He was pretty certain of that, although he couldn't quite work out how it had happened. And he was in awe of Granny Weatherwax.

He followed her meekly toward the dungeons, hurrying to keep up with her long stride.

"What's happening, Mistress Weatherwax?"

"Got something to show you."

"You mentioned elves."

"That's right."

"I thought they were a fairy story."

"Well?"

"I mean . . . you know . . . an old wives' tale?"

"So?"

Granny Weatherwax seemed to generate a gyroscopic field—if you started out off-balance, she saw to it that you remained there.

He tried again.

"Don't exist, is what I'm trying to say."

Granny reached a dungeon door. It was mainly age-blackened oak, but with a large barred grille occupying some of the top half.

"In there."

Verence peered inside.

"Good grief!"

"I got Shawn to unlock it. I don't reckon anyone else saw us come in. Don't tell anyone. If the dwarfs and the trolls find out, they'll tear the walls apart to get him out."

"Why? To kill him?"

"Of course. They've got better memories than humans."

"What am *I* supposed to do with it?"

"Just keep it locked up. How should I know? I've got to think!"

Verence peered in again at the elf. It was lying curled up in the center of the floor.

"*That's* an elf? But it's . . . just a long, thin human with a foxy face. More or less. I thought they were supposed to be beautiful?"

"Oh, they are when they're conscious," said Granny, waving a hand vaguely. "They project this . . . this . . . when people look at them, they see beauty, they see something they want to please. They can look just like you want them to look. 'S'called *glamour*. You can tell when elves are around. People act funny. They stop thinking clear. Don't you know anything?"

"I thought . . . elves were just stories . . . like the Tooth Fairy . . ."

"Nothing funny about the Tooth Fairy," said Granny. "Very hard-working woman. I'll never know how she manages with the ladder and everything. No. Elves are real. Oh, drat. Listen . . ."

She turned, and held up a finger.

"Feudal system, right?"

"What?"

"Feudal system! Pay attention. Feudal system. King on top, then barons and whatnot, then everyone else . . . witches off to one side a bit," Granny added diplomatically. She steepled her fingers. "Feudal system. Like them pointy buildings heathen kings get buried in. Understand?"

"Yes."

"Right. That's how the elves see things, yes? When they get into a world, everyone else is on the bottom. Slaves. Worse than slaves. Worse than animals, even. They take what they want, and they want everything. But worst of all, the worst bit is . . .

they read your mind. They hear what you think, and in self-defense you think what they want. *Glamour.* And it's barred windows at night, and food out for the fairies, and turning around three times before you talks about 'em, and horseshoes over the door."

"I thought that sort of thing was, you know," the king grinned sickly, "folklore?"

"Of course it's folklore, you stupid man!"

"I *do* happen to be king, you know," said Verence reproachfully.

"You stupid king, your majesty."

"Thank you."

"I mean it doesn't mean it's not true! Maybe it gets a little muddled over the years, folks forget details, they forget *why* they do things. Like the horseshoe thing."

"I know my granny had one over the door," said the king.

"There you are. Nothing to do with its shape. But if you lives in an old cottage and you're poor, it's probably the nearest bit of iron with holes in it that you can find."

"Ah."

"The thing about elves is they've got no . . . begins with m." Granny snapped her fingers irritably.

"Manners?"

"Hah! Right, but no."

"Muscle? Mucus? Mystery?"

"No. No. No. Means like . . . seein' the other person's point of view."

Verence tried to see the world from a Granny Weatherwax perspective, and suspicion dawned.

"Empathy?"

"Right. None at all. Even a hunter, a good hunter, can feel for the quarry. That's what makes 'em a good hunter. Elves aren't like that. They're cruel for fun, and they can't understand things like mercy. They can't understand that anything apart from themselves might have feelings. They laugh a lot, especially if they've caught a lonely human or a dwarf or a troll. Trolls might be made out of rock, your majesty, but I'm telling you that a troll is your brother compared to elves. In the head, I mean."

"But why don't I know all this?"

"Glamour. Elves are beautiful. They've got," she spat the word, "*style*. Beauty. Grace. That's what matters. If cats looked like frogs we'd realize what nasty, cruel little bastards they are. Style. That's what people remember. They remember the glamour. All the rest of it, all the truth of it, becomes . . . old wives' tales."

"Magrat's never said anything about them."

Granny hesitated.

"Magrat doesn't know too much about elves," she said. "Hah. She ain't even a *young* wife yet. They're not something that gets talked about a lot these days. It's not *good* to talk about them. It's better if everyone forgets about them. They . . . come when they're called. Not called like 'Cooee.' Called inside people's heads. It's enough for people just to want them to be here."

Verence waved his hands in the air.

"I'm still learning about monarchy," he said. "I don't understand this stuff."

"You don't have to understand. You're a king.

Listen. You know about weak places in the world?
Where it joins other worlds?"

"No."

"There's one up on the moor. That's why the
Dancers were put up around it. They're a kind of
wall."

"Ah."

"But sometimes the barriers between worlds is
weaker, see? Like tides. At circle time."

"Ah."

"And if people act stupidly then, even the Dancers
can't keep the gateway shut. 'Cos where the world's
thin, even the wrong thought can make the link."

"Ah."

Verence felt the conversation had orbited back to
that area where he could make a contribution.

"Stupidly?" he said.

"Calling them. Attracting them."

"Ah. So what do I do?"

"Just go on reigning. I think we're safe. They
can't get through. I've stopped the girls, so there'll
be no more channeling. You keep this one firmly
under lock and key, and *don't tell Magrat.* No sense
in worrying her, is there? *Something* came through,
but I'm keeping an eye on it."

Granny rubbed her hands together in grim sat-
isfaction.

"I think I've got it sorted," she said.

She blinked.

She pinched the bridge of her nose.

"What did I just say?" she said.

"Uh. You said you thought you'd got it sorted,"
said the king.

Granny Weatherwax blinked.

"That's right," she said. "I said that. Yes. And I'm in the castle, aren't I? Yes."

"Are you all right, Mistress Weatherwax?" said the king, his voice taut with sudden worry.

"Fine, fine. Fine. In the castle. And the children are all right, too?"

"Sorry?"

She blinked again.

"What?"

"You don't look well . . ."

Granny screwed up her face and shook her head.

"Yes. The castle. I'm me, you're you, Gytha's upstairs with Magrat. That's right." She focused on the king. "Just a bit of . . . of overtiredness there. Nothing to worry about. Nothing to worry about at all."

Nanny Ogg looked doubtfully at Magrat's preparation.

"A mouldy bread poultice doesn't sound very magical to *me*," she said.

"Goodie Whemper used to swear by it. But I don't know what we can do about the coma."

Magrat thumbed hopefully through the crackling, ancient pages. Her ancestral witches had written things down pretty much as they occurred to them, so that quite important spells and observations would be interspersed with comments about the state of their feet.

"It says here, '*The smalle pointy stones sometimes found are knowne as Elf-shot, beinge the heads of Elf arrows from Times Past.*' That's all I can find. And there's a drawing. But *I've* seen these little stones around, too."

"Oh, there's lots of them," said Nanny, bandaging Diamanda's shoulder. "Dig 'em up all the time, in my garden."

"But elves don't shoot people! Elves are *good*."

"They probably just fired at Esme and the girl in fun, like?"

"But—"

"Look, dear, you're going to be queen. It's an important job. You look after the king now, and let me and Esme look after . . . other stuff."

"Being Queen? It's all tapestry and walking around in unsuitable dresses! I know Granny. She doesn't like anything that's . . . that's got style and grace. She's so *sour*."

"I daresay she's got her reasons," said Nanny amiably. "Well, that's got the girl patched up. What shall we do with her now?"

"We've got dozens of spare bedrooms," said Magrat, "and they're all ready for the guests. We can put her in one of them. Um. Nanny?"

"Yes?"

"Would you like to be a bridesmaid?"

"Not really, dear. Bit old for that sort of thing." Nanny hovered. "There isn't anything you need to ask me, though, is there?"

"What do you mean?"

"What with your mum being dead and you having no female relatives and everything . . ."

Magrat still looked puzzled.

"After the wedding, is what I'm hinting about," said Nanny.

"Oh, *that*. No, most of that's being done by a caterer. The cook here isn't much good at canapes and things."

Nanny looked carefully at the ceiling.

"And what about after that?" she said. "If you catch my meaning."

"I'm getting a lot of girls in to do the clearing up. Look, don't worry. I've thought of everything. I wish you and Granny wouldn't treat me as if I don't know *anything*."

Nanny coughed. "Your man," she said. "Been around a bit, I expect? Been walking out with dozens of young women, I've no doubt."

"Why do you say that? I don't think he has. Fools don't have much of a private life and, of course, he's been very busy since he's been king. He's a bit shy with girls."

Nanny gave up.

"Oh, well," she said, "I'm sure you'll work it all out as you—"

Granny and the king reappeared.

"How's the girl?" said Granny.

"We took out the arrow and cleaned up the wound, anyway," said Magrat. "But she won't wake up. Best if she stays here."

"You sure?" said Granny. "She needs keeping an eye on. I've got a spare bedroom."

"She shouldn't be moved," said Magrat, briskly.

"They've put their mark on her," said Granny. "You sure you know how to deal with it?"

"I do know it's quite a nasty wound," said Magrat, briskly.

"I ain't exactly thinking about the wound," said Granny. "She's been touched by them is what I mean. She's—"

"I'm sure I know how to deal with a sick person," said Magrat. "I'm not *totally* stupid, you know."

"She's not to be left alone," Granny persisted.

"There'll be plenty of people around," said Verence. "The guests start arriving tomorrow."

"Being alone isn't the same as not having other people around," said Granny.

"This is a *castle*, Granny."

"Right. Well. We won't keep you, then," said Granny. "Come, Gytha."

Nanny Ogg helped herself to an elderly lamb chop from under one of the silver covers, and waved it vaguely at the royal pair.

"Have fun," she said. "Insofar as that's possible."

"Gytha!"

"Coming."

Elves are wonderful. They provoke wonder.

Elves are marvelous. They cause marvels.

Elves are fantastic. They create fantasies.

Elves are glamorous. They project glamour.

Elves are enchanting. They weave enchantment.

Elves are terrific. They beget terror.

The thing about words is that meanings can twist just like a snake, and if you want to find snakes look for them behind words that have changed their meaning.

No one ever said elves are *nice*.

Elves are *bad*.

* * *

"Well, that's it," said Nanny Ogg, as the witches walked out over the castle's drawbridge. "Well done, Esme."

"It ain't over," said Granny Weatherwax.

"You said yourself they can't get through now. No one else round here's going to try any magic at the stones, that's sure enough."

"Yes, but it'll be circle time for another day or so yet. Anything could happen."

"That Diamanda girl's out of it, and you've put the wind up the others," said Nanny Ogg, tossing the lamb bone into the dry moat. "Ain't no one else going to call 'em, I know that."

"There's still the one in the dungeon."

"You want to get rid of it?" said Nanny. "I'll send our Shawn to King Ironfoundersson up at Copperhead, if you like. Or I could hop on the old broomstick meself and go and drop the word to the Mountain King. The dwarfs and trolls'll take it off our hands like a shot. No more problem."

Granny ignored this.

"There's something else," she said. "Something we haven't thought of. She'll still be looking for a way."

They'd reached the town square now. She surveyed it. Of course, Verence was king and that was right and proper, and this was his kingdom and that was right and proper too. But in a deeper sense the kingdom belonged to her. And to Gytha Ogg, of course. Verence's writ only ran to the doings of mankind; even the dwarfs and trolls didn't acknowledge him as king, although they were very polite about it. But when it came to the trees and the rocks and the soil, Granny Weatherwax saw it as *hers*. She was sensitive to its moods.

It was still being watched. She could sense the watchfulness. Sufficiently close examination changes the thing being observed, and what was being observed was the whole country. The whole country was under attack, and here she was, her mind unraveling . . .

"Funny thing," said Nanny Ogg, to no one in particular, "while I was sitting up there at the Dancers this morning I thought, funny thing . . ."

"What're you going on about now?"

"I remember when I was young there was a girl like Diamanda. Bad-tempered and impatient and talented and a real pain in the bum to the old witches. I don't know if you happen to remember her, by any chance?"

They passed Jason's forge, which rang to the sound of his hammer.

"I never forgot her," said Granny, quietly.

"Funny thing, how things go round in circles . . ."

"No they don't," said Granny Weatherwax firmly. "I wasn't like *her*. You know what the old witches round here were like. Set in their ways. No more than a bunch of old wart-charmers. And I wasn't rude to them. I was just . . . firm. Forthright. I stood up for meself. Part of being a witch is standing up for yourself—you're *grinning*."

"Just wind, I promise."

"It's completely different with her. No one's ever been able to say I wasn't open to new ideas."

"Well known for being open to new ideas, you

are," said Nanny Ogg. "I'm always saying, that Esme Weatherwax, she's always open to new ideas."

"Right." Granny Weatherwax looked up at the forested hills around the town, and frowned.

"The thing is," she said, "girls these days don't know how to think with a clear mind. You've got to think clearly and not be distracted. That's Magrat for you, always being distracted. It gets in the way of doing the proper thing." She stopped. "I can feel her, Gytha. The Queen of the Fairies. She can get her mind past the stones. Blast that girl! She's got a way in. She's everywhere. Everywhere I look with my mind, I can smell her."

"Everything's going to be all right," said Nanny, patting her on the shoulder. "You'll see."

"She's looking for a way," Granny repeated.

"Good morrow, brothers, and wherehap do we whist this merry day?" said Carter the baker.

The rest of the Lancre Morris Men looked at him.

"You on some kind of medication or what?" said Weaver the thatcher.

"Just trying to enter into the spirit of the thing," said Carter.

"That's how rude mechanicals talk."

"Who're rude mechanicals?" said Baker the weaver.

"They're the same as Comic Artisans, I think," said Carter the baker.

"I asked my mum what artisans are," said Jason.

"Yeah?"

"They're us."

"And we're Rude Mechanicals as well?" said Baker the weaver.

"I reckon."

"Bum!"

"Well, we certainly don't talk like these buggers in the writing," said Carter the baker. "I never said 'fol-de-rol' in my life. And I can't understand any of the jokes."

"You ain't supposed to understand the jokes, this is a *play*," said Jason.

"Drawers!" said Baker the weaver.

"Oh, shut up. And push the cart."

"Don't see why we couldn't do the Stick and Bucket Dance . . ." mumbled Tailor the other weaver.

"We're *not* doing the Stick and Bucket dance! I never want to hear any more ever about the Stick and Bucket dance! I still get twinges in my knee! So shut up about the Stick and Bucket dance!"

"Belly!" shouted Baker, who wasn't a man to let go of an idea.

The cart containing the props bumped and skidded on the rutted track.

Jason had to admit that Morris dancing was a lot easier than acting. People didn't keep turning up to watch and giggle. Small children didn't stand around jeering. Weaver and Thatcher were in almost open rebellion now, and mucking up the words. The evenings were becoming a constant search for somewhere to rehearse.

Even the forest wasn't private enough. It was amazing how people would just happen to be passing.

Weaver stopped pushing, and wiped his brow.

"You'd have thought the Blasted Oak would've been safe," he said. "Half a mile from the nearest path, and damn me if after five minutes you can't move for charcoal burners, hermits, trappers, tree tappers, hunters, trolls, bird-limers, hurdle-makers, swine-herds, truffle hunters, dwarfs, bodgers and suspicious buggers with big coats on. I'm surprised there's room in the forest for the bloody trees. Where to now?"

They'd reached a crossroads, if such it could be called.

"Don't remember this one," said Carpenter the poacher. "Thought I knew all the paths around here."

"That's 'cos you only ever sees 'em in the dark," said Jason.

"Yeah, everyone knows 'tis your delight on a shining night," said Thatcher the carter.

" 'Tis his delight *every* night," said Jason.

"Hey," said Baker the weaver, "we're getting really *good* at this rude mechanism, ain't we?"

"Let's go right," said Jason.

"Nah, it's all briars and thorns that way."

"All right, then, left then."

"It's all winding," said Weaver.

"What about the middle road?" said Carter.

Jason peered ahead.

There was a middle track, hardly more than an animal path, which wound away under shady trees. Ferns grew thickly alongside it. There was a general green, rich, dark feel to it, suggested by the word "bosky."*

His blacksmith's senses stood up and screamed.

"Not that way," he said.

---

*i.e., having a lot of bosk.

"Ah, come *on*," said Weaver. "What's wrong with it?"

"Goes up to the Dancers, that path does," said Jason. "Me mam said no one was to go up to the Dancers 'cos of them young women dancing round 'em in the nudd."

"Yeah, but they've been stopped from that," said Thatcher. "Old Granny Weatherwax put her foot down hard and made 'em put their drawers on."

"And they ain't to go there anymore, neither," said Carter. "So it'll be nice and quiet for the rehearsing."

"Me mam said no one was to go there," said Jason, a shade uncertainly.

"Yeah, but she probably meant . . . you know . . . with magical intent," said Carter. "Nothing magical about prancing around in wigs and stuff."

"Right," said Thatcher. "*And* it'll be really private."

"*And*," said Weaver, "*if* any young women fancies sneaking back up there to dance around without their drawers on, we'll be sure to see 'em."

There was a moment of absolute, introspective silence.

"I reckon," said Thatcher, voicing the unspoken views of nearly all of them, "we owes it to the community."

"We-ell," said Jason, "me mam said . . ."

"Anyway, your mum's a fine one to talk," said Weaver. "My dad said that when he was young, your mum hardly ever had—"

"Oh, all right," said Jason, clearly outnumbered. "Can't see it can do any harm. We're only actin'. It's

. . . it's *make-believe*. It's not as if it's anything *real*. But no one's to do any dancing. Especially, and I want everyone to be absolutely def'nite about this, the Stick and Bucket dance."

"Oh, we'll be acting all right," said Weaver. "And keeping watch as well, o'course."

"It's our duty to the community," said Thatcher, again.

"Make-believe is bound to be all right," said Jason, uncertainly.

Clang boinng clang ding . . .

The sound echoed around Lancre.

Grown men, digging in their gardens, flung down their spades and hurried for the safety of their cottages . . .

Clang boinnng goinng ding . . .

Women appeared in doorways and yelled desperately for their children to come in at once . . .

. . . BANG buggrit Dong boinng . . .

Shutters thundered shut. Some men, watched by their frightened families, poured water on the fire and tried to stuff sacks up the chimney . . .

Nanny Ogg lived alone, because she said old people needed their pride and independence. Besides, Jason lived on one side, and he or his wife whatshername could easily be roused by means of a boot applied heavily to the wall, and Shawn lived on the other side and Nanny had got him to fix up a long length of string with some tin cans on it in case *his* presence was required. But this was only for emergencies, such as when she wanted a cup of tea or felt bored.

Bond drat *clang* . . .

Nanny Ogg had no bathroom but she *did* have a tin bath, which normally hung on a nail on the back of the privy. Now she was dragging it indoors. It was almost up the garden, after being bounced off various trees, walls, and garden gnomes on the way.

Three large black kettles steamed by her fireside. Beside them were half a dozen towels, the loofah, the pumice stone, the soap, the soap for when the first soap got lost, the ladle for fishing spiders out, the waterlogged rubber duck with the prolapsed squeaker, the bunion chisel, the big scrubbing brush, the small scrubbing brush, the scrubbing brush on a stick for difficult crevices, the banjo, the thing with the pipes and spigots that no one ever really knew the purpose of, and a bottle of *Klatchian Nights* bath essence, one drop of which could crinkle paint.

Bong clang slam . . .

Everyone in Lancre had learned to recognize Nanny's pre-ablutive activities, out of self-defense.

"But it ain't April!" neighbors told themselves, as they drew the curtains.

In the house just up the hill from Nanny Ogg's cottage Mrs. Skindle grabbed her husband's arm.

"The goat's still outside!"

"Are you mad? I ain't going out there! Not now!"

"You know what happened last time! It was paralyzed all down one side for three days, man, and we couldn't get it down off the roof!"

Mr. Skindle poked his head out of the door. It had all gone quiet. Too quiet.

"She's probably pouring the water in," he said.

"You've got a minute or two," said his wife. "Go on, or we'll be drinking yogurt for weeks."

Mr. Skindle took down a halter from behind the door, and crept out to where his goat was tethered near the hedge. It too had learned to recognize the bathtime ritual, and was rigid with apprehension.

There was no point in trying to drag it. Eventually he picked it up bodily.

There was a distant but insistent sloshing noise, and the bonging sound of a floating pumice stone bouncing on the side of a tin bath.

Mr. Skindle started to run.

Then there was the distant tinkle of a banjo being tuned.

The world held its breath.

Then it came, like a tornado sweeping across a prairie.

"AAaaaaeeeeeee—"

Three flowerpots outside the door cracked, one after the other. Shrapnel whizzed past Mr. Skindle's ear.

"—wizzaaardsah staaafff has a knobontheend, knobontheend—"

He threw the goat through the doorway and leapt after it. His wife was waiting, and slammed the door shut behind him.

The whole family, including the goat, got under the table.

It wasn't that Nanny Ogg sang badly. It was just that she could hit notes which, when amplified by a tin bath half full of water, ceased to be sound and became some sort of invasive presence.

There had been plenty of singers whose high

notes could smash a glass, but Nanny's high C could clean it.

The Lancre Morris Men sat glumly on the turf, passing an earthenware jug between them. It had not been a good rehearsal.

"Don't work, does it?" said Thatcher.

" 'S'not funny, that I do know," said Weaver. "Can't see the king killing himself laughing at us playing a bunch of mechanical artisans not being very good at doin' a play."

"You're just no good at it," said Jason.

"We're *sposed* to be no good at it," said Weaver.

"Yeah, but you're no good at acting like someone who's no good at acting," said Tinker. "I don't know how, but you ain't. You can't expect all the fine lords and ladies—"

A breeze blew over the moor, tasting of ice at mid-summer.

"—to laugh at us not being any good at being no good at acting."

"I don't see what's funny about a bunch of rude artisans trying to do a play anyway," said Weaver.

Jason shrugged.

"It says all the gentry—"

A tang on the wind, the sharp tin taste of snow . . .

"—in Ankh-Morpork laughed at it for weeks and weeks," he said. "It was on Broad Way for three months."

"What's Broad Way?"

"That's where all the theaters are. The Dysk, Lord Wynkin's Men, the Bearpit . . ."

"They'd laugh at any damn thing down there,"

said Weaver. "Anyway, they all think we'm all sim-
pletons up here. They all think we say oo-aah and
sings daft folk songs and has three brain cells hud-
dlin' together for warmth 'cos of drinking scumble
all the time."

"Yeah. Pass that jug."

"Swish city bastards."

"They don't know what it's like to be up to the
armpit in a cow's backside on a snowy night. Hah!"

"And there ain't one of 'em that—what're you
talking about? You ain't got a cow."

"No, but I know what it's like."

"They don't know what it's like to get one wellie
sucked off in a farmyard full of gyppoe and that
horrible moment where you waves the foot around
knowin' that wherever you puts it down it's going to
go through the crust."

The stoneware jug glugged gently as it was passed
from hand to unsteady hand.

"True. That's very true. And you ever seen 'em
Morris dancing? 'Nuff to make you hang up your
hanky."

"What, Morris dancing in a *city*?"

"Well, down in Sto Helit, anyway. Bunch o' soft
wizards and merchants. I watched 'em a whole hour
and there wasn't even a groinin'."

"Swish city bastards. Comin' up here, takin' our
jobs . . ."

"Don't be daft. They don't know what a proper
job is."

The jug glugged, but with a deeper tone, suggest-
ing that it contained a lot of emptiness.

"Bet *they've* never been up to the armpit—"

"The point *is*. The point *is*. The point. The point *is*. Hah. All laughin' at decent rude artisans, eh? I mean. I mean. I mean. What's it all about? I mean. I mean. I mean. Play's all about some mechanical . . . rude buggers makin' a pig's ear out of doin' a play about a bunch of lords and ladies—"

A chill in the air, sharp as icicles . . .

"It needs something else."

"Right. Right."

"A mythic element."

"Right. My point. My point. My point. Needs a plot they can go home whistlin'. Exactly."

"So it should be done here, in the open air. Open to the sky and the hills."

Jason Ogg wrinkled his brows. They were always pretty wrinkled anyway, whenever he was dealing with the complexities of the world. Only when it came to iron did he know exactly what to do. But he held up a wavering finger and tried to count his fellow thespians. Given that the jug was now empty, this was an effort. There seemed, on average, to be seven other people. But he had a vague, nagging feeling that something wasn't right.

"Out here," he said, uncertainly.

"Good idea," said Weaver.

"Wasn't it your idea?" said Jason.

"I thought *you* said it."

"I thought *you* did."

"Who cares who said it?" said Thatcher. " 'S'a good idea. Seems . . . right."

"What was that about the miffic quality?"

"What's miffic?"

"Something you've got to have," said Weaver, theatrical expert. "Very important, your miffics."

"Me mam said no one was to go—" Jason began.

"We shan't be doing any dancing or anything," said Carter. "I can see you don't want people skulking around up here by 'emselves, doin' magic. But it can't be wrong if everyone comes here. I mean, the king and everyone. Your mam, too. Hah, I'd like to see any girls with no drawers on get past her!"

"I don't think it's just—" Jason began.

"And the other one'll be there, too," said Weaver.

They considered Granny Weatherwax.

"Cor, she frightens the life out of me, her," said Thatcher, eventually. "The way she looks right through you. I wouldn't say a word against her, mark you, a fine figure of a woman," he said loudly, and then added rather more quietly, "but they do say she creeps around the place o'nights, as a hare or a bat or something. Changes her shape and all. Not that I believes a word of it," he raised his voice, then let it sink again, "but old Weezen over in Slice told me once he shot a hare in the leg one night and next day she passed him on the lane and said 'Ouch' and gave him a right ding across the back of his head."

"My dad said," said Weaver, "that one day he was leading our old cow to market and it took ill and fell down in the lane near her cottage and he couldn't get it to move and he went up to her place and he knocked on the door and she opened it and before he could open his mouth she said, 'Yer cow's ill, Weaver' . . . just like that . . . And then she said—"

"Was that the old brindled cow what your dad had?" said Carter.

"No, it were my uncle had the brindled cow, we had the one with the crumpled horn," said Weaver. "Anyway—"

"Could have sworn it was brindled," said Carter. "I remember my dad looking at it over the hedge one day and saying, 'That's fine brindling on that cow, you don't get brindling like that these days.' That was when you had that old field alongside Cabb's Well."

"We never had that field, it was my cousin had that field," said Weaver. "Anyway—"

"You sure?"

"*Anyway*," said Weaver, "she said, 'You wait there, I'll give you something for it,' and she goes out into her back kitchen and comes back with a couple of big red pills, and she—"

"How'd it get crumpled, then?" said Carter.

"—*and she* gave him one of the pills and said, 'What you do, you raise the old cow's tail and shove this pill where the sun don't shine, and in half a minute she'll be up and running as fast as she can,' and he thanked her, and then as he was going out of the door he said, 'What's the other pill for?' and she gave him a look and said, 'Well, you *want* to catch her, don't you?' "

"That'd be that deep valley up near Slice," said Carter.

They looked at him.

"What, exactly, are you talking about?" said Weaver.

"It's right behind the mountain," said Carter,

nodding knowingly. "Very shady there. That's what she meant, I expect. The place where the sun doesn't shine. Long way to go for a pill, but I suppose that's witches for you."

Weaver winked at the others.

"Listen," he said, "I'm telling you she meant . . . well, where the monkey put his nut."

Carter shook his head.

"No monkeys in Slice," he said. His face became suffused with a slow grin. "Oh, I get it! She was daft!"

"Them playwriters down in Ankh," said Baker, "boy, they certainly know about us. Pass me the jug."

Jason turned his head again. He was getting more and more uneasy. His hands, which were always in daily contact with iron, were itching.

"Reckon we ought to be getting along home now, lads," he managed.

" 'S'nice night," said Baker, staying put. "Look at them stars a-twinklin'."

"Turned a bit cold, though," said Jason.

"Smells like snow," said Carter.

"Oh, yeah," said Baker. "That's right. Snow at midsummer. That's what they get where the sun don't shine."

"Shutup, shutup, shutup," said Jason.

"What's up with you?"

"It's wrong! We shouldn't be up here! Can't you *feel* it?"

"Oh, sit down, man," said Weaver. "It's fine. Can't feel nothing but the air. And there's still more scumble in the jug."

Baker leaned back.

"I remember an old story about this place," he said. "Some man went to sleep up here once, when he was out hunting."

The bottle glugged in the dusk.

"So what? I can do that," said Carter. "I go to sleep every night, reg'lar."

"Ah, but *this* man, when he woke up and went home, his wife was carrying on with someone else and all his children had grown up and didn't know who he was."

"Happens to me just about every day," said Weaver gloomily.

Baker sniffed.

"You know, it *does* smell a bit like snow. You know? That kind of sharp smell."

Thatcher leaned back, cradling his head on his arm.

"Tell you what," he said, "if I thought my old woman'd marry someone else and my hulking great kids'd bugger off and stop eating up the larder every day I'd come up here with a blanket like a shot. Who's got that jug?"

Jason took a pull out of nervousness, and found that he felt better as the alcohol dissolved his synapses.

But he made an effort.

"Hey, lads," he slurred, " 've got 'nother jug coolin' in the water trough down in the forge, what d'you say? We could all go down there now. Lads? Lads?"

There was the soft sound of snoring.

"Oh, *lads*."

Jason stood up.

The stars wheeled.

Jason fell down, very gently. The jug rolled out of his hands and bounced across the grass.

The stars twinkled, the breeze was cold, and it smelled of snow.

The king dined alone, which is to say, he dined at one end of the big table and Magrat dined at the other.

But they managed to meet up for a last glass of wine in front of the fire.

They always found it difficult to know what to say at moments like this. Neither of them was used to spending what might be called quality time in the company of another person. The conversation tended toward the cryptic.

And mostly it was about the wedding. It's *different*, for royalty. For one thing, you've already got everything. The traditional wedding list with the complete set of Tupperware and the twelve-piece dining set looks a bit out of place when you've already got a castle with so many furnished rooms that have been closed up for so long that the spiders have evolved into distinct species in accordance with strict evolutionary principles. And you can't simply multiply it all up and ask for An Army in a Red and White Motif to match the kitchen wallpaper. Royalty, when they marry, either get very small things, like exquisitely constructed clockwork eggs, or large bulky items, like duchesses.

And then there's the guest list. It's bad enough at an ordinary wedding, what with old relatives who dribble and swear, brothers who get belligerent after one drink, and various people who Aren't Talking to other people because of What They Said About Our Sharon. Royalty has to deal with entire *countries* who get belligerent after one drink, and entire kingdoms who Have Broken Off Diplomatic Relations after what the Crown Prince Said About Our Sharon. Verence had managed to work that all out, but then there were the species to consider. Trolls and dwarfs got on all right in Lancre by the simple expedient of having nothing to do with one another, but too many of them under one roof, especially if drink was flowing, and especially if it was flowing in the direction of the dwarfs, and people would Be Breaking People's Arms Off because of what, more or less, Their Ancestors Said About Our Sharon.

And then there's other things . . .

"How's the girl they brought in?"

"I've told Millie to keep an eye on her. What are they doing, those two?"

"I don't know."

"You're king, aren't you?"

Verence shifted uneasily.

"But they're witches. I don't like to ask them questions."

"Why not?"

"They might give me answers. And then what would I do?"

"What did Granny want to talk to you about?"

"Oh . . . you know . . . things . . ."

"It wasn't about . . . sex, was it?"

Verence suddenly looked like a man who had been expecting a frontal attack and suddenly finds nasty things happening behind him.

"No! Why?"

"Nanny was trying to give me motherly advice. It was all I could do to keep a straight face. Honestly, they both treat me as if I'm a big child."

"Oh, no. Nothing like that."

They sat on either side of the huge fireplace, both crimson with embarrassment.

Then Magrat said: "Er . . . you did send off for that book, did you? You know . . . the one with the woodcuts?"

"Oh, yes. Yes, I did."

"It ought to have arrived by now."

"Well, we only get a mail coach once a week. I expect it'll come tomorrow. I'm fed up with running down there every week in case Shawn gets there first."

"You *are* king. You could tell him not to."

"Don't like to, really. He's so keen."

A large log crackled into two across the iron dogs.

"Can you really get books about . . . that?"

"You can get books about *anything*."

They both stared at the fire. Verence thought: she doesn't like being a queen, I can see that, but that's what you *are* when you marry a king, all the books say so . . .

And Magrat thought: he was much nicer when he was a man with silver bells on his hat and slept every night on the floor in front of his master's door. I could talk to him then . . .

Verence clapped his hands together.

"Well, that's about it, then. Busy day tomorrow, what with all the guests coming and everything."

"Yes. It's going to be a long day."

"Very nearly *the* longest day. Haha."

"Yes."

"I expect they've put warming pans in our beds."

"Has Shawn got the hang of it now?"

"I hope so. I can't afford any more mattresses."

It was a *great* hall. Shadows piled up in the corners, clustered at either end.

"I suppose," said Magrat, very slowly, as they stared at the fire, "they haven't really had many books here in Lancre. Up until now."

"Literacy is a great thing."

"They got along without them, I suppose."

"Yes, but not properly. Their husbandry is really very primitive."

Magrat looked at the fire. Their wifery wasn't up to much either, she thought.

"So we'd better be off to bed, then, do you think?"

"I suppose so."

Verence took down two silver candlesticks, and lit the candles with a taper. He handed one to Magrat.

"Goodnight, then."

"Goodnight."

They kissed, and turned away, and headed for their own rooms.

The sheets on Magrat's bed were just beginning to turn brown. She pulled out the warming pan and dropped it out of the window.

She glared at the garderobe.

Magrat was probably the only person in Lancre who worried about things being biodegradable. Everyone else just hoped things would last and knew that damn near everything went rotten if you left it long enough.

At home—correction, at the cottage where she *used to live*—there had been a privy at the bottom of the garden.

She'd approved of it. With a regular bucket of ashes and a copy of last year's *Almanack* on a nail and a bunch-of-grapes cutout on the door it functioned quite effectively. About once every few months she'd have to dig a big hole and get someone to help her move the shed itself.

The garderobe was this: a sort of small roofed-in room inside the wall, with a wooden seat positioned over a large square hole that went down all the way to the foot of the castle wall far below, where there was an opening from which biodegradability took place once a week by means of an organo-dynamic process known as Shawn Ogg and his wheelbarrow. That much Magrat understood. It kind of fitted in with the whole idea of royalty and commonality. What shocked her were the hooks.

They were for storing clothes in the garderobe. Millie had explained that the more expensive furs and things were hung there. Moths were kept away by the draught from the hole and . . . the smell.*

Magrat had put her foot down about that, at least.

Now she lay in bed and stared at the ceiling.

Of course she *wanted* to marry Verence, even with his weak chin and slightly runny eyes. In the pit of the night Magrat knew that she was in no position to be choosy, and getting a king in the circumstances was a stroke of luck.

It was just that she *had* preferred him when he'd

---

*Really true. That's why people stand aside when kings go past.

been a Fool. There's something about a man who tinkles gently as he moves.

It was just that she could see a future of bad tapestry and sitting looking wistfully out of the window.

It was just that she was fed up with books of etiquette and lineage and *Twurp's Peerage* of the Fifteen Mountains and the Sto Plains.

You had to know this kind of thing, to be a queen. There were books full of the stuff in the Long Gallery, and she hadn't even explored the far end. How to address the third cousin of an earl. What the pictures on shields meant, all those lions passant and regardant. And the clothes weren't getting any better. Magrat had drawn the line at a wimple, and she wasn't at all happy about the big pointy hat with the scarf dangling from it. It probably looked beautiful on the Lady of Shallot, but on Magrat it looked as though someone had dropped a big ice cream on her neck.

Nanny Ogg sat in front of her fire in her dressing gown, smoking her pipe and idly cutting her toenails. There was the occasional ping and ricochet from distant parts of the room, and a small tinkle as an oil lamp was smashed.

Granny Weatherwax lay on her bed, still and cold. In her blue-veined hands, the words: I ATE'NT DEAD . . .

Her mind drifted across the forest, searching, searching . . .

The trouble was, she could not go where there were no eyes to see or ears to hear.

So she never noticed the hollow near the stones, where eight men slept.

And dreamed . . .

Lancre is cut off from the rest of the lands of mankind by a bridge over Lancre Gorge, above the shallow but poisonously fast and treacherous Lancre River.*

The coach pulled up at the far end.

There was a badly painted red, black, and white post across the road.

The coachman sounded his horn.

"What's up?" said Ridcully, leaning out of the window.

"Troll bridge."

"Whoops."

After a while there was a booming sound under the bridge, and a troll clambered over the parapet. It was quite overdressed, for a troll. In addition to the statutory loincloth, it was wearing a helmet. Admittedly it had been designed for a human head, and was attached to the much larger troll head by string, but there probably wasn't a better word than "wearing."

"What's up?" said the Bursar, waking up.

"There's a troll on the bridge," said Ridcully, "but it's underneath a helmet, so it's probably official and will get into serious trouble if it eats people.** Nothing to worry about."

The Bursar giggled, because he was on the up-

---

*The Lancratians did not consider geography to be a very original science.

**Troll, a lifeform on silicon rather than carbon, can't in fact digest people. But there's always someone ready to give it a try.

curve of whatever switchback his mind was currently riding.

The troll appeared at the coach window.

"Afternoon, your lordships," it said. "Customs inspection."

"I don't think we have any," babbled the Bursar happily. "I mean, we used to have a tradition of rolling boiled eggs downhill on Soul Cake Tuesday, but—"

"I means," said the troll, "do you have any beer, spirits, wines, liquors, hallucinogenic herbage, or books of a lewd or licentious nature?"

Ridcully pulled the Bursar back from the window.

"No," he said.

"No?"

"No."

"Sure?"

"Yes."

"Would you like some?"

"We haven't even got," said the Bursar, despite Ridcully's efforts to sit on his head, "any *billygoats*."

There are some people that would whistle "Yankee Doodle" in a crowded bar in Atlanta.

Even these people would consider it tactless to mention the word "billygoat" to a troll.

The troll's expression changed very slowly, like a glacier eroding half a mountain. Ponder tried to get under the seat.

"So we'll just *trit-trot* along, shall we?" said the Bursar, his voice by now slightly muffled.

"He doesn't mean it," said the Archchancellor quickly. "It's the dried frog talking."

"You don't want to eat *me*," said the Bursar.

"You want to eat my *brother*, he's much mfmfph mfmfph . . ."

"Well, now," said the troll, "seems to me that—" He spotted Casanunda.

"Oh-*ho*," he said, "*dwarf* smuggling, eh?"

"Don't be ridiculous, man," said Ridcully, "there's no such thing as dwarf smuggling."

"Yeah? Then what's that you've got there?"

"I'm a giant," said Casanunda.

"Giants are a lot bigger."

"I've been ill."

The troll looked perplexed. This was post-graduate thinking for a troll. But he was looking for trouble. He found it on the roof of the coach, where the Librarian had been sunbathing.

"What's in that sack up there?"

"That's not a sack. That's the Librarian."

The troll prodded the large mass of red hair.

"Ook . . ."

"What? A monkey?"

"Oook?"

Several minutes later, the travelers leaned on the parapet, looking down reflectively at the river far below.

"Happen often, does it?" said Casanunda.

"Not so much these days," said Ridcully. "It's like—what's that word, Stibbons? About breedin' and passin' on stuff to yer kids?"

"Evolution," said Ponder. The ripples were still sloshing against the banks.

"Right. Like, my father had a waistcoat with embroidered peacocks on it, and he left it to me, and now I've got it. They call it hereditarery—"

"No, that's not—" Ponder began, with no hope whatsoever that Ridcully would listen.

"—so anyway, most people left back home know the difference between apes and monkeys now," said Ridcully. "Evolution, that is. It's hard to breed when you've got a headache from being bounced up and down on the pavement."

The ripples had stopped now.

"Do you think trolls can swim?" said Casanunda.

"No. They just sink and walk ashore," said Ridcully. He turned, and leaned back on his elbows. "This really takes me back, you know. The old Lancre River. There's trout down there that'd take your arm off."

"Not just trout," said Ponder, watching a helmet emerge from the water.

"And limpid pools further up," said Ridcully. "Full of, of, of . . . limpids, stuff like that. And you can bathe naked and no one'd see. And water meadows full of . . . water, don'tyerknow, and flowers and stuff." He sighed. "You know, it was on this very bridge that she told me she—"

"He's got out of the river," said Ponder. But the troll wasn't moving very fast, because the Librarian was nonchalantly levering one of the big stones out of the parapet.

"On this very bridge I asked—"

"That's a big club he's got," said Casanunda.

"This bridge, I may say, was where I nearly—"

"Could you stop holding that rock in such a provocative way?" said Ponder.

"Oook."

"It'd be a help."

"The actual bridge, if anyone's interested, is where my whole life took a diff—"

"Why don't we just go on?" said Ponder. "He's got a steep climb."

"Good thing for him he hasn't got up here, eh?" said Casanunda. Ponder swiveled the Librarian around and pushed him toward the coach.

"This is the bridge, in fact, where—"

Ridcully turned around.

"Are you coming or not?" said Casanunda, with the reins in his hand.

"I was actually having a quality moment of misty nostalgic remembrance," said Ridcully. "Not that any of you buggers noticed, of course."

Ponder held the door open.

"Well, you know what they say. You can't cross the same river twice, Archchancellor," he said.

Ridcully stared at him.

"Why not? This is a *bridge*."

On the roof of the coach the Librarian picked up the coach-horn, bit the end of it reflectively—well, you never knew—and then blew it so hard that it uncurled.

It was early morning in Lancre town, and it was more or less deserted. Farmers had got up hours before to curse and swear and throw a bucket at the cows and had then gone back to bed.

The sound of the horn bounced off the houses.

Ridcully leapt out of the coach and took a deep, theatrical breath.

"Can't you smell that?" he said. "That's real fresh mountain air, that is." He thumped his chest.

"I've just trodden in something rural," said Ponder. "Where is the castle, sir?"

"I think it could be that huge black towering thing looming over the town," said Casanunda.

The Archchancellor stood in the middle of the square and turned slowly with his arms spread wide.

"See that tavern?" he said. "Hah! If I had a penny for every time they threw me out of there, I'd have . . . five dollars and thirty-eight pence. And over there is the old forge, and there's Mrs. Persifleur's, where I had lodgings. See that peak up there? That's Copperhead, that is. I climbed that one day with old Carbonaceous the troll. Oh, great days, great days. And see that wood down there, on the hill? That's where she—"

His voice trailed into a mumble. "Oh, my word. It all comes back to me . . . What a summer *that* was. They don't make 'em like *that* anymore." He sighed. "You know," he said, "I'd give *anything* to walk through those woods with her again. There were so many things we never—oh, well. Come on."

Ponder looked around at Lancre. He'd been born and raised in Ankh-Morpork. As far as he was concerned, the countryside was something that happened to other people, and most of them had four legs. As far as he was concerned, the countryside was like raw chaos before the universe, which was to say something with cobbles and walls, something *civilized*, was created.

"This is the capital city?" he said.

"More or less," said Casanunda, who tended to feel the same way about places that weren't paved.

"I bet there's not a single delicatessen anywhere," said Ponder.

"And the beer here," said Ridcully, "the beer here—well, you'd just better taste the beer here! And there's stuff called scumble, they make it from apples and . . . and damned if I know what else they put in it, except you daren't pour it into metal mugs. You ought to try it, Mr. Stibbons. It'd put hair on your chest. And yours—" he turned to the next one down from the coach, who turned out to be the Librarian.

"Oook?"

"Well, I, er, I should just drink anything you like, in your case," said Ridcully.

He hauled the mail sack down from the roof.

"What do we do with this?" he said.

There were ambling footsteps behind him, and he turned to see a short, red-faced youth in ill-fitting and baggy chain-mail, which made him look like a lizard that had lost a lot of weight very quickly.

"Where's the coach driver?" said Shawn Ogg.

"He's ill," said Ridcully. "He had a sudden attack of bandits. What do we do with the mail?"

"I take the palace stuff, and we generally leave the sack hanging up on a nail outside the tavern so that people can help themselves," said Shawn.

"Isn't that dangerous?" said Ponder.

"Don't think so. It's a strong nail," said Shawn, rummaging in the sack.

"I meant, don't people steal letters?"

"Oh, they wouldn't do that, they wouldn't do that. One of the witches'd go and stare at 'em if they did that." Shawn stuffed a few packages under his arm and hung the sack on the aforesaid nail.

"Yes, that's another thing they used to have round here," said Ridcully. "Witches! Let me tell you about the witches round here—"

"Our mum's a witch," said Shawn conversationally, rummaging in the sack.

"As fine a body of women as you could hope to meet," said Ridcully, with barely a hint of mental gear-clashing. "And not a bunch of interfering power-mad old crones at all, whatever anyone might say."

"Are you here for the wedding?"

"That's right. I'm the Archchancellor of Unseen University, this is Mr. Stibbons, a wizard, this—where are you? Oh, there you are—this is Mr. Casanunda—"

"Count," said Casanunda. "I'm a Count."

"Really? You never said."

"Well, you don't, do you? It's not the first thing you say."

Ridcully's eyes narrowed.

"But I thought dwarfs didn't have titles," he said.

"I performed a small service for Queen Agantia of Skund," said Casanunda.

"Did you? My word. How small?"

"Not that small."

"My word. And *that's* the Bursar, and *this* is the Librarian." Ridcully took a step backward, waved his hands in the air, and silently mouthed the words: Don't Say Monkey.

"Pleased to meet you," said Shawn, politely.

Ridcully felt moved to investigate.

"The Librarian," he repeated.

"Yes. You said." Shawn nodded at the orang-utan. "How d'you do?"

"Ook."

"You might be wondering why he looks like that," Ridcully prompted.

"No, sir."

"No?"

"My mum says none of us can help how we're made," said Shawn.

"What a singular lady. And what is her name?" said Ridcully.

"Mrs. Ogg, sir."

"Ogg? Ogg? Name rings a bell. Any relation to Sobriety Ogg?"

"He was my dad, sir."

"Good grief. Old Sobriety's son? How *is* the old devil?"

"Dunno, sir, what with him being dead."

"Oh dear. How long ago?"

"These past thirty years," said Shawn.

"But you don't look any older than twen—" Ponder began. Ridcully elbowed him sharply in the ribcage.

"This is the countryside," he hissed. "People do things differently here. And more often." He turned back to Shawn's pink and helpful face.

"Things seem to be waking up a bit," he said, and indeed shutters were coming down around the square. "We'll get some breakfast in the tavern. They used to do wonderful breakfasts." He sniffed again, and beamed.

"Now *that*," he said, "is what *I* call fresh air."

Shawn looked around carefully.

"Yes, sir," he said. "That's what we call it, too."

There was the sound of someone frantically running, and then a pause, and King Verence II appeared around the corner, walking slowly and calmly with a very red face.

"Certainly gives people a rosy complexion," said Ridcully cheerfully.

"It's the king!" hissed Shawn. "And me without my trumpet!"

"Um," said Verence. "Post been yet, Shawn?"

"Oh, yes, sire!" said Shawn, almost as flustered as the king. "Got it right here. Don't you worry about it! I'll open it all up and have it on your desk right away, sire!"

"Um . . ."

"Something the matter, sire?"

"Um . . . I think perhaps . . ."

Shawn was already tearing at the wrappers.

"Here's that book on etiquette you've been waiting for, sire, and the pig stockbook, and . . . what's this one . . . ?"

Verence made a grab for it. Shawn automatically tried to hang on to it. The wrapping split, and the large bulky book thumped on to the cobbles. Its fluttering pages played their woodcuts to the breeze.

They looked down.

"Wow!" said Shawn.

"My word," said Ridcully.

"Um," said the king.

"Oook?"

Shawn picked up the book very, very carefully, and turned a few pages.

"Hey, look at this one! He's doing it with his feet! I didn't know you could do it with your feet!" He nudged Ponder Stibbons. "Look, sir!"

Ridcully peered at the king.

"You all right, your majesty?" he said.

Verence squirmed.

"Um . . ."

"And, look, here's one where both chaps are doing it with sticks . . ."

"What?" said Verence.

"Wow," said Shawn. "Thank you, sire. This is going to really come in handy, I can tell you. I mean, I've picked up bits and pieces here and there, but—"

Verence snatched the book from Shawn's hands and looked at the title page.

"'Martial Arts'? *Martial* Arts. But I'm sure I wrote Marit—"

"Sire?"

There was one exquisite moment while Verence fought for mental balance, but he won.

"Ah. Yes. Right. Uh. Well, yes. Uh. Of course. Yes. Well, you see, a well-trained army is . . . is essential to the security of any kingdom. That's right. Yes. Fine. Magrat and me, we thought . . . yes. It's for you, Shawn."

"I'll start practicing right away, sire!"

"Um. Good."

Jason Ogg awoke, and wished he hadn't.

Let's be clear. Many authorities have tried to describe a hangover. Dancing elephants and so on are often employed for this purpose. The descriptions never work. They always smack of, hoho, here's one for the lads, let's have some hangover machismo, hoho, landlord, another nineteen pints of lager, hey, we supped some stuff last night, hoho . . .

Anyway, you can't describe a scumble hangover.

The *best* bit of it is a feeling that your teeth have dissolved and coated themselves on your tongue.

Eventually the blacksmith sat up and opened his eyes.*

His clothes were soaked with dew.

His head felt full of wisps and whispers.

He stared at the stones.

The scumble jar was lying in the leather. After a moment or two he picked it up, and took an experimental swig. It was empty.

He nudged Weaver in the ribs with his boot.

"Wake up, you old bugger. We've been up here all night!"

One by one, the Morris Men made the short but painful journey into consciousness.

"I'm going to get some stick from our Eva when I get home," moaned Carter.

"You might not," said Thatcher, who was on his hands and knees looking for his hat. "Maybe when you gets 'ome she'll have married someone else, eh?"

"Maybe a hundred years'll have gone past," said Carter, hopefully.

"Cor, I hope so," said Weaver, brightening up. "I had sevenpence invested in The Thrift Bank down in Ohulan. I'll be a millionaire at complicated interest. I'll be as rich as Creosote."

"Who's Creosote?" said Thatcher.

"Famous rich bugger," said Baker, fishing one of his boots out of a peat pool. "Foreign."

"Wasn't he the one, everything he touched turned to gold?" said Carter.

---

*Insert the usual "red-hot curried marbles" description here, if you like.

"Nah, that was someone else. Some king or other. That's what happens in foreign parts. One minute you're all right, next minute, everything you touch turns to gold. He was plagued with it."

Carter looked puzzled.

"How did he manage when he had to—"

"Let that be a lesson to you, young Carter," said Baker. "You stay here where folks are sensible, not go gadding off abroad where you might suddenly be holding a fortune in your hands and not have anything to spend it on."

"We've slept out here all night," said Jason uncertainly. "That's dangerous, that is."

"You're right there, Mr. Ogg," said Carter. "I think something went to the toilet in my ear."

"I mean strange things can enter your head."

"That's what I mean, too."

Jason blinked. He was certain he'd dreamed. He could *remember* dreaming. But he couldn't remember what the dream had been about. But there was still the feeling in his head of voices talking to him, but too far away to be heard.

"Oh, well," he said, managing to stand up at the third attempt, "probably no harm done. Let's get on home and see what century it is."

"What century *is* it, anyway?" said Thatcher.

"Century of the Fruitbat, isn't it?" said Baker.

"Might not be anymore," said Carter hopefully.

It turned out that it was, indeed, the Century of the Fruitbat. Lancre didn't have much use for units of time any smaller than an hour or larger than a year, but people were clearly putting up bunting in the town square and a gang of men were erecting the Maypole. Someone was nailing up a very badly painted picture of Verence and Magrat under which was the slogan: God Bles Their Majestieys.

With hardly a word exchanged, the men parted and staggered their separate ways.

A hare lolloped through the morning mist until it reached the drunken, ancient cottage in its clearing in the woods.

It reached a tree stump between the privy and The Herbs. Most woodland animals avoided The Herbs. This was because animals that didn't avoid The Herbs over the past fifty years had tended not to have descendants. A few tendrils waved in the breeze and this was odd because there wasn't any breeze.

It sat on the stump.

And then there was a sensation of movement. Something left the hare and moved across the air to an open upstairs window. It was invisible, at least to normal eyesight.

The hare changed. Before, it had moved with purpose. Now it flopped down and began to wash its ears.

After a while the back door opened and Granny Weatherwax walked out stiffly, holding a bowl of bread and milk. She put it down on the step and turned back without a second glance, closing the door again behind her.

The hare hopped closer.

It's hard to know if animals understand obligations, or the nature of transactions. But that doesn't matter. They're built into witchcraft. If you want to really upset a witch, do her a favor which she has no means of repaying. The unfulfilled obligation will nag at her like a hangnail.

Granny Weatherwax had been riding the hare's mind all night. Now she owed it something. There'd be bread and milk left outside for a few days.

You had to repay, good or bad. There was more than one type of obligation. That's what people never really understood, she told herself as she stepped back into the kitchen. Magrat hadn't understood it, nor that new girl. Things had to balance. You couldn't set out to be a good witch or a bad witch. It never worked for long. All you could try to be was a *witch*, as hard as you could.

She sat down by the cold hearth, and resisted a temptation to comb her ears.

They had broken in somewhere. She could feel it in the trees, in the minds of tiny animals. *She* was planning something. Something soon. There was of course nothing special about midsummer in the occult sense, but there was in the minds of people. And the minds of people was where elves were strong.

Granny knew that sooner or later she'd have to face the Queen. Not Magrat, but the real Queen.

And she would lose.

She'd worked all her life on controlling the insides of her own head. She'd prided herself on being the best there was.

But no longer. Just when she needed all her self reliance, she couldn't rely on her mind. She could sense the probing of the Queen—she could remember the feel of that mind, from all those decades ago.

And she seemed to have her usual skill at Borrowing. But *herself*—if she didn't leave little notes for herself, she'd be totally at sea. Being a witch meant knowing exactly who you were and where you were, and she was losing the ability to know both. Last night she'd found herself setting the table for two people. She'd tried to walk into a room she didn't have. And soon she'd have to fight an elf.

If you fought an elf and lost . . . then, if you were lucky, you would die.

Magrat was brought breakfast in bed by a giggling Millie Chillum.

"Guests are arriving already, ma'am. And there's flags and everything down in the square! *And* Shawn has found the coronation coach!"

"How can you lose a coach?" said Magrat.

"It was locked up in one of the old stables, ma'am. He's giving it a fresh coat of gold paint right now."

"But we're going to be married *here*," said Magrat. "We don't have to go anywhere."

"The king said perhaps you could both ride around a bit. Maybe as far as Bad Ass, he said. With Shawn Ogg as a military escort. So people can wave and shout hooray. And then come back here."

Magrat put on her dressing gown and crossed to the tower window. She could see down over the outer walls and into Lancre town square, which was already quite full of people. It would have been a market day in any case, but people were erecting benches as well and the Maypole was already up. There were even a few dwarfs and trolls, politely maintaining a distance from one another.

"I just saw a monkey walk across the square," said Magrat.

"The whole world's coming to Lancre!" said Millie, who had once been as far as Slice.

Magrat caught sight of the distant picture of herself and her fiancé.

"This is stupid," she said to herself, but Millie heard her and was shocked.

"What *can* you mean, ma'am?"

Magrat spun around.

"All this! For *me*!"

Millie backed away in sudden fright.

"I'm just Magrat Garlick! Kings ought to marry princesses and duchesses and people like that! People who are *used* to it! I don't want people shouting hooray just because I've gone by in a coach! And especially not people who've known me all my life! All this—this," her frantic gesture took in the hated garderobe, the huge four-poster bed, and the dressing room full of stiff and expensive clothes, "this *stuff* . . . it's not for *me*! It's for some kind of *idea*. Didn't you ever get those cut-outs, those dolls, you know, when you were a girl . . . dolls you cut out, and there were cut-out clothes as well? And you could make her anything you wanted? That's *me*! It's . . . it's like the bees! I'm being turned into a queen whether I want to or not! That's what's happening to me!"

"I'm sure the king bought you all those nice clothes because—"

"I don't mean just *clothes*. I mean people'd be shouting hooray if—if *anyone* went past in the coach!"

"But you were the one who fell in love with the king, ma'am," said Millie, bravely.

Magrat hesitated for a moment. She'd never quite analyzed that emotion. Eventually she said, "No. He wasn't king then. No one knew he was going to be king. He was just a sad, nice little man in a cap and bells who everyone ignored."

Millie backed away a bit more.

"I expect it's nerves, ma'am," she gabbled. "Everyone feels nervous on the day before their wedding. Shall I . . . shall I see if I can make you some herbal—"

"I'm *not* nervous! And I can do my own herbal tea if I happen to want any!"

"Cook's very particular who goes into the herb garden, ma'am," said Millie.

"I've *seen* that herb garden! It's all leggy sage and yellowy parsley! If you can't stuff it up a chicken's bum, she doesn't think it's an herb! Anyway . . . who's queen in this vicinity?"

"I thought you didn't want to be, ma'am?" said Millie.

Magrat stared at her. For a moment she looked as if she was arguing with herself.

Millie might not have been the best-informed girl in the world, but she wasn't stupid. She was at the door and through it just as the breakfast tray hit the wall.

Magrat sat down on the bed with her head in her hands.

She didn't want to be queen. Being a queen was like being an actor, and Magrat had never been any good at acting. She'd always felt she wasn't very good at being Magrat, if it came to that.

The bustle of the pre-nuptial activities rose up from the town. There'd be folkdancing, of course—there seemed to be no way of preventing it—and probably folksinging would be perpetrated. And there'd be dancing bears and comic jugglers and the greasy pole competition, which for some reason Nanny Ogg always won. And bowling-with-a-pig. And the bran tub, which Nanny Ogg usually ran; it was a brave man who plunged his hand into a bran tub stocked by a witch with a broad sense of humor. Magrat had always liked the fairs. Up until now.

Well, there were still some things she could do.

She dressed herself in her commoner's clothes for the last time, and let herself out and down the back stairs to the widdershins tower and the room where Diamanda lay.

Magrat had instructed Shawn to keep a good fire going in the grate, and Diamanda was still sleeping, peacefully, the unwakeable sleep.

Magrat couldn't help noticing that Diamanda was strikingly good-looking and, from what she'd heard, quite brave enough to stand up to Granny Weatherwax. She could hardly wait to get her better so that she could envy her properly.

The wound seemed to be healing up nicely, but there seemed to be—

Magrat strode to the bellpull in the corner and hauled on it.

After a minute or two Shawn Ogg arrived, panting. There was gold paint on his hands.

"*What*," said Magrat, "are all *these* things?"

"Um. Don't like to say, ma'am . . ."

"One happens to be . . . very nearly . . . the queen," said Magrat.

"Yes, but the king said . . . well, *Granny* said—"

"Granny Weatherwax does not happen to rule the kingdom," said Magrat. She hated herself when she spoke like this, but it seemed to work. "And anyway she's not here. One *is* here, however, and if you don't tell one what's going on I'll see to it that you do all the dirty jobs around the palace."

"But I do all the dirty jobs anyway," said Shawn.

"I shall see to it that there are dirtier ones."

Magrat picked up one of the bundles. It was made up of strips of sheet wrapped around what turned out to be an iron bar.

"They're all around her," she said. "Why?"

Shawn looked at his feet. There was gold paint on his boots, too.

"Well, our mum said . . ."

"Yes?"

"Our mum said I was to see to it that there was iron round her. So me and Millie got some bars from down the smithy and wrapped 'em up like this and Millie packed 'em round her."

"Why?"

"To keep away the . . . the Lords and Ladies, ma'am."

"What? That's just old superstition! Anyway, everyone knows elves were good, whatever Granny Weatherwax says."

Behind her, Shawn flinched. Magrat pulled the wrapped iron lumps out of the bed and tossed them into the corner.

"No old wives' tales here, thank you very much. Is there anything else people haven't been telling me, by any chance?"

Shawn shook his head, guiltily aware of the thing in the dungeon.

"Huh! Well, go away. Verence wants the kingdom to be modern and efficient, and that means no horseshoes and stuff around the place. Go on, go away."

"Yes, Miss Queen."

At least I can do something positive around here, Magrat told herself.

Yes. Be sensible. Go and see him. Talk. Magrat clung to the idea that practically anything could be sorted out if only people talked to one another.

"Shawn?"

He paused at the door.

"Yes, ma'am?"

"Has the king gone down to the Great Hall yet?"

"I think he's still dressing, Miss Queen. He hasn't rung for me to do the trumpet, I know that."

In fact, Verence, who didn't like going everywhere preceded by Shawn's idea of a fanfare, had already gone downstairs incognito. But Magrat slipped along to his room, and knocked on the door.

Why be bashful? It'd be *her* room as well from tomorrow, wouldn't it? She tried the handle. It turned. Without quite willing it, Magrat went in.

Rooms in the castle could hardly be said to belong to anyone in any case. They'd had too many occupants over the centuries. The very atmosphere was the equivalent of those walls scattered with outbreaks of drawing-pin holes where last term's occupants hung the posters of rock groups long disbanded. You couldn't stamp your personality on that stone. It stamped back harder.

For Magrat, stepping into a man's bedroom was like an explorer stepping on to that part of the map marked Here Be Dragons.*

And it wasn't exactly what it ought to have been.

Verence had arrived at the bedroom concept fairly late in life. When he was a boy, the entire family slept on straw in the cottage attic. As an apprentice in the Guild of Joculators, he'd slept on a pallet in a long dormitory of other sad, beaten young men. When he was a fully fledged Fool he'd slept, by tradition, curled up in front of his master's door. Suddenly, at a later age than is usual, he'd been introduced to the notion of soft mattresses.

And now Magrat was privy to the big secret.

It hadn't worked.

There was the Great Bed of Lancre, which was said to be able to sleep a dozen people, although in what circumstances and why it should be necessary history had never made clear. It was huge and made of oak.

It was also, very clearly, unslept in.

Magrat pulled back the sheets, and smelled the scorched smell of linen. But it also smelled unaired, as if it hadn't been slept in.

---

*In the case of the *a*-Ω Street Mappe of Ankh-Morpork, this would be The Sunshine Home for Sick Dragons in Morphic Street, Please Leave Donations of Coal by Side Door. Remember, A Dragon is For Life, Not Just for Hogswatchnight.

She stared around the room until her eye lit on the little still-life by the door. There was a folded nightshirt, a candlestick, and a small pillow.

As far as Verence had been concerned, a crown merely changed which side of the door you slept.

Oh, gods. He'd always slept in front of the door of his master. And now he was king, he slept in front of the door to his kingdom.

Magrat felt her eyes fill with tears.

You couldn't help loving someone as soppy as that.

Fascinated, and aware that she was where she technically shouldn't be, Magrat blew her nose and explored further. A heap of discarded garments by the bed suggested that Verence had mastered the art of hanging up clothes as practiced by half the population of the world, and also that he had equally had difficulty with the complex topological maneuvers necessary to turn his socks the right way out.

There was a tiny dressing table and a mirror. Stuck to the mirror frame was a dried and faded flower that looked, to Magrat, very like the ones she habitually wore in her hair.

She shouldn't have gone on looking. She admitted that to herself, afterward. But she seemed to have no self-control.

There was a wooden bowl in the middle of the dresser table, full of odd coins, bits of string, and the general detritus of the nightly emptied pocket.

And a folded paper. Much folded, as if it had stayed in said pocket for some time.

She picked it up, and unfolded it.

* * *

There were little kingdoms all over the hubward slopes of the Ramtops. Every narrow valley, every ledge that something other than a goat could stand on, was a kingdom. There were kingdoms in the Ramtops so small that, if they were ravaged by a dragon, and that dragon had been killed by a young hero, and the king had given him half his kingdom as per Section Three of the Heroic Code, then there wouldn't have *been* any kingdom left. There were wars of annexation that went on for years just because someone wanted a place to keep the coal.

Lancre was one of the biggest kingdoms. It could actually afford a standing army.*

Kings and queens and various sub-orders of aristocracy were even now streaming over Lancre bridge, watched by a sulking and soaking-wet troll who had given up on bridge-keeping for the day.

The Great Hall had been thrown open. Jugglers and fire-eaters strolled among the crowd. Up in the minstrels gallery a small orchestra was playing the Lancre one-string fiddle and famed Ramtop bagpipes, but fortunately they were more or less drowned out by the noise of the crowd.

Nanny Ogg and Granny Weatherwax moved through said crowd. In deference to this being a festive occasion, Nanny Ogg had exchanged her normal black pointy hat for one the same shape but in red, with wax cherries on it.

"All the hort mond are here," Nanny observed,

---

*Shawn Ogg.**

**Except when he was lying down.

taking a drink off a passing tray. "Even some wizards from Ankh-Morpork, our Shawn said. One of them said I had a fine body, he said. Been tryin' to remember all morning who that could have been."

"Spoiled for choice," said Granny, but it was automatic nastiness, with no real heart to it. It worried Nanny Ogg. Her friend seemed preoccupied.

"There's some *gentry* we don't want to see here," said Granny. "I won't be happy until all this is over."

Nanny Ogg craned to try and see over the head of a small emperor.

"Can't see Magrat around," she said. "There's Verence talking to some other kings, but can't see our Magrat at *all*. Our Shawn said Millie Chillum said she was just a bag of nerves this morning."

"All these high-born folks," said Granny, looking around at the crowned heads. "I feel like a fish out of water."

"Well, the way I see it, it's up to you to make your own water," said Nanny, picking up a cold roast chicken leg from the buffet and stuffing it up a sleeve.

"Don't drink too much. We've got to keep alert, Gytha. Remember what I said. Don't let yourself get distracted—"

"That's never the delectable Mrs. Ogg, is it?"

Nanny turned.

There was no one behind her.

"Down here," said the voice.

She looked down, into a wide grin.

"Oh, blast," she said.

"It's me, Casanunda," said Casanunda, who was dwarfed still further by an enormous* powdered wig. "You remember? We danced the night away in Genua?"

"No we didn't."

"Well, we could have done."

"Fancy you turning up here," said Nanny, weakly. The thing about Casanunda, she recalled, was that the harder you slapped him down the faster he bounced back, often in an unexpected direction.

"Our stars are entwined," said Casanunda. "We're fated for one another. I wants your body, Mrs. Ogg."

"I'm still using it."

And while she suspected, quite accurately, that this was an approach the world's second greatest lover used on anything that appeared to be even vaguely female, Nanny Ogg had to admit that she was flattered. She'd had many admirers in her younger days, but time had left her with a body that could only be called comfortable and a face like Mr. Grape the Happy Raisin. Long-banked fires gave off a little smoke.

Besides, she'd rather *liked* Casanunda. Most men were oblique in their approach, whereas his direct attack was refreshing.

"It'd never work," she said. "We're basically in-

---

*But not huge, by wig standards. There have, in the course of decadent history, been many large wigs, often with built-in gewgaws to stop people having to look at boring hair all the time. There had been ones big enough to contain pet mice or clockwork ornaments. Mme. Cupidor, mistress of Mad King Soup II, had one with a bird cage in it, but on special state occasions wore one containing a perpetual calendar, a floral clock, and a take-away linguini shop.

compatible. When I'm 5' 4" you'll still only be 3' 9".
Anyway, I'm old enough to be your mother."

"You can't be. My mother's nearly 300, and she's
got a better beard than you."

And of course that was another point. By dwarf
standards, Nanny Ogg was hardly more than a
teenager.

"La, sir," she said, giving him a playful tap that
made his ears ring, "you do know how to turn a
simple country girl's head and no mistake!"

Casanunda picked himself up and adjusted his
wig happily.

"I like a girl with spirit," he said. "How about you
and me having a little tête-à-tête when this is over?"

Nanny Ogg's face went blank. Her cosmopolitan
grip of language had momentarily let her down.

"Excuse me a minute," she said. She put her drink
down on his head and pushed through the crowd
until she found a likely looking duchess, and prodded her in the bustle regions.

"Hey, your grace, what's a tater tate?"

"I beg your pardon?"

"A tater tate? Do you do it with your clothes on
or what?"

"It means an intimate meeting, my good woman."

"Is that all? Oh. Ta."

Nanny Ogg elbowed her way back to the vibrat-
ing dwarf.

"You're on," she said.

"I thought we could have a little private dinner,
just you and me," said Casanunda. "In one of the
taverns?"

Never, in a long history of romance, had Nanny

Ogg ever been taken out for an intimate dinner. Her courtships had been more noted for their quantity than their quality.

"OK," was all she could think of to say.

"Dodge your chaperone and meet me at six o'clock?"

Nanny Ogg glanced at Granny Weatherwax, who was watching them disapprovingly from a distance.

"She's not my—" she began.

Then it dawned on her that Casanunda couldn't possibly have really thought that Granny Weatherwax was chaperoning her.

Compliments and flattery had also been very minor components in the machinery of Nanny Ogg's courtships.

"Yes, all right," she said.

"And now I shall circulate, so that people don't talk and ruin your reputation," said Casanunda, bowing and kissing Nanny Ogg's hand.

Her mouth dropped open. No one had ever kissed her hand before, either, and certainly no one had ever worried about her reputation, least of all Nanny Ogg.

As the world's second greatest lover bustled off to accost a countess, Granny Weatherwax—who had been watching from a discreet distance*—said, in an amiable voice: "You haven't got the morals of a cat, Gytha Ogg."

"Now, Esme, you know that's not true."

"All right. You *have* got the morals of a cat, then."

"That's better."

---

*i.e., far enough so's not to look like you're intruding on the conversation, but close enough to get a pretty good idea of what is going on.

Nanny Ogg patted her mass of white curls and wondered if she had time to go home and put her corsets on.

"We must stay on our guard, Gytha."

"Yes, yes."

"Can't let other considerations turn our heads."

"No, no."

"You're not listening to a word I say, are you?"

"What?"

"You could at least find out why Magrat isn't down here."

"All right."

Nanny Ogg wandered off, dreamily.

Granny Weatherwax turned—

—there should have been violins. The murmur of the crowd should have faded away, and the crowd itself should have parted in a quite natural movement to leave an empty path between her and Ridcully.

There should have been violins. There should have been *something*.

There shouldn't have been the Librarian accidentally knuckling her on the toe on his way to the buffet, but this, in fact, there was.

She hardly noticed.

"Esme?" said Ridcully.

"Mustrum?" said Granny Weatherwax.

Nanny Ogg bustled up.

"Esme, I saw Millie Chillum and she said—"

Granny Weatherwax's vicious elbow jab winded her. Nanny took in the scene.

"Ah," she said, "I'll just, I'll just . . . I'll just go away, then."

The gazes locked again.

The Librarian knuckled past again with an entire display of fruit.

Granny Weatherwax paid him no heed.

The Bursar, who was currently on the median point of his cycle, tapped Ridcully on the shoulder.

"I say, Archchancellor, these quails' eggs are amazingly go—"

"DROP DEAD. Mr. Stibbons, fish out the frog pills and keep knives away from him, please."

The gazes locked again.

"Well, well," said Granny, after a year or so.

"This must be some enchanted evening," said Ridcully.

"Yes. That's what I'm afraid of."

"That really *is* you, isn't it?"

"It's really me," said Granny.

"You haven't changed a bit, Esme."

"Nor have you, then. You're *still* a rotten liar, Mustrum Ridcully."

They walked toward one another. The Librarian shuttled between them with a tray of meringues. Behind them, Ponder Stibbons groveled on the floor for a spilled bottle of dried frog pills.

"Well, well," said Ridcully.

"Fancy that."

"Small world."

"Yes indeed."

"You're you and I'm me. Amazing. And it's here and now."

"Yes, but *then* was *then*."

"I sent you a lot of letters," said Ridcully.

"Never got 'em."

There was a glint in Ridcully's eye.

"That's odd. And there was me putting all those destination spells on them too," he said. He gave her a critical up-and-down glance. "How much do you weigh, Esme? Not a spare ounce on you, I'll be bound."

"What do you want to know for?"

"Indulge an old man."

"Nine stones, then."

"Hmm . . . should be about right . . . three miles hubward . . . you'll feel a slight lurch to the left, nothing to worry about . . ."

In a lightning movement, he grabbed her hand. He felt young and light-headed. The wizards back at the University would have been astonished.

"Let me take you away from all this."

He snapped his fingers.

There has to be at least an approximate conservation of mass. It's a fundamental magical rule. If something is moved from A to B, something that was at B has got to find itself at A.

And then there's momentum. Slow as the disc spins, various points of its radii are moving at different speeds relative to the Hub, and a wizard projecting himself any distance toward the Rim had better be prepared to land jogging.

The three miles to Lancre Bridge merely involved a faint tug, which Ridcully had been ready for, and he landed leaning up against the parapet with Esme Weatherwax in his arms.

The customs troll who had until a fraction of a second previously been sitting there ended up lying full length on the floor of the Great Hall, coincidentally on top of the Bursar.

Granny Weatherwax looked over at the rushing water, and then at Ridcully.

"Take me back this instant," she said. "You've got no right to do that."

"Dear me, I seem to have run out of power. Can't understand it, very embarrassing, fingers gone all limp," said Ridcully. "Of course, we could walk. It's a lovely evening. You always did get lovely evenings here."

"It was all fifty or sixty years ago!" said Granny. "You can't suddenly turn up and say all those years haven't happened."

"Oh, I know they've happened all right," said Ridcully. "I'm the head wizard now. I've only got to give an order and a thousand wizards will . . . uh . . . disobey, come to think of it, or say 'What?', or start to argue. But they have to take notice."

"I've been to that University a few times," said Granny. "A bunch of fat old men in beards."

"That's right! That's *them*!"

"A lot of 'em come from the Ramtops," said Granny. "I knew a few boys from Lancre who became wizards."

"Very magical area," Ridcully agreed. "Something in the air."

Below them, the cold black waters raced, always dancing to gravity, never flowing uphill.

"There was even a Weatherwax as Archchancellor, years ago," said Ridcully.

"So I understand. Distant cousin. Never knew him," said Granny.

They both stared down at the river for a moment. Occasionally a twig or a branch would whirl along in the current.

"Do you remember—"

"I have a . . . very good memory, thank you."

"Do you ever wonder what life would have been like if you'd said yes?" said Ridcully.

"No."

"I suppose we'd have settled down, had children, grandchildren, that sort of thing . . ."

Granny shrugged. It was the sort of thing romantic idiots said. But there was something in the air tonight . . .

"What about the fire?" she said.

"What fire?"

"Swept through our house just after we were married. Killed us both."

"*What* fire? I don't know anything about any fire?"

Granny turned around.

"Of course not! It didn't happen. But the point is, it *might* have happened. You can't say 'if *this* didn't happen then *that* would have happened' because you don't *know* everything that might have happened. You might think something'd be good, but for all you know it could have turned out horrible. You can't say 'If only I'd . . . ' because you could be wishing for *anything*. The point is, you'll never know. You've gone past. So there's no use thinking about it. So I don't."

"The Trousers of Time," said Ridcully, moodily. He picked a fragment off the crumbling stonework and dropped it into the water. It went *plunk*, as is so often the case.

"What?"

"That's the sort of thing they go on about in the High Energy Magic building. And they call themselves wizards! You should hear them talk. The buggers wouldn't know a magic sword if it bit them on the knee. That's young wizards today. Think they bloody invented magic."

"Yes? You should see the girls that want to be witches these days," said Granny Weatherwax. "Velvet hats and black lipstick and lacy gloves with no fingers to 'em. Cheeky, too."

They were side by side now, watching the river.

"Trousers of Time," said Ridcully. "One of you goes down one leg, one of you goes down the other. And there's all these continuinuinuums all over the place. When I was a lad there was just one decent universe and this was *it*, and all you had to worry about was creatures breaking through from the Dungeon Dimensions, but at least there was this actual damn universe and you knew where you stood. Now it turns out there's millions of the damn things. And there's this damn cat they've discovered that you can put in a box and it's dead and alive at the same time. Or something. And they all run around saying marvelous, marvelous, hooray, here comes another quantum. Ask 'em to do a decent levitation spell and they look at you as if you've started to dribble. You should hear young Stibbons talk. Went on about me not inviting me to my own wedding. Me!"

From the side of the gorge a kingfisher flashed, hit the water with barely a ripple, and ricocheted away with something silver and wriggly in its beak.

"Kept going on about everything happening at the same time," Ridcully went on morosely. "Like there's no such thing as a choice. You just decide which leg you're heading for. *He* says that we *did* get married, see. He says all the things that might have been have to be. So there's thousands of me out there who never became a wizard, just like there's thousands of you who, oh, answered letters. Hah! To *them*, *we're* something that might have been. Now, d'you call that proper thinking for a growing lad? When *I* started wizarding, old 'Tudgy' Spold was Archchancellor, and if any young wizard'd even *mentioned* that sort of daft thing, he'd feel a staff across his backside. Hah!"

Somewhere far below, a frog plopped off a stone.

"Mind you, I suppose we've all passed a lot of water since then."

It dawned gently on Ridcully that the dialogue had become a monologue. He turned to Granny, who was staring round-eyed at the river as if she'd never seen water before.

"Stupid, stupid, stupid," she said.

"I beg your pardon? I was only—"

"Not *you*. I wasn't talking to *you*. Stupid! I've been *stupid*. But I *ain't* been daft! Hah! And I thought it was my memory going! And it was, too. It was going and fetching!"

"What?"

"I was getting scared! Me! And not thinking clear! Except I *was* thinking clear!"

"What!"

"Never mind! Well, I won't say this hasn't been . . . nice," said Granny. "But I've got to get back. Do the thing with the fingers again. And hurry."

Ridcully deflated a little.

"Can't," he said.

"You did it just now."

"That's the point. I wasn't joking when I said I couldn't do it again. It takes a lot out of you, transmigration."

"You used to be able to do it all the time, as I recall," said Granny. She risked a smile. "Our feet hardly touched the ground."

"I was younger then. Now, once is enough."

Granny's boots creaked as she turned and started to walk quickly back toward the town. Ridcully lumbered after her.

"What's the hurry?"

"Got important things to do," said Granny, without turning around. "Been letting everyone down."

"Some people might say *this* is important."

"No. It's just personal. Personal's not the same as important. People just think it is."

"*You're doing it again!*"

"What?"

"I don't know what the other future would have been like," said Ridcully, "but I for one would have liked to give it a try."

Granny paused. Her mind was crackling with relief. Should she tell him about the memories? She opened her mouth to do so, and then thought again. No. He'd get soppy.

"I'd have been crabby and bad-tempered," she said, instead.

"That goes without saying."

"Hah! And what about you? I'd have put up with all your womanizing and drunkenness, would I?"

Ridcully looked bewildered.

"What womanizing?"

"We're talking about *what might have been*."

"But I'm a wizard! We hardly ever womanize. There's laws about it. Well . . . rules. Guidelines, anyway."

"But you wouldn't have been a wizard then."

"And I'm hardly ever drunk."

"You would have been if you'd been wedded to me."

He caught up with her.

"Even young Ponder doesn't think like this," he said. "You've made up your mind that it would have been dreadful, have you?"

"Yes."

"Why?"

"Why'd you think?"

"I asked *you*!"

"I'm too busy for this," said Granny. "Like I said, personal ain't the same as important. Make yourself useful, Mr. Wizard. You know it's circle time, don't you?"

Ridcully's hand touched the brim of his hat.

"Oh, yes."

"And you know what that means?"

"They tell me it means that the walls between realities get weaker. The circles are . . . what's the word Stibbons uses? Isoresons. They connect levels of, oh, something daft . . . similar levels of reality. Which is bloody stupid. You'd be able to walk from one universe to another."

"Ever tried it?"

"No!"

"A circle is a door half open. It doesn't need much to open it up all the way. Even belief'll do it. That's why they put the Dancers up, years ago. We got the dwarfs to do it. Thunderbolt iron, those stones. There's something special about 'em. They've got the love of iron. Don't ask me how it works. Elves hate it even more than ordinary iron. It . . . upsets their senses, or something. But minds can get through . . ."

"Elves? Everyone knows elves don't exist anymore. Not proper elves. I mean, there's a few folk who say they're elves—"

"Oh, yeah. Elvish ancestry. Elves and humans breed all right, as if *that's* anything to be proud of. But you just get a race o'skinny types with pointy ears and a tendency to giggle and burn easily in sunshine. I ain't talking about *them*. There's no harm in them. I'm talking about real wild elves, what we ain't seen here for—"

The road from the bridge to the town curved between high banks, with the forest crowding in on either side and in places even meeting overhead. Thick ferns, already curling like green breakers, lined the clay banks.

They rustled.

The unicorn leapt on the road.

Thousands of universes, twisting together like a rope being plaited from threads . . .

There's bound to be leakages, a sort of mental equivalent of the channel breakthrough on a cheap hi-fi that gets you the news in Swedish during quiet bits in the music. Especially if you've spent your life using your mind as a receiver.

Picking up the thoughts of another human being is very hard, because no two minds are on the same, er, wavelength.

But somewhere out there, at the point where the parallel universes tangle, are a million minds just like yours. For a very obvious reason.

Granny Weatherwax smiled.

Millie Chillum and the king and one or two hangers-on were clustered around the door to Magrat's room when Nanny Ogg arrived.

"What's happening?"

"I know she's in there," said Verence, holding his crown in his hands in the famous *Ai*-Señor-Mexican-Bandits-Have-Raided-Our-*Village* position. "Millie heard her shout go away and I think she threw something at the door."

Nanny Ogg nodded sagely.

"Wedding nerves," she said. "Bound to happen."

"But we're all going to attend the Entertainment," said Verence. "She really ought to attend the Entertainment."

"Well, I dunno," said Nanny. "Seeing our Jason and the rest of 'em prancing about in straw wigs . . . I mean, they mean well, but it's not something a young—a fairly young—girl has to see on the night before her nuptials. You asked her to unlock the door?"

"I did better than that," said Verence. "I *instructed* her to. That was right, wasn't it? If even Magrat won't obey me, I'm a poor lookout as king."

"Ah," said Nanny, after a moment's slow consideration. "You've not entirely spent a lot of time in female company, have you? In a generalized sort of way?"

"Well, I—"

The crown spun in Verence's nervous fingers. Not only had the bandits invaded the village, but the Magnificent Seven had decided to go bowling instead.

"Tell you what," said Nanny, patting him on the back, "you go and preside over the Entertainment and hobnob with the other nobs. I'll see to Magrat, don't you worry. I've been a bride three times, and that's only the official score."

"Yes, but she should—"

"I think if we go easy on the 'shoulds,'" said Nanny, "we might all make it to the wedding. Now, off you all go."

"Someone ought to stay here," said Verence. "Shawn will be on guard, but—"

"No one's going to invade, are they?" said Nanny. "Let me sort this out."

"Well . . . if you're sure . . ."

"Go on!"

Nanny Ogg waited until she heard them go down the main staircase. After a while a rattle of coaches and general shouting suggested that the wedding party was leaving, minus the bride-to-be.

She counted to a hundred, under her breath.

Then:

"Magrat?"

"Go away!"

"I know how it is," said Nanny. "I was a bit worried on the night before my wedding." She refrained from adding: because there was a reasonable chance Jason would turn up as an extra guest.

"I am not worried! I am *angry*!"

"Why?"

"You know!"

Nanny took off her hat and scratched her head.

"You've got me there," she said.

"And *he* knew. I *know* he knew, and I know who told him," said the muffled voice behind the door. "It was all arranged. You must all have been laughing!"

Nanny frowned at the impassive woodwork.

"Nope," she said. "Still all at sea this end."

"Well, I'm not saying any more."

"Everyone's gone to the Entertainment," said Nanny Ogg. No reply.

"And later they'll be back."

A further absence of dialogue.

"Then there'll be carousing and jugglers and fellas that put weasels down their trousers," said Nanny.

Silence.

"And then it'll be tomorrow, and then what're you going to do?"

Silence.

"You can always go back to your cottage. No one's moved in. Or you can stop along of me, if you like. But you'll have to decide, d'you see, because you can't stay locked in there."

Nanny leaned against the wall.

"I remember years ago my granny telling me about Queen Amonia, well, I say queen, but she never was queen except for about three hours because of what I'm about to unfold, on account of them playing hide-and-seek at the wedding party and her hiding in a big heavy old chest in some attic and the lid slamming shut and no one finding her for seven months, by which time you could definitely say the wedding cake was getting a bit stale."

Silence.

"Well, if you ain't telling me, I can't hang around all night," said Nanny. "It'll all be better in the morning, you'll see."

Silence.

"Why don't you have an early night?" said Nanny. "Our Shawn'll do you a hot drink if you ring down. It's a bit nippy out here, to tell you the truth. It's amazing how these old stone places hang on to the chill."

Silence.

"So I'll be off then, shall I?" said Nanny, to the unyielding silence. "Not doing much good here, I can see that. Sure you don't want to talk?"

Silence.

"Stand before your god, bow before your king, and kneel before your man. Recipe for a happy life, that is," said Nanny, to the world in general. "Well, I'm going away now. Tell you what, I'll come back early tomorrow, help you get ready, that sort of thing. How about it?"

Silence.

"So that's all sorted out then," said Nanny. "Cheerio."

She waited a full minute. By rights, by the human mechanics of situations like this, the bolts should have been drawn back and Magrat should have peeped out into the corridor, or possibly even called out to her. She did not.

Nanny shook her head. She could think of at least three ways of getting into the room, and only one of them involved going through the door. But there was a time and a place for witchcraft, and this wasn't it. Nanny Ogg had led a long and generally happy life by knowing when not to be a witch, and this was one of those times.

She went down the stairs and out of the castle. Shawn was standing guard at the main gate, surreptitiously practicing karate chops on the evening air. He stopped and looked embarrassed as Nanny Ogg approached.

"Wish I was going to the Entertainment, Mum."

"I daresay the king will be very generous to you come payday on account of your duty," said Nanny Ogg. "Remind me to remind him."

"Aren't you going?"

"Well, I'm . . . I'm just going for a stroll into town," said Nanny. "I expect Esme went with 'em, did she?"

"Couldn't say, Mum."

"Just a few things I got to do."

She hadn't gone much further before a voice behind her said, "Ello, oh moon of my delight."

"You do sneak up on people, Casanunda."

"I've arranged for us to have dinner at the Goat and Bush," said the dwarf Count.

"Ooo, that's a horrible expensive place," said Nanny Ogg. "Never eaten there."

"They've got some special provisions in, what with the wedding and all the gentry here," said Casanunda. "I've made special arrangements."

These had been quite difficult.

Food as an aphrodisiac was not a concept that

had ever caught on in Lancre, apart from Nanny Ogg's famous Carrot and Oyster Pie.* As far as the cook at the Goat and Bush was concerned, food and sex were only linked in certain humorous gestures involving things like cucumbers. He'd never heard of chocolate, banana skins, avocado and ginger, marshmallow, and the thousand other foods people had occasionally employed to drive an A-to-B freeway through the rambling pathways of romance. Casanunda had spent a busy ten minutes sketching out a detailed menu, and quite a lot of money had changed hands.

He'd arranged a careful romantic candlelit supper. Casanunda had always believed in the *art* of seduction.

Many tall women accessible by stepladder across the continent had reflected how odd it was that the dwarfs, a race to whom the aforesaid art of seduction consisted in the main part of tactfully finding out what sex, underneath all that leather and chainmail, another dwarf *was*, had generated someone like Casanunda.

It was as if Eskimos had produced a natural expert in the care and attention of rare tropical plants. The great pent-up waters of dwarfish sexuality had found a leak at the bottom of the dam—small, but with enough power to drive a dynamo.

Everything that his fellow dwarfs did very occasionally as nature demanded he did all the time, sometimes in the back of a sedan chair and once upside down in a tree—but, and this is important,

---

*Carrots so you can see in the dark, she'd explain, and oysters so's you've got something to look at.

with care and attention to detail that was typically dwarfish. Dwarfs would spend months working on an exquisite piece of jewelry, and for broadly similar reasons Casanunda was a popular visitor to many courts and palaces, for some strange reason generally while the local lord was away. He also had a dwarfish ability with locks, always a useful talent for those awkward moments *sur la boudoir*.

And Nanny Ogg was an attractive lady, which is not the same as being beautiful. She fascinated Casanunda. She was an incredibly comfortable person to be around, partly because she had a mind so broad it could accommodate three football fields and a bowling alley.

"I wish I had my crossbow," muttered Ridcully. "With *that* head on my wall I'd always have a place to hang my hat."

The unicorn tossed its head and pawed the ground. Steam rose from its flanks.

"I ain't sure that would work," said Granny. "You sure you've got no whoosh left in them fingers of yours?"

"I could create an illusion," said the wizard. "That's not hard."

"It wouldn't work. The unicorn is an elvish creature. Magic don't work on 'em. They see through illusions. They ought to, they're good enough at 'em. How about the bank? Reckon you could scramble up it?"

They both glanced at the banks. They were red clay, slippery as priests.

"Let's walk backward," said Granny. "Slowly."

"How about its mind? Can you get in?"

"There's someone in there already. The poor thing's her pet. It obeys only her."

The unicorn walked after them, trying to watch both of them at the same time.

"What shall we do when we come to the bridge?"

"You can still swim, can't you?"

"The river's a long way down."

"But there's a deep pool there. Don't you remember? You dived in there once. One moonlit night . . ."

"I was young and foolish then."

"Well? You're old and foolish now."

"I thought unicorns were more . . . fluffy."

"See clear! Don't let the glamour get you! See what's in front of your eyes! It's a damn great horse with a horn on the end!" said Granny.

The unicorn pawed the ground.

Granny's feet scraped the bridge.

"Got here by accident, can't get back," she said. "If'n there'd been one of us it'd be charging by now. We're about halfway across the bridge—"

"Lot of snow runoff in that river," said Ridcully, doubtfully.

"Oh, yes," said Granny. "See you at the weir."

And she was gone.

The unicorn, which had been trying to decide between targets, was left with Ridcully.

It could count up to one.

It lowered its head.

Ridcully had never liked horses, animals which seemed to him to have only the weakest possible grip on sanity.

As the unicorn charged, he vaulted the parapet and dropped, without much aerodynamic grace, into the icy waters of the Lancre.

The Librarian liked the stage. He was always in the front seat on the first night of a new production at any of Ankh's theaters, his prehensile abilities allowing him to clap twice as hard as anyone else or, if necessary, hurl peanut shells.

And he was feeling let down. There were hardly any books in the castle, except for serious volumes on etiquette and animal breeding and estate management. As a rule, royalty doesn't read much.

He wasn't expecting to be amazed at the Entertainment. He'd peered behind the bit of sacking that was doing service as a dressing room, and seen half a dozen heavily built men arguing with one another. This did not bode well for an evening of thespianic splendor, although there was always the possibility that one of them might hit another one in the face with a custard pie.*

He had managed to get the three of them seats in the front row. This wasn't according to the rules of precedence, but it was amazing how everyone

---

*The Librarian, an ape of simple but firmly held tastes, considered an episode with custard pies, buckets of whitewash, and especially that bit when someone takes someone else's hat off, fills it with something oozy, and replaces it on the deadpan head while the orchestra plays "WHAH . . . Whah . . . whah . . . whaaa . . ." to be an absolutely essential part of any theatrical performance. Since a roasted peanut is a dangerous and painful item when hurled with pinpoint accuracy, directors in Ankh-Morpork had long ago taken the hint. This made some of the *grand guignol* melodramas a little unusual, but it was considered that plays like "The Blood-Soaked Tragedy of the Mad Monk of Quirm (with Custard-Pie scene)" were far better than being deaf in one ear for five days.

squeezed up to make room. He'd also found some peanuts. No one ever knew how he managed that.

"Oook?"

"No, thank you," said Ponder Stibbons. "They give me wind."

"Oook?"

"I like to listen to a man who likes to talk! Whoops! Sawdust and treacle! Put that in your herring and smoke it!"

"I don't think he wants one," said Ponder.

The curtain went up, or at least was pulled aside by Carter the baker.

The Entertainment began.

The Librarian watched in deepening gloom. It was amazing. Normally he quite liked a badly acted play, provided enough confectionery stayed airborne, but these people weren't even good at bad acting. Also, no one seemed to be on the point of throwing anything.

He fished a peanut out of the bag and rolled it in his fingers, while staring intently at the left ear of Tailor the other weaver.

And felt his hair rise. This is very noticeable on an orang-utan.

He glanced up at the hill behind the erratic actors, and growled under his breath.

"Oook?"

Ponder nudged him.

"Quiet!" he hissed. "They're getting the hang of it . . ."

There was an echo to the voice of the one in the straw wig.

"What'd she say?" said Ponder.

"Oook!"

"How'd she do that? That's good makeup, that—"

Ponder fell silent.

Suddenly the Librarian felt very alone.

Everyone else in the audience had their gaze fastened firmly on the turf stage.

He moved a hand up and down in front of Stibbons's face.

The air was wavering over the hill, and the grass on its side moved in a way that made the ape's eyes ache.

"Oook?"

Over the hill, between the little stones, it began to snow.

"*Oook?*"

Alone in her room, Magrat unpacked the wedding dress.

And that was another thing.

She ought to have been *involved* in the dress, at least. She was going to—*would have been* the one wearing it, after all. There should have been weeks of choosing the material, and fittings, and changing her mind, and changing the material, and changing the pattern, and more fittings . . .

. . . although of course she was her own woman and didn't need that kind of thing at all . . .

. . . but she should have had the *choice*.

It was white silk, with a tasteful amount of lace. Magrat knew she wasn't much up on the language of dressmaking. She knew what things *were*, she just didn't know the *names*. All those ruches and pleats and gores and things.

She held the dress against her and gave it a critical examination.

There was a small mirror against the wall.

After a certain amount of internal tussling Magrat gave in and tried the dress on. It wasn't as if she'd be wearing it tomorrow. If she never did try it on, she'd always wonder if it had fitted.

It fitted. Or, rather, it didn't fit but in a flattering way. Whatever Verence had paid, it had been worth it. The dressmaker had done cunning things with the material, so that it went in where Magrat went straight up and down and billowed out where Magrat didn't.

The veil had silk flowers on the headband.

I'm not going to start crying again, Magrat told herself. I'm going to stay angry. I'm going to wind up the anger until it's thick enough to become rage, and when they come back I shall—

—what?

She could try being icy. She could sweep majestically past them . . . this was a good dress for that . . . and that'd teach them.

And then what? She couldn't stay here, not with everyone knowing. And they'd find out. About the letter. News went around Lancre faster than turpentine through a sick donkey.

She'd have to go away. Perhaps find somewhere where there were no witches and start up again, although at the moment her feelings about witches were such that she'd prefer practically any other profession, insofar as there *were* other professions for an ex-witch.

Magrat stuck out her chin. The way she felt now,

with the bile bubbling like a hot spring, she'd *create* a new profession. One that with any luck didn't involve men and meddling old women.

And she'd keep that damn letter, just to remind her.

All the time she'd wondered how Verence was able to have things arranged weeks before she got back, and it was as simple as this. How they must have laughed . . .

It occurred briefly to Nanny Ogg that she really should be somewhere else, but at her time of life invitations to intimate candlelit suppers were not a daily occurrence. There had to be a time when you stopped worrying about the rest of the world and cared a little for yourself. There had to be a time for a quiet, inner moment.

"This is damn good wine," she said, picking up another bottle. "What did you say it's called?" She peered at the label. "Chateau Maison? Chat-eau . . . that's foreign for cat's water, you know, but that's only their way, I know it ain't real cat's water. Real cat's water is sharper." She hammered the cork into the bottle with the end of her knife, then stuck her finger over the neck and gave it a vigorous shaking "to mix the goodness in."

"But I don't hold with drinking it out of ladies' boots," she said. "I know it's supposed to be the thing to do, but I can't see what's so wonderful about walking home with your boots full of wine. Ain't you hungry? If you don't want that bit of gristle, I'll eat it. Any more of them lobsters? Never had lobster before. And that mayonnaise. And them little eggs stuffed with stuff. Mind you, that bramble jam tasted of fish, to my mind."

"'S caviar," murmured Casanunda.

He was sitting with his chin on his hand, watching her in rapt infatuation.

He was, he was surprised to find, enjoying himself immensely while not horizontal.

He knew how this sort of dinner was supposed to go. It was one of the basic weapons in the seducer's armory. The amoratrix was plied with fine wines and expensive yet light dishes. There was much knowing eye contact across the table, and tangling of feet underneath it. There was much pointed eating of pears and bananas and so on. And thus the ship of temptation steered, gently yet inexorably, to a good docking.

And then there was Nanny Ogg.

Nanny Ogg appreciated fine wine in her very own way. It would never have occurred to Casanunda that anyone would top up white wine with port merely because she'd reached the end of the bottle.

As for the food . . . well, she enjoyed that, too. Casanunda had never seen that elbow action before. Show Nanny Ogg a good dinner and she went at it with knife, fork, and rammer. Watching her eat a lobster was a particular experience he would not forget in a hurry. They'd be picking bits of claw out of the woodwork for weeks.

And the asparagus . . . he might actually *try* to forget Nanny Ogg putting away asparagus, but he suspected the memory would come creeping back.

It must be a witch thing, he told himself. They're

always very clear about what they want. If you climbed cliffs and braved rivers and ski'd down mountains to bring a box of chocolates to Gytha Ogg, she'd have the nougat centers out of the bottom layer even before you got your crampons off. That's *it*. Whatever a witch does, she does one hundred percent.

Hubba, hubba!

"Ain't you going to eat all those prawns? Just push the plate this way, then."

He had tried a little footsie to keep his hand in, as it were, but an accidental blow on the ankle from one of Nanny's heavy iron-nailed boots had put a stop to that.

And then there had been the gypsy violinist. At first Nanny had complained about people playin' the fiddle while she was trying to concentrate on her eatin', but between courses she'd snatched it off the man, thrown the bow into a bowl of camellias, retuned the instrument to something approaching a banjo, and had given Casanunda three rousing verses of what, him being foreign, she chose to call *Il Porcupino Nil Sodomy Est*.

Then she'd drunk more wine.

What also captivated Casanunda was the way Nanny Ogg's face became a mass of cheerful horizontal lines when she laughed, and Nanny Ogg laughed a lot.

In fact Casanunda was finding, through the faint haze of wine, that he was actually having fun.

"I take it there is no Mr. Ogg?" he said, eventually.

"Oh, yes, there's a Mr. Ogg," said Nanny. "We buried him years ago. Well, we had to. He was dead."

"It must be very hard for a woman living all alone?"

"Dreadful," said Nanny Ogg, who had never prepared a meal or wielded a duster since her eldest daughter had been old enough to do it for her, and who had at least four meals cooked for her every day by various terrified daughters-in-law.

"It must be especially lonely at night," said Casanunda, out of habit as much as anything else.

"Well, there's Greebo," said Nanny. "He keeps my feet warm."

"Greebo—"

"The cat. I say, do you think there's any pudding?"

Later, she asked for a doggy bottle.

Mr. Brooks the beekeeper ladled some greenish, foul-smelling liquid out of the saucepan that was always simmering in his secret hut, and filled his squirter.

There was a wasps' nest in the garden wall. It'd be a mortuary by morning.

That was the thing about bees. They always guarded the entrance to the hive, with their lives if necessary. But wasps were adept at finding the odd chink in the woodwork around the back somewhere and the sleek little devils'd be in and robbing the hive before you knew it. Funny. The bees in the hive'd let them do it, too. They guarded the entrance, but if a wasp found another way in, they didn't know what to do.

He gave the plunger a push. A stream of liquid bubbled out and left a smoking streak on the floor.

Wasps looked pretty enough. But if you were for bees, you had to be against wasps.

There seemed to be some sort of party going on in the hall. He vaguely remembered getting an invitation but, on the whole, that sort of thing never really caught his imagination. And especially now. Things were wrong. None of the hives showed any signs of swarming. Not one.

As he passed the hives in the dusk he heard the humming. You got that, on a warm night. Battalions of bees stood at the hive entrance, fanning the air with their wings to keep the brood cool. But there was also the roar of bees circling the hive.

They were angry, and on guard.

There was a series of small weirs just on the borders of Lancre. Granny Weatherwax hauled herself up on to the damp woodwork, and squelched to the bank where she emptied her boots.

After a while a pointy wizard's hat drifted downriver, and rose to reveal a pointy wizard underneath it. Granny lent a hand to help Ridcully out of the water.

"There," she said, "bracing, wasn't it? Seemed to me you could do with a cold bath."

Ridcully tried to clean some mud out of his ear. He glared at Granny.

"Why aren't you wet?"

"I am."

"No you're not. You're just damp. I'm wet through. How can you float down a river and just be damp?"

"I dries out quick."

Granny Weatherwax glared up the rocks. A short distance away the steep road ran on to Lancre, but there were other, more private ways known to her among the trees.

"So," she said, more or less to herself. "She wants to stop me going there, does she? Well, we'll see about that."

"Going where?" said Ridcully.

"Ain't sure," said Granny. "All I know is, if she don't want me to go there, that's where I'm going. But I hadn't bargained on you turnin' up and having a rush of blood to the heart. Come on."

Ridcully wrung out his robe. A lot of the sequins had come off. He removed his hat and unscrewed the point.

Headgear picks up morphic vibrations. Quite a lot of trouble had once been caused in Unseen University by a former Archchancellor's hat, which had picked up too many magical vibrations after spending so much time on wizardly heads and had developed a personality of its very own. Ridcully had put a stop to this by having his own hat made to particular specifications by an Ankh-Morpork firm of completely insane hatters.

It was not a normal wizard hat. Few wizards have ever made much use of the pointy bit, except maybe to keep the odd pair of socks in it. But Ridcully's hat had small cupboards. It had surprises. It had four telescopic legs and a roll of oiled silk in the brim that extended downward to make a small but serviceable tent, and a patent spirit stove just above it. It had inner pockets with three days' supply of iron rations. And the tip unscrewed to dispense an adequate supply of spirituous liquors for use in emergencies, such as when Ridcully was thirsty.

Ridcully waved the small pointed cup at Granny. "Brandy?" he said.

"What *have* you got on your head?"

Ridcully felt his pate gingerly.

"Um . . ."

"Smells like honey and horse apples to me. And what's *that* thing?"

Ridcully lifted the small cage off his head. There was a small treadmill in it, in a complex network of glass rods. A couple of feeding bowls were visible. And there was a small, hairy and currently quite wet mouse.

"Oh, it's something some of the young wizards came up with," said Ridcully diffidently. "I said I'd . . . try it out for them. The mouse hair rubs against the glass rods and there's sparks, don't'y'know, and . . . and . . ."

Granny Weatherwax looked at the Archchancellor's somewhat grubby hair and raised an eyebrow.

"My word," she said. "What will they think of next?"

"Don't really understand how it works, Stibbons is the man for this sort of thing, I thought I'd help them out . . ."

"Lucky you were going bald, eh?"

In the darkness of her sickroom Diamanda opened her eyes, if they were *her* eyes. There was a pearly sheen to them.

The song was as yet only on the threshold of hearing.

And the world was different. A small part of her mind was still Diamanda, and looked out through the mists of enchantment. The world was a pattern of fine silver lines, constantly moving, as though everything was coated with filigree. Except where there was iron. There the lines were crushed and tight and bent. There, the whole world was invisible. Iron distorted the world. Keep away from iron.

She slipped out of bed, using the edge of the blanket to grasp the door handle, and opened the door.

Shawn Ogg was standing very nearly to attention.

Currently he was guarding the castle and Seeing How Long He Could Stand On One Leg.

Then it occurred to him that this wasn't a proper activity for a martial artist, and he turned it into No. 19, the Flying Chrysanthemum Double Drop Kick.

After a while he realized that he had been hearing something. It was vaguely rhythmical, and put him in mind of a grasshopper chirruping. It was coming from inside the castle.

He turned carefully, keeping alert in case the massed armies of Foreign Parts tried to invade while his back was turned.

This needed working out. He wasn't on guard from things inside the castle, was he? "On guard" meant things outside. That was the point of castles. That's why you had all the walls and things. He'd got the big poster they gave away free with *Jane's All the World's Siege Weapons*. He knew what he was talking about.

Shawn was not the quickest of thinkers, but his

thoughts turned inexorably to the elf in the dungeon. But that was locked up. He'd locked the door himself. And there was iron all over the place, and Mum had been very definite about the iron.

Nevertheless . . .

He was methodical about it. He raised the drawbridge and dropped the portcullis and peered over the wall for good measure, but there was just the dusk and the night breeze.

He could *feel* the sound now. It seemed to be coming out of the stone, and had a saw-toothed edge to it that grated on his nerves.

It couldn't have got out, could it? No, it stood to reason. People hadn't gone around building dungeons you could get out of.

The sound swung back and forth across the scale.

Shawn leaned his rusty pike against the wall and drew his sword. He knew how to use it. He practiced for ten minutes every day, and it was one sorry hanging sack of straw when *he'd* finished with it.

He slipped into the keep by the back door and sidled along the passages toward the dungeon. There was no one else around. Of course, everyone was at the Entertainment. And they'd be back any time now, carousing all over the place.

The castle felt big, and old, and cold.

Any time now.

Bound to.

The noise stopped.

Shawn peered around the corner. There were the steps, there was the open doorway to the dungeons.

"Stop!" shouted Shawn, just in case.

The sound echoed off the stones.

"Stop! Or . . . or . . . or . . . Stop!"

He eased his way down the steps and looked through the archway.

"I warn you! I'm learning the Path of the Happy Jade Lotus!"

There was the door to the cell, standing ajar. And a white-clad figure next to it.

Shawn blinked.

"Aren't you Miss Tockley?"

She smiled at him. Her eyes glowed in the dim light.

"You're wearing chain-mail, Shawn," she said.

"What, miss?" He glanced at the open door again.

"That's terrible. You must take it off, Shawn. How can you hear with all that stuff around your ears?"

Shawn was aware of the empty space behind him. But he daren't look around.

"I can hear fine, miss," he said, trying to ease himself around so that his back was against a wall.

"But you can't hear *truly*," said Diamanda, drifting forward. "The iron makes you deaf."

Shawn was not yet used to thinly clad young women approaching him with a dreamy look on their faces. He fervently wished he could take the Path of the Retreating Back.

He glanced sideways.

There was a tall skinny shape outlined in the open cell doorway. It was standing very carefully, as if it wanted to keep as far away from its surroundings as possible.

Diamanda was smiling at him in a funny way.

He ran.

* * *

Somehow, the woods had changed. Ridcully was certain that in his youth they'd been full of bluebells and primroses and—and bluebells and whatnot and so on. Not bloody great briars all over the place. They snagged at his robe and once or twice some tree-climbing equivalent knocked his hat off.

What made it worse was that Esme Weatherwax seemed to avoid all of them.

"How do you manage that?"

"I just know where I am all the time," said Granny.

"Well? I know where *I* am, too."

"No you don't. You just happen to be present. That's not the same."

"Well, do you happen to know where a proper path is?"

"This is a short cut."

"Between two places where you're not lost, d'you mean?"

"I keep *tellin'* you, I ain't lost! I'm . . . directionally challenged."

"Hah!"

But it was a fact about Esme Weatherwax, he had to admit. She might be lost, and he had reason to suspect this was the case now, unless there were in this forest two trees with exactly the same arrangement of branches *and* a strip of his robe caught on one of them, but she did have a quality that in anyone not wearing a battered pointy hat and an antique black dress might have been called poise. Absolute poise. It would be hard to imagine her making an awkward movement unless she wanted to.

He'd seen that years ago, although of course at

the time he'd just been amazed at the way her shape fitted perfectly into the space around it. And—

He'd got caught up *again*.

"Wait a minute!"

"Entirely the wrong sort of clothes for the country!"

"I wasn't expecting a hike through the woods! This is a ceremonial damn costume!"

"Take it off, then."

"Then how will anyone know I'm a wizard?"

"I'll be sure to tell them!"

Granny Weatherwax was getting rattled. She was also, despite everything that she'd said, getting lost. But the point was that you couldn't get lost between the weir at the bottom of the Lancre rapids and Lancre town itself. It was uphill all the way. Besides, she'd walked through the local forests all her life. They were *her* forests.

She was pretty sure they'd passed the same tree twice. There was a bit of Ridcully's robe hanging on it.

It was like getting lost in her own garden.

She was also sure she'd seen the unicorn a couple of times. It was tracking them. She'd tried to get into its mind. She might as well have tried to climb an ice wall.

It wasn't as if her own mind was tranquil. But now at least she knew she was sane.

When the walls between the universes are thin, when the parallel strands of If bunch together to pass through the Now, then certain things leak across. Tiny signals, perhaps, but audible to a receiver skilled enough.

In her head were the faint, insistent thoughts of a thousand Esme Weatherwaxes.

Magrat wasn't sure what to pack. Most of her original clothes seemed to have evaporated since she'd been in the castle, and it was hardly good manners to take the ones Verence had bought for her. The same applied to the engagement ring. She wasn't sure if you were allowed to keep it.

She glared at herself in the mirror.

She'd have to stop thinking like this. She seemed to have spent her whole life trying to make herself small, trying to be polite, apologizing when people walked over her, trying to be *good-mannered*. And what had happened? People had treated her as if she was small and polite and good-mannered.

She'd stick the, the, the *damn* letter on the mirror, so they'd all know why she'd gone.

She'd a *damn* good mind to go off to one of the cities and become a courtesan.

Whatever *that* was.

And then she heard the singing.

It was, without a doubt, the most beautiful sound Magrat had ever heard. It flowed straight through the ears and into the hindbrain, into the blood, into the bone . . .

A silk camisole dropped from her fingers on to the floor.

She wrenched at the door, and a tiny part of her mind still capable of rational thought remembered about the key.

The song filled the passageway. She gripped some

folds of the wedding dress to make running easier and hurried toward the stairs . . .

Something bulleted out of another doorway and bore her to the floor.

It was Shawn Ogg. Through the chromatic haze she could see his worried face peering out from its hood of rusty—

—iron.

The song changed while staying the same. The complex harmonies, the fascinating rhythm did not alter but suddenly grated, as if she was hearing the song through different ears.

She was dragged into the doorway.

"Are you all right, Miss Queen?"

"What's happening?"

"Dunno, Miss Queen. But I think we've got elves."

"Elves?"

"And they've got Miss Tockley. Um. You know you took the iron away—"

"What *are* you talking about, Shawn?"

Shawn's face was white.

"That one down the dungeons started singing, and they'd put their mark on her, so she's doing what they want—"

"Shawn!"

"And Mum said they don't kill you, if they can help it. Not right away. You're much more fun if you're not dead."

Magrat stared at him.

"I had to run away! She was trying to get my hood off! I had to leave her, miss! You understand, miss?"

"Elves?"

"You got to hold on to something iron, miss! They hate iron!"

She slapped his face, hurting her fingers on the mail.

"You're gabbling, Shawn!"

"They're out there, miss! I heard the drawbridge go down! They're out there and we're in here and they don't kill you, they keep you alive—"

"Stand to attention, soldier!"

It was all she could think of. It seemed to work. Shawn pulled himself together.

"Look," said Magrat, "everyone knows there really aren't any elves any mo . . ." Her voice faded. Her eyes narrowed. "Everyone but Magrat Garlick knows different, yes?"

Shawn shook. Magrat grabbed his shoulders.

"Me mum and Mistress Weatherwax said you wasn't to know!" Shawn wailed. "They said it was witch business!"

"And where are they now, when they've got some witch business to mind?" said Magrat. "I don't see them, do you? Are they behind the door? No! Are they under the bed? How strange, they're not . . . there's just me, Shawn Ogg. And if you don't tell me everything you know right now I'll make you regret the day I was born."

Shawn's Adam's apple bobbed up and down as he considered this. Then he shook himself free of Magrat's grasp and listened at the door.

The singing had stopped. For a moment Magrat thought she heard footsteps outside the door, hurrying away.

"Well, Miss Queen, our mum and Mistress Weatherwax was up at the Dancers—"

Magrat listened.

Finally she said, "And where's everyone now?"

"Dunno, miss. All gone to the Entertainment . . . but they ought to've been back by now."

"Where's the Entertainment?"

"Dunno, miss. Miss?"

"Yes?"

"Why've you got your wedding dress on?"

"Never you mind."

"It's unlucky for the groom to see the bride in her dress before the wedding," said Shawn, taking refuge in run-of-the-mill idiocies to relieve his terror.

"It will be for him if I see him first," snarled Magrat.

"Miss?"

"Yes?"

"I'm feared about what's happened to everyone. Our Jason said they'd be back in an hour or so, and that was hours ago."

"But there's almost a hundred guests and everyone from the town, practically. Elves couldn't do anything to them."

"They wouldn't have to, miss." Shawn went to the unglazed window. "Look, miss. I can drop down on to the granary in the stable yard from here. It's thatch, I'll be all right. Then I can sneak around the kitchens and out by the little gate by the hubward tower with military precision."

"What for?"

"To get help, miss."

"But you don't know if there's any help to *get*."

"Can you think of anything else, miss?"

She couldn't.

"It's very . . . brave of you, Shawn," said Magrat.

"You stay here and you'll be right as rain," said Shawn. "Tell you what . . . How about if I lock the door and take the key with me? Then even if they sing at you they *can't* get you to open the door."

Magrat nodded.

Shawn tried to smile. "Wish we had another suit of mail," he said. "But it's all in the armory."

"I'll be fine," said Magrat. "Off you go, then."

Shawn nodded. He waited for a moment on the window ledge, and then dropped into the darkness.

Magrat pushed the bed against the door and sat on it.

It occurred to her that she should have gone as well. But that would mean leaving the castle empty, and that didn't feel right.

Besides, she was scared.

There was one candle in the room, and that was half burned down. When it was gone, there'd be nothing but the moonlight. Magrat had always liked moonlight. Up to now.

It was quiet outside. There should be the noises of the town.

It crept over her that letting Shawn go away with a key to the door was not a wholly sensible thing, because if they caught him they could open—

There was a scream, which went on for a long time.

And then the night rolled back in again.

After a few minutes there was a scrabbling at the

lock, such as might be made by someone trying to manipulate a key held in several thicknesses of cloth, so as not to come into contact with the iron.

The door began to open, and wedged up against the bed.

"Will you not step outside, lady?"

The door creaked again.

"Will you not come dance with us, pretty lady?"

The voice had strange harmonics and an echo that buzzed around the inside of the head for several seconds after the last word had been spoken.

The door burst open.

Three figures slid into the room. One looked up the bed, and the others poked into dark corners. Then one of them crossed to the window and looked out.

The crumbling wall stretched down to the thatched roof entirely unoccupied.

The figure nodded to two more shapes in the courtyard, its blond hair glowing in the moonlight.

One of them pointed up, to where a figure, its long white dress billowing in the breeze, was climbing up the wall of the keep.

The elf laughed. This was going to be more enjoyable than it'd suspected.

Magrat pulled herself over the windowsill and collapsed, panting, on the floor. Then she staggered across to the door, which was missing its key. But there were two heavy wooden bars, which she slotted into place.

There was a wooden shutter for the window.

They'd never let her get away with it again. She'd

been expecting an arrow but . . . no, something as simple as that wouldn't have been enough fun.

She glared at the darkness. So . . . there was this room. She didn't even know which one it was. She found a candlestick and a bundle of matches and, after some scrabbling, got it lit.

There were some boxes and cases piled by the bed. So . . . a guest room.

The thoughts trickled through the silence of her brain, one after another.

She wondered if they'd sing to her, and if she could stand it again. Maybe if you knew what to expect . . .

There was a gentle tap at the door.

"We have your *friends* downstairs, lady. Come dance with me."

Magrat stared desperately around the room.

It was as featureless as guest bedrooms everywhere. Jug and basin on a stand, the horrible garderobe alcove inadequately concealed behind a curtain, the bed which had a few bags and bundles tossed on it, a battered chair with all the varnish gone and a small square of carpet made gray with age and ground-in dust.

The door rattled. "Let me in, sweet lady."

The window was no escape this time. There was the bed to hide under, and that'd work for all of two seconds, wouldn't it?

Her eye was drawn by some kind of horrible magic back to the room's garderobe, lurking behind its curtain.

Magrat lifted the lid. The shaft was definitely wide enough to admit a body. Garderobes were notorious in that respect. Several unpopular kings had met their end, as it were, in the garderobe, at the hands of an assassin with good climbing ability, a spear, and a fundamental approach to politics.

Something hit the door hard.

"Lady, shall I sing to you?"

Magrat reached a decision.

It was the hinges that gave way eventually, the rusty bolts finally losing their grip on the stone.

The alcove's half-drawn curtain moved in the breeze.

The elf smiled, strode to the curtain, and pulled it aside.

The oak lid was up.

The elf looked down.

Magrat rose up behind it like a white ghost and hit it hard across the back of the neck with the chair, which shattered.

The elf tried to turn and keep its balance, but there was still enough chair left in Magrat's hands for her to catch it on the desperate upswing. It toppled backward, flailed at the lid, and only succeeded in pulling it shut behind it. Magrat heard a thump and a scream of rage as it dropped into the noisome darkness. It'd be too much to hope that the fall would kill it. After all, it'd land in something soft.

"Not just high," said Magrat to herself, "but stinking."

Hiding under the bed is only good for about two seconds, but sometimes two seconds is enough.

She let go of the chair. She was shaking. But she was still alive, and that felt good. That's the thing about being alive. You're alive to enjoy it.

Magrat peered out into the passage.

She had to move. She picked up a stricken chair leg for the little comfort that it gave, and ventured out.

There was a scream again, from the direction of the Great Hall.

Magrat looked the other way, toward the Long Gallery. She ran. There had to be a way out, somewhere, some gate, some window . . .

Some enterprising monarch had glazed the windows some time ago. The moonlight shone through in big silver blocks, interspersed with squares of deep shadow.

Magrat ran from light to shade, light to shade, down the endless room. Monarch after monarch flashed past, like a speeded-up film. King after king, all whiskers and crowns and beards. Queen after queen, all corsages and stiff bodices and Lappet-faced wowhawks and small dogs and—

Some shape, some trick of moonlight, some expression on a painted face somehow cut through her terror and caught her eye.

That was a portrait she'd never seen before. She'd never walked down this far. The idiot vapidity of the assembled queens had depressed her. But this one . . .

This one, somehow, reached out to her.

She stopped.

It couldn't have been done from life. In the days of *this* queen, the only paint known locally was a sort of blue, and generally used on the body. But a few generations ago King Lully I had been a bit of a historian and a romantic. He'd researched what was known of the early days of Lancre, and where actual evidence had been a bit sparse he had, in the best traditions of the keen ethnic historian, inferred from revealed self-evident wisdom* and extrapolated from associated sources.** He'd commissioned the portrait of Queen Ynci the Short-Tempered, one of the founders of the kingdom.

She had a helmet with wings and a spike on it and a mass of black hair plaited into dreadlocks with blood as a setting lotion. She was heavily made-up in the woad-and-blood-and-spirals school of barbarian cosmetics. She had a 42 D-cup breastplate and shoulder pads with spikes. She had knee pads with spikes on, and spikes on her sandals, and a rather short skirt in the fashionable tartan and blood motif. One hand rested nonchalantly on a double-headed battle axe with a spike on it, the other caressed the hand of a captured enemy warrior. The rest of the captured enemy warrior was hanging from various pine trees in the background. Also in the picture was Spike, her favorite war pony, of the now extinct Lancre hill breed which was the same general shape and disposition as a barrel of gunpowder, and her war chariot, which picked up the popular spiky theme. It had wheels you could shave with.

Magrat stared.

They'd never mentioned this.

They'd told her about tapestries, and embroidery, and farthingales, and how to shake hands with lords. They'd never told her about spikes.

There was a sound at the end of the gallery, from

---

*Made it up.

**Had read a lot of stuff that other people had made up, too.

back the way she'd come. She grabbed her skirts and ran.

There were footsteps behind her, and laughter.

Left down the cloisters, then along the dark passage above the kitchens, and past the—

A shape moved in the shadows. Teeth flashed. Magrat raised the chair leg, and stopped in mid-strike.

"Greebo?"

Nanny Ogg's cat rubbed against her legs. His hair was flat against his body. This unnerved Magrat even more. This was *Greebo*, undisputed king of Lancre's cat population and father of most of it, in whose presence wolves trod softly and bears climbed trees. He was frightened.

"Come here, you bloody idiot!"

She grabbed him by the scruff of his scarred neck and ran on, while Greebo gratefully sank his claws into her arm to the bone* and scrambled up to her shoulder.

She must be somewhere near the kitchen now, because that was Greebo's territory. This was an unknown and shadowy area, terror incognita, where the flesh of carpets and the plaster pillars ran out and the stone bone of the castle showed through.

She was sure there were footsteps behind her, very fast and light.

If she hurried around the next corner—

In her arms, Greebo tensed like a spring. Magrat stopped.

Around the next corner—

---

*"He's just an old soppy really"—from the Nanny Ogg Book of Cat Sayings.

Without her apparently willing it, the hand holding the broken wood came up, moving slowly back.

She stepped to the corner and stabbed in one movement. There was a triumphant hiss which turned into a screech as the wood scraped down the side of the waiting elf's neck. It reeled away. Magrat bolted for the nearest doorway, weeping in panic, and wrenched at the handle. It swung open. She darted through, slammed the door, flailed in the dark for the bars, felt them clonk home, and collapsed on to her knees.

Something hit the door outside.

After a while Magrat opened her eyes, and then wondered if she really had opened her eyes, because the darkness was no less dark. There was a feeling of space in front of her. There were all sorts of things in the castle, old hidden rooms, anything . . . there could be a pit there, there could be *anything*. She fumbled for the doorframe, guided herself upright, and then groped cautiously in the general direction of the wall.

There was a shelf. This was a candle. And this was a bundle of matches.

So, she insisted above her own heartbeat, this was a room that got used recently. Most people in Lancre still used tinderboxes. Only the king could afford matches all the way from Ankh-Morpork. Granny Weatherwax and Nanny Ogg got them too, but they didn't buy them. They got given them. It was easy to get given things, if you were a witch.

Magrat lit the stub of candle, and turned to see what kind of room she'd scuttled into.

Oh, no . . .

* * *

"Well, well," said Ridcully. "There's a familiar tree."

"Shut up."

"I thought *someone* said we just had to walk uphill," said Ridcully.

"Shut up."

"I remember once when we were in these woods you let me—"

"Shut up."

Granny Weatherwax sat down on a stump.

"We're being mazed," she said. "Someone's playing tricks on us."

"I remember a story once," said Ridcully, "where these two children were lost in the woods and a lot of birds came and covered them with leaves." Hope showed in his voice like a toe peeking out from under a crinoline.

"Yes, that's just the sort of bloody stupid thing a bird would think of," said Granny. She rubbed her head.

"*She's* doing it," she said. "It's an elvish trick. Leading travelers astray. She's mucking up my head. My actual head. Oh, she's good. Making us go where she wants. Making us go round in circles. Doing it to *me*."

"Maybe you've got your mind on other things," said Ridcully, not quite giving up hope.

"Course I've got my mind on other things, with you falling over all the time and gabbling a lot of nonsense," said Granny. "If Mr. Cleverdick Wizard hadn't wanted to dredge up things that never existed in the first place I wouldn't be here, I'd be in the center of things, knowing what's going on." She clenched her fists.

"Well, you don't have to be," said Ridcully. "It's a fine night. We could sit here and—"

"You're falling for it too," said Granny. "All that dreamy-weamy, eyes-across-a-crowded-room stuff. Can't imagine how you keep your job as head wizard."

"Mainly by checking my bed carefully and makin' sure someone else has already had a slice of whatever it is I'm eating," said Ridcully, with disarming honesty. "There's not much to it, really. Mainly it's signin' things and having a good shout—"

Ridcully gave up.

"Anyway, you looked pretty surprised when you saw me," he said. "Your face went white."

"Anyone'd go white, seeing a full-grown man standing there looking like a sheep about to choke," said Granny.

"You really don't let up, do you?" said Ridcully. "Amazing. You don't give an inch."

Another leaf drifted past.

Ridcully didn't move his head.

"You know," he said, his voice staying quite level, "either autumn comes really early in these parts, or the birds here are the ones out of that story I mentioned, or someone's in the tree above us."

"I know."

"You know?"

"Yes, because I've been paying attention while you were dodging the traffic in Memory Lane," said Granny. "There's at least five of 'em, and they're right above us. How's those magic fingers of yours?"

"I could probably manage a fireball."

"Wouldn't work. Can you carry us out of here?"

"Not both of us."

"Just you?"

"Probably, but I'm not going to leave you."

Granny rolled her eyes. "It's true, you know," she said. "All men are swains. Push off, you soft old bugger. They're not intending to kill me. At least, not yet. But they don't hardly know nothing about wizards and they'll chop you down without thinking."

"Now who's being soft?"

"I don't want to see you dead when you could be doin' something useful."

"Running away isn't useful."

"It's going to be a lot more useful than staying here."

"I'd never forgive myself if I went."

"And I'd never forgive you if you stayed, and I'm a lot more unforgiving than you are," said Granny. "When it's all over, try to find Gytha Ogg. Tell her to look in my old box. She'll know what's in there. And if you don't go now—"

An arrow hit the stump beside Ridcully.

"The buggers are *firing* at me!" he shouted. "If I had my crossbow—"

"I should go and get it, then," said Granny.

"Right! I'll be back instantly!"

Ridcully vanished. A moment later several lumps of castle masonry dropped out of the space he had just occupied.

"That's him out of the way, then," said Granny, to no one in particular.

She stood up, and gazed around at the trees.

"All right," she said, "here I am. I ain't running. Come and get me. Here I am. All of me."

Magrat calmed down. Of course it existed. Every castle had one. And of course this one was used. There was a trodden path through the dust to the rack a few feet away from the door, where a few suits of unraveling chain-mail hung on a rack, next to the pikes.

Shawn probably came in here every day.

It was the armory.

Greebo hopped down from Magrat's shoulders and wandered off down the cobwebbed avenues, in his endless search for anything small and squeaky.

Magrat followed him, in a daze.

The kings of Lancre had never thrown anything away. At least, they'd never thrown anything away if it was possible to kill someone with it.

There was armor for men. There was armor for horses. There was armor for fighting dogs. There was even armor for ravens, although King Gurnt the Stupid's plan for an aerial attack force had never really got off the ground. There were more pikes, and swords, cutlasses, rapiers, epees, broadswords, flails, morningstars, maces, clubs, and huge knobs with spikes. They were all piled together and, in those places where the roof had leaked, were rusted into a lump. There were longbows, short bows, pistol bows, stirrup bows, and crossbows, piled like firewood and stacked with the same lack of care.

Odd bits of armor were piled in more heaps, and were red with rust. In fact rust was everywhere. The whole huge room was full of the death of iron.

Magrat went on, like some clockwork toy that won't change direction until it bumps into something.

The candlelight was reflected dully in helmets and breastplates. The sets of horse armor in particular were terrible, on their rotting wooden frames—they stood like exterior skeletons, and, like skeletons, nudged the mind into thoughts of mortality. Empty eye sockets stared sightlessly down at the little candlelit figure.

"Lady?"

The voice came from outside the door, far behind Magrat. But it echoed around her, bouncing off the centuries of moldering armaments.

They can't come in here, Magrat thought. Too much iron. In here, I'm safe.

"If lady wants to play, we will fetch her friends."

As Magrat turned, the light caught the edge of something, and gleamed.

Magrat pulled aside a huge shield.

"Lady?"

Magrat reached out.

"Lady?"

Magrat's hands held a rusty iron helmet, with wings.

"Come dance at the wedding, lady."

Magrat's hands closed on a well-endowed breastplate, with spikes.

Greebo, who had been tracking mice through a prone suit of armor, stuck his head out of a leg.

A change had come over Magrat. It showed in her breathing. She'd been panting, with fear and exhaustion. Then, for a few seconds, there was no sound of her breathing at all. And finally it returned. Slowly. Deeply. Deliberately.

Greebo saw Magrat, who he'd always put down as basically a kind of mouse in human shape, lift the hat with the wings on it and put it on her head.

Magrat knew all about the power of hats.

In her mind's ear she could hear the rattle of the chariots.

"Lady? We will bring your friends to sing to you."

She turned.

The candlelight sparkled off her eyes.

Greebo drew back into the safety of his armor. He recalled a particular time when he'd leapt out on a vixen. Normally Greebo could take on a fox without raising a sweat but, as it turned out, this one had cubs. He hadn't found out until he chased her into her den. He'd lost a bit of one ear and quite a lot of fur before he'd got away.

The vixen had a very similar expression to the one Magrat had now.

"Greebo? Come here!"

The cat turned and tried to find a place of safety in the suit's breastplate. He was beginning to doubt he'd make it through the knight.

Elves prowled the castle gardens. They'd killed the fish in the ornamental pond, eventually.

Mr. Brooks was perched on a kitchen chair, working at a crevice in the stable wall.

He'd been aware of some sort of excitement, but

it was involving humans and therefore of secondary importance. But he did notice the change in the sound from the hives, and the splintering of wood.

A hive had already been tipped over. Angry bees clouded around three figures as feet ripped through comb and honey and brood.

The laughter stopped as a white-coated, veiled figure appeared over the hedge. It raised a long metal tube.

No one ever knew what Mr. Brooks put in his squirter. There was old tobacco in it, and boiled-up roots, and bark scrapings, and herbs that even Magrat had never heard of. It shot a glistening stream over the hedge which hit the middle elf between the eyes, and sprayed over the other two.

Mr. Brooks watched dispassionately until their struggles stopped.

"Wasps," he said.

Then he went and found a box, lit a lantern and, with great care and delicacy, oblivious to the stings, began to repair the damaged combs.

Shawn couldn't feel much in his arm anymore, except in the hot dull way that indicated at least one broken bone, and he knew that two of his fingers shouldn't be looking like that. He was sweating, despite being only in his vest and drawers. He should never have taken his chain-mail off, but it's hard to say no when an elf is pointing a bow at you. Shawn knew what, fortunately, many people didn't—chain-mail isn't much defense against an arrow. It certainly isn't when the arrow is being aimed between your eyes.

He'd been dragged along the corridors to the

armory. There were at least four elves, but it was hard to see their faces. Shawn remembered when the traveling Magic Lanthorn show had come to Lancre. He'd watched entranced as different pictures had been projected on to one of Nanny Ogg's bedsheets. The elf faces put him in mind of that. There were eyes and a mouth in there somewhere, but everything else seemed to be temporary, the elves' features passing across their faces like the pictures on the screen.

They didn't say much. They just laughed a lot. They were a merry folk, especially when they were twisting your arm to see how far it could go.

The elves spoke to one another in their own language. Then one of them turned to Shawn, and indicated the armory door.

"We wish the lady to come out," it said. "You must say to her, if she does not come out, we will play with you some more."

"What will you do to us if she *does* come out?" said Shawn.

"Oh, we shall still play with you," said the elf. "That's what makes it so much fun. But she must hope, must she not? Talk to her now."

He was pushed up to the door. He knocked on it, in what he hoped was a respectful way.

"Um. Miss Queen?"

Magrat's voice was muffled.

"Yes?"

"It's me, Shawn."

"I know."

"I'm out here. Um. I think they've hurt Miss Tockley. Um. They say they'll hurt me some more if you don't come out. But you don't have to come out because they daren't come in there because of all the iron. So I shouldn't listen to them if I was you."

There were some distant clankings, and then a *twang*.

"Miss Magrat?"

"Ask her," said the elf, "if there is any food and water in there."

"Miss, they say—"

One of the elves jerked him away. Two of them took up station either side of the doorway, and one put his pointed ear to it.

Then it knelt down and peered through the keyhole, taking care not to come too near the metal of the lock.

There was a sound no louder than a click. The elf remained motionless for a moment, and then keeled over gently, without a sound.

Shawn blinked.

There was about an inch of crossbow bolt sticking out of its eye. The feathers had been sheared off by its passage through the keyhole.

"Wow," he said.

The armory door swung open, revealing nothing but darkness.

One of the elves started to laugh.

"So much for him," it said. "How stupid . . . Lady? Will you listen to your warrior?"

He gripped Shawn's broken arm, and twisted.

Shawn tried not to scream. Purple lights flashed in front of his eyes. He wondered what would happen if he passed out.

He wished his mum was here.

"Lady," said the elf, "if you—"

"All right," said Magrat's voice, from somewhere in the darkness. "I'm going to come out. You must promise not to hurt me."

"Oh, indeed I do, lady."

"And you'll let Shawn go."

"Yes."

The elves on either side of the doorway nodded at each other.

"Please?" Magrat pleaded.

"Yes."

Shawn groaned. If it had been Mum or Mistress Weatherwax, they'd have fought to the death. Mum was right—Magrat always was the nice soft one . . .

. . . who'd just fired a crossbow through a keyhole.

Some eighth sense made Shawn shift his weight. If the elf relaxed his grip for just one second, Shawn was ready to stagger.

Magrat appeared in the doorway. She was carrying an ancient wooden box with the word "Candles" on the side in peeling paint.

Shawn looked hopefully along the corridor.

Magrat smiled brightly at the elf beside him. "This is for you," she said, handing over the box. The elf took it automatically. "But you mustn't open it. And remember you promised not to hurt me."

The elves closed in behind Magrat. One of them raised a hand, with a stone knife in it.

"Lady?" said the elf holding the box, which was rocking gently in its hands.

"Yes?" said Magrat, meekly.

"I lied to you."

The knife plunged toward her back.

And shattered.

The elf looked at Magrat's innocent expression, and opened the box.

Greebo had spent an irritating two minutes in that box. Technically, a cat locked in a box may be alive or it may be dead. You never know until you look. In fact, the mere act of opening the box will determine the state of the cat, although in this case there were three determinate states the cat could be in: these being Alive, Dead, and Bloody Furious.

Shawn dived sideways as Greebo went off like a Claymore mine.

"Don't worry about him," said Magrat dreamily, as the elf flailed at the maddened cat. "He's just a big softy."

She drew a knife out of the folds of her dress, turned, and stabbed the elf behind her. It wasn't an accurate thrust, but it didn't have to be. Not with an iron blade.

She completed the movement by daintily raising the hem of her dress and kicking the third elf just under the knee.

Shawn saw a flash of metal as her foot retreated under the silk again.

She elbowed the screaming elf aside, trotted into the doorway, and came back with a crossbow.

"Shawn," she said, "which one hurt you?"

"All of them," said Shawn, weakly. "But the one fighting Greebo stabbed Diamanda."

The elf pulled Greebo off his face. Green-blue blood was streaming from a dozen wounds and Greebo hung on to its arm as he was flailed against the wall.

"Stop it," said Magrat.

The elf looked down at the bow, and froze.

"I will not beg for mercy," it said.

"Good," said Magrat, and fired.

That left one elf rolling in circles on the flagstones, clutching at its knee.

Magrat stepped daintily over the body of another elf, vanished into the armory for a moment, and came back with an axe.

The elf stopped moving, and focused all its attention on her.

"Now," said Magrat, conversationally, "I'm not going to lie to you about your chances, because you haven't got any. I'm going to ask you some questions. But first of all, I'm going to get your attention."

The elf was expecting it, and managed to roll aside as the axe splintered the stones.

"Miss?" said Shawn weakly, as Magrat raised the axe again.

"Yes?"

"Mum says they don't feel pain, miss."

"No? But they can certainly be put to inconvenience."

Magrat lowered the axe.

"Of course, there's armor," she said. "We could put this one in a suit of armor. How about it?"

"No!"

The elf tried to pull away across the floor.

"Why not?" said Magrat. "Better than axes, yes?"

"No!"

"Why not?"

"It is like being buried in the earth," hissed the elf. "No eyes, no ears, no mouth!"

"Chain-mail, then," said Magrat.

"No!"

"Where is the king? Where is everyone?"

"I will not say!"

"All right."

Magrat vanished into the armory again, and came back dragging a suit of chain-mail.

The elf tried to scramble away.

"You won't get it on," said Shawn, from where he lay. "You'll never get it over its arms—"

Magrat picked up the axe.

"Oh, no," said Shawn. "Miss!"

"You will never get him back," said the elf. "She has him."

"We shall see," said Magrat. "All right, Shawn. What shall we do with it?"

In the end they dragged it into a storeroom next to the dungeon and manacled it to the bars of the window. It was still whimpering at the touch of the iron as Magrat slammed the door.

Shawn was trying to keep at a respectful distance. It was the way Magrat kept smiling all the time.

"Now let's have a look at that arm of yours," she said.

"I'm all right," said Shawn, "but they stabbed Diamanda in the kitchen."

"Was it her I heard screaming?"

"Uh. Partly. Uh." Shawn stared down in fascination at the dead elves as Magrat stepped over them.

"You killed them," he said.

"Did I do it wrong?"

"Um. No," said Shawn cautiously. "No, you did it . . . quite well, really."

"And there's one in the pit," said Magrat. "You know . . . *the* pit. What day is it?"

"Tuesday."

"And you clean it out on . . . ?"

"Wednesdays. Only I missed last Wednesday because I had—"

"Then we probably don't need to worry about it. Are there any more around?"

"I . . . don't think so. Uh. Miss Queen?"

"Yes, Shawn?"

"Could you put the axe down, please? I'd feel a lot better if you put the axe down. The axe, Miss Queen. You keep swinging it about. It could go off at any second."

"What axe?"

"The one you're holding."

"Oh, *this* axe." Magrat appeared to notice it for the first time. "That arm looks bad. Let's get down to the kitchen and I'll splint it. Those fingers don't look good, either. Did they kill Diamanda?"

"I don't know. And I don't know *why*. I mean, she was *helping* them."

"Yes. Wait a moment." Magrat disappeared one more time into the armory, and came back carrying a sack. "Come on. Greebo!"

Greebo gave her a sly look, and stopped washing himself.

"D'you know a funny thing about Lancre?" said Magrat, as they sidled down the stairs.

"What's that, miss?"

"We never throw anything away. And you know another thing?"

"No, miss."

"They couldn't have painted her from life, of course. I mean, people didn't paint portraits in those days. But the *armor* . . . hah! All they had to do was look. And you know what?"

Shawn suddenly felt frightened. He'd been scared before, but it had been immediate and physical. But Magrat, like this, frightened him more than the elves. It was like being charged by a sheep.

"No, miss?" he said.

"No one told me about her. You'd think it's all tapestry and walking around in long dresses!"

"What, miss?"

Magrat waved an arm expressively.

"All this!"

"Miss!" said Shawn, from knee level.

Magrat looked down.

"What?"

"Please put the axe down!"

"Oh. Sorry."

Hodgesaargh spent his nights in a little shed adjoining the mews. He too had received an invitation to the wedding, but it had been snatched from his hand and eaten in mistake for one of his fingers by Lady Jane, an ancient and evil-tempered gyrfalcon. So he'd gone through his usual nightly routine, bathing his wounds and eating a meal of stale bread and ancient cheese and going to bed early to bleed gently by candlelight over a copy of *Beaks and Talons.*

He looked up at a sound from the mews, picked up the candlestick, and wandered out.

An elf was looking at the birds. It had Lady Jane perched on its arm.

Hodgesaargh, like Mr. Brooks, didn't take much interest in events beyond his immediate passion. He was aware that there were a lot of visitors in the castle and, as far as he was concerned, anyone looking at the hawks was a fellow enthusiast.

"That's my best bird," he said proudly. "I've nearly got her trained. She's very good. I'm training her. She's very intelligent. She knows eleven words of command."

The elf nodded solemnly. Then it slipped the hood off the bird's head, and nodded toward Hodgesaargh.

"Kill," it commanded.

Lady Jane's eyes glittered in the torchlight. Then she leapt, and hit the elf full in the throat with two sets of talons and a beak.

"She does that with me, too," said Hodgesaargh. "Sorry about that. She's very intelligent."

Diamanda was lying on the kitchen floor, in a pool of blood. Magrat knelt beside her.

"She's still alive. Just." She grabbed the hem of her dress, and tried to rip it.

"Damn the thing. Help me, Shawn."

"Miss?"

"We need bandages!"

"But—"

"Oh, stop gawping."

The skirt tore. A dozen lace roses unraveled.

Shawn had never been privy to what queens wore

under their clothes, but even starting with certain observations concerning Millie Chillum and working his way up, he'd never considered metal underwear.

Magrat thumped the breastplate.

"Fairly good fit," she said, defying Shawn to point out that in certain areas there was quite a lot of air between the metal and Magrat. "Not that a few tucks and a rivet here and there wouldn't help. Don't you think it looks good?"

"Oh, yes," said Shawn. "Uh. Sheet iron is really *you*."

"You really think so?"

"Oh, yes," said Shawn, inventing madly. "You've got the figure for it."

She set and splinted his arm and fingers, working methodically, using strips of silk as bandages. Diamanda was less easy. Magrat cleaned and stitched and bandaged, while Shawn sat and watched, trying to ignore the insistent hot-ice pain from his arm.

He kept repeating, "They just laughed and stabbed her. She didn't even try to run away. It was like they were *playing*."

For some reason Magrat shot a glance at Greebo, who had the decency to look embarrassed.

"Pointy ears and hair you want to stroke," she said, vaguely. "And they can fascinate you. And when they're happy they make a pleasing noise."

"What?"

"Just thinking to myself." Magrat stood up. "OK. I'll build up the fire and fetch a couple of crossbows and load them up for you. And you keep the door shut and let no one in, d'you hear? And if I don't come back . . . try and go somewhere where there's people. Get up to the dwarfs at Copperhead. Or the trolls."

"What are you going to do?"

"I'm going to see what's happened to everyone."

Magrat opened the sack she'd brought down from the armory. There was a helmet in it. It had wings on, and to Shawn's mind was quite impractical.* There was also a pair of mail gloves and a choice assortment of rusty weaponry.

"But there's probably more of those things out there!"

"Better out there than in here."

"Can you fight?"

"Don't know. Never tried," said Magrat.

"But if we wait here, someone's bound to come."

"Yes. I'm afraid they will."

"What I mean is, you don't have to do this!"

"Yes I do. I'm getting married tomorrow. One way or the other."

"But—"

"Shut up!"

She's going to get killed, Shawn thought. It's not enough to be able to pick up a sword. You have to know which end to poke into the enemy. I'm supposed to be on guard and she's going to get killed—

But—

But—

She shot one of them in the eye, right through

---

*He knew this because the previous month's issue of *Popular Armor* had run a feature entitled "We Test The Top Twenty Sub-$50 Helmets." It had also run a second feature called "Battleaxes: We Put The Ten Best Through Their Paces" and had advertised for half a dozen new testers.

the keyhole. I couldn't have done that. I'd have said something like "Hands up!" first. But they were in the way and she just . . . got them out of her way.

She's still going to die. She's just probably going to die bravely.

I wish my mum was here.

Magrat finished rolling up the stained remnant of the wedding dress and stowed it in the sack.

"Have we got any horses?"

"There's . . . elf horses in the courtyard, miss. But I don't think you'll be able to ride one."

It struck Shawn immediately that this wasn't the right thing to say.

It was black, and larger than what Magrat had to think of as a human horse. It rolled red eyes at her, and tried to get into position to kick.

Magrat managed to mount only by practically tethering every leg to the rings in the stable wall, but when she was on, the horse changed. It had the docility of the severely whipped, and seemed to have no mind of its own.

"It's the iron," said Shawn.

"What does it do to them? It can't *hurt*."

"Don't know, miss. Seems they just freeze up, kind of thing."

"Drop the portcullis after I'm through."

"Miss—"

"Are you going to tell me not to go?"

"But—"

"Shut up, then."

"But—"

"I remember a folksong about a situation just like

this," said Magrat. "This girl had her fiancé stolen by the Queen of the Elves and she didn't hang around whining, she jolly well got on her horse and went and rescued him. Well, I'm going to do that too."

Shawn tried to grin.

"You're going to *sing*?" he said.

"I'm going to fight. I've got everything to fight for, haven't I? And I've tried everything else."

Shawn wanted to say: but that's not the same! Going and fighting when you're a real person isn't like folksongs! In real life you die! In folksongs you just have to remember to keep one finger in your ear and how to get to the next chorus! In real life no one goes wack-fol-a-diddle-di-do-sing-too-rah-li-ay!

But he *said*:

"But, miss, if you don't come back—"

Magrat turned in the saddle.

"I'll be back."

Shawn watched her urge the sluggish horse into a trot and disappear over the drawbridge.

"Good luck!" he shouted.

Then he lowered the portcullis and went back into the keep, where there were three loaded cross-bows on the kitchen table.

There was also the book on martial arts that the king had sent for specially.

He pumped up the fire, turned a chair to face the door, and turned to the Advanced Section.

Magrat was halfway down the road to the square when the adrenaline wore off and her past life caught up with her.

She looked down at the armor, and the horse, and thought: I'm out of my mind.

It was that bloody letter. And I was frightened. I thought I'd show everyone what I'm made of. And now they'll probably find out: I'm made of lots of tubes and greeny purple wobbly bits.

I was just lucky with those elves. And I didn't think. As soon as I think, I get things wrong. I don't think I'll be that lucky again . . .

Luck?

She thought wistfully of her bags of charms and talismans at the bottom of the river. They'd never really worked, if her life was anything to go by, but maybe—it was a horrible thought—maybe they'd just stopped it getting *worse*.

There were hardly any lights in the town, and a lot of the houses had their shutters up.

The horse's hooves clattered loudly on the cobbles. Magrat peered into the shadows. Once, they'd just been shadows. Now they could be gateways to anything.

Clouds were pressing in from the Hub. Magrat shivered.

This was something she'd never seen before.

It was true night.

Night had fallen in Lancre, and it was an old night. It was not the simple absence of day, patrolled by the moon and stars, but an extension of something that had existed long before there was any light to define it by absence. It was unfolding itself from under tree roots and inside stones, crawling back across the land.

Magrat's sack of what she considered to be essential props might be at the bottom of the river but she had been a witch for more than ten years, and she could feel the terror in the air.

People remember badly. But *societies* remember well, the *swarm* remembers, encoding the information to slip it past the censors of the mind, passing it on from grandmother to grandchild in little bits of nonsense they won't bother to forget. Sometimes the truth keeps itself alive in devious ways despite the best efforts of the official keepers of information. Ancient fragments chimed together now in Magrat's head.

Up the airy mountain, down the rushy glen . . .

From ghosties and bogles and long-leggity beasties . . .

My mother said I never should . . .

We dare not go a-hunting, for fear . . .

And things that go bump . . .

Play with the fairies in the wood . . .

Magrat sat on the horse she didn't trust and gripped the sword she didn't know how to use while the ciphers crept out of memory and climbed into a shape.

They steal cattle and babies . . .

They steal milk . . .

They love music, and steal away musicians . . .

In fact they steal everything.

We'll never be as free as them, as beautiful as them, as clever as them, as light as them; we are animals.

Chilly wind soughed in the forest beyond the town. It had always been a pleasant forest to walk in at nights but now, she knew, it would not be so again. The trees would have eyes. There would be distant laughter in the wind.

What they take is everything.

Magrat spurred the horse into a walk. Somewhere in the town a door slammed shut.

And what they give you is fear.

There was the sound of hammering from across the street. A man was nailing something on his door. He glanced around in terror, saw Magrat, and darted inside.

What he had been nailing on the door was a horseshoe.

Magrat tied the horse firmly to a tree and slid off its back. There was no reply to her knocking.

Who was it who lived here? Carter the weaver, wasn't it, or Weaver the baker?

"Open up, man! It's me, Magrat Garlick!"

There was something white beside the doorstep. It turned out to be a bowl of cream.

Again, Magrat thought of the cat Greebo. Smelly, unreliable, cruel, and vindictive—but who purred nicely, and had a bowl of milk every night.

"Come on! Open up!"

After a while the bolts slid back, and an eye was applied to a very narrow crack.

"Yes?"

"You're Carter the baker, aren't you?"

"I'm Weaver the thatcher."

"And you know who I am?"

"Miss Garlick?"

"Come on, let me in!"

"Are you alone, miss?"

"*Yes.*"

The crack widened to a Magrat width.

There was one candle alight in the room. Weaver

backed away from Magrat until he was leaning awk-wardly over the table. Magrat peered around him.

The rest of the Weaver family were hiding under the table. Four pairs of frightened eyes peered up at Magrat.

"What's going on?" she said.

"Er . . ." said Weaver. "Didn't recognize you in your flying hat, miss . . ."

"I thought you were doing the Entertainment? What's happened? Where is everyone? *Where is my going-to-be-husband?*"

"Er . . ."

Yes, it *was* probably the helmet. That's what Magrat decided afterward. There are certain items, such as swords and wizards' hats and crowns and rings, which pick up something of the nature of their owners. Queen Ynci had probably never sewn a tapestry in her life and undoubtedly had a temper shorter than a wet cowpat.* It was better to think that something of her had rubbed off on the helmet and was being transmitted to Magrat like some kind of royal scalp disease. It was better to let Ynci take over.

She grabbed Weaver by his collar.

"If you say 'Er' one more time," she said, "I'll chop your ears off."

"Er . . . aargh . . . I mean, miss . . . it's the Lords and Ladies, miss!"

"It really *is* the elves?"

"Miss!" said Weaver, his eyes full of pleading. "Don't say it! We heard 'em go down the street.

---

*The shortest unit of *time* in the multiverse is the New York Second, defined as the period of time between the traffic lights turning green and the cab behind you honking.

Dozens of 'em. And they've stolen old Thatcher's cow and Skindle's goat and they broke down the door of—"

"Why'd you put a bowl of milk out?" Magrat demanded.

Weaver's mouth opened and shut a few times. Then he managed: "You see, my Eva said her granny always put a bowl of milk out for them, to keep them hap—"

"I see," said Magrat, icily. "And the king?"

"The king, miss?" said Weaver, buying time.

"The king," said Magrat. "Short man, runny eyes, ears that stick out a bit, unlike other ears in this vicinity very shortly."

Weaver's fingers wove around one another like tormented snakes.

"Well . . . well . . . well . . ."

He caught the look on Magrat's face, and sagged.

"We done the play," he said. "I *told* 'em, let's do the Stick and Bucket Dance instead, but they were set on this play. And it all started all right and then, and then, and then . . . suddenly *They* were there, hundreds of 'em, and everyone was runnin', and someone bashed into me, and I rolled into the stream, and then there was all this noise, and I saw Jason Ogg hitting four elves with the first thing he could get hold of—"

"Another elf?"

"Right, and then I found Eva and the kids, and then lots of people were running like hell for home, and there were these—Gentry on horseback, and I could hear 'em laughing, and we got home and Eva said to put a horseshoe on the door and—"

"What about the king?"

"Dunno, miss. Last I remember, he was laughin' at Thatcher in his straw wig."

"And Nanny Ogg and Granny Weatherwax? What happened to them?"

"Dunno, miss. Don't remember seein' 'em, but there was people runnin' everywhere—"

"And where was all this?"

"Miss?"

"Where did it happen?" said Magrat, trying to speak slowly and distinctly.

"Up at the Dancers, miss. You know. Them old stones."

Magrat let him go.

"Oh, yes," she said. "Don't tell Magrat, Magrat's not to know about this sort of thing. The Dancers? Right."

"It wasn't us, miss! It was only make-believe!"

"Hah!"

She unbolted the door again.

"Where're you going, miss?" said Weaver, who was not a competitor in the All-Lancre Uptake Stakes.

"Where d'you think?"

"But, miss, you can't take iron—"

Magrat slammed the door. Then she kicked the bowl of milk so hard that it sprayed across the street.

Jason Ogg crawled cautiously through the dripping bracken. There was a figure a few feet away. He hefted the stone in his hand—

"Jason?"

"Is that you, Weaver?"

"No, it's me—Tailor."

"Where's everyone else?"

"Tinker'n Baker found Carpenter just now. Have you seen Weaver?"

"No, but I saw Carter and Thatcher."

Mist curled up as the rain drummed into the warm earth. The seven surviving Morris Men crawled under a dripping bush.

"There's going to be hell to pay in the morning!" moaned Carter. "When she finds us we're done for!"

"We'll be all right if we can find some iron," said Jason.

"Iron don't have no effect on her! She'll tan our hides for us!"

Carter clutched his knees to his chest in terror.

"Who?"

"Mistress Weatherwax!"

Thatcher jabbed him in the ribs. Water cascaded off the leaves above them and funneled down every neck.

"Don't be so daft! You saw them things! What're you worrying about that old baggage for?"

"She'll tan our hides for us, right enough! 'Twas all our fault, she'll say!"

"I just hopes she gets a chance," muttered Tinker.

"We are," said Thatcher, "between a rock and a hard place."

"No we ain't," sobbed Carter. "I been there. That's that gorge just above Bad Ass. We ain't there! I wish we was there! We're under this bush! And they'll be looking for us! And so shall she!"

"What happened when we was doing the Ent—" Carpenter began.

"I ain't asking that question right now," said Jason. "The question I'm asking right now is, how do we get home tonight?"

"She'll be waiting for us!" Carter wailed.

There was a tinkle in the darkness.

"What've you got there?" said Jason.

"It's the props sack," said Carter. "You said as how it was my job to look after the props sack!"

"You dragged *that* all the way down here?"

"I ain't about to get into more trouble 'cos of losing the props sack!"

Carter started to shiver.

"If we gets back home," said Jason, "I'm going to talk to our mam about getting you some of these new dried frog pills."

He pulled the sack toward him and undid the top.

"There's our bells in here," he said, "and the sticks. And who told you to pack the accordion?"

"I thought we might want to do the Stick and—"

"*No one's* ever to do the Stick and—"

There was a laugh, away on the rain-soaked hill, and a crackling in the bracken. Jason suddenly felt the focus of attention.

"They're out there!" said Carter.

"And we ain't got any weapons," said Tinker.

A set of heavy brass bells hit him in the chest.

"Shut up," said Jason, "and put your bells on. Carter?"

"They're waiting for us!"

"I'll say this just once," said Jason. "*After tonight* no one's ever to talk about the Stick and Bucket dance ever again. All right?"

* * *

The Lancre Morris Men faced one another, rain plastering their clothes to their bodies.

Carter, tears of terror mingling with makeup and the rain, squeezed the accordion. There was the long-drawn-out chord that by law must precede all folk music to give bystanders time to get away.

Jason held up his hand and counted his fingers.

"One, two . . ." His forehead wrinkled. "One, two, three . . ."

". . . four . . ." hissed Tinker.

". . . four," said Jason. "Dance, lads!"

Six heavy ash sticks clashed in mid-air.

". . . one, two, forward, one, back, *spin* . . ."

Slowly, as the leaky strains of *Mrs. Widgery's Lodger* wound around the mist, the dancers leapt and squelched their way slowly through the night . . .

". . . two, back, *jump* . . ."

The sticks clashed again.

"They're watching us!" panted Tailor, as he bounced past Jason, "I can *see* 'em!"

". . . one . . . two . . . they won't do nothing 'til the music stops! . . . back, two, *spin* . . . they loves music! . . . forward, hop, *turn* . . . one and six, beetle crushers! . . . hop, back, *spin* . . ."

"They're coming out of the bracken!" shouted Carpenter, as the sticks met again.

"I *see* 'em . . . two, three, forward, turn . . . Carter . . . back, spin . . . you do a double . . . two, back . . . wandering angus down the middle . . ."

"I'm losing it, Jason!"

"Play! . . . two, three, *spin* . . ."

"They're all round us!"

"*Dance!*"

"They're watching us! They're closing in!"

". . . *spin*, back . . . jump . . . we're nearly at the road . . ."

"Jason!"

"Remember when . . . three, turn . . . we won the cup against Ohulan Casuals? . . . *spin* . . ."

The sticks met, with a thump of wood against wood. Clods of earth were kicked into the night.

"Jason, you don't mean—"

". . . back, two . . . *do it* . . ."

"Carter's getting . . . one, two . . . out of wind . . ."

". . . two, spin . . ."

"The accordion's melting, Jason," sobbed Carter.

". . . one, two, forward . . . bean setting!"

The accordion wheezed. The elves pressed in. Out of the corner of his eye Jason saw a dozen grinning, fascinated faces.

"Jason!"

". . . one, two . . . Carter into the middle . . . one, two, spin . . ."

Seven pairs of boots thudded down . . .

"*Jason!*"

". . . one, two . . . spin . . . ready . . . one, two . . . back . . . back . . . one, two . . . turn . . . *KILL* . . . and back, one, two . . ."

The inn was a wreck. The elves had stripped it of everything edible and rolled out every barrel, although a couple of rogue cheeses in the cellar had put up quite a fight.

The table had collapsed. Lobster claws and candlesticks lay among the ruined meal.

Nothing moved.

Then someone sneezed, and some soot fell into the empty grate, followed by Nanny Ogg and, eventually, by the small, black, and irate figure of Casanunda.

"Yuk," said Nanny, looking around at the debris. "This really is the *pips*."

"You should have let me fight them!"

"There were too many of them, my lad."

Casanunda threw his sword on the floor in disgust.

"We were just getting to know one another properly and fifty elves burst into the place! Damn! This kind of thing happens to me all the time!"

"That's the best thing about black, it doesn't show the soot," said Nanny Ogg vaguely, dusting herself off. "They managed it, then. Esme was right. Wonder where she is? Oh, well. Come on."

"Where're we going?" said the dwarf.

"Down to my cottage."

"Ah!"

"To get my broomstick," said Nanny Ogg firmly. "I ain't having the Queen of the Fairies ruling *my* children. So we'd better get some help. This has gone too far."

"We could go up into the mountains," said Casanunda, as they crept down the stairs. "There's thousands of dwarfs up there."

"No," said Nanny Ogg. "Esme won't thank me for this, but I'm the one who has to wave the bag o' sweets when she overreaches herself . . . and I'm thinking about someone who *really* hates the Queen."

"You won't find anyone who hates her worse than dwarfs do," said Casanunda.

"Oh, you will," said Nanny Ogg, "if you knows where to look."

The elves had been into Nanny Ogg's cottage, too. There weren't two pieces of furniture left whole.

"What they don't take they smash," said Nanny Ogg.

She stirred the debris with her foot. Glass tinkled.

"That vase was a present from Esme," she said, to the unfeeling world in general. "Never liked it much."

"Why'd they do it?" said Casanunda, looking around.

"Oh, they'd smash the world if they thought it'd make a pretty noise," said Nanny. She stepped outside again and felt around under the eaves of the low thatched roof, and pulled out her broomstick with a small grunt of triumph.

"I always shove it up there," she said, "otherwise the kids nick it and go joy-riding. You ride behind me, and I say this against my better judgement."

Casanunda shuddered. Dwarfs are generally scared of heights, since they don't often have the opportunity to get used to them.

Nanny scratched her chin, making a sandpapery sound.

"And we'll need a crowbar," she said. "There'll be one in Jason's forge. Hop on, my lad."

"I really wasn't expecting this," said Casanunda, feeling his way on to the broomstick with his eyes shut. "I was looking forward to a convivial evening, just me and you."

"It *is* just me and you."

"Yes, but I hadn't assumed there'd be a broomstick involved."

The stick left the ground slowly. Casanunda clung miserably to the bristles.

"Where're we going?" he said weakly.

"Place I know, up in the hills," said Nanny. "Ages since I've been there. Esme won't go near it, and Magrat's too young to be tole. I used to go there a lot, though. When I was a girl. Girls used to go up there if they wanted to get—oh, bugger . . ."

"What?"

"Thought I saw something fly across the moon, and I'm damn sure it wasn't Esme."

Casanunda tried to look around while keeping his eyes shut.

"Elves can't fly," he muttered.

"That's all *you* know," said Nanny. "They ride yarrow stalks."

"Yarrow stalks?"

"Yep. Tried it meself, once. You can get some lift out of 'em, but it plays merry hell with the gussets. Give me a nice bundle of bristles every time. Anyway," she nudged Casanunda, "you should be right at home on one of these. Magrat says a broomstick is one of them sexual metaphor things."*

Casanunda had opened one eye just long enough to see a rooftop drift silently below him. He felt sick.

"The difference being," said Nanny Ogg, "that a broomstick stays up longer. And you can use it to keep the house clean, which is more than you can say for—are you all right?"

---

*Although this is a phallusy.

"I really don't like this at all, Mrs. Ogg."

"Just trying to cheer you up, Mr. Casanunda."

"'Cheer' I like, Mrs. Ogg," said the dwarf, "but can we avoid the 'up'?"

"Soon be down."

"*That* I like."

Nanny Ogg's boots scraped along the hard-packed mud of the smithy's yard.

"I'll leave the magic running, won't be a mo," she said. Ignoring the dwarf's bleat for help, she hopped off the stick and disappeared through the back door.

The elves hadn't been there, at least. Too much iron. She pulled a crowbar from the toolbench and hurried out again.

"You can hold this," she said to Casanunda. She hesitated. "Can't have too much luck, can we?" she said, and scurried back into the forge. This time she was out again much faster, slipping something into her pocket.

"Ready?" she said.

"No."

"Then let's go. And keep a look out. With your eyes open."

"I'm looking for elves?" said Casanunda, as the stick rose into the moonlight.

"Could be. It wasn't Esme, and the only other one ever flying around here is Mr. Ixolite the banshee, and he's very good about slipping us a note under the door when he's going to be about. For air traffic control, see?"

Most of the town was dark. The moonlight made a black and silver checkerboard across the country. After a while, Casanunda began to feel better about things. The motion of the broomstick was actually quite soothing.

"Carried lots of passengers, have you?" he said.

"On and off, yes," said Nanny.

Casanunda appeared to be thinking about things. And then he said, in a voice dripping with scientific inquiry, "Tell me, has anyone ever tried to mak—"

"No," said Nanny Ogg firmly. "You'd fall off."

"You don't know what I was going to ask."

"Bet you half a dollar?"

They flew in silence for a couple of minutes, and then Casanunda tapped Nanny Ogg on the shoulder.

"Elves at three o'clock!"

"That's all right, then. That's hours away."

"I mean they're over there!"

Nanny squinted at the stars. Something ragged moved across the night.

"Oh, blast."

"Can't you outfly them?"

"Nope. They can put a girdle round the world in forty minutes."

"Why? It's not that fat," said Casanunda, who was feeling in the mood for a handful of dried frog pills.

"I mean they're *fast*. We can't outrun 'em, even if we lost some weight."

"I think I'm losing a tiny bit," said Casanunda, as the broomstick dived toward the trees.

Leaves scraped on Nanny Ogg's boots. Moonlight glinted briefly off ash-blond hair, away to her left.

"Bugger, bugger, *bugger*."

Three elves were keeping station with the broomstick. That was the thing about elves. They chased you till you dropped, until your blood was curdling with dread; if a dwarf wanted you dead, on the other hand, they'd simply cut you in half with an axe first chance they got. But that was because dwarfs were a lot nicer than elves.

"They're gaining on us!" said Casanunda.

"Got the crowbar?"

"Yes!"

"Right . . ."

The broomstick zigzagged over the silent forest. One of the elves drew its sword and swung down. Knock them down into the trees, leave them alive as long as possible . . .

The broomstick went into reverse. Nanny Ogg's head and legs went forward, so that partly she was sitting on her hands but mainly she was sitting on nothing. The elf swooped toward her, laughing—

Casanunda stuck out the crowbar.

There was a sound very like *doioinng.*

The broomstick jerked ahead again, dumping Nanny Ogg in Casanunda's lap.

"Sorry."

"Don't mention it. In fact, do it again if you like."

"Get him, did you?"

"Took his breath away."

"Good. Where're the others?"

"Can't see them."

Casanunda grinned madly.

"We showed them, eh?"

Something went *zip* and stuck into Nanny Ogg's hat.

"They know we've got iron," she said. "They won't come close again. They don't need to," she added bitterly.

The broomstick swerved around a tree and plowed through some bracken. Then it swung out on to an overgrown path.

"They aren't following us anymore," said Casanunda, after a while. "We've frightened them off, yes?"

"Not us. They're nervy of going close to the Long Man. It's not their turf. Huh, look at the state of this path. There's *trees* growing in it now. When I was a girl, you wouldn't find a blade of grass growing on the path." She smiled at a distant memory. "Very popular place on a summer night, the Long Man was."

There was a change in the texture of the forest now. It was old even by the standards of Lancre forestry. Beards of moss hung from gnarled low branches. Ancient leaves crackled underfoot as the witch and the dwarf flew between the trees. Something heard them and crashed away through the thick undergrowth. By the sound of it, it was something with horns.

Nanny let the broomstick glide to a halt.

"There," she said, pushing aside a bracken frond, 'the Long Man.' "

Casanunda peered under her elbow.

"Is that all? It's just an old burial mound."

"Three old burial mounds," said Nanny.

Casanunda took in the overgrown landscape.

"Yes, I see them," he said. "Two round ones and a long one. Well?"

"The first time I saw 'em from the air," said Nanny, "I nearly fell off the bloody broomstick for laughin'."

There was one of those pauses known as the delayed drop while the dwarf worked out the topography of the situation.

Then:

"Blimey," said Casanunda. "I thought the people who built burial mounds and earthworks and things were serious druids and people like that, not . . . not people who drew on privy walls with 200,000 tons of earth, in a manner of speaking."

"Doesn't sound like you to be shocked by that sort of thing."

She could have sworn the dwarf was blushing under his wig.

"Well, there's such a thing as *style*," said Casanunda. "There's such a thing as subtlety. You don't just shout: I've got a great big tonker."

"It's a bit more complicated than that," said Nanny, pushing through the bushes. "Here it's the landscape saying: I've got a great big tonker. That's a dwarf word, is it?"

"Yes."

"It's a good word."

Casanunda tried to untangle himself from a briar.

"Esme doesn't ever come up here," said Nanny, from somewhere up ahead. "She says it's bad enough about folksongs and maypoles and suchlike, without the whole scenery getting suggestive. 'Course," she went on, "this was never intended as a women's place. My great-gran said in the real old days the men used to come up for strange rites what no women ever saw."

"Except your great-grandmother, who hid in the bushes," said Casanunda.

Nanny stopped dead.

"How did you know *that*?"

"Let's just say I'm developing a bit of an insight into Ogg womanhood as well, Mrs. Ogg," said the dwarf. A thorn bush had ripped his coat.

"She said they just used to build sweat lodges and smell like a blacksmith's armpit and drink scumble and dance around the fire with horns on and piss in the trees any old how," said Nanny. "She said it was a bit sissy, to be honest. But I always reckon a man's got to be a man, even if it *is* sissy. What happened to your wig?"

"I think it's on that tree back there."

"Still got the crowbar?"

"Yes, Mrs. Ogg."

"Here we are, then."

They had arrived at the foot of the long mound. There were three large irregular stones there, forming a low cave. Nanny Ogg ducked under the lintel into the fusty and somewhat ammonia-scented darkness.

"About here'd do," she said. "Got a match?"

The sulfurous glow revealed a flat rock with a crude drawing scratched on it. Ochre had been rubbed into the lines. They showed a figure of an owl-eyed man wearing an animal skin and horns.

In the flickering light he seemed to dance.

There was a runic inscription underneath.

"Anyone ever worked out what that says?" said Casanunda.

Nanny Ogg nodded.

"It's a variant of Oggham," she said. "Basically, it means 'I've Got a Great Big Tonker.'"

"Oggham?" said the dwarf.

"My family has been in these, how shall I put it, in these parts for a very long time," said Nanny.

"Knowing you is a real education, Mrs. Ogg," said Casanunda.

"Everyone says that. Just shove the crowbar down the side of the stone, will you? I've always wanted an excuse to go down there."

"What *is* down there?"

"Well, it leads into Lancre Caves. They run everywhere, I've heard. Even up to Copperhead. There's supposed to be an entrance in the castle, but I've never found it. But mainly they lead to the world of the elves."

"I thought the Dancers led to the world of the elves?"

"This is the *other* world of the elves."

"I thought they only had one."

"They don't talk about this one."

"And you want to go into it?"

"Yes."

"You want to *find* elves?"

"That's right. Now, are you going to stand here all night, or are you going to crowbar that stone?" She gave him a nudge. "There's *gold* down there, you know."

"Oh, yes, thanks very much," said Casanunda sarcastically. "That's speciesist, that is. Just because I am . . . vertically disadvantaged, you're trying to get round me with gold, yes? Dwarfs are just a lot of appetites on legs, that's what you think. Hah!"

Nanny sighed.

"Oh, all right," she said. "Tell you what . . . when

we get back home, I'll bake you some proper dwarf bread, how about that?"

Casanunda's face split into a disbelieving grin.

"Real dwarf bread?"

"Yes. I reckon I've still got the recipe, and anyway it's been weeks since I emptied out the cat box."*

"Well, all right—"

Casanunda rammed one end of the crowbar under the stone and pulled on it with dwarfish strength. After a moment's resistance the stone swung up.

There were steps below, thick with earth and old roots.

Nanny started down them without a look back, and then realized that the dwarf wasn't following.

"What's the matter?"

"Never liked dark and enclosed spaces much."

"What? You're a *dwarf.*"

"*Born* a dwarf, *born* a dwarf. But I even get nervous when I'm hiding in wardrobes. That's a bit of a drawback in my line of work."

"Don't be daft. I'm not scared."

"You're not me."

"Tell you what—I'll bake 'em with extra gravel."

"Ooh . . . you're a temptress, Mrs. Ogg."

"And bring the torches."

The caves were dry, and warm. Casanunda trotted along after Nanny, anxious to stay in the torchlight.

"You haven't been down here before?"

---

*There are many recipes for the flat round loaves of Lancre dwarf bread, but the common aim of all of them is to make a field ration that is long-lasting, easily packed, and can disembowel the enemy if skimmed through the air hard enough. Edibility is a kind of optional extra. Most recipes are a closely guarded secret, apart from the gravel.

"No, but I know the way."

After a while Casanunda began to feel better. The caves were better than wardrobes. For one thing, you weren't tripping over shoes all the time, and there probably wasn't much chance of a sword-wielding husband opening the door.

In fact, he began to feel happy.

The words rose unbidden into his head, from somewhere in the back pocket of his genes.

"Hiho, hiho—"

Nanny Ogg grinned in the darkness.

The tunnel opened into a cavern. The torchlight picked up the suggestion of distant walls.

"This it?" said Casanunda, gripping the crowbar.

"No. This is something else. We . . . know about this place. It's mythical."

"It's not real?"

"Oh, it's real. *And* mythical."

The torch flared. There were hundreds of dust-covered slabs ranged around the cavern in a spiral; at the center of the spiral was a huge bell, suspended from a rope that disappeared into the darkness of the ceiling. Just under the hanging bell was one pile of silver coins and one pile of gold coins.

"Don't touch the money," said Nanny. "'Ere, watch this, my dad told me about this, it's a good trick."

She reached out and tapped the bell very gently, causing a faint *ting*.

Dust cascaded off the nearest slab. What Casanunda had thought was just a carving sat up, in a creaky way. It was an armed warrior. Since he'd sat up he almost certainly was alive, but he looked as though he'd gone from life to rigor mortis without passing through death on the way.

He focused deepset eyes on Nanny Ogg.

"What bloody tyme d'you call *thys*, then?"

"Not time yet," said Nanny.

"What did you goe and bang the bell for? I don't know, I haven't had a wynke of sleep for two hundred years, some sodde alwayes bangs the bell. Go *awaye*."

The warrior lay back.

"It's some old king and his warriors," whispered Nanny, as they hurried away. "Some kind of magical sleep, I'm told. Some old wizard did it. They're supposed to wake up for some final battle when a wolf eats the sun."

"Those wizards, always smoking *something*," said Casanunda.

"Could be. Go right here. Always go right."

"We're walking in a circle?"

"A spiral. We're right under the Long Man now."

"No, that can't be right," said Casanunda. "We climbed down a hole under the Long Man . . . hold on . . . you mean we're in the place where we started and it's a different place?"

"You're getting the hang of this, I can see that."

They followed the spiral.

Which, at length, brought them to a door, of sorts.

The air was hotter here. Red light glowed from side passages.

Two massive stones had been set up against a rock wall, with a third stone across them. Animal skins hung across the crude entrance thus formed; wisps of steam curled around them.

"They got put up at the same time as the Dancers," said Nanny, conversationally. "Only the hole here's vertical, so they only needed three. Might as well leave your crowbar here and take your boots off if they've got nails in 'em."

"These boots were stitched by the finest shoemaker in Ankh-Morpork," said Casanunda, "and one day I shall pay him."

Nanny pulled aside the skins.

Steam billowed out.

There was darkness inside, thick and hot as treacle and smelling of a fox's locker room. As Casanunda followed Nanny Ogg he sensed unseen figures in the reeking air, and heard the silence of murmured conversations suddenly curtailed. At one point he thought he saw a bowl of red hot stones, and then a shadowy hand moved across them and upturned a ladle, hiding them in steam.

This can't be inside the Long Man, he told himself. That's an earthworks, this is a long tent of skins.

They can't both be the same thing.

He realized he was dripping with sweat.

Two torches became visible as the steam swirled, their light hardly more than a red tint to the darkness. But they were enough to show a huge sprawled figure lying by another bowl of hot stones.

It looked up. Antlers moved in the damp, clinging heat.

"Ah. Mrs. Ogg."

The voice was like chocolate.

"Y'lordship," said Nanny.

"I suppose it is too much to expect you to kneel?"

"Yes indeed, y'honor," said Nanny, grinning.

"You know, Mrs. Ogg, you have a way of showing respect to your god that would make the average atheist green with envy," said the dark figure. It yawned.

"Thank you, y'grace."

"No one even dances for me now. Is that too much to ask?"

"Just as you say, y'lordship."

"You witches don't believe in me anymore."

"Right again, your hornishness."

"Ah, little Mrs. Ogg—and how, having got in here, do you possibly think you are going to get out?" said the slumped one.

"Because I have iron," said Nanny, her voice suddenly sharp.

"Of course you have not, little Mrs. Ogg. No iron can enter this realm."

"I have the iron that goes everywhere," said Nanny.

She took her hand out of her apron pocket, and held up a horseshoe.

Casanunda heard scuffles around him, as the hidden elves fought to get out of the way. More steam hissed up as a brazier of hot stones was overturned.

"Take it away!"

"I'll take it away when I go," said Nanny. "Now you listen to me. She's making trouble again. You've got to put a stop to it. Fair's fair. We're not having all the Old Trouble again."

"Why should I do that?"

"You want her to be powerful, then?"

There was a snort.

"You can't ever rule again, back in the world," said Nanny. "There's too much music. There's too much iron."

"Iron rusts."

"Not the iron in the head."

The King snorted.

"Nevertheless . . . even that . . . one day . . ."

"One day." Nanny nodded. "Yes. I'll drink to that. One day. Who knows? One day. Everyone needs 'one day.' But it ain't today. D'you see? So you come on out and balance things up. Otherwise, this is what I'll do. I'll get 'em to dig into the Long Man with iron shovels, y'see, and they'll say, why, it's just an old earthworks, and pensioned-off wizards and priests with nothin' better to do will pick over the heaps and write dull old books about burial traditions and suchlike, and that'll be another iron nail in your coffin. And I'd be a little bit sorry about that, 'cos you know I've always had a soft spot for you. But I've got kiddies, y'see, and they don't hide under the stairs because they're frit of the thunder, and they don't put milk out for the elves, and they don't hurry home because of the night, and before we go back to them dark old ways *I'll see you nailed.*"

The words sliced through the air.

The horned man stood up. And further up. His antlers touched the roof.

Casanunda's mouth dropped open.

"So you see," said Nanny, subsiding, "not today. One day, maybe. You just stay down here and sweat it out 'til One Day. But not today."

"I . . . will decide."

"Very good. You decide. And I'll be getting along."

The horned man looked down at Casanunda.

"What are *you* staring at, dwarf?"

Nanny Ogg nudged Casanunda.

"Go on, answer the nice gentleman."

Casanunda swallowed.

"Blimey," he said, "you don't half look like your picture."

In a narrow little valley a few miles away a party of elves had found a nest of young rabbits which, in conjunction with a nearby antheap, kept them amused for a while.

Even the meek and blind and voiceless have gods.

Herne the Hunted, god of the chased, crept through the bushes and wished fervently that *gods* had gods.

The elves had their backs to him as they hunkered down to watch closely.

Herne the Hunted crawled under a clump of bramble, tensed, and sprang.

He sank his teeth in an elf's calf until they met, and was flung away as it screamed and turned.

He dropped and ran.

That was the problem. He wasn't built to fight, there was not an ounce of predator in him. Attack and run, that was the only option.

And elves could run faster.

He bounced over logs and skidded through drifts of leaves, aware even as his vision fogged that elves were overtaking him on either side, pacing him, waiting for him to . . .

The leaves exploded. The little god was briefly aware of a fanged shape, all arms and vengeance. Then there were a couple of disheveled humans, one of them waving an iron bar around its head.

Herne didn't wait to see what happened next. He dived through the apparition's legs and ran on, but a distant warcry echoed in his long, floppy ears:

"Why, certainly, I'll have your whelk! How do we do it? Volume!"

Nanny Ogg and Casanunda walked in silence back to the cave entrance and the flight of steps. Finally, as they stepped out into the night air, the dwarf said, "Wow."

"It leaks out even up here," said Nanny. "Very mackko place, this."

"But I mean, good grief—"

"He's brighter than she is. Or more lazy," said Nanny. "He's going to wait it out."

"But he was—"

"They can look like whatever they want, to us," said Nanny. "We see the shape we've given 'em." She let the rock drop back, and dusted off her hands.

"But why should he want to stop her?"

"Well, he's her husband, after all. He can't stand her. It's what you might call an open marriage."

"Wait *what* out?" said Casanunda, looking around to see if there were anymore elves.

"Oh, you know," said Nanny, waving a hand. "All this iron and books and clockwork and universities and reading and suchlike. He reckons it'll all pass, see. And one day it'll all be over, and people'll look up at the skyline at sunset and there *he'll* be."

Casanunda found himself turning to look at the sunset beyond the mound, half-imagining the huge figure outlined against the afterglow.

"One day he'll be back," said Nanny softly. "When even the iron in the head is rusty."

Casanunda put his head on one side. You don't move around among a different species for most of your life without learning to read a lot of their body language, especially since it's in such large print.

"You won't entirely be sorry, eh?" he said.

"Me? I don't want 'em back! They're untrustworthy and cruel and arrogant parasites and we don't need 'em one bit."

"Bet you half a dollar?"

Nanny was suddenly flustered.

"Don't you look at me like that! Esme's right. Of course she's right. We don't want elves anymore. Stands to reason."

"Esme's the short one, is she?"

"Hah, no, Esme's the tall one with the nose. You know her."

"Right, yes."

"The short one is Magrat. She's a kind-hearted soul and a bit soft. Wears flowers in her hair and believes in songs. I reckon she'd be off dancing with the elves quick as a wink, her."

More doubts were entering Magrat's life. They concerned crossbows, for one thing. A crossbow is a very useful and usable weapon designed for speed and convenience and deadliness in the hands of the inexperienced, like a faster version of an out-of-code TV dinner. But it is designed to be used once, by someone who has somewhere safe to duck while they reload. Otherwise it is just so much metal and wood with a piece of string on it.

Then there was the sword. Despite Shawn's misgivings, Magrat did in theory know what you did with a sword. You tried to stick it into the enemy by a vigorous arm motion, and the enemy tried to stop you. She was a little uncertain about what happened next. She hoped you were allowed another go.

She was also having doubts about her armor. The helmet and the breastplate were OK, but the rest of it was chain-mail. And, as Shawn Ogg knew, chain-mail from the point of view of an arrow can be thought of as a series of loosely connected holes.

The rage was still there, the pure fury still gripped her at the core. But there was no getting away from the fact that the heart it gripped was surrounded by the rest of Magrat Garlick, spinster of this parish and likely to remain so.

There were no elves visible in the town, but she could see where they had been. Doors hung off their hinges. The place looked as though it had been visited by Genghiz Cohen.*

Now she was on the track that led to the stones. It was wider than it had been; the horses and carriages had churned it on the way up, and the fleeing people had turned it into a mire on the way down.

She knew she was being watched, and it almost came as a relief when three elves stepped out from under the trees before she'd even lost sight of the castle.

---

*Hence the term "wholesale destruction."

The middle one grinned.

"Good evening, girl," it said. "My name is Lord Lankin, and you will curtsy when you talk to me."

The tone suggested that there was absolutely no possibility that she would disobey. She felt her muscles strain to comply.

Queen Ynci wouldn't have obeyed . . .

"I happen to be practically the queen," she said.

It was the first time she'd looked an elf in the face when she was in any condition to notice details. This one was currently wearing high cheekbones and hair tied in a ponytail; it wore odds and ends of rags and lace and fur, confident in the knowledge that anything would look good on an elf.

It wrinkled its perfect nose at her.

"There is only one Queen in Lancre," it said. "And you are, most definitely, not her."

Magrat tried to concentrate.

"Where is she, then?" she said.

The other two raised their bows.

"You are looking for the Queen? Then we will take you to her," Lankin stated. "And, lady, should you be inclined to make use of that nasty iron bow there are more archers hidden in the trees."

There was indeed a rustling in the trees on one side of the track, but it was followed by a thump. The elves looked disconcerted.

"Get out of my way," said Magrat.

"I think you have a very wrong idea," said the elf. Its smile widened, but vanished when there was another sylvan crash from the other side of the track.

"We felt you coming all the way up the track,"

said the elf. "The brave girl off to rescue her lover! Oh, the romance! Take her."

A shadow rose up behind the two armed elves, took a head in either hand, and banged them together.

The shadow stepped forward over their bodies and, as Lankin turned, caught it with one roundarm punch that picked it up and slammed it into a tree.

Magrat drew her sword.

Whatever this was, it looked worse than elves. It was muddy and hairy and almost troll-like in its build, and it reached out for the bridle with an arm that seemed to extend forever. She raised the sword—

"Oook?"

"Put the sword down, *please*, miss!"

The voice came from somewhere behind her, but it sounded human and worried. Elves never sounded worried.

"Who are you?" she said, without turning around. The monster in front of her gave her a big, yellow-toothed grin.

"Um, I'm Ponder Stibbons. A wizard. And *he's* a wizard, too."

"He's got no clothes on!"

"I could get him to have a bath, if you like," said Ponder, slightly hysterically. "He always puts on an old green dressing gown when he's had a bath."

Magrat relaxed a bit. No one who sounded like that could be much of a threat, except to themselves.

"Whose side are you on, Mr. Wizard?"

"How many are there?"

"Oook?"

"When I get off this horse," said Magrat, "it'll

bolt. So can you ask your . . . friend to let go of the bridle? He'll be hurt."

"Oook?"

"Um. Probably not."

Magrat slid off. The horse, relieved of the presence of iron, bolted. For about two yards.

"Oook."

The horse was struggling to get back on its feet.

Magrat blinked.

"Um, he's just a bit annoyed at the moment," said Ponder. "One of the . . . elves . . . shot him with an arrow."

"But they do that to control people!"

"Um. He's not a person."

"Oook!"

"Genetically, I mean."

Magrat had met wizards before. Occasionally one visited Lancre, although they didn't stay very long. There was something about the presence of Granny Weatherwax that made them move on.

They didn't look like Ponder Stibbons. He'd lost most of his robe and, of his hat, only the brim remained. Most of his face was covered in mud, and there was a multicolored bruise over one eye.

"Did they do *that* to you?"

"Well, the mud and the torn clothes is just from, you know, the forest. And we've run into—"

"Ook."

"—*over* elves a few times. But *this* is when the Librarian hit me."

"Oook."

"Thank goodness," Ponder added. "Knocked me cold. Otherwise I'd be like the others."

A foreboding of a conversation to come swept over Magrat.

"What others?" she snapped.

"Are you alone?"

"What others?"

"Have you any *idea* what's been happening?"

Magrat thought about the castle, and the town.

"I might be able to hazard a guess," she said.

Ponder shook his head.

"It's worse than that," he said.

"What others?" said Magrat.

"I think there's definitely been a cross-continuum breakthrough, and I'm sure there's a difference in energy levels."

"But what *others*?" Magrat insisted.

Ponder Stibbons glanced nervously at the surrounding forest.

"Let's get off the path. There's a lot more elves back there."

Ponder disappeared into the undergrowth. Magrat followed him, and found a second wizard propped against a tree like a ladder. He had a huge smile creasing his face.

"The Bursar," said Ponder. "I think we may have overdone the dried frog pills a bit." He raised his voice. "How . . . are . . . you . . . doing . . . sir?"

"Why, I'll have a little of the roast weasel, if you would be so good," said the Bursar, beaming happily at nothing.

"Why's he gone so stiff?" said Magrat.

"We think it's some kind of side effect," said Ponder.

"Can't you do anything about it?"

"What, and have nothing to cross streams on?"

"Call again tomorrow, baker, and we'll have a crusty one!" said the Bursar.

"Besides, he seems quite happy," said Ponder. "Are you a warrior, miss?"

"What?" said Magrat.

"Well, I mean, the armor and everything . . ."

Magrat looked down. She was still holding the sword. The helmet kept falling over her eyes, but she'd padded it a bit with a scrap of wedding dress.

"I . . . er . . . yes. Yes, that's right. That's what I am," she said. "Absolutely. Yes."

"Here for the wedding, I expect. Like us."

"That's right. Definitely here for the wedding. That's true." She changed her grip on the sword. "Now tell me what happened," she said. "Paying particular attention to what happened to the others."

"Well . . ." Ponder absentmindedly picked up a corner of his torn robe and began to screw it up in his fingers. "We all went to see this Entertainment, you see. A play. You know. Acting? And, and it was very funny. There were all these yokels in their big boots and everything, straw wigs and everything, clumping around pretending to be lords and ladies and everything, and getting it all wrong. It was very funny. The Bursar laughed at them a lot. Mind you, he's been laughing at trees and rocks, too. But everyone was having fun. And then . . . and then . . ."

"I want to know everything," said Magrat.

"Well . . . well . . . then there was this bit I can't really remember. It was something to do with the acting, I think. I mean, suddenly . . . suddenly it all seemed *real*. Do you know what I mean?"

"No."

"There was this chap with a red nose and bandy legs and he was playing the Queen of the Fairies or something and suddenly he was still him but . . . everything felt . . . everything round me just vanished, there was just the actors . . . and there was this hill . . . I mean, they must have been good, because I really believed . . . I think at some point I remember someone asking us to clap our hands . . . and everyone was looking very strange and there was this singing and it was wonderful and . . . and . . ."

"Oook."

"Then the Librarian hit me," said Ponder simply.

"Why?"

"Best if he tells it in his own words," said Ponder.

"Ooook ook eek. Ook! Ook!"

"Cough, Julia! Over the bender!" said the Bursar.

"I didn't understand what the Librarian said," said Magrat.

"Um. We were all present at an interdimensional rip," said Ponder. "Caused by belief. The play was the last little thing that opened it up. There must have been a very delicate area of instability very close. It's hard to describe, but if you had a rubber sheet and some lead weights I could demonstrate—"

"You're trying to tell me those . . . *things* exist because people believe in them?"

"Oh, no. I imagine they exist anyway. They're *here* because people believe in them *here*."

"Ook."

"He ran off with us. They shot an arrow at him."

"Eeek."

"But it just made him itch."

"Ook."

"Normally he's as gentle as a lamb. Really he is."

"Ook."

"But he can't abide elves. They smell wrong to him."

The Librarian flared his nostrils.

Magrat didn't know much about jungles, but she thought about apes in trees, smelling the rank of the tiger. Apes never admired the sleek of the fur and the burn of the eye, because they were too well aware of the teeth of the mouth.

"Yes," she said, "I expect they would. Dwarfs and trolls hate them, too. But I think they don't hate them as much as I do."

"You can't fight them all," said Ponder. "They're swarming like bees up there. There's flying ones, too. The Librarian says they made people get fallen trees and things and push those, you know, those stones down? There were some stones on the hill. They attacked them. Don't know why."

"Did you see any witches at the Entertainment?" said Magrat.

"Witches, witches . . ." muttered Ponder.

"You couldn't have missed them," said Magrat. "There'd be a thin one glaring at everyone and a small fat one cracking nuts and laughing a lot. And they'd be talking to each other very loudly. And they'd both have tall pointy hats."

"Can't say I noticed them," said Ponder.

"Then they couldn't have been there," said Magrat. "Being noticed is what being a witch is all about." She was about to add that she'd never been good at it, but didn't. Instead she said: "I'm going on up there."

"You'll need an army, miss. I mean, you'd have been in trouble just now if the Librarian hadn't been up in the trees."

"But I haven't got an army. So I'm going to have to try by myself, aren't I?"

This time Magrat managed to spur the horse into a gallop.

Ponder watched her go.

"You know, folksongs have got a lot to answer for," he said to the night air.

"Oook."

"She's going to get utterly killed."

"Oook."

"Hello, Mr. Flowerpot, two pints of eels if you would be so good."

"Of course, it could be her destiny, or one of those sort of things."

"Oook."

"Millennium hand and shrimp."

Ponder Stibbons looked embarrassed.

"Anyone want to follow her?"

"Oook."

"Whoops, there he goes with his big clock."

"Was that a 'yes'?"

"Oook."

"Not yours, his."

"Flobby wobbly, here comes our jelly."

"I think that probably counts as a 'yes'," said Ponder, reluctantly.

"Oook?"

"I've got a lovely new vest."

"But look," said Ponder, "the graveyards are full of people who rushed in bravely but unwisely."

"Ook."

"What'd he say?" said the Bursar, passing briefly through reality on his way somewhere else.

"I think he said, 'Sooner or later the graveyards are full of *everybody*,'" said Ponder. "Oh, blast. Come on."

"Yes indeedy," said the Bursar, "hands up the mittens, Mr. Bosun!"

"Oh, shut up."

Magrat dismounted and let the horse go.

She knew she was near the Dancers now. Colored light flickered in the sky.

She wished she could go home.

The air was colder here, far too cold for a mid-summer night. As she plodded onward, flakes of snow swirled in the breeze and turned to rain.

Ridcully materialized inside the castle, and then clung on to a pillar for support until he got his breath back. Transmigration always made blue spots appear in front of his eyes.

No one noticed him. The castle was in turmoil.

Not everyone had run home. Armies had marched across Lancre many times over the last few thousand years, and the recollection of the castle's thick *safe* walls had been practically engraved in the folk memory. *Run to the castle*. And now it held most of the little country's population.

Ridcully blinked. People were milling around and being harangued by a small young man in loose-fitting chain-mail and one arm in a sling, who seemed to be the only person with any grip on things.

When he was certain he could walk straight, Ridcully headed toward him.

"What's going on, young—" he began, and then stopped. Shawn Ogg looked around.

"The scheming minx!" said Ridcully, to the air in general. "'Oh, go back and get it then,' she said, and I fell right for it! Even if I *could* cut the mustard again I don't know where we were!"

"Sir?" said Shawn.

Ridcully shook himself. "What's happening?" he said.

"I don't know!" said Shawn, who was almost in tears. "I think we're being attacked by elves! Nothing anyone's telling me's making any sense! Somehow they arrived during the Entertainment! Or something!"

Ridcully looked around at the frightened, bewildered people.

"And Miss Magrat's gone out to fight them *alone*!"

Ridcully looked perplexed.

"Who's Miss Magrat?"

"She's going to be queen! The bride! You know? Magrat Garlick?"

Ridcully's mind could digest one fact at a time.

"What's she gone out for?"

"They captured the king!"

"Did you know they've got Esme Weatherwax as well?"

"What, Granny Weatherwax?"

"I came back to rescue her," said Ridcully, and

then realized that this sounded either nonsense or cowardly.

Shawn was too upset to notice. "I just hope they're not collecting witches," he said. "They'll need our mum to get the complete set."

"They ain't got me, then," said Nanny Ogg, behind him.

"Mum? How did you get in?"

"Broomstick. You'd better get some people with bows up on the roof. I came down that way. So can others."

"What're we going to *do*, Mum?"

"There's bands of elves all over the place," said Nanny, "and there's a big glow over the Dancers—"

"We must attack them!" shouted Casanunda. "Give 'em a taste of cold steel!"

"Good man, that dwarf!" said Ridcully. "That's right! I'll get my crossbow!"

"There's too many of them," said Nanny flatly.

"Granny and Miss Magrat are out there, Mum," said Shawn. "Miss Magrat came over all strange and put on armor and went out to fight *all* of them!"

"But the hills are crawling with elves," said Nanny. "It's a double helping of hell with extra devils. Certain death."

"It's certain death anyway," said Ridcully. "That's the thing about Death, certainty."

"We'd have no chance at all," said Nanny.

"Actually, we'd have one chance," said Ridcully. "I don't understand all this continuinuinuum stuff, but from what young Stibbons says it means that everything has to happen somewhere, d'y'see, so that means it *could* happen here. Even if it's a million to one chance, ma'am."

"That's all very well," said Nanny, "but what you're saying is, for every Mr. Ridcully that survives tonight's work, 999,999 are going to get killed?"

"Yes, but I'm not bothered about those other buggers," said Ridcully. "They can look after themselves. Serve 'em right for not inviting me to their weddings."

"What?"

"Nothing."

Shawn was hopping from one foot to the other.

"We ought to be fighting 'em, Mum!"

"Look at everyone!" said Nanny. "They're dog tired and wet and confused! That's not an army!"

"Mum, Mum, Mum!"

"What?"

"I'll pussike 'em up, Mum! That's what you have to do before troops go into battle, Mum! I read about that in books! You can take a rabble of thingy and make the right kind of speech and pussike them up and turn 'em into a terrible fighting force, Mum!"

"They look terrible anyway!"

"I mean terrible like fierce, Mum!"

Nanny Ogg looked at the hundred or so Lancre subjects. The thought of them managing to fight anyone at all took some getting used to.

"You been studyin' this, Shawn?" she inquired.

"I've got five years' worth of *Bows and Ammo*, Mum," said Shawn reproachfully.

"Give it a try, then. If you think it'll work."

Trembling with excitement, Shawn climbed on

to a table, drew his sword with his good hand, and banged it on the planks until people were silent.

He made a speech.

He pointed out that their king had been captured and their prospective queen had gone out to save him. He pointed out their responsibility as loyal subjects. He pointed out that other people currently not here but at home hiding under the bed would, after the glorious victory, wish they'd been there too instead of under the aforesaid bed which they were hiding under, you know, the bed he'd just mentioned. In fact it was *better* that there were so few here to face the enemy, because that meant that there would be a higher percentage of honor per surviving head. He used the word "glory" three times. He said that in times to come people would look back on this day, whatever the date was, and proudly show their scars, at least those who'd *survived* would show their scars, and be very proud and probably have drinks bought for them. He advised people to imitate the action of the Lancre Reciprocating Fox and stiffen some sinews while leaving them flexible enough so's they could move their arms and legs, in fact, probably it'd be better to relax them a bit now and stiffen them properly when the time came. He suggested that Lancre expected everyone to do their duty. And um. And uh. Please?

The silence that followed was broken by Nanny Ogg, who said, "They're probably considering it a bit, Shawn. Why don't you take Mr. Wizard here up to his room and help him with his crossbow?"

She nodded meaningfully in the direction of the stairs.

Shawn wavered, but not for long. He'd seen the glint in his mother's eye.

When he'd gone, Nanny climbed up on the same table.

"Well," she said, "it's like this. If you go out there you may have to face elves. But if you stops here, you *definitely* have to face me. Now, elves is worse than me, I'll admit. But I'm persistent."

Weaver put up a tentative hand.

"Please, Mrs. Ogg?"

"Yes, Weaver?"

"What exactly *is* the action of the Reciprocating Fox?"

Nanny scratched her ear.

"As I recall," she said, "its back legs go like *this* but its front legs go like *this*."

"No, no, no," said Quarney the storekeeper. "It's its *tail* that goes like *that*. Its legs go like *this*."

"That's not reciprocating, that's just oscillating," said someone. "You're thinking of the Ring-tailed Ocelot."

Nanny nodded.

"That's settled, then," she said.

"Hold on, I'm not sure—"

"*Yes*, Mr. Quarney?"

"Oh . . . well . . ."

"Good, good," said Nanny, as Shawn reappeared. "They was just saying, our Shawn, how they was swayed by your speech. Really pussiked up."

"Cor!"

"They're ready to follow you into the jaws of hell itself, I expect," said Nanny.

Someone put up their hand.

"Are you coming too, Mrs. Ogg?"

"I'll just stroll along behind," said Nanny.

"Oh. Well. Maybe *as far as* the jaws of hell, then."

"Amazing," said Casanunda to Nanny, as the crowd filed reluctantly toward the armory.

"You just got to know how to deal with people."

"They'll follow where an Ogg leads?"

"Not exactly," said Nanny, "but if they know what's good for 'em they'll go where an Ogg follows."

Magrat stepped out from under the trees, and the moorland lay ahead of her.

A whirlpool of cloud swirled over the Dancers, or at least, over the place where the Dancers had been. She could make out one or two stones by the flickering light, lying on their side or rolled down the slope of the hill.

The hill itself glowed. Something was wrong with the landscape. It curved where it shouldn't curve. Distances weren't right. Magrat remembered a woodcut shoved in as a place marker in one of her old books. It showed the face of an old crone but, if you stared at it, you saw it was also the head of a young woman; a nose became a neck, an eyebrow became a necklace. The images seesawed back and forth. And like everyone else, she'd squinted herself silly trying to see them both at the same time.

The landscape was doing pretty much the same thing. What was a hill was also *at the same time* a vast snowbound panorama. Lancre and the land of the elves were trying to occupy the same space.

The intrusive country wasn't having it all its own way. Lancre was fighting back.

There was a circle of tents just on the cusp of the warring landscapes, like a beachhead on an alien shore. They were brightly colored. Everything about the elves was beautiful, until the image tilted, and you saw it from the other side . . .

Something was happening. Several elves were on horseback, and more horses were being led between the tents.

It looked as though they were breaking camp.

The Queen sat on a makeshift throne in her tent. She sat with her elbow resting on one arm of the throne and her fingers curling pensively around her mouth.

There were other elves seated in a semicircle, except that "seated" was a barely satisfactory word. They lounged; elves could make themselves at home on a wire. And here there was more lace and velvet and fewer feathers, although it was hard to know if it meant that these were aristocrats—elves seemed to wear whatever they felt like wearing, confident of looking absolutely stunning.*

Every one of them watched the Queen, and was a mirror of her moods. When she smiled, they smiled. When she said something she thought was amusing, they laughed.

Currently the object of her attention was Granny Weatherwax.

---

*The Monks of Cool, whose tiny and exclusive monastery is hidden in a really cool and laid-back valley in the lower Ramtops, have a passing-out test for a novice. He is taken into a room full of all types of clothing and asked: Yo,** my son, which of these is the most stylish thing to wear? And the correct answer is: Hey, whatever I select.

**Cool, but not necessarily up to date.

"What is happening, old woman?" she said.

"It ain't easy, is it?" said Granny. "Thought it *would* be easy, didn't you?"

"You've done some magic, haven't you? Something is fighting us."

"No magic," said Granny. "No magic at all. It's just that you've been away too long. Things change. The land belongs to humans now."

"That can't be the case," said the Queen. "Humans take. They plough with iron. They ravage the land."

"Some do, I'll grant you that. Others put back more'n they take. They put back love. They've got soil in their bones. They tell the land what it is. That's what humans are for. Without humans, Lancre'd just be a bit of ground with green bits on it. They wouldn't even know they're trees. We're all down here together, madam—us and the land. It's not just land anymore, it's a country. It's like a horse that's been broken and shod or a dog that's been tamed. Every time people put a plough in the soil or planted a seed they took the land further away from you," said Granny. "Things change."

Verence sat beside the Queen. His pupils were tiny pinpoints; he smiled faintly, permanently, in a way very reminiscent of the Bursar.

"Ah. But when we are *married*," said the Queen, "the land must accept me. By your own rules. I know how it works. There's more to being a king than wearing a crown. The king and the land are one. The king and the queen are one. And I shall be queen."

She smiled at Granny. There was an elf on either side of her and, Granny knew, at least one behind her. Elves were not given to introspection; if she moved without permission, she'd die.

"What *you* shall be is something I have yet to decide," said the Queen. She held up an exquisitely thin hand and curled the thumb and forefinger into a ring, which she held up to her eye.

"And now someone comes," she said, "with armor that doesn't fit and a sword she cannot use and an axe she can hardly even lift, because it is so *romantic*, is it not? What is her name?"

"Magrat Garlick," said Granny.

"She is a mighty enchantress, is she?"

"She's good with herbs."

The Queen laughed.

"I could kill her from here."

"Yes," said Granny, "but that wouldn't be much fun, would it? Humiliation is the key."

The Queen nodded.

"You know, you think very much like an elf."

"I think it will soon be dawn," said Granny. "A fine day. Clear light."

"Not soon enough." The Queen stood up. She glanced at King Verence for a moment, and changed. Her dress went from red to silver, catching the torchlight like glittering fish scales. Her hair unraveled and reshaped itself, became corn blond. And a subtle ripple of alterations flowed across her face before she said, "What do you think?"

She looked like Magrat. Or, at least, like Magrat wished she looked and maybe as Verence always thought of her. Granny nodded. As one expert to another, she recognized accomplished nastiness when she saw it.

"And you're going to face her like that," she said.

"Certainly. Eventually. At the finish. But don't feel sorry for her. She's only going to die. Would you like me to show you what *you* might have been?"

"No."

"I could do it easily. There are other times than this. I could show you *grandmother* Weatherwax."

"No."

"It must be terrible, knowing that you have no friends. That no one will care when you die. That you never touched a heart."

"Yes."

"And I'm sure you think about it . . . in those long evenings when there's no company but the ticking of the clock and the coldness of the room and you open the box and look at—"

The Queen waved a hand vaguely as Granny tried to break free.

"Don't kill her," she said. "She *is* much more fun alive."

Magrat stuck the sword in the mud and hefted the battleaxe.

Woods pressed in on either side. The elves would have to come this way. There looked like hundreds of them and there was only one Magrat Garlick.

She knew there was such a thing as heroic odds. Songs and ballads and stories and poems were *full* of stories about one person single-handedly taking on and defeating a vast number of enemies.

Only now was it dawning on her that the trouble was that they were songs and ballads and stories and poems because they dealt with things that were, not to put too fine a point on it, untrue.

She couldn't, now she had time to think about it, ever remember an example from *history*.

In the woods to one side of her an elf raised its bow and took careful aim.

A twig snapped behind it. It turned.

The Bursar beamed.

"Whoopsy daisy, old trouser, my bean's all runny."

The elf swung the bow.

A pair of prehensile feet dropped out of the greenery, gripped it by the shoulders, and pulled it upward sharply. There was a crack as its head hit the underside of a branch.

"Oook."

"Move right along!"

On the other side of the path another elf took aim. And then its world flowed away from it . . .

This is the inside of the mind of an elf:

Here are the normal five senses but they are all subordinate to the sixth sense. There is no formal word for it on the Discworld, because the force is so weak that it is only ever encountered by observant blacksmiths, who call it the Love of Iron. Navigators might have discovered it were it not that the Disc's standing magical field is much more reliable. But bees sense it, because bees sense everything. Pigeons navigate by it. And everywhere in the multiverse elves use it to know exactly where they are.

It must be hard for humans, forever floundering through inconvenient geography. Humans are always slightly lost. It's a basic characteristic. It explains a lot about them.

Elves are never lost at all. It's a basic characteristic. It explains a lot about them.

Elves have absolute position. The flow of the silvery force dimly outlines the landscape. Creatures generate small amounts of it themselves, and become perceptible in the flux. Their muscles crackle with it, their minds buzz with it. For those who learn how, even thoughts can be read by the tiny local changes in the flow.

For an elf, the world is something to reach out and take. Except for the terrible metal that drinks the force and deforms the flux universe like a heavy weight on a rubber sheet and blinds them and deafens them and leaves them rudderless and more alone than most humans could ever be . . .

The elf toppled forward.

Ponder Stibbons lowered the sword.

Almost everyone else would not have thought much about it. But Ponder's wretched fate was to look for patterns in an uncaring world.

"But I hardly touched him," he said, to no one except himself.

" 'And I kissed her in the shrubbery where the nightingales'—sing it, you bastards! Two, three!"

They didn't know where they were. They didn't know where they'd been. They were not fully certain who they were. But the Lancre Morris Men had reached some sort of state now where it was easier to go on than stop. Singing attracted elves, but singing also fascinated them . . .

The dancers whirled and hopped, gyrated and skipped along the paths. They pranced through isolated hamlets, where elves left whoever they were torturing to draw closer in the light of the burning buildings . . .

"'With a WACK foladiddle-di-do, sing too-rah-li-ay!'"

Six sticks did their work, right on the beat.

"Where're we goin', Jason?"

"I reckon we've gone down Slippery Hollow and're circling back toward the town," said Jason, hopping past Baker. "Keep goin', Carter!"

"The rain's got in the keys, Jason!"

"Don't matter! They don't know the difference! It's good enough for folk music!"

"I think I broke my stick on that last one, Jason!"

"Just you keep dancing, Tinker! Now, lads . . . how about *Gathering Peasecods*? We might as well get some practice in, since we're here . . ."

"There's some people up ahead," said Tailor, as he skipped past, "I can see torches an' that."

"Human, two, three, or more elves?"

"Dunno!"

Jason spun and danced back.

"Is that you, our Jason?"

Jason cackled as the voice echoed among the dripping trees.

"It's our mam! And our Shawn. And—and lots of people! We've made it, lads!"

"Jason," said Carter.

"Yes?"

"I ain't sure I can stop!"

The Queen examined her face in a mirror attached to the tent pole.

"Why?" said Granny. "What is it *you* see?"

"Whatever I want to see," said the Queen. "You know that. And now . . . let us ride to the castle. Tie her hands together. But leave her legs free."

It rained again, gently, although around the stones it turned to sleet. The water dripped off Magrat's hair and temporarily unraveled the tangles.

Mist coiled out from among the trees where summer and winter fought.

Magrat watched the elven court mount up. She made out the figure of Verence, moving like a puppet. And Granny Weatherwax, tied behind the Queen's horse by a long length of rope.

The horses splashed through the mud. They had silver bells on their harness, dozens of them.

The elves in the castle, the night of ghosts and shadows, all of this was just a hard knot in her memory. But the jingling of the bells was like a nail-file rubbed across her teeth.

The Queen halted the procession a few yards away.

"Ah, the brave girl," she said. "Come to save her fiancé, all alone? How sweet. Someone kill her."

An elf spurred its horse forward, and raised its sword. Magrat gripped the battleaxe.

Somewhere behind her a bowstring slammed against wood. The elf jerked. So did one behind it. The arrow kept going, curving a little as it passed over one of the fallen Dancers.

Then Shawn Ogg's ragbag army charged out from under the trees, except for Ridcully, who was feverishly trying to rewind his crossbow.

The Queen did not look surprised.

"And there's only about a hundred of them," she said. "What do you think, Esme Weatherwax? A valiant last stand? It's so beautiful, isn't it? I love the way humans think. They think like songs."

"You get down off that horse!" Magrat shouted.

The Queen smiled at her.

Shawn felt it. Ridcully felt it. Ponder felt it. The glamour swept over them.

Elves feared iron, but they didn't need to go near it.

You couldn't fight elves, because you were so much more worthless than them. It was *right* that you should be so worthless. And they were so beautiful. And you weren't. You were always the one metaphorically picked last for any team, even after the fat kid with one permanently blocked runny nostril; you were always the one who wasn't told the rules until you'd lost, and then wasn't told the *new* rules; you were the one who always knew that everything interesting was happening to other people. All those hot self-consuming feelings were rolled together. You couldn't fight an elf. Someone as useless as you, as stolid as you, as *human* as you, could never win; the universe wasn't built like that—

Hunters say that, just sometimes, an animal will step out of the bushes and stand there waiting for the spear . . .

Magrat managed to half-raise the axe, and then her hand slumped to her side. She looked down. The correct attitude of a human before an elf was one of shame. She had shouted so *coarsely* at something as beautiful as an elf . . .

The Queen dismounted and walked over to her.

"Don't touch her," said Granny.

The Queen nodded.

"You can resist," she said. "But you see, it doesn't matter. We can take Lancre without a fight. There is nothing you can do about it. Look at the brave little army, standing like sheep. Humans are so *enthusiastic*."

Granny looked at her boots.

"You can't rule while I'm alive," she said.

"There's no trickery here," said the Queen. "No silly women with bags of sweets."

"You noticed that, did you?" said Granny. "Gytha meant well, I expect. Daft old biddy. Mind if I sit down?"

"Of course you may," said the Queen. "You are an old woman now, after all."

She nodded to the elves. Granny subsided gratefully on to a rock, her hands still tied behind her.

"That's the thing about witchcraft," she said. "It doesn't exactly keep you young, but you do stay old for longer. Whereas you, of course, do not age," she added.

"Indeed, we do not."

"But I suspect you may be capable of being *reduced*."

The Queen's smile didn't vanish, but it *did* freeze, as smiles do when their owner is not certain about what has just been said and isn't sure what to say next.

"You meddled in a play," said Granny. "I believe you don't realize what you've done. Plays and books . . . you've got to keep an eye on the buggers. They'll turn on you. I mean to see that they do." She nodded amicably at an elf covered in woad and badly tanned skins. "Ain't that so, Fairy Peaseblossom?"

The Queen's brows knotted.

"But that is not his name," she said.

Granny Weatherwax gave the Queen a bright smile.

"We shall see," she said. "There's a lot more humans these days, and lots of them live in cities, and they don't know much about elves one way or another. And they've got iron in their heads. You're too late."

"No. Humans always need us," said the Queen.

"They don't. Sometimes they want you. That's different. But all you can give 'em is gold that melts away in the morning."

"There are those who would say that gold for one night is enough."

"No."

"Better than iron, you stupid old hag, you stupid child who has grown older and done nothing and been nothing."

"No. It's just soft and shiny. Pretty to look at and no damn use at all," said Granny, her voice still quite calm and level. "But this is a real world, madam. That's what I had to learn. And real people in it. You got no right to 'em. People've got enough to cope with just being people. They don't need you swanking around with your shiny hair and shiny eyes and shiny gold, going sideways through life, always young, always singing, never *learning*."

"You didn't always think like this."

"That was a long time ago. And, my lady, old I may be, and hag I may be, but stupid I ain't. You're no kind of goddess. I ain't against gods and goddesses, in their place. But they've got to be the ones we make ourselves. Then we can take 'em to bits for the parts when we don't need 'em anymore, see? And elves far away in fairyland, well, maybe that's something people need to get 'emselves through the iron times. But I ain't having elves *here*. You make us want what we can't have and what you give us is worth nothing and what you take is everything and all there is left for us is the cold hillside, and emptiness, and the laughter of the elves."

She took a deep breath. "So bugger off."

"Make us, *old* woman."

"I thought you'd say that."

"We don't want the world. Just this little kingdom will do. And we will take it, whether it wants us or not."

"Over my dead body, madam."

"If that is a condition."

The Queen lashed out mentally, like a cat.

Granny Weatherwax winced, and leaned backward for a moment.

"Madam?"

"Yes?" said the Queen.

"There aren't any rules, are there?"

"Rules? What are rules?" said the Queen.

"I thought so," said Granny. "Gytha Ogg?"

Nanny managed to turn her head.

"Yes, Esme?"

"My box. You know. The one in the dresser. You'll know what to do."

Granny Weatherwax smiled. The Queen swayed sideways, as if she'd been slapped.

"You *have* learned," she said.

"Oh, yes. You know I never entered your circle. I could see where it led. So I had to *learn*. All my life. The hard way. And the hard way's pretty hard, but not so hard as the easy way. I learned. From the trolls and the dwarfs and from people. Even from pebbles."

The Queen lowered her voice.

"You will not be killed," she whispered. "I promise you that. You'll be left alive, to dribble and gibber and soil yourself and wander from door to door for scraps. And they'll say: there goes the mad old woman."

"They say that now," said Granny Weatherwax. "They think I can't hear."

"But inside," said the Queen, ignoring this, "inside I'll keep just a part of you which looks out through your eyes and knows what you've become.

"And there will be none to help," said the Queen. She was closer now, her eyes pinpoints of hatred. "No charity for the mad old woman. You'll see what you have to eat to stay alive. And we'll be with you all the time inside your head, just to remind you. You could have been the great one, there was so much you could have done. And inside you'll know it, and you'll plead all the dark night long for the silence of the elves."

The Queen wasn't expecting it. Granny Weatherwax's hand shot out, pieces of rope falling away from it, and slapped her across the face.

"You threaten me with *that*?" she said. "*Me?* Who am becoming *old*?"

The elf woman's hand rose slowly to the livid mark across her cheek. The elves raised their bows, waiting for an order.

"Go back," said Granny. "You call yourself some kind of goddess and you know nothing, madam, nothing. What don't die can't live. What don't live can't change. What don't change can't learn. The smallest creature that dies in the grass knows more than you. You're right. I'm older. You've lived longer than me but I'm older than you. And better'n you. And, madam, that ain't hard."

The Queen struck wildly.

The rebounded force of the mental blow knocked Nanny Ogg to her knees. Granny Weatherwax blinked.

"A good one," she croaked. "But still I stand, and still I'll not kneel. And still I have strength—"

An elf keeled over. This time the Queen swayed.

"Oh, and I have no time for this," she said, and snapped her fingers.

There was a pause. The Queen glanced around at her elves.

"They can't fire," said Granny. "And you wouldn't want that, would you? So simple an end?"

"You can't be holding them! You have not that much power!"

"Do you want to find out how much power I have, madam? Here, on the grass of Lancre?"

She stepped forward. Power crackled in the air. The Queen had to step back.

"My own turf?" said Granny.

She slapped the Queen again, almost gently.

"What's this?" said Granny Weatherwax. "Can't

you resist me? Where's *your* power now, madam? Gather your power, madam!"

"You foolish old *crone*!"

It was felt by every living creature for a mile around. Small things died. Birds spiraled out of the sky. Elves and humans alike dropped to the ground, clutching their heads.

And in Granny Weatherwax's garden the bees rose out of their hives.

They emerged like steam, colliding with one another in their rush to get airborne. The deep gunship hum of the drones underpinned the frantic roars of the workers.

But, louder than the drones, was the piccolo piping of the queens.

The swarms spiraled up over the clearing, circled once, and then broke and headed away. Others joined them, out of backyard skeps and hollow trees, blackening the sky.

After a while, order became apparent in the great circling cloud. The drones flew on the wings, throbbing like bombers. The workers were a cone made up of thousands of tiny bodies. And at its tip, a hundred queens flew.

The fields lay silent after the arrow-shaped swarm of swarms had gone.

Flowers stood alone and uncourted. Nectar flowed undrunk. Blossoms were left to go fertilize themselves.

The bees headed toward the Dancers.

Granny Weatherwax dropped to her knees, clutching at her head.

"No—"

"Oh, but yes," said the Queen.

Esme Weatherwax raised her hands. The fingers were curled tightly with effort and pain.

Magrat found she could move her eyes. The rest of her felt weak and useless, even with chain-mail and the breastplates. So this was it. She could feel the ghost of Queen Ynci laughing scornfully from a thousand years ago. *She'd* not give up. Magrat was just another one of those dozens of simpering stiff women who'd just hung around in long dresses, ensuring the royal succession—

Bees poured down out of the sky.

Granny Weatherwax turned her face toward Magrat.

Magrat heard the voice clearly in her head.

"You want to be queen?"

And she was free.

She felt the weariness drop away from her and it also felt as though pure Queen Ynci poured out of the helmet.

More bees rained down, covering the slumped figure of the old witch.

The Queen turned, and her smile froze as Magrat straightened up, stepped forward and, with hardly a thought in her head, raised the battleaxe and brought it around in one long sweep.

The Queen moved faster. Her hand snaked out and gripped Magrat's wrist.

"Oh yes," she said, grinning into Magrat's face. "Really? You think so?"

She twisted. The axe dropped from Magrat's fingers.

"And you wanted to be a *witch*?"

Bees were a brown fog, hiding the elves—too small to hit, impervious to glamour, but determined to kill.

Magrat felt the bone scrape.

"The old witch is finished," said the Queen, forcing Magrat down. "I won't say she wasn't good. But she wasn't good *enough*. And you certainly aren't."

Slowly and inexorably, Magrat was forced downward.

"Why don't *you* try some magic?" said the Queen.

Magrat kicked. Her foot caught the Queen on the knee, and she heard a crack. As she staggered back Magrat launched herself forward and caught her around the waist, bearing her to the ground.

She was amazed at the lightness. Magrat was skinny enough, but the Queen seemed to have no weight at all.

"Why," she said, pulling herself up until the Queen's face was level with hers, "you're *nothing*. It's all in the mind, isn't it? Without the glamour, you're—"

—an almost triangular face, a tiny mouth, the nose hardly existing at all, but eyes larger than human eyes and now focused on Magrat in pinpoint terror.

"Iron," whispered the Queen. Her hands gripped Magrat's arms. There was no strength there. An elf's strength lay in persuading others they were weak.

Magrat could feel her desperately trying to enter her mind, but it wasn't working. The helmet—

—was lying several feet away, in the mud.

She just had time to wish she hadn't noticed that

before the Queen attacked again, exploding into her uncertainty like a nova.

She was nothing. She was insignificant. She was so worthless and unimportant that even something completely worthless and exhaustively unimportant would consider her beneath contempt. In laying hands upon the Queen she truly deserved an eternity of pain. She had no control of her body. She did not deserve any. She did not deserve a thing.

The disdain sleeted over her, tearing the planetary body of Magrat Garlick to pieces.

She'd never be any good. She'd never be beautiful, or intelligent, or strong. She'd never be anything at all.

Self-confidence? Confidence in what?

The eyes of the Queen were all she could see. All she wanted to do was lose herself in them . . .

And the ablation of Magrat Garlick roared on, tearing at the strata of her soul . . .

. . . exposing the core.

She bunched up a fist and hit the Queen between the eyes.

There was a moment of terminal perplexity before the Queen screamed, and Magrat hit her again.

Only one queen in a hive! Slash! Stab!

They rolled over, landing in the mud. Magrat felt something sting her leg, but she ignored it. She took no notice of the noise around her, but she *did* find the battleaxe under her hand as the two of them landed in a peat puddle. The elf scrabbled at her but this time without strength, and Magrat managed to push herself to her knees and raise the axe—

—and *then* noticed the silence.

It flowed over the Queen's elves and Shawn Ogg's makeshift army as the glamour faded.

There was a figure silhouetted against the setting moon.

Its scent carried on the dawn breeze.

It smelled of lions' cages and leaf mold.

"*He's* back," said Nanny Ogg. She glanced sideways and saw Ridcully, his face glowing, raising his crossbow.

"Put it down," she said.

"Will you look at the horns on that thing—"

"*Put it down.*"

"But—"

"It'd go right through him. Look, you can see that tree through him. He's not really here. He can't get past the doorway. But he can send his thoughts."

"But I can *smell*—"

"If he was really here, we wouldn't still be standing up."

The elves parted as the King walked through. His hind legs hadn't been designed for bipedal walking; the knees were the wrong way round and the hooves were over-large.

It ignored them all and strutted slowly to the fallen Queen. Magrat pulled herself to her feet and hefted the axe uncertainly.

The Queen uncoiled, leaping up and raising her hands, her mouth framing the first words of some curse—

The King held out a hand, and said nothing.

Only Magrat heard it.

Something about meeting by moonlight, she said later.

* * *

And they awoke.

The sun was well over the Rim. People pulled themselves to their feet, staring at one another.

There was not an elf in sight.

Nanny Ogg was the first to speak. Witches can generally come to terms with what actually *is*, instead of insisting on *what ought to be*.

She looked up at the moors. "The first thing we do," she said, "the *first* thing, is put back the stones."

"The second thing," corrected Magrat.

They both looked down at the still body of Granny Weatherwax. A few stray bees were flying disconsolate circles in the grass near her head.

Nanny Ogg winked at Magrat.

"You did well there, girl. Didn't think you had it in you to survive an attack like that. It fairly had *me* widdling myself."

"I've had practice," said Magrat darkly.

Nanny Ogg raised her eyebrows, but made no further comment. Instead she nudged Granny with her boot.

"Wake up, Esme," she said. "Well done. We won."

"Esme?"

Ridcully knelt down stiffly and picked up one of Granny's arms.

"It must have taken it out of her, all that effort," burbled Nanny. "Freeing Magrat and everything—"

Ridcully looked up.

"She's dead," he said.

He thrust both arms underneath the body and got unsteadily to his feet.

"Oh, she wouldn't do a thing like that," said Nanny,

but in the voice of someone whose mouth is running on automatic because their brain has shut down.

"She's not breathing and there's no pulse," said the wizard.

"She's probably just resting."

"Yes."

Bees circled, high in the blue sky.

Ponder and the Librarian helped drag the stones back into position, occasionally using the Bursar as a lever. He was going through the rigid phase again.

They were unusual stones, Ponder noticed—quite hard, and with a look about them that suggested that once, long ago, they had been melted and cooled.

Jason Ogg found him standing deep in thought by one of them. He was holding a nail on a piece of string. But, instead of hanging from the string, the nail was almost at right angles, and straining as if desperate to reach the stone. The string thrummed. Ponder watched it as though mesmerized.

Jason hesitated. He seldom encountered wizards and wasn't at all sure how you were supposed to treat them.

He heard the wizard say: "It sucks. But *why* does it suck?"

Jason kept quiet.

He heard Ponder say: "Maybe there's iron and . . . and iron that loves iron? Or male iron and female iron? Or common iron and royal iron? Some iron contains something else? Some iron makes a weight in the world and other iron rolls down the rubber sheet?"

The Bursar and the Librarian joined him, and watched the swinging nail.

"Damn!" said Ponder, and let go of the nail. It hit the stone with a *plink*.

He turned to the others with the agonized expression of a man who has the whole great whirring machinery of the Universe to dismantle and only a bent paper clip to do it with.

"What ho, Mr. Sunshine!" said the Bursar, who was feeling almost cheerful with the fresh air and lack of shouting.

"Rocks! Why am I messing around with lumps of stone? When did they ever tell anyone anything?" said Ponder. "You know, sir, sometimes I think there's a great ocean of truth out there and I'm just sitting on the beach playing with . . . with *stones*."

He kicked the stone.

"But one day we'll find a way to sail that ocean," he said. He sighed. "Come on. I suppose we'd better get down to the castle."

The Librarian watched them join the procession of tired men who were staggering down the valley.

Then he pulled at the nail a few times, and watched it fly back to the stone.

"Oook."

He looked up into the eyes of Jason Ogg.

Much to Jason's surprise, the orang-utan winked.

Sometimes, if you pay real close attention to the pebbles you find out about the ocean.

The clock ticked.

In the chilly morning gloom of Granny Weatherwax's cottage, Nanny Ogg opened the box.

Everyone in Lancre knew about Esme Weatherwax's mysterious box. It was variously rumored to contain books of spells, a small private universe, cures for all ills, the deeds of lost lands and several tons of gold, which was pretty good going for something less than a foot across. Even Nanny Ogg had never been told about the contents, apart from the will.

She was a bit disappointed but not at all surprised to find that it contained nothing more than a couple of large envelopes, a bundle of letters, and a miscellaneous assortment of common items in the bottom.

Nanny lifted out the paperwork. The first envelope was addressed to her, and bore the legend: To Gytha Ogge, Reade This NOWE.

The second envelope was a bit smaller and said: The Will of Esmerelda Weatherwax, Died Midsummer's Eve.

And then there was a bundle of letters with a bit of string round them. They were very old; bits of yellowing paper crackled off them as Magrat picked them up.

"They're all letters to her," she said.

"Nothing odd about that," said Nanny. "Anyone can get letters."

"And there's all this stuff at the bottom," said Magrat. "It looks like pebbles."

She held one up.

"This one's got one of those curly fossil things in it," she said. "And this one . . . looks like that red rock the Dancers were made of. It's got a darning needle stuck to it. How strange."

"She always paid attention to small details, did Esme. Always tried to see inside to the real thing."

They were both silent for a moment, and the silence wound out around them and filled the kitchen, to be sliced into gentle pieces by the soft ticking of the clock.

"I never thought we'd be doing this," said Magrat, after a while. "I never thought we'd be reading her will. I thought she'd keep on going forever."

"Well, there it is," said Nanny. "Tempus fuggit."

"Nanny?"

"Yes, love?"

"I don't understand. She was your friend but you don't seem . . . well . . . upset?"

"Well, I've buried a few husbands and one or two kiddies. You get the hang of it. Anyway, if she hasn't gone to a better place she'll damn well be setting out to improve it."

"Nanny?"

"Yes, love?"

"Did *you* know anything about the letter?"

"What letter?"

"The letter to Verence."

"Don't know anything about any letter to Verence."

"He must have got it *weeks* before we got back. She must have sent it even before we got to Ankh-Morpork."

Nanny Ogg looked, as far as Magrat could tell, genuinely blank.

"Oh, hell," said Magrat. "I mean *this* letter."

She fished it out of the breastplate.

"See?"

Nanny Ogg read:

"Dear sire, This is to inform youe that Magrate

Garlick will bee retouning to Lancre on or aboute Blind Pig Tuesday. Shee is a Wet Hen but shee is clean and has got Good Teeth. If you wishes to marrie her, then starte arranging matters without delae, because if you just proposes and similar she will lede you a Dance because there is noone like Magrat for getting in the way of her own life. She does not Knoe her own Mind. You aere Kinge and you can doe what you like. You muste present her with a Fate Accompli. PS. I hear there is talk aboute making witches pay tax, no kinges of Lancre has tried this for many a Year, you could profit from their example. Yrs. in good health, at the moment. A FRIEND (MSS)."

The ticking of the clock stitched the blanket of silence.

Nanny Ogg turned to look at it.

"She *arranged* it all!" said Magrat. "You know what Verence is like. I mean, she hardly disguised who she was, did she? And I got back and it was all *arranged*—"

"What would you have done if nothing had been arranged?" said Nanny.

Magrat looked momentarily taken aback.

"Well, I would . . . I mean, if he had . . . I'd—"

"You'd be getting married today, would you?" said Nanny, but in a distant voice, as if she was thinking about something else.

"Well, that depends on—"

"You want to, don't you?"

"Well, yes, of course, but—"

"That's nice, then," said Nanny, in what Magrat thought of as her nursery voice.

"Yes, but she pushed me on one side and shut me up in the castle and I got so wound up—"

"You were so angry that you actually stood up to the Queen. You actually laid hands on her," said Nanny. "Well done. The old Magrat wouldn't have done that, would she? Esme could always see the real thing. Now nip out of the back door and look at the log pile, there's a love."

"But I hated her and hated her and now she's dead!"

"Yes, dear. Now go and tell Nanny about the log pile."

Magrat opened her mouth to frame the words "I happen to be very nearly queen" but decided not to. Instead she graciously went outside and looked at the log pile.

"It's quite high," she said, coming back and blowing her nose. "Looks like it's just been stacked."

"And she wound up the clock yesterday," said Nanny. "And the tea caddy's half full, I just looked."

"Well?"

"She wasn't sure," said Nanny. "Hmm."

She opened the envelope addressed to her. It was larger and flatter than the one holding the will, and contained a single piece of card.

Nanny read it, and let it drop on to the table.

"Come on," she said. "We ain't got much time!"

"What's the matter?"

"And bring the sugar bowl!"

Nanny wrenched open the door and hurried toward her broomstick.

"Come on!"

Magrat picked up the card. The writing was familiar. She'd seen it several times before, when calling on Granny Weatherwax unexpectedly.

It said: I ATE'NT DEAD.

"Halt! Who goes there?"

"What're you doing on guard with your arm in a sling, Shawn?"

"Duty calls, Mum."

"Well, let us in right now."

"Are you Friend or Foe, Mum?"

"Shawn, this is almost-Queen Magrat here with me, all right?"

"Yes, but you've got to—"

"Right now!"

"Oooaaaww, Mum!"

Magrat tried to keep up with Nanny as she scurried through the castle.

"The wizard was right. She was dead, you know. I don't blame you for hoping, but I can tell when people are dead."

"No, you can't. I remember a few years ago you came running down to my house in tears and it turned out she was just off Borrowing. That's when she started using the sign."

"But—"

"She wasn't sure what was going to happen," said Nanny. "That's good enough for me."

"Nanny—"

"You never know until you look," said Nanny Ogg, expounding her own Uncertainty Principle.

Nanny kicked open the doors to the Great Hall.

"What's all this?"

Ridcully got up from his chair, looking embarrassed.

"Well, it didn't seem right to leave her all alone—"

"Oh dear, oh dear," said Nanny, gazing at the solemn tableau.

"Candles and lilies. I bet you pinched 'em yourself, out of the garden. And then you all shut her away indoors like this."

"Well—"

"And no one even thought to leave a damn window open! Can't you *hear* them?"

"Hear what?"

Nanny looked around hurriedly and picked up a silver candlestick.

"No!"

Magrat snatched it out of her hand.

"This happens to be," winding her arm back, "very nearly," taking aim, "*my* castle—"

The candlestick flew up, turning end over end, and hit a big stained glass window right in the center.

Fresh sunlight extruded down to the table, visibly moving in the Disc's slow magical field. And down it, like marbles down a chute, the bees cascaded.

The swarm settled on the witch's head, giving the impression of a very dangerous wig.

"What did you—" Ridcully began.

"She's going to swank about this for *weeks*," said Nanny. "No one's ever done it with bees. Their mind's everywhere, see? Not just in one bee. In the whole swarm."

"What are you—"

Granny Weatherwax's fingers twitched.

Her eyes flickered.

Very slowly, she sat up. She focused on Magrat and Nanny Ogg with some difficulty, and said:

"I wantzzz a bunzzch of flowerszz, a pot of honey, and someone to szzzting."

"I brung the sugar bowl, Esme," said Nanny Ogg.

Granny eyed it hungrily, and then looked at the bees that were taking off from her head like planes from a stricken carrier.

"Pour a dzzrop of water on it, then, and tip it out on the table for them."

She stared triumphantly at their faces as Nanny Ogg bustled off.

"I done it with beezzz! *No one* can do it with beezzz, and I *done* it! You endzzz up with your mind all flying in different directionzzz! You got to be *good* to do it with beezzz!"

Nanny Ogg sloshed the bowl of makeshift syrup across the table. The swarm descended.

"You're alive?" Ridcully managed.

"That's what a univerzzity education doezz for you," said Granny, trying to massage some life into her arms. "You've only got to be sitting up and talking for five minutzz and they can work out you're alive."

Nanny Ogg handed her a glass of water. It hovered in the air for a moment and then crashed to the floor, because Granny had tried to grasp it with her fifth leg.

"Zzorry."

"I knew you wasn't certain!" said Nanny.

"Czertain? Of courze I waz certain! Never in any doubt whatsoever."

Magrat thought about the will.

"You never had a moment's doubt?"

Granny Weatherwax had the grace not to look her in the eye. Instead, she rubbed her hands together.

"What's been happening while I've been away?"

"Well," said Nanny, "Magrat stood up to the—"

"Oh, I knew she'd do *that*. Had the wedding, have you?"

"Wedding?" The rest of them exchanged glances.

"Of course not!" said Magrat. "Brother Perdore of the Nine Day Wonderers was going to do it and he was knocked out cold by an elf, and anyway people are all—"

"Don't let's have any excuses," said Granny briskly. "Anyway, a senior wizard can conduct a service at a pinch, ain't that right?"

"I, I, I *think* so," said Ridcully, who was falling behind a bit in world events.

"Right. A wizard's only a priest without a god and a damp handshake," said Granny.

"But half the guests have run away!" said Magrat.

"We'll round up some more," said Granny.

"Mrs. Scorbic will never get the wedding feast done in time!"

"You'll have to *tell* her to," said Granny.

"The bridesmaids aren't here!"

"We'll make do."

"I haven't got a dress!"

"What's that you've got on?"

Magrat looked down at the stained chain-mail, the mud-encrusted breastplate, and the few damp remnants of white silk that hung over them like a ragged tabard.

"Looks good to me," said Granny. "Nanny'll do your hair."

Magrat reached up instinctively, removed the winged helmet, and patted her hair. Bits of twigs and fragments of heather had twisted themselves in it with comb-breaking complexity. It never looked good for five minutes together at the best of times; now it was a bird's nest.

"I think I'll leave it," she said.

Granny nodded approvingly.

"That's the way of it," she said. "It's not what you've got that matters, it's how you've got it. Well, we're just about ready, then."

Nanny leaned toward her and whispered.

"What? Oh, yes. Where's the groom?"

"He's a bit muzzy. Not sure what happened," said Magrat.

"Perfectly normal," said Nanny, "after a stag night."

There were difficulties to overcome:

"We need a Best Man."

"Ook."

"Well, at least put some clothes on."

Mrs. Scorbic the cook folded her huge pink arms.

"Can't be done," she said firmly.

"I thought perhaps just some salad and quiche and some light—" Magrat said, imploringly.

The cook's whiskery chin stuck out firmly.

"Them elves turned the whole kitchen upside down," she said. "It's going to take me days to get it straight. Anyway, everyone knows raw vegetables are bad for you, and I can't be having with them eggy pies."

Magrat looked beseechingly at Nanny Ogg; Granny Weatherwax had wandered off into the gardens, where she was getting a tendency to stick her nose in flowers right out of her system.

"Nothin' to do with me," said Nanny. "It's not my kitchen, dear."

"No, it's *mine*. I've been cook here for years," said Mrs. Scorbic, "and I knows how things should be done, and I'm not going to be ordered around in my own kitchen by some chit of a girl."

Magrat sagged. Nanny tapped her on the shoulder.

"You might need this at this point," she said, and handed Magrat the winged helmet.

"The king's been very happy with—" Mrs. Scorbic began.

There was a click. She looked down the length of a crossbow and met Magrat's steady gaze.

"Go ahead," said the Queen of Lancre softly, "bake my quiche."

Verence sat in his nightshirt with his head in his hands. He could remember hardly anything about the night, except a feeling of coldness. And no one seemed very inclined to tell him.

There was a faint creak as the door opened.

He looked up.

"Glad to see you're up and about already," said Granny Weatherwax. "I've come to help you dress."

"I've looked in the garderobe," said Verence. "The . . . elves, was it? . . . they ransacked the place. There's nothing I can wear."

Granny looked around the room. Then she went to a low chest and opened it. There was a faint tinkling of bells, and a flash of red and yellow.

"I *thought* you never threw them away," she said. "And you ain't put on any weight, so they'll still fit. On with the motley. Magrat'll appreciate it."

"Oh, no," said Verence. "I'm very firm about this. I'm king now. It'd be demeaning for Magrat to marry a Fool. I've got a position to maintain, for the sake of the kingdom. Besides, there *is* such a thing as pride."

Granny stared at him for so long that he shifted uncomfortably.

"Well, there is," he said.

Granny nodded, and walked toward the doorway.

"Why're you leaving?" said Verence nervously.

"I ain't leaving," said Granny, quietly, "I'm just shutting the door."

And then there was the incident with the crown.

Ceremonies and Protocols of The Kingdom of Lancre was eventually found after a hurried search of Verence's bedroom. It was very clear about the procedure. The new queen was crowned, by the king, as part of the ceremony. It wasn't technically difficult for any king who knew which end of a queen was which, which even the most inbred king figured out in two goes.

But it seemed to Ponder Stibbons that the ritual wobbled a bit at this point.

It seemed, in fact, that just as he was about to lower the crown on the bride's head he glanced across the hall to where the skinny old witch was standing. And nearly everyone else did too, including the bride.

The old witch nodded very slightly.

Magrat was crowned.

Wack-fol-a-diddle, etc.

The bride and groom stood side by side, shaking hands with the long line of guests in that dazed fashion normal at this point in the ceremony.

"I'm sure you'll be very happy—"

"Thank you."

"Ook!"

"Thank you."

"Nail it to the counter, Lord Ferguson, and damn the cheesemongers!"

"Thank you."

"Can I kiss the bride?"

It dawned on Verence that he was being addressed by fresh air. He looked down.

"I'm sorry," he said, "you are—?"

"My card," said Casanunda.

Verence read it. His eyebrows rose.

"Ah," he said. "Uh. Um. Well, well, well. Number two, eh?"

"I try harder," said Casanunda.

Verence looked around guiltily, and then bent down until his mouth was level with the dwarf's ear.

"Could I have a word with you in a minute or two?"

The Lancre Morris Men got together again for the first time at the reception. They found it hard to talk to one another. Several of them jigged up and down absentmindedly as they talked.

"All right," said Jason, "anyone remember? Really remember?"

"I remember the start," said Tailor the other weaver. "Definitely remember the start. And the dancing in the woods. But the Entertainment—"

"There was elves in it," said Tinker the tinker.

"That's why it all got buggered up," said Thatcher the carter. "There was a lot of shouting, too."

"There was someone with horns on," said Carter, "and a great big—"

"It was all," said Jason, "a bit of a dream."

"Hey, look over there, Carter," said Weaver, winking at the others, "there's that monkey. You've got something to ask it, ain't you?"

Carter blinked. "Coo, yes," he said.

"Shouldn't waste a golden opportunity if I was you," said Weaver, with the happy malice often shown by the clever to the simple.

The Librarian was chatting to Ponder and the Bursar. He looked around as Carter prodded him.

"You've been over to Slice, then, have you?" he said, in his cheery open way.

The Librarian gave him a look of polite incomprehension.

"Oook?"

Carter looked perplexed.

"That's where you put your nut, ain't it?"

The Librarian gave him another odd look, and shook his head.

"Oook."

"Weaver!" Carter shouted, "the monkey says he didn't put his nut where the sun don't shine! You said he did! You didn't, did you? He said you did."

He turned to the Librarian. "He didn't, Weaver. See, I knew you'd got it wrong. You're *daft*. There's no monkeys in Slice."

Silence flowed outward from the two of them.

Ponder Stibbons held his breath.

"This is a lovely party," said the Bursar to a chair, "I wish I was here."

The Librarian picked up a large bottle from the table. He tapped Carter on the shoulder. Then he poured him a large drink and patted him on the head.

Ponder relaxed and turned back to what he was doing. He'd tied a knife to a bit of string and was gloomily watching it spin round and round . . .

On his way home that night Weaver was picked up by a mysterious assailant and dropped into the Lancre. No one ever found out why. Do not meddle in the affairs of wizards, especially simian ones. They're not all that subtle.

Others went home that night.

"She'll be getting ideas above her station in life," said Granny Weatherwax, as the two witches strolled through the scented air.

"She's a *queen*. That's pretty high," said Nanny Ogg. "Almost as high as witches."

"Yes . . . well . . . but you ain't got to give yourself airs," said Granny Weatherwax. "We're *advantaged*, yes, but we act with modesty and we don't Put Ourselves Forward. No one could say I haven't been decently modest all my life."

"You've always been a bit of a shy violet, I've always said," said Nanny Ogg. "I'm always telling people, when it comes to humility you won't find anyone more humile than Esme Weatherwax."

"Always keep myself to myself and minded my own business—"

"Barely known you were there half the time," said Nanny Ogg.

"I was *talking*, Gytha."

"Sorry."

They walked along in silence for a while. It was a warm dry evening. Birds sang in the trees.

Nanny said, "Funny to think of our Magrat being married and everything?"

"What do you mean, everything?"

"Well, *you* know—*married*," said Nanny. "I gave her a few tips. Always wear something in bed. Keeps a man interested."

"You always wore your hat."

"Right."

Nanny waved a sausage on a stick. She always believed in stocking up on any free food that was available.

"I thought the wedding feast was very good, didn't you? And Magrat looked radiant, I thought."

"*I* thought she looked hot and flustered."

"That *is* radiant, with brides."

"You're right, though," said Granny Weatherwax, who was walking a little way ahead. "It was a good dinner. I never had this Vegetarian Option stuff before."

"When I married Mr. Ogg, we had three dozen oysters at *our* wedding feast. Mind you, they didn't all work."

"And I like the way they give us all a bit o' the wedding cake in a little bag," said Granny.

"Right. You know, they says, if you puts a bit under your pillow, you dream of your future husb . . ." Nanny Ogg's tongue tripped over itself.

She stopped, embarrassed, which was unusual in an Ogg.

"It's all right," said Granny. "I don't mind."

"Sorry, Esme."

"Everything happens somewhere. I know. I *know*. Everything happens somewhere. So it's all the same in the end."

"That's very continuinuinuum thinking, Esme."

"Cake's nice," said Granny, "but . . . right now . . . don't know why . . . what I could really do with, Gytha, right now . . . is a sweet."

The last word hung in the evening air like the echo of a gunshot.

Nanny stopped. Her hand flew to her pocket, where the usual bag of fluff-encrusted boiled sweets resided. She stared at the back of Esme Weatherwax's head, at the tight bun of gray hair under the brim of the pointy hat.

"Sweet?" she said.

"I expect you've got another bag now," said Granny, without looking around.

"Esme—"

"You got anything to say, Gytha? About bags of sweets?"

Granny Weatherwax still hadn't turned around.

Nanny looked at her boots.

"No, Esme," she said meekly.

"I knew you'd go up to the Long Man, you know. How'd you get in?"

"Used one of the special horseshoes."

Granny nodded. "You didn't ought to have brung him into it, Gytha."

"Yes, Esme."

"He's as tricky as she is."

"Yes, Esme."

"You're trying preemptive meekness on me."

"Yes, Esme."

They walked a little further.

"What was that dance your Jason and his men did when they'd got drunk?" said Granny.

"It's the Lancre Stick and Bucket Dance, Esme."

"It's legal, is it?"

"Technically they shouldn't do it when there's women present," said Nanny. "Otherwise it's sexual morrisment."

"And I thought Magrat was very surprised when you recited that poem at the reception."

"Poem?"

"The one where you did the gestures."

"Oh, that poem."

"I saw Verence making notes on his napkin."

Nanny reached again into the shapeless recesses of her clothing and produced an entire bottle of champagne you could have sworn there was no room for.

"Mind you, I thought she looked happy," she said. "Standing there wearing about half of a torn muddy dress and chain-mail underneath. Hey, d'you know what she told me?"

"What?"

"You know that ole painting of Queen Ynci? You know, the one with the iron bodice? Her with all the spikes and knives on her chariot? Well, she said she was sure the . . . the spirit of Ynci was helping her. She said she wore the armor and she did things she'd never dare do."

"My word," said Granny, noncommittally.

"Funny ole world," agreed Nanny.

They walked in silence for a while.

"So you didn't tell her that Queen Ynci never existed, then?"

"No point."

"Old King Lully invented her entirely 'cos he thought we needed a bit of romantic history. He was a bit mad about that. He even had the armor made."

"I know. My great-grandma's husband hammered it out of a tin bath and a couple of saucepans."

"But you didn't think you ought to tell her that?"

"No."

Granny nodded.

"Funny thing," she said, "even when Magrat's completely different, she's just the same."

Nanny Ogg produced a wooden spoon from somewhere in her apron. Then she raised her hat and carefully lifted down a bowl of cream, custard, and jelly which she had secreted there.*

"Huh. I really don't know why you pinches food the whole time," said Granny. "Verence'd give you a bathful of the stuff if you asked. You know he don't touch custard himself."

---

*Nanny Ogg was also a great picker-up of unconsidered trifles.

"More fun this way," said Nanny. "I deserve a bit of fun."

There was a rustling in the thick bushes and the unicorn burst through.

It was mad. It was angry. It was in a world where it did not belong. And it was being driven.

It pawed the ground a hundred yards away, and lowered its horn.

"Whoops," said Nanny, dropping her just desserts. "Come on. There's a tree here, *come on*."

Granny Weatherwax shook her head.

"No. I ain't runnin' this time. She couldn't get me before and she's tryin' through an *animal*, eh?"

"Will you look at the size of the horn on that thing?"

"I can see clear enough," said Granny calmly.

The unicorn lowered its head and charged. Nanny Ogg reached the nearest tree with low branches and leapt upward . . .

Granny Weatherwax folded her arms.

"Come *on*, Esme!"

"No. I ain't been *thinking* clear enough, but I am now. There's some things I don't have to run from."

The white shape bulleted down the avenue of trees, a thousand pounds of muscle behind twelve inches of glistening horn. Steam swirled behind it.

"*Esme!*"

Circle time was ending. Besides, she knew now why her mind had felt so unravelled, and that was a help. She couldn't hear the ghostly thoughts of all the other Esme Weatherwaxes anymore.

Perhaps some lived in a world ruled by elves. Or had died long ago. Or were living what they thought were happy lives. Granny Weatherwax seldom wished for anything, because wishing was soppy, but she felt a tiny regret that she'd never be able to meet them.

Perhaps some were going to die, now, here on this path. Everything you did meant that a million copies of you did something else. Some were going to die. She'd sensed their future deaths . . . the deaths of Esme Weatherwax. And couldn't save them, because chance did not work like that.

On a million hillsides the girl ran, on a million bridges the girl chose, on a million paths the woman stood . . .

All different, all one.

All she could do for all of them was be herself, here and now, as hard as she could.

She stuck out a hand.

A few yards away the unicorn hit an invisible wall. Its legs flailed as it tried to stop, its body contorted in pain, and it slid the rest of the way to Granny's feet on its back.

"Gytha," said Granny, as the beast tried to get upright, "you'll take off your stockings and knot 'em into a halter and pass it to me carefully."

"Esme . . ."

"What?"

"Ain't got no stockings on, Esme."

"What about the lovely red and white pair I gave you on Hogswatchnight? I knitted 'em myself. You know how I hates knitting."

"Well, it's a warm night. I likes to, you know, let the air circulate."

"I had the devil of a time with the heels."

"Sorry, Esme."

"At least you'll be so good as to run up to my place and bring everything that's in the bottom of the dresser."

"Yes, Esme."

"But before that you'll call in at your Jason's and tell him to get the forge good and hot."

Nanny Ogg stared down at the struggling unicorn. It seemed to be stuck, terrified of Granny but at the same time quite unable to escape.

"Oh, Esme, you're never going to ask our Jason to—"

"I won't *ask* him to do anything. And I ain't *asking* you, neither."

Granny Weatherwax removed her hat, skimming it into the bushes. Then, her eyes never leaving the animal, she reached up to the iron-gray bun of her hair and removed a few crucial pins.

The bun uncoiled a waking snake of fine hair, which unwound down to her waist when she shook her head a couple of times.

Nanny watched in paralyzed fascination as she reached up again and broke a single hair at its root.

Granny Weatherwax's hands made a complicated motion in the air as she made a noose out of something almost too thin to see. She ignored the thrashing horn and dropped it over the unicorn's neck. Then she pulled.

Struggling, its unshod hooves kicking up great clods of mud, the unicorn struggled to its feet.

"That'll never hold it," said Nanny, sidling around the tree.

"I could hold it with a cobweb, Gytha Ogg. With a *cobweb*. Now go about your business."

"Yes, Esme."

The unicorn threw back its head and screamed.

Half the town was waiting as Granny led the beast into Lancre, hooves skidding on the cobbles, because when you tell Nanny Ogg you tell everyone.

It danced at the end of the impossibly thin tether, kicking out at the terminally unwary, but never quite managing to pull free.

Jason Ogg, still in his best clothes, was standing nervously at the open doorway to the forge. Superheated air vibrated over the chimney.

"Mister Blacksmith," said Granny Weatherwax, "I have a job for you."

"Er," said Jason, "that's a unicorn, is that."

"Correct."

The unicorn screamed again, and rolled mad red eyes at Jason.

"No one's ever put shoes on a unicorn," said Jason.

"Think of this," said Granny Weatherwax, "as your big moment."

The crowd clustered round, trying to see and hear while keeping out of the way of the hooves.

Jason rubbed his chin with his hammer.

"I don't know—"

"Listen to me, Jason Ogg," said Granny, hauling on the hair as the creature skittered around in a circle, "you can shoe anything anyone brings you. And there's a price for that, ain't there?"

Jason gave Nanny Ogg a panic-stricken look. She had the grace to look embarrassed.

"She never told me about it," said Granny, with

her usual ability to read Nanny's expression through the back of her own head.

She leaned closer to Jason, almost hanging from the plunging beast. "The price for being able to shoe anything, anything that anyone brings you . . . is having to shoe anything anyone brings you. The price for being the best is always . . . having to *be* the best. And you pays it, same as me."

The unicorn kicked several inches of timber out of the door frame.

"But iron—" said Jason. "And nails—"

"Yes?"

"Iron'll kill it," said Jason. "If I nail iron to 'n, I'll kill 'n. Killing's not part of it. I've never killed anything. I was up all night with that ant, it never felt a thing. I won't hurt a living thing that never done me no harm."

"Did you get that stuff from my dresser, Gytha?"

"Yes, Esme."

"Bring it in here, then. And you, Jason, you just get that forge hot."

"But if I nail iron to it I'll—"

"Did I say anything about iron?"

The horn took a stone out of the wall a foot from Jason's head. He gave in.

"You'll have to come in to keep it calm, then," he said. "I've never shod a stallion like this'n without two men and a boy a-hanging on to it."

"It'll do what it's told," Granny promised. "It can't cross me."

"It murdered old Scrope," said Nanny Ogg. "I wouldn't mind him killing it."

"Then shame on you, woman," said Granny. "It's

an animal. Animals can't murder. Only us superior races can murder. That's one of the things that sets us apart from animals. Give me that sack."

She towed the fighting animal through the big double doors and a couple of the villagers hurriedly swung them shut. A moment later a hoof kicked a hole in the planking.

Ridcully arrived at a run, his huge crossbow slung over his shoulder.

"They told me the unicorn had turned up again!"

Another board splintered.

"In there?"

Nanny nodded.

"She dragged it all the way down from the woods," she said.

"But the damn thing's savage!"

Nanny Ogg rubbed her nose. "Yes, well . . . but she's qualified, ain't she? When it comes to unicorn taming. Nothing to do with witchcraft."

"What d'you mean?"

"I thought there was *some* things *everyone* knew about trapping unicorns," said Nanny archly. "Who could trap 'em, is what I am delicately hintin' at. She always *could* run faster'n you, could Esme. She could outdistance any man."

Ridcully stood there with his mouth open.

"Now, *me*," said Nanny, "I'd always trip over first ole tree root I came to. Took me ages to find one, sometimes."

"You mean after I went she never—"

"Don't get soft ideas. It's all one at our time o'life anyway," said Nanny. "It'd never have crossed her mind if you hadn't turned up." An associated thought seemed to strike her. "You haven't seen Casanunda, have you?"

" 'Ello, my little rosebud," said a cheerful, hopeful voice.

Nanny didn't even turn around.

"You do turn up where people aren't looking," she said.

"Famed for it, Mrs. Ogg."

There was silence from inside the forge. Then they could make out the tap-tap-tap of Jason's hammer.

"What they doing in there?" said Ridcully.

"It's stopping it kicking, whatever it is," said Nanny.

"What was in the sack, Mrs. Ogg?" said Casanunda.

"What she told me to get," said Nanny. "Her old silver tea set. Family heirloom. I've only ever seen it but twice, and once was just now when I put it in the sack. I don't think she's ever used it. It's got a cream jug shaped like a humorous cow."

More people had arrived outside the forge. The crowd stretched all the way across the square.

The hammering stopped. Jason's voice, quite close, said:

"We're coming out now."

"They're coming out now," said Nanny.

"What'd she say?"

"She said they're coming out now."

"They're coming out now!"

The crowd pulled back. The doors swung open.

Granny emerged, leading the unicorn. It walked sedately, muscles moving under its white coat like frogs in oil. And its hooves clattered on the cobbles. Ridcully couldn't help noticing how they shone.

It walked politely alongside the witch until she reached the center of the square. Then she turned it loose, and gave it a light slap on the rump.

It whinnied softly, turned, and galloped down the street, toward the forest . . .

Nanny Ogg appeared silently behind Granny Weatherwax as she watched it go.

"Silver shoes?" she said quietly. "They'll last no time at all."

"And silver nails. They'll last for long enough," said Granny, speaking to the world in general. "And *she'll* never get it back, though she calls it for a thousand years."

"Shoeing the unicorn," said Nanny, shaking her head. "Only you'd think of shoeing a unicorn, Esme."

"I've been doing it all my life," said Granny.

Now the unicorn was a speck on the moorland. As they watched, it disappeared into the evening gloom.

Nanny Ogg sighed, and broke whatever spell there was.

"So that's it, then."

"Yes."

"Are you going to the dance up at the castle?"

"Are you?"

"Well . . . Mr. Casanunda did ask if I could show him the Long Man. You know. Properly. I suppose it's him being a dwarf. They're very interested in earthworks."

"Can't get enough of them," said Casanunda.

Granny rolled her eyes.

"Act your age, Gytha."

"Act? Don't have to act, can do it automatic," said Nanny. "Acting half my age . . . now *that's* the difficult trick. Anyway, you didn't answer me."

To the surprise of Nanny, and of Ridcully, and possibly even of Granny Weatherwax herself, she slipped her arm around Ridcully's arm.

"Mr. Ridcully and I are going to have a stroll down to the bridge."

"We are?" said Ridcully.

"Oh, that's *nice*."

"Gytha Ogg, if you keep on looking at me like that I shall give you a right ding around the ear."

"Sorry, Esme," said Nanny.

"Good."

"I expect you want to talk about old times," Nanny volunteered.

"Maybe old times. Maybe other times."

The unicorn reached the forest, and galloped onward.

The waters of the Lancre gushed below. No one crossed the same water twice, even on a bridge.

Ridcully dropped a pebble. It went *plunk*.

"It all works out," said Granny Weatherwax, "somewhere. Your young wizard knows that, he just puts daft words around it. He'd be quite bright, if only he'd look at what's in front of him."

"He wants to stay here for a while," said Ridcully gloomily. He flicked another pebble into the depths. "Seems fascinated by the stones. I can't say no, can I? The king's all for it. He says other kings have always had fools, so he'll try having a wise man around, just in case that works better."

Granny laughed.

"And there's young Diamanda going to be up and about any day now," she said.

"What do you mean?"

"Oh, nothing. That's the thing about the future. It could turn out to be *anything*. And everything."

She picked up a pebble. It hit the water at the same time as one of Ridcully's own, making a double *plunk*.

"Do you think," said Ridcully, "that . . . somewhere . . . it all went right?"

"Yes. Here!"

Granny softened at the sight of his sagging shoulders.

"But there, too," she said.

"What?"

"I mean that somewhere Mustrum Ridcully married Esmerelda Weatherwax and they lived—" Granny gritted her teeth "—lived happily ever after. More or less. As much as anyone does."

"How d'you know?"

"I've been picking up bits of her memories. She seemed happy enough. And I ain't easily pleased."

"How can you *do* that?"

"I try to be good at everything I do."

"Did she say anything about—"

"She didn't say nothing! She don't know we exist! Don't ask questions! It's enough to know that everything happens somewhere, isn't it?"

Ridcully tried to grin.

"Is that the best you can tell me?" he said.

"It's the best there is. Or the next best thing."

* * *

Where does it end?*

On a summer night, with couples going their own ways, and silky purple twilight growing between the trees. From the castle, long after the celebrations had ended, faint laughter and the ringing of little silver bells. And from the empty hillside, only the silence of the elves.

---

*When Hwel the playwright turned up with the rest of the troupe next day they told him all about it, and he wrote it down. But he left out all the bits that wouldn't fit on a stage, or were too expensive, or which he didn't believe. In any case, he called it *The Taming of the Vole*, because no one would be interested in a play called *Things that Happened on A Midsummer Night*.